For Real

How long can he outrun the secrets?

Staci Stallings

Spirit Light Publishing

For Real

Publisher's Note: This is a work of fiction. Names, places, characters, and incidents either are the product of the author's imagination or are used fictitiously, and any resemblance to actual persons, living or dead, events, or locales is entirely coincidental.

All the characters and events portrayed in this book are fictitious.

Cover Design: Allan Kristopher Palor
Contact info: allan.palor@yahoo.com
Interior Formatting: Ellen C. Maze, The Author's Mentor,
www.theauthorsmentor.com
Author Website: http://www.stacistallings.com

Spirit Light Publishing
ISBN-13: 978-0615718064
ISBN-10: 061571806X

Also available in eBook publication

Spirit Light Publishing

PRINTED IN THE UNITED STATES OF AMERICA

~*~

Partners don't come along very often,
and it seems God sends them to me at just the right time.
To Aki, my cover designer extraordinaire!
You are the miracle I needed who showed up
at just the right moment.
Amazing how God can make a connection despite
miles, age, and calling. You are awesome!
Thank you so much, my friend!

For Real

If he can just outrun the secrets...

One

Two months, eight days, nineteen hours, and a handful of minutes—that's how long it had been since Melody Todd's heart had forever given up hope of being anyone's someone. It wasn't that she wanted to give up hope, but she hadn't exactly had a choice. When Miss Perfection walks in the door, how could anyone else have any kind of chance?

Annoyed with life in general, she flipped her long, course blonde hair over her shoulder as she bent next to the rack of shoelaces that had been dismantled piece-by-piece throughout the day. With an audible sigh, she picked up three plastic holders and replaced them on the rack. Midnight Madness sales were bad enough, but holding one on Leap Year Day somehow seemed unconscionable. True if she was at home, she would only be studying, but even that seemed like a step up from Galaxy Shoes on a sale day.

The test in biology she had yet to study for crossed her mind as the last set of shoelaces found its home. As she stepped away from the rack, her gaze chanced across her watch. Once again she sighed. Eight o'clock already and not only had she not studied like she'd promised herself she would, she hadn't even eaten since before noon. Why she agreed to work these ridiculous hours she couldn't quite remember at the moment. It had something to do with making enough to afford tuition because the scholarship she'd needed hadn't come through. Yeah, it was something like that, she thought as she straightened the rack of backpacks.

"Melody," Nathan, the night manager, said in the whiny voice that raked across her brain like a jagged fingernail.

"What?" she asked, drawing the syllable out into two.

"Look, I admire your forward thinking in getting this picked up, but not at the expense of letting a customer walk out the door." He pointed across three rows of shelves to an expanse of light green stretched across two nicely rounded shoulders. "Unless you want me to make this commission."

Melody shot him a shut-up look and turned to stride down the aisle. "I've got it." With purposeful steps she rounded her way into the aisle where the customer was even as she made sure that Farin was safely up front ringing up another customer. Yes, she had this one all to herself. Now if only she could make the sale. "May I help you?"

It wasn't until he turned around that she realized he wasn't examining his own shoes but those of the small boy at his feet. "We're fine," the man said quickly. "We're just looking."

"Oh," Melody said, wishing she was better at high-pressured sales tactics. "I was just…" At that moment her brain caught up with her gaze and throttled her to a head-jerking stop. "Blaine?"

With a start the young man, dressed in smart charcoal pants and a light green dress shirt set off with a green and blue necktie, stopped his assessment of the little boy's shoes and turned to her. "Melody?"

High-pressured sales tactics flew right out of her head. "Hey," she said brightly, and without thinking, she reached over to give him a hug. "It's been awhile."

"Yeah, it has." He accepted the sideways hug with a smile. "What've you been up to?"

"Oh, you know, selling shoes—or trying to." She shrugged and smiled at him as her thoughts turned to her own disheveled appearance. Coolly her hand went up and flipped a shock of hair back over her shoulder.

He glanced down to assess the child's progress. "I didn't know you worked here."

"About three years now." Her brain snapped back into sales mode. "So if there's anything I can help you with…"

With a slightly embarrassed gaze, he glanced down again at the child standing at his feet. "We were just looking for a good deal on some school shoes."

"School shoes," Melody said with a nod and a smile to the

small brown-toned face staring up at her. She carefully bent down to the little boy. "You got anything special in mind?"

The boy cowered into Blaine's pant leg.

"We were thinking about these," Blaine said as he picked up the box, "but they're a little steep."

Melody glanced at the box in his hand, trying not to notice the chocolate brown of his eyes. "Hmm. Yeah, those are good—all leather uppers, but if you just want some good, basic tennis shoes, we've got these over here." She stood, looked over the selection to her right, reached out for one, and stopped. "What size does he wear?"

"Umm, well, he was in a four last we checked, but…"

"So we need to figure out a size, then we'll worry about a style." With the precision of a hundred thousand times of practice, she whipped the size plate off the top of the shelves. "Here we go." She bent back down and then decided even that was too uncomfortable so she twisted her feet under her and sat down. "Can you put your foot right here?"

The little boy stared at her skeptically. Putting a strong hand on his shoulder, Blaine led him around his leg. "Come on, Dylan. It's okay." With just more than a little coaxing, Blaine got the boy's foot onto the apparatus.

Quickly Melody measured the small foot. "I think a four-and-a-half would work." She turned back for the shoe shelves. Two swipes and she had three boxes in her hands. "Let's start with these." As she bent to the floor, she swung her hair over her shoulder. "So, Dylan, how's school?"

"Fine," the little voice answered as Blaine helped him slide up on the bench seat.

"What grade are you in—first?"

"Second," he answered softly.

In no time Melody had the shoe laced. Her hands worked to put a shoe on the little foot even as her mind worked through a million questions that had nothing to do with school. One date and one… well, she had never been real sure what that was, but it was definitely something you wouldn't have gone on if you had a wife and child at home. Furtively she checked Blaine's ring finger, left hand. No ring, but then that didn't always mean anything. "Second grade. Are you getting really smart in second grade?"

"I know how to spell knuckle," the little boy offered.

"Oh, yeah? How?" she challenged.

"K-N-U-C-K-L-E," he said slowly as she worked a shoe onto his other foot.

"Wow. That's really good. I couldn't spell that until at least third grade." She caught the smile he beamed up at Blaine and didn't miss the sweet, kind, brown eyes that beamed one right back. Carefully she leaned back. "These are four-and-a-halves, but they might not have enough growing room in them. See what you think."

Smoothly Blaine dropped to one knee and felt the toe of the shoe. "How do they feel?"

"Good," the little boy answered with a hesitant nod.

"How about you walk around in them a little?" Melody suggested.

Slowly the little frame slid off the bench and took three uncertain steps away and then came back. Blaine watched him closely as Melody fought to keep her concentration on the little boy and away from the young man observing him. Dylan slid in between Blaine's knees as Blaine put a hand under his arm. "What do you think?"

The two little shoulders reached for the ceiling.

"We could try a half size bigger," Melody said when Blaine's silence dragged on a little too long.

"We probably ought to."

She swung back into professional mode, and in no time Dylan was walking in the larger shoes.

"What do you think?" Blaine asked to no one in particular. Concentrating on his feet, Dylan nodded. When he made it back to them, Melody reached down and tested the toe.

"You'll probably want the bigger ones," she said. "Otherwise you'll have to be in here again in a month when he grows." As soon as she said it, she wished she had given the opposite advice. However, it was too late to take it back because Blaine nodded.

"Then we'll take them," he said decisively but wavered in the next second. "Oh, how much are they?"

"$30, but tonight it's half off," Melody said as she stowed the unwanted shoes back in the other box.

"Can't beat a deal like that," Blaine said. He started to take the shoes off but stopped. "Can he wear them out?"

She shrugged. "Sure." Quickly she replaced the other shoes

as well, but she noticed the rag-tag pair of shoes Blaine picked up from the floor. It didn't take much to see how fast he threw them into the new box and closed it. When he glanced at her, she saw the embarrassment scrawl across his face, but she smiled it away. "You need anything else? A backpack? Shoelaces?"

His smile stretched tighter than the grimace had. "Nope, I think this will get it."

Nathan would probably give her a demerit for not getting them to buy something else, but at the moment she didn't care about anything other than the two people walking with her to the checkout. She wanted to say something to fill the silence between them, but she could think of nothing. She was glad to see that Farin was nowhere in sight.

"I saw Eve the other day," Blaine finally said as they reached the front.

Melody's heart collapsed around the name, but she willed her voice not to register that fact. "Oh, yeah?"

"Yeah, she and A.J. are getting a house out in Rolling Hills."

"Oh, really?" Hurt, unseen to that moment, flooded through Melody's chest. "I hadn't heard that. Cool." Fighting to take her mind off of the conversation's track, she busied herself with the register. "That'll be $16.85."

He handed her a twenty and waited for the change. She didn't want to look at him. There were too many things she didn't want him to see. Quickly she exchanged the money, handed it to him, and slid the receipt into the bag. She folded the plastic handles and handed the bag over the counter. "Your receipt's in the bag."

For one solid second after the bag was in his hands, Blaine didn't move. He had such a nice face, conventional and yet striking. "I guess I'll see you later then?"

"Yeah, later," she said with a quick nod as she pushed her hair over her ear.

One more awkward pause and Blaine reached down for Dylan's hand. "Well, 'bye."

She mumbled something—presumably good-bye but for all she could tell it could've been 'how could you do this to me?' Granted, he hadn't really done anything more egregious than innocently end up on the semi-same date with her, but still. Just the thought of his poor car, the stench of vomit and the sound of her moans filling it, threatened to make her sick all over again.

That hadn't been her fault of course. The name A.J. streaked through her mind as the memory rewound a bit more, and she threw a box that had fallen on the floor under the counter a little harder than she really had to.

A.J.

A.J. and little Miss Perfection. Heat rose in her at the very thought of them. Now they were buying a house together. Thrilling. She was absolutely thrilled for them. She kicked another box under the counter. Of all the bad dates she had ever been on, and there had been many, that day at AstroWorld had been the very worst. There had been a time when she had kept up with A.J. feat for feat, but apparently that time had passed.

It was Greased Lightnin's 360-loop that ultimately got her, and in that second she had lost every shred of dignity she had managed to muster in the past 25 years. Of course Blaine, or more precisely, Blaine's car had been the unfortunate recipient of the fall-out from that bad decision. And while Blaine was making an emergency trip to get her home, Miss Perfect had made her move on A.J. Things had never been the same since.

Even as the thoughts continued, Melody yanked two boxes up from the floor next to the women's shelves. Her heart dove for the floor at the mere thought of A.J., her best friend in the whole world. Now he was gone, making a life for himself with her. Her. Eve What's Her Name. So, now they had a house. So, what? They were married. Right? A.J. and Miss Perfect Wonderful, Fantastic Eve were married. And now they were living happily ever after just like the storybook said they would.

Swiping her cheek with one hand and slamming another box onto the shelf with the other, Melody tried to stow the lump in her throat as easily. There had been a time in what seemed a different lifetime that she would've been the first one A.J. would've called with news like this. But now… Now she had to hear it from some semi-acquaintance who only knew her because she'd used him to make A.J. jealous. She snorted softly. "Well, that worked."

With a swift kick she corralled two more boxes to the shelves. "It's over, Mel. It's over. Get over it, and move on already. Just get that through your thick skull, and we'll all be better off." Unfortunately her head wasn't the only part of her not getting the message.

Blaine Donovan checked the plate glass window once more from the safety of the darkened parking lot. She was busy—working. She wasn't watching him. That was a good thing, he told himself as he hustled Dylan into the beat up, green Toyota. At least that way she wouldn't notice his current mode of transportation. Not that it made any difference to him if she wondered, he reasoned as he yanked twice to get the door opened and then jumped into the driver's side, grabbed his glasses off the dashboard, and prayed that Lillian would start just one more time. "Just get me out of here, Baby," he pleaded as he pumped the accelerator before cranking the starter. If only she would get him safely into the middle of an intersection before she decided to die for good, at least he could handle that.

Still pumping the gas, he prodded the little car out of the lot as his gaze found the rearview mirror, and he just had to smile with the sigh. Melody. She was still as nice as he remembered. Sweet and unassuming. Fun even—as long as she wasn't throwing up in your best friend's car. A genuine laugh escaped at that thought, and he squeezed his eyes closed at the memory.

It had cost almost a hundred bucks that he didn't have to get that car back to good enough so that Peyton hadn't noticed. Not that Peyton noticed much of anything when it came to stuff he owned—especially cars. Blaine had lost count of the number of cars Peyton had wrecked since their senior year in high school. First it was a Mazda, cute little metallic number that probably set Peyton's dad back more than ten grand or three. Then there was the red Firebird. That one only lasted a month or so. Then only six months before E-Day as Blaine had affectionately begun remembering it, Peyton got the gold Porsche Carrera GT. Cool. It was the coolest car Blaine had ever seen with the leather seats and the computerized everything.

Blaine still remembered pulling up to Eve's apartment in that car. He had felt like a million and one bucks in it. And walking her out to get in that car… Man, it was the greatest moment of his life. What happened next he still wasn't real clear about—except that by the time he left the amusement park, he was coming to the rescue of a very sick Melody who couldn't walk two steps without him holding her up, and Eve was permanently in the arms of someone he'd never even heard of prior to that day.

The ride home was when the little Carrera had been baptized. He shook his head at the memory. Melody had apologized until she could hardly keep her head up. He still remembered her leaning against the bucket seat nearly lying in the trunk for how far back he had laid it. Without a doubt at that moment she was the sickest human being he had ever seen.

How much of that ride she remembered he had no idea. Most of it she spent moaning and barely holding the green in her face from coming up again. Thankfully when he dropped her off, no one had been at her house because explaining her state and why she was coming home with a guy she didn't even know might not have been pleasant. He had spent the next four hours trying to make the car semi-presentable again, and it was well after midnight when he had dropped it off at Peyton's, grabbed Lillian and headed back across town to the little dump he called home.

A rock descended to his chest when he thought about the place he still reluctantly called home. His gaze traveled from the traffic outside the window to the child in the seat next to him. Asleep already. Poor little guy. Blaine checked his watched with a short sigh. 9:34. Dylan should've been in bed an hour ago. He didn't need to be out shopping. He needed to be at home in his bed getting a good night's sleep for school tomorrow.

Blaine shook his head without shaking it and refocused on the road. It couldn't be helped. He didn't get out of class until 8:00, and there was simply no time between work and class. He shoved his cramped schedule away from his consciousness. It was depressing, but only if he thought about it.

Allowing whatever less depressing thought that wanted to take over in, he drifted back to Melody and the panic that had set in the night she had called him a few weeks later. Had it been him who had thrown up in her car, he would never have made that call. No way. No how. They should've given her a courage award for that one. It still surprised him that they had ended up with A.J., Eve and the gang on that date too. No matter how hard he tried, he couldn't quite get all of the pieces of that puzzle to line up in his head.

Eve was as nice as she had always been to him, and the others were pleasant enough although he really didn't know them well enough to know if that's how they always were or if there was something else going on. It was only A.J. who hadn't seemed all that happy about Blaine's presence. Okay, at the amusement park, Blaine could understand the animosity now. Eve had apologized about it the next Monday. But how long could a guy hold a grudge against an innocent bystander? Apparently, with A.J., a long time.

No, it was plenty clear that A.J. Knight had a chip on his shoulder, and Blaine had dealt with enough chips in his time to know you can either knock them off or steer clear. He was sincerely glad that steering clear was the easiest fork in that road. As he turned into the little driveway, he prayed that the light blue flashes of light through the open front window meant his mother had already passed out on the couch.

The blinding light of the refrigerator stung Melody's overtired eyes. Biology was going to kill her. She rummaged past the mayonnaise and milk and grabbed a yogurt from the back. What she really wanted was chips, but she had sworn on Monday that she was going to start sticking to her diet. Never on the slim side, her freshman 15 had turned into the sophomore 40. That fact wasn't lost on her consciousness. However, as she filled her glass with stale-tasting water, sympathy for her situation invaded her body, and she grabbed the chips anyway.

She needed something. Something to make it through this night—if not this whole crummy semester. First there was Biology that she hated. She had thought the principles of marketing class would be fun until she figured out on the third class that all the teacher did was talk about guns and deer. And then there was math. How they had talked her into taking math and biology at the same time, she would never know.

In her room, she threw the bag of chips onto the bed with a crunch, grabbed her book off the desk and replaced it with the yogurt. With a flop she fell onto the bed and reached for a chip. "The five parts of the circulatory system are…"

He was missing something, Blaine thought as he scanned back across the textbook page. His fingers rested on his head, his thumb holding up the edge of his glasses that he only wore for reading and close-up work. Drafting 202. He should've known this stuff forward and backward by now, and yet somehow this point was eluding him. It just couldn't be this hard. Slowly word-by-word he reread the section that he should've already had memorized. Still what it said was exactly what he was doing, and it wasn't working. In frustration he stood from the little kitchen table and strode over to the refrigerator. One hand slid down to keep his tie in place as he opened the door and scanned the contents. He pulled out a Coke and then looked down at his attire and sighed. Nearly three o'clock in the morning and he was still in the same clothes he'd put on at seven the morning before.

Somehow, some way he was going to have to get a little sleep. He couldn't keep up with this schedule much longer. He popped the Coke open and took a sip. But what were his options? Cut down on work? They'd all starve. Not go to school? No, that wasn't an option he would even consider. He had worked too hard to this point. He wasn't going to back out now.

Straddling the chair, he sat back down, sighed, scratched his head, and stared at the book lying open on the table. Only then did his gaze slide from the printed words up to the four-color illustration at the top and then to the one small angle in the corner. With a clank the Coke can hit the table, and he grabbed his pencil. "Oh, please, please, please, let this work," he breathed, knowing if it didn't he might very well show up for work in five hours in those exact same clothes.

Two

Life had become one slow, irritating grind by mid-March. Biology was still giving Melody fits, and if she pulled a D in math, she might have to throw a party to celebrate. Who she would even invite at this point was a mystery considering the only people she ever saw were her family, co-workers, and the other students who were struggling almost as much as she was. Still, passing math had to be worth something.

It was math that she was feverishly working on as she drove manically through the early evening Houston traffic three days before Spring Break. Equations, formulas. 2 + 17X… Who cared? Certainly not her. She stuck the pencil in her mouth as she turned a corner.

"No," she muttered through the pencil as her gaze swept across the parking lot that was jammed with cars. "Oh, come on. I'm not that late."

She maneuvered the car around first one line and then a second. A frustrated growl crawled into her throat. "I should've left before Farin got there. She does this to me every single time." Her hands worked the steering wheel back out onto the busy street. The library was a hike and a half, but it was her only good option. Watching for even a single small break in the traffic, she sat in the turning lane, her left foot tapping in consternation on the floorboard. "Are you kidding me?" she asked when no opening appeared. "Come on."

Finally a hole the size of a pin opened, and Melody careened through it. On the other side when she realized she hadn't been pulverized by the oncoming pickup, she breathed a short sigh of relief. There were three parking places left at the far end of the lot.

As soon as the car stopped, she threw it into park, yanked her book and papers off of the seat, and grabbed her backpack without bothering to actually put the book into it.

Her feet beat a quick path across the parking lot and back to the jam-packed street. Yanking her courage to her, she dashed between the oncoming traffic barely making it to the center of the street without getting hit. "Would a crossover be too much to ask?" she asked no one in particular. A tiny break and she ran for it again. Heaving from the exertion not to mention the fright, she pulled her books up tighter and hurried past the cars lining the parking lot. School was hard enough. It really shouldn't be life-threatening to get there, she thought as she pulled her backpack up on her shoulder.

When she pulled the door open to the Admin Building, a gust of frigid air hit her smack in the face and whisked through the bundle of stringy blonde hair clamped carelessly at the top of her head. "Welcome to Alaska." Pushing her feet forward, she trudged to the bottom of the first of three flights of stairs. One more tug to keep her backpack on her shoulder and she started up.

Just across the hall, Blaine was having his own problems. The carefully constructed project he had finished at two the morning before hadn't faired very well on his walk to the Admin Building. With each step, tiny pieces of architecture were slowly ungluing themselves. He had just set the project on the little bench so he could retrieve the fourth plastic window that had made a suicide dive when he glanced up and saw her. The recognition hit him square, and for a solid second he froze. Melody.

At least he thought it was Melody. Her hair was wrapped on the top of her head and stuck out at weird angles in all directions. She looked tired, like she'd been up studying all night. He shook his head and breathed a small laugh as she disappeared up the stairs above him—her and every other poor, unfortunate human being within these walls.

With that thought, he stuck the window back in place on the miniature condominium and pressed extra hard for good measure. Then carefully he picked up the project. As he started up the stairs adjacent but opposite the ones she had just ascended, he wondered to himself what she was doing here. Going to school—obviously, but he couldn't remember ever seeing her around before. Not that he was all that social himself. Scooting in under the wire and jumping up to leave as soon as the professor said, "That's it," he wasn't exactly the type to stand around chit-chatting and getting to know everyone.

On each level that he climbed, he wondered if she had stopped there. Reality was she could be in any one of these classrooms, taking just about anything. The Admin Building was home to everything except the administration. They had bailed long before Blaine started what seemed eons ago. Two years—this associate degree was supposed to take two little years, and yet he had somehow managed to stretch that out to almost five. After next semester, he would have to decide on a next step. For now the next step was somehow getting through Modern Architecture.

When class broke three hours later, Blaine hauled himself out of the seat and smoothed the wrinkles out of his brush-polished gray slacks. His foot screamed in pain as he put his weight on it again. The outside of his shoe felt like a solid block of wood against the blister he knew was there without even seeing it. He kicked his heel back against the riser trying to get the shoe to give his foot just a little more room.

"Hey, Blaine, good project," Lana McCalaster said from behind him. "Great lines."

"Oh, thanks." He swung his backpack to his shoulder and stepped aside to let Lana out in front of him. "Yours was good too."

At floor level, her soft blonde hair swung gently over her shoulder as she looked back at him, waiting just a beat for him to catch up. "You going out of town for Spring Break?"

"Oh, you know," he said with a shrug. "A bunch of us will probably go down to Corpus or something."

"Corpus?" she asked in clear horror.

"One of the guys has a beach house down there," Blaine said, falling easily into the made up world he inhabited on occasions like this. He shrugged. "I wanted Florida, but the guys couldn't afford it."

"Oh." She nodded in understanding. "Well, Corpus won't be so bad."

"Yeah, that's what I keep telling myself," he said as they reached the stairs and started down.

The second Melody caught sight of Blaine rounding the railing of the second staircase opposite from the one her foot had just reached, her heart stopped, and she almost pitched headlong down the next flight. Soft blue-gray pinstriped shirt, perfectly pressed gray slacks, the bright satin blue tie just a fuzz of a shade darker than the shirt. She knew it was him. It had to be. No one else had that silhouette.

That unbelievably handsome silhouette that she had fallen so in love with as she lay as motionless as possible on the seat beside him all the way home from the amusement park. She had never been sicker in her life, and yet he never flinched. Even when she threw up all over the beautiful soft beige leather of his car seats, he just kept looking at her with that I-really-wish-I-could-do-something-to-help-you look. If it had been her, she would've thrown the other person out, and yet he had stopped and helped her clean as much of it off of her as she could, then got her a bag and a Sprite. Her own mother couldn't have cared as much.

All the way home she had laid on that seat, and every time her eyes unglued themselves from her bottom lashes, she was grateful for that silhouette. Careful to stay out of his sight now, she followed him down. He was talking to Miss Perfection 2. That figured. Wavy blonde hair—the kind that looks like silk. She had a slender to the point of non-existent body, perfect shoulders, perfect waist, perfect outfit. Perfect. Perfect. Perfect. It was sickening.

Melody yanked her backpack up against her neck and tried to look somewhere else. Blaine was a nice guy—not to even mention rich and handsome. A prize catch in any girl's book. Melody knew better than anyone else what that meant. Nice, rich, handsome guys weren't exactly lined up at her doorstep. In fact besides A.J. and Bobby she'd never even been out on a real date, and she wondered now if those two even counted.

By the time she reached the bottom step, he was gone—lost in the throng of students hurriedly leaving the halls of higher education. Oh, well. It was a nice thought, but even if she got up the nerve to talk to him, what would she say? He would be nice.

She would fumble around trying to figure out something to say that didn't sound hopelessly stupid, and then he would be gone. Yes, she knew this routine, and for his sake, she hoped they wouldn't have to stumble through it again.

Lillian crawled slowly up the little driveway. Her tires crunched on the small stones. She rolled to a stop, and Blaine cut the headlights. Night had fallen across Houston long before. With the practice of a hundred thousand times he cranked down the window and reached to the door handle outside. A little persuasion and the door popped open. He quickly rolled the window back up and grabbed his backpack.

Somewhere down the block he heard the slamming of a door and indiscriminant yelling. Ah, another night in the throes of ghettoland. Trying not to listen to the sounds that disgusted him, he climbed the three steps to his own kitchen door. Once again he vowed it was only a matter of time before he got out of this place. No one deserved to live like this, and he was determined to get Dylan out of here at the first chance he got. However, he'd been promising himself that for ten years, and the fact that it still hadn't happened yanked a sigh out of his soul.

The screen door squeaked in protest as he pulled on the little handle. He popped the second door loose from its frame and shook his head. Why didn't his mother get it that leaving the doors unlocked was dangerous in any neighborhood? In this one it was suicide. With a quick turn he locked that door and sighed when the blinking of the television lights flashed across the threadbare curtain that shaded nothing. He strode into the living room, glanced at the couch where his mother lay. The empty bottle of vodka lay on the floor next to her, making the entire room reek.

"Do it," he told himself as he turned the knob to shut the television off. "Just do it, and don't think about it." He swiped the vodka bottle off the floor and kicked the chip bag in front of him to the garbage. Then he went back and checked the front door, which was unlocked as well. His spirit registered his irritation although outwardly he simply went through the motions he had long ago memorized.

Down the darkened hallway he padded until he got to the first room where he cracked the door and peeked in. As always, the sight brought a soft, sad smile to his face. Even in the midst of chaos and insanity, the little angel boy could look like peace itself. As he did every night of his life, Blaine stood there and breathed a promise to that sleeping figure. "I'm going to get you out of here, Dylan. I swear."

Then softly he closed the door, and went back out to the kitchen to start his fourth shift of the day.

By Wednesday of Spring Break Blaine knew he had to do something about his shoes. The hole that had started between the sole and the upper was ripping wider by the minute, and his toes felt like chopped spaghetti by noon every day.

During his lunch break that afternoon he had casually sauntered by the shoe department of Harmon's and glanced at the tags. He wasn't obvious enough to attract Kenneth's attention, which was good because even with his employee discount, there was no way he would ever be able to afford the shoes laid out for the masses.

A thought crossed his mind, but he quickly batted that away. She would think he was stalking her if he showed up at Galaxy Shoes again. But then again, she might not even be working tonight. It was a good possibility that she went off somewhere on vacation. It wasn't like he knew her schedule or anything.

So as he whoofed his half of a tuna sandwich down in the break room, he decided that after work he would make a short pit stop just to see what kind of a selection they had.

Melody didn't see him come in later that afternoon. She was elbow deep in boxes and shoes from the last customer who had tried on every single pair of size tens in the store and then decided he didn't like any of them. That was a great way to kill a commission check, she thought as she stuffed the last pair of shoes back in the box and stood to start the arduous task of putting them all back.

"Excuse me," the soft voice said behind her. "Umm, I was wondering…"

She whirled around, and the middle of her heart collapsed around the sight. "Blaine?"

He smiled as though at a joke only he knew. "I thought that might be you."

Whipping her hair over her ear, she bent down for two of the boxes. "Yeah. Who else would it be drowning in shoe boxes?"

He laughed and then glanced back at the shelves. "Hey, I was wondering if you knew why there are no size tens anywhere."

With a laugh, she held up the two boxes in her hands. "Because they're all right here waiting to be put back up."

"Oh. Well, how convenient." Blaine glanced down at the boxes in her hands and then all the way to those stacked at her feet. "You mind if I try a few on before you put them back? It would sure save me some time."

She shrugged. "They're all yours."

He sat down on the little stool and then looked back up at her skeptically.

"Oh," she said, sensing his discomfort. "I'll just be over here if you need anything."

"I'll remember that," he said with a smooth smile. He brushed the white and peach striped tie down as he reached for the first box.

With a nod, she drifted out of sight but furtively kept her attention on him as he went about choosing a pair of shoes. There was just no other way to say it. He was gorgeous. He had traded in the blue shirt for a light peach number that brought out the lighter highlights in his brown hair. Too bad she didn't know he was coming in, she would've taken a little extra time to put herself together this morning. She pulled her fingers through her past-shoulder-length hair and flipped it over her shoulder and then yanked at the awful dull purple Galaxy Shoes polo she was forced to wear. After nearly nine hours, she was quite sure she looked atrocious. Which of course was about the way things always went.

Blaine was careful to tuck his old shoes in the crease behind the stool in case she came back. Truthfully he hadn't wanted her to leave, but when he realized she might actually see how bad his shoes looked, he was glad she had. However, when he'd narrowed the choice to three pairs, he really needed a better opinion than his own. He looked around the store and noticed her straightening a wall of socks just beyond the shelving.

"Melody?" he called, and she turned. He loved the brightness of her eyes and her smile.

"Did you make a decision?" Leaving the socks piled six high, she strode over to him. Her periwinkle Galaxy Shoes knit shirt brought out the blue of her eyes. Periwinkle, he thought with a thwack. Only guys who worked in the clothing industry knew there was such a thing. Still, he liked what it did for her eyes.

He shook his head in frustration as he held his hands out from his sides to examine the shiny black shoes currently in residence on his feet. "I was hoping you were better at this than I am."

She laughed as she came all the way over to him. "Hey, they're your shoes."

Spinning the toe of his shoe so it picked up his heel, he twisted to the side to look in the little floor mirror. "I know. I just have a hard time telling how they look. You mind?"

"Hey, what's a salesgirl for?" Sitting down on the stool he had vacated, she crossed her legs before crossing her hands on her knees. "Let's see the options."

"Well, there's this one." He handed her one pair. "It's nice looking, but I'm not sure I like the stitching along the side."

She took the shoe from him and pulled the tongue up. "Man-made upper. It'll fall apart in a week."

"Ah, bad choice." He took the shoe from her and stuffed it back in its box. "How about this one?"

Carefully she examined the next choice. "Leather. That's good. Yeah. That one would work."

"And this one?" he asked, slipping the one on his right foot off and handing it to her, wishing he didn't notice how nice it was to be so close to her or how horrible his feet smelled from being on them all day. His heart was pounding in his ears so loud, he was sure she could hear it too.

She examined the shoe carefully and then handed it back. "That one will work too."

He wished it was easier to not notice how relaxed and normal she was. For some unknown reason he liked that about her. She was just Melody, not Melody-trying-to-be-Fabulous. It was a nice change from the girls he was normally around. "Great." He looked at the two shoes now in his hands. Both were deep brown and but for the different stitching, there really wasn't much difference.

"Why don't you try them on? Maybe we can eliminate one that way."

Figuring it was worth a try, he bent and put the first shoe back on.

"Now, walk," she commanded.

He looked at her in surprise. "Where?"

"Anywhere. Around the shelves. Up and down the aisle. Just walk."

Slowly, feeling her gaze going with him, he walked around the shelves.

"How do they feel?"

"A little tight," he admitted.

"Tight is not good."

Blaine bounced twice on the toes. "Won't they stretch out?"

"Better to get one that fits right out of the box. Here. Try this one."

He swapped the shoes out and then stood to try them out.

"Better?" she asked.

"Still tight," he said, shaking his head.

"Okay. Then why don't we try a 10 ½?"

"But I wear a ten."

"Just for the funny of it, let's try one."

He shrugged and sat down on the bench she had vacated to remove the shoes. When she returned with the bigger shoe, he slipped them on his feet, and instantly his little toe said, "Ah."

"Better?" she asked.

He tested them out on the floor. "Much."

"Walk."

Dutifully he stood and walked around the shelves again, even bouncing in the shoes a little when his feet felt the newfound freedom. "Wow. These are much better."

"How do you like the style?"

He looked down and nodded, but then thought better of giving his own opinion. Back on her side of the shelves, he turned slightly. "What do you think?"

She folded her arms as she scrutinized his feet. "It's a good color. It'll go with anything. I think it's good." Then she seemed to catch herself. "But it doesn't really matter what I think."

Trying not to be obvious, Blaine glanced at the box, but she caught just enough of his gaze to understand. "They're originally

$60, but they're on clearance for $45."

He was genuinely touched although she had no idea how much that comment helped and she was just doing her job. Gratefully he smiled at her. "Then I'll take them."

"Cool," she said as though she hadn't expected to make the sale. "I can take them to the front for you if you'd like."

"Oh." He glanced back at the pair in the crease behind the chair. "I think I'll wear them—if you don't mind."

"Let me see the two right quick."

He handed them to her not really understanding. Quickly she checked under the tongue of each.

"It's a pair." She handed them back. "I'll just meet you up front."

"Be there in a second."

As soon as she was gone, he gathered up his old shoes and stuffed them into the box, carefully covering them with the tissue paper. Then he glanced around to make sure he wasn't leaving anything behind. The area was stacked with boxes just like he found it. His gaze caught the Size 10 stamped on the side of one of the boxes. No wonder the other ones had never felt quite right. With a shrug he started to the front.

Melody had just reached the counter when Farin Jerell, the manager on duty, slipped up beside her. "Oo, who's the dish?"

"Dish?" Melody asked as she began typing in her code.

"The guy," Farin said as she smoothed out the non-existent wrinkles at the stomach of her orange stretch shirt that was living up to its name. "He is unbelievable."

Barely glancing up, Melody caught Farin's meaning. "Oh, Blaine? He's just a friend of mine."

A good six inches shorter than Melody who wasn't exactly tall, Farin had a flitty, fairy quality to her that annoyed Melody to no end. "So, you know him then?" Farin asked.

"Yeah. Why?" Melody asked, but didn't bother to get the answer because Blaine picked that moment to approach the counter. She smiled at him. Not the fake smile she usually used, but a real smile that reached her toes with its happiness. Farin was right. He was gorgeous. Out of her league, but gorgeous nonetheless. Thankful that Farin had vacated the front of the store,

Melody finished punching in her code. "Would you like some socks to go with that today?"

He glanced at the display. "No, I think I'm good there."

"Okay. Phone number?"

Just then Farin reappeared at her elbow. "Melody. You have a phone call."

Melody turned in surprise. "A call?" She never got calls.

"In the back. I'm sorry. It sounded important," Farin said.

"Oh, well…" Melody glanced back at Blaine. "Umm…"

"It's okay. I'll handle this one." Farin smiled at Blaine sweetly. She took hold of Melody and pulled her from the computer. "Don't worry. You'll get the commission."

"O…Okay." Melody backed to the end of the counter. "I guess I'll see you later, Blaine."

He smiled. "Yeah. Later."

Seeing no other option, she turned and headed for the back.

The petite raven-headed girl stepped into Melody's spot. "Phone number?"

Blaine's attention stayed with Melody a second more as she disappeared through the shelves of shoes.

"Hello. Earth to Blaine," the girl said, and he shook himself out of the trance.

"Oh, umm… 555-4357."

"And how do you want to pay for this?"

He pulled out his checkbook, scribbled the numbers down, and signed it. Handing it over to her, he glanced back to where Melody had gone, absurdly hoping she would make it back before he had to leave.

"So Blaine Donovan," the girl said, surveying the check, "you got a place to where those nice, new shoes?"

"A place…? Umm. Work?" He picked up the box and slid it under his arm.

Farin laughed as she punched in his information. "No, I didn't mean work. I meant…well, I was just thinking, some of us are going out Friday night. End of Spring Break kind of thing. You wouldn't be interested, would you?"

Blaine's attention crashed from the back to the checkout counter. "Oh, I don't…"

"Ah, come on," Farin said with a quick wink. "You know what they say, 'All work and no play makes Blaine a dull boy.' What do you say? I can call you tomorrow night with the details."

"But you don't…" Then he caught sight of the computer and understood all too well. "Oh, sure. I guess so."

"Cool," she said happily. "Oh, I'm Farin by the way."

He took the hand she offered and tried to smile. Only then did he realize how beautiful she really was. A great offer from a beautiful girl. Where was his head? Charm machine—On. "Well, hello, Farin, it's nice to meet you. I'm…"

"Blaine," she said with a coy laugh. "I know."

His smile said it all.

By the time Melody returned to the front, Blaine was gone.

"There was no one on the phone, Farin," she said more than mildly annoyed.

"Oh, really?" Farin asked as though she was concerned by that. "Hmm. I guess it wasn't as important as they thought it was."

"Guess not," Melody said still not happy. "Linda called while I was back there though. She was wondering if you got that shipment of Aerosoles this morning."

"Okay, I'll be sure to give her a call in a few," Farin said and rechecked the counter. "Can you handle everything out here?"

Considering there wasn't another customer in the whole store, that answer was pretty easy. "Sure. No problem."

In a way Blaine never expected to hear from Farin again but in another, he wasn't all that surprised when the phone rang the next evening.

"Hey, Blaine, what are you up to?" Sweet. She sounded so very sweet.

He repositioned the phone at his ear as his gaze shifted to the open architecture book across the room on the table. "Just hanging out, how about you?"

"Putting together our little outing for tomorrow night. You still going to be able to make it?"

"Umm, what time did you say again?"

"We'll probably meet at The Bar Houston around ten. Don't

want to get there too early you know."

"Oh, of course not. Who else is coming?" Not that he would know any of the others, but just in case.

"Everybody's not nailed down yet, but probably Ben and Karen, and maybe Ty and Delise. I thought I'd call Eddie and Kyla too, but who ever knows with those two."

"Oh, yeah," he said suddenly realizing this sounded like the loading of the Ark.

"You know, Blaine." Farin said his name slowly and with emphasis. "I was also wondering… I mean not that you have to or anything, but well, my car's in the shop. I'm sure it's out of your way, and all but…"

His head clicked on what she was saying. "Oh, I could pick you up if you want."

"Could you? That would really be so great because I hate sitting on that console in Karen's car. I'll be at work until nine. Why don't you just swing by there?"

"Sounds good." He made quick three mental notes to himself at the same time. Babysitter. Peyton. No overtime for tomorrow.

"I spoke to Mrs. Sanchez today," Melody's mother said as she sat in the living room watching the mouse race around the virtual track on the television the next afternoon.

"Oh, yeah?" she said not really hearing the other end of the conversation.

"You'll never guess who's back in town."

"Who?"

Big dramatic pause that Melody didn't even hear. "Bobby Wilson."

"That's nice."

"Nice? Did you hear what I said? Bobby Wilson is back in town," her mother repeated. "And Vera said he's back to stay this time. Got a job over in the paint store down on 157th. I think he's going to be the manager or something."

"That's nice," Melody said again as she continued to roll the mouse ball around the screen.

"Whatever happened with you and him anyway?" her mother asked as she sat down in the faded brown chair to watch her daughter.

"Me and Bobby?"

"Yeah."

Melody shrugged. "I don't know. I guess we just went in different directions." That and she caught him with Roxie Gallegos, but that was more information than her mother needed to know.

"He was always such a nice boy. So polite. And now that he's got his education behind him…"

Melody sighed as the mouseball veered one second too long on the round bridge and plunged to his death in the ether below. "Bobby's not my type."

"What, not your type? He's a nice guy with a steady job and a paycheck. How is that not your type?"

"Trust me, Mom. He's not." Melody switched off the game box and pulled herself up from the floor. "I think I'm going to call it a night."

"Rather than stay down here and talk to me."

"Rather than stay down here and let you fix me up." Melody smiled in spite of herself. She couldn't be too mad. She'd fixed too many people up in her time to get angry.

"I just want you to be happy," her mother said, pouting.

"I am happy, Mom. Me, myself, and I—we are very happy."

"But you're 26 years old. Shouldn't you be out at least looking?"

"Good night, Mom," she called as she mounted the stairs.

"You could do worse!" her mother called.

Worse than Bobby Wilson? That would be a stretch.

Three

"I hope Nathan gets here pretty soon," Farin said on Friday evening as she stood behind Melody and looked out the storefront window.

"Got a hot date?" Melody asked as she worked with the computer. Farin always had a hot date, and Nathan always found a way to be late enough to send her into a conniption. As far as Melody could see everything was right on schedule.

"The hottest," Farin breathed. She leaned backward on the counter and smiled at Melody. "Remember that guy from the other night?"

There were a lot of guys from the other night that Farin had drooled over.

"Which one? The one who talked on his cell the whole time?"

"No, dummy. That guy you knew. Blaine."

With that name, all of the air whooshed out of Melody's lungs.

"You know, your friend Blaine?" Farin went to work rifling through the price codes.

Melody had to clear her throat to get anything out. "Hmm. I didn't know you knew him all that well."

"I don't really, but he called me last night, and I figured you know, I'm not doing anything tonight so why not?"

'Why not?'—Farin Jerell summed up in two words.

Farin turned from the register. "So, come on, Mel, give me the low down on him. You said you're friends. What do I need to know?"

Melody shrugged as though it mattered nothing to her. "He's

a nice guy. I'm sure you'll love him."

Just then through the glass of the front window, Melody saw it, and what was left of her breath vanished. The gold-bronze Carrera just as she remembered it. He parked at the curb, and when he stepped out, Farin fairly squealed with delight.

"Oh, my… You're kidding me. Melody! You didn't tell me he drives a Porsche."

She couldn't breathe. "Yeah. I must've forgotten that detail."

Wishing she could hide even as the bells at the door rang, Melody spun and went to busy herself repositioning the purses and bags along the side wall. How she continually found herself watching guys she really liked being swept off their feet and carried away by beautiful women, she had no idea. It just wasn't fair. Oh, to be a thousand miles away where she wouldn't be subjected to hearing them.

"Hi, Blaine." Farin's silky-sweet voice carried easily over to Melody.

What she wouldn't give to disappear. This was all so in-your-face unfair.

"Hi. Are you ready?"

"Yeah, just let me get my stuff from the back." Farin sauntered to the back, and the sway of her hiphuggers was so obvious Melody wanted to crawl in a hole.

Rolling her eyes and barely shaking her head, she went back to sorting the purses. They weren't Prada. They weren't even Prada knock-offs. The dreariness of her life weighed down on her. If only she was Farin or Eve…

"Hey." The word was soft and careful behind her.

Melody turned to find Blaine smiling from where he stood at the closest counter to her. Even his eyes seemed to glint with a hope that she might want to say hi. Her smile drifted through her. "Hey." She bent and swiped a turquoise purse from the floor. "Big date, I see."

His smile fell as did his gaze. He crossed his arms and leaned against the pane glass with the big, yellow letters screaming "Spring Sale." In a white shirt and charcoal jacket, he looked like he was posing for GQ. She hated that. It hurt her heart. His chocolate-colored locks fell down to one side—waved just so. They were longer than she'd ever seen them.

"I guess," he said, glancing back to the storeroom. His gaze slid back to her. "So, you're working again I see."

"Yep." Hanging the last purse on the rack, she straightened her shirt and strode over to the counter. "Can't live on Daddy's money like other people."

Blaine kicked away from the window and followed her. "You got anybody in mind when you say that?" He crossed his arms again, standing feet planted solidly, blocking her escape from the registers.

She felt the scowl more than she saw it, but before she could reply, Farin made her grand entrance. Tight black dress and heels taller than a Houston Rocket, she looked made for the clubs.

Taking a full step backward, Blaine appraised her. "Wow."

Melody spun to look at Blaine who had obviously forgotten she was even on the planet. His smile was that of a guy seeing the best T-bone broiled to perfection. He stepped around the counter, and if a bomb had gone off, he wouldn't have noticed.

Farin beamed at the attention. "You like?" She spun slowly, her hands dancing in the air with her black sequined purse.

"Very nice," he breathed. At her side, he laced his fingers through hers, making Melody's stomach feel like she was again on Greased Lightnin'. "Shall we?"

A giggle was his only answer. They started for the door, and just as they got there, another customer came in. This guy gave Farin a once-over as well as the two of them crossed into the darkness beyond. Feeling like the ugly duckling in a pond full of swans, Melody stuffed her hatred of all things guys down into who-cares.

"Can I help you?"

Some absurd part of him wished Melody was still looking when he got to the car with Farin. They made a good couple—she inches shorter but striking an awesome figure in that dress. However, when he opened the door and helped Farin in, his gaze slid back to the windows. Melody was nowhere to be seen. That irritated him.

He ran around and got in, purposely putting the sunroof back.

"Nice," Farin said so smoothly Blaine wondered what else she had in mind other than dancing. Her hand came across and rubbed across the back of his on the gearshift. Any question was answered with that gesture.

"The Bar Houston?" he asked.

"Or your place."

Blaine glanced over at her. "Let's start with dancing, and then we'll see."

"Your call."

From the time they left until the time Melody went to bed, nothing went right. It took an hour more than normal to close up, what with the stockroom in disaster mode. She tripped on a hole in the parking lot, nearly sprawling herself in the path of on-coming traffic, and the burger she stopped to get on the way home was cold and greasy.

"Ugh." Making as much noise as she could, she slumped over the table and chewed each bite with a vengeance. Halfway through the burger, it hit her that this was probably why she was so fat. Eating at all hours of the night, inhaling burgers because salad was too difficult. At that thought, she flipped the last half of the burger to the table and sighed.

As much as she hated to admit it, the reason guys like Blaine didn't take a second look at her like they did at the Farins of the world was because she wasn't rail thin and stacked in all the right places. She could never pull off that dress Farin had worn. It would've looked like someone painted it on. Disgusted with herself and life, she chunked the burger into the trash and plucking at her work shirt because it stunk, she went upstairs to take a shower.

Her mother was long-since in bed as she would've been if she didn't have to have funds to be able to continue her education. In the bathroom, she laughed at that. Education. Meant to further her miserable single life. The truth was guys didn't want an education. They wanted a bubblehead with a knockout body like Farin. Melody glanced in the mirror, and the disgust deepened. She looked like she'd been deep-fried with her burger.

Nothing about her looked even remotely right. Her make-up was a mess. Her hair was worse. In her jeans and stupid light blue shirt, she looked like someone who should be working at the Waffle Wagon. Turning so she wouldn't have to be more humiliated, she started peeling off her clothes. No wonder guys ran the other direction, so would she.

Just because it would be the final nail in her coffin of gloom, she stepped on the scales. What she'd already known stared back at her. The question of what Farin saw when she looked at those numbers wafted over Melody. Farin didn't think twice about the size of her latest outfit. "Oh, yes. A size two please."

Abhorrence at the loathsome mess her body was in snaked through Melody. But the facts were clear. If she wanted a guy, any guy, to ever notice her, she would have to make some serious changes. Vowing that starting tomorrow, she would start dieting and exercising and stick to it this time, she got in the shower. It was one thing to want to diet. It was another to know you had no choice.

"And then we broke out the rum shots," Farin said as she practically draped herself over Blaine in the round booth. "Jacqueline was puking before we got back to the dorms. It was hilarious."

"Jacqueline never could handle her liquor," the girl on the other side of Blaine who was Farin's roommate said just before she downed another Jell-o shot. When she came back to earth, she ogled Blaine. "Or her men."

"O-kay." Blaine retraced his gaze out to the dance floor. "Come on, Farin. Let's go dance."

"Dancing?" Farin giggled in that little girl way that crawled right across Blaine's nerves. "Me like." She flipped her hair over her shoulder as she glanced back at her friend.

Blaine wanted nothing of seeing that exchange so he grabbed her hand and kept walking. On the dance floor he watched as Farin slid her shoulders through the beat, keeping her gaze only on him. How someone could seduce someone in open public like that with no qualms at all, he had no idea. Maybe some guys thought that was sexy, and some might even take her up on the offer she was obviously giving. For him, he glanced around them to see if anyone was staring at them as humiliation crept up his chest.

However, the others seemed to be in their own little worlds, so he swallowed, turned to Farin and tried to smile. When that song ended, a slower one took its place, and without asking, Farin stepped into his arms. Blaine fought with his feet to keep them moving—back and forth, back and forth. He glanced down at her, the tresses of auburn snaking down the outline of his jacket as her face nestled next to him. She was nuzzling there, burrowing into him.

On his back, her hand worked its way up past the break in his jacket and to his waistline. He fought not to squirm out of her grasp. It was odd how she could be so into this and have no idea that he so wasn't. Praying that the song would end before she went too far, Blaine glanced around again at the other couples. Most were doing just what she was. Some going even farther in the dim light. But instead of that easing the qualms, it increased them. Why had he agreed to this? What was he thinking?

The song ended, and moving away ever-so-slightly, Farin angled her gaze up to him through the heavily massacred eyelashes. Her smile spoke of finding a quiet place and letting nature take its course. Blaine purposely moved his gaze from hers.

"You know," she said, lifting her shoulders as they neared the table. "It's almost midnight. What do you say we go back to your place for some real fun?"

My place? The thought was so absurd, Blaine almost laughed out loud. "Oh. You're not having fun here?"

"Well, yeah, but…"

He waited for her to scoot into the booth. Nothing in him wanted to be near the girl downing Jell-o shots like candy. Wasted was clearly getting closer by the second. It was at that moment that he realized Farin had reached into her tiny purse and pulled out a cigarette. His stomach roiled at the thought.

She put it to her lips and with that same look in her eye held the lighter up to him. "It's just not the same if I do it."

Wishing the floor would open up and take him, Blaine tried to smile as he took the lighter from her. Girls like this were so predictable and so annoying. He tried not to think about it as he lit the cigarette for her. She inhaled and blew a long line of smoke into the air.

"Ah. That's so much better." It was then that her hand slid under the table and found his thigh. "Don't you think?"

Blaine sucked in the gasp. Taking hold of her hand lest it get too carried away, he fought not to let his shift away from her land him on the floor. "You know, Farin." He cleared his throat when she blew another stream of smoke his direction. "It is getting kind of late."

Glee sprang to her eyes, but she covered it well. "I thought you'd never ask."

"I… Well… Okay." He slid from the booth, hoping upon hope that he could get her home without major humiliation for one of them though that didn't look promising. Some not-so-subtle something told him she might not take no for an answer.

"We're going back," Farin said, emphasizing the word 'back.'

"Oh," her roommate said, her gaze dulled by the weight of the alcohol. "'s okay. I'll just crash at Eddie's."

The fact that Eddie had been dancing the entire night with some girl named Tiffany apparently made little difference to Jell-o girl.

"Cool," Farin said. "See ya in the morning."

"Yeah."

There were no words to express how desperately Blaine wanted out of this situation. Truth be told, one part of him had known she was like this when he first met her. And part of him knew he had to be an idiot not to be falling all over her like most guys in his place would. However, the longer he was with her, the more he simply wanted not to be.

She maintained the smoking party-girl thing all the way to the car. As they stepped up to it, however, the understanding that their first battle had arrived crashed into him.

"Uh, I'd rather you didn't smoke in the car," Blaine said, assessing the weave of her steps and wondering just how many she'd had.

"Oh, come on. One little cigarette won't hurt your precious car."

"Yeah. Well, I just don't want to get that started. I don't like the smell."

Farin leaned into him and took a big sniff of his jacket. "You smell just like it. What's the difference?"

Understanding of just how badly he reeked made him wrinkle his nose even as he reached for her cigarette. "That's beside the point. I don't want Pey… my car to smell like a tobacco factory." He managed to grab the cigarette without burning his hand or hers. He threw it to the ground and ground it out with the toe of his shoe.

Petulant, Farin crossed her arms as he unlocked the car.

When he turned, he found her, bottom lip curled under and a glint in her eye. Before he could think another thought, she launched herself at him. His hands went out on both sides as she kissed him soundly. She tasted about as good as she smelled.

With both hands, he pushed her backward. "Hey. Hey! Farin. Whoa."

"What? I'm just giving you a little preview." She came at him again, but he dodged her and opened the door. With a long clearly confused look, she stepped past him and folded onto the seat.

Blaine closed the door and walked around to his side, side-stepping the couple currently pressed against the huge, red 4 X 4 next to them. He was beginning to remember why he didn't do this more. "Tell me how to get to your dorm again."

True to form, Farin draped herself over the console and onto his shoulder, her hand drifting once again atop his thigh. It took everything in him to ignore it.

He started the car. "Uh, your dorm?"

"We could go to your place." Her lips angled for his neck.

Shrugging her off, he put the car in drive. "My place is across town. It's late, and I've got work in the morning."

She seemed surprised by that but gave him the directions as he'd asked. Although she only partially resumed her seat, never had he been so grateful for a gearshift and bucket seats. Nonetheless, the reprieve didn't last long. The fact that "no" wasn't in her vocabulary became abundantly clear the farther they drove. Had he been the kind of guy to accept such an offer, he was quite sure there would've been no complaints. As it was, he had far too many things to worry about in his life without complicating it by getting someone pregnant.

With everything in him, he was thrilled to see the dorm when they pulled up. He got out, helped her out, and wondered how quickly he could get rid of her.

"You're really not coming up?" she asked, fairly hanging from him as they made their way up to the dorm doors. Her steps swayed on the weight of the alcohol. "You don't know what you're missing."

"Huh. I think I'd better get home." He almost lost his balance when she stumbled on a crack in the sidewalk and yanked him sideways. "Whoa. Careful there." Bracing himself to hold her up, Blaine opened the heavy door. "And we're here. Finally."

"You really don't have to leave." The fact that she was still trying despite his 17,000 protests sounded more desperate each time. "Kyla isn't going to be back tonight. We'll have the room all to ourselves."

In the bright lights of the dorm foyer, Blaine felt conspicuous at best. He couldn't help but notice the looks the three coeds gave them as they strode out the doors. "No, Farin. I really have to go." He leaned her up against the wall lest she fall when he let her go.

"But we were just starting to have fun." A devilish glint jumped to her eyes as she anchored her wrists across his shoulders. "Ten minutes. I'll make it worth your while."

She leaned toward him, her eyes falling closed with each movement. Her hand slipped between them, and his alert systems screamed to life.

"Hey, Farin. Look. I'm serious. I have to go." Taking both of her hands in his, he shoved them toward her. He leveled his gaze at her although petulant and drunk, he was sure she would never truly understand what he was telling her. "I have to go."

Making sure she was leaning on the wall, he let her go and headed back for the doors. Of course, a gentleman wouldn't leave her like that, but a lady wouldn't throw herself at the first moving target she met either.

"Call me!" she yelled after him.

In disbelief, Blaine picked up his hand to wave over his shoulder even as he pushed through the doors into the cool night air. Air. It felt glorious. He was still an hour from making it home, and concern flowed through him again when he thought about the smell in the car. Once inside, he knew it was as bad as he'd feared. There was really no other option. As he pulled into the late night traffic, he rolled both windows down, turned the air on high, and prayed for a really stiff breeze. The only good thing was this night was now in the past.

By the time Melody got to work on Monday evening, all she'd had since Saturday morning was five celery sticks, ten carrots, one salad, and two glasses of water. The diet was going pretty well, save for the headache she now carried with her everywhere. On Saturday she'd actually gone to the gym and worked out for two hours. The fact that she couldn't move on Sunday was remedied with two doses of Advil and half a bottle of ointment from her mother's medicine cabinet. She still hadn't lost any weight, but that was only a matter of time.

"You're late," Farin said two seconds after Melody walked in the back.

"Late? I'm supposed to start at five."

"Nathan redrew the schedules. You were supposed to be here at four." Farin practically threw the schedule in her face.

"He… what?" Panic flooded through her. "I can't be here at four on Mondays. I have class."

"Not my problem." Farin flounced out.

Melody let out a low guttural sound and went to find Nathan. This had better be a really bad April Fool's Day joke.

"Hey, Blaine. How's life for the most handsome guy in the men's department?" Eve Knight, with her sky high heels and swank outfits, could always perk up any visit to the break room. She strode across the room, dark hair flowing down her back, oblivious to the stares of the two new assistants at Harmon's.

"Eve." Blaine's smile was never far behind when she showed up. "Come on, have a seat. You finished with the fall line buy yet?" He spun a chair her direction.

Two seconds to grab a small frappuccino and Eve accepted the chair. She flipped her hair back over her shoulder, revealing a fall of aqua and silver lamé strips. "Almost."

"So, how's the new house? Did y'all get moved?" Blaine sipped his Dr. Pepper. It wasn't as flashy as the other offerings, but it was cheaper.

"Ugh. I'm so tired of boxes. I could scream."

"Yeah." He took a head-to-toe inventory of her. "It looks like you're really overdoing it there."

She laughed and waved a set of long, tanned fingers at him. "The guys did most of it. A.J., Gabe, Jeff. They've been at it for two weeks now. But we finally got all the boxes over on Saturday. It's amazing how much stuff two people can accumulate in such a short time."

Aside from the recent nuptials, which Blaine had not been invited to, he didn't really know much about her life outside of the store. Of course there was that one date, which turned into a non-date, but he no longer counted that. "So is this wonderful new place somewhere close?"

Her eyelashes covered half of her eyes as she glanced at him. "No, we went the suburb route. A.J.'s even thinking about transferring out there."

It would be better if they could have a conversation without it involving A.J., but they never did.

"Oh, really? And you?"

Eve stretched her long legs and downed the last of her drink. "I'm keeping my options open. Who knows? Maybe in a couple months I'll have a good reason to quit and just stay home."

A full second elapsed before Blaine caught the intent of her words. Protective admiration poured through him as he sat up. "Really? And this will be expected?"

With a soft smile, she shrugged. "We'll see."

The sight of A.J.'s old car parked in front of Mrs. Knight's house as Melody drove past made her push on the brake. Her gaze snagged and held on it. It could only mean one thing. One person. For a breath of a second she considered stopping, but then the thought of seeing the two of them together roiled through her empty stomach.

Forget it, Mel. If he'd wanted to talk to you, he'd have done it by now. He's got her. Why would he want to waste any time with you?

At that moment the front door swung open, and A.J. looking more handsome than he ever had stepped out and bounded down the stairs. That cap, perpetually backward, reminded her of how he used to be, and her heart danced with the thoughts. His gaze traced to the roadway, and surprise catapulted to his face. He picked his hand up in a wave, and Melody still staring very nearly hit a parked car sitting at the next house. It snagged her attention a mere two seconds before disaster. Swerving, she slammed on the brakes and ended up dead center on the street.

The breaths came in heaves as she fought to explain to herself that she hadn't actually hit the thing. It was then she saw him approach and heard the tapping at her window. Fighting the humiliation, she reached for the window control and let it slide down between them.

"Mel, are you all right? You almost took out that car."

"Yeah." She was still gasping. "I'm fine. I just…"

A horn behind her blared, yanking both of their attentions to it. His returned to the car before hers did.

"You'd better get out of the street. Why don't you pull in right up here?" He pointed to the curb next to the house two down from his.

She was so close, so unbelievably close to her own house that she could see it even from where she sat. The thought of simply driving off crossed through her consciousness, but she couldn't do that to him. As much as she wanted to, she just couldn't.

With shaking hands, she parked the car and did her best impression of being excited to see him when she got out. However, between the near-collision and the lack-of-food, her body was holding on by a mere thread. She fought not to let the headache take her down with it. "Hi." Stumbling on the curb, she barely caught her balance as he came abreast of her. "S-sorry about that."

"Mel?" There was concern dripping from the question and his gaze. "Are you sure you're okay?"

She laughed, a hollow, off-handed laugh. "Of course. I'm fine. I'm just surprised to see you slumming in these parts that's all."

The barb hit him square, and he backed up a step. His gaze slid back to his mom's house. "I was just coming to get the rest of my stuff out of mom's garage. Now that I have room…"

A knife like she'd never felt went right through her, but she breathed, fighting to stay on her feet. "Yeah, I heard you got a new place."

A.J.'s gaze swung back to her, and his dark eyes narrowed. "How'd you hear…" The clouds cleared. "Oh, Mom."

Defiance swept through her. "No, actually Blaine. Blaine Donovan. You remember him. The guy who took Eve to the park that day." She was being cruel, and she knew it. Nubbing the toe of her shoe into the curb, she looked up at him.

His reaction couldn't have been any better. The almond eyes widened like saucers, and his mouth fell a full inch open. Fighting to recover, he tucked his hands into the crooks of his armpits and leaned back on the waist-high chain link fence. "I didn't know you ever saw him anymore."

One tiny piece of her said she should be honest, but the rest of her hurt too much. She shrugged. "We've seen each other off-and-on." Okay. It wasn't a total lie. "We're mostly just friends."

"But?" A.J. could always read her loud-and-clear.

"Well." She dipped her head to her shoulder and let her gaze fall to the concrete. "I don't have any better prospects. So…"

When she looked up, the fact that A.J. was about to spit nails was abundantly clear. She glanced down the block at his vehicle, and it occurred to her that this might be the last time they would ever stand out here like this again. So many times before floated through her memory, and each and every one brought a fresh wave of pain.

"You're taking the trap set then?" she asked, feeling the words run her through. How she would ever be able to stand there and watch him drive away was beyond her.

A.J. shrugged, a hard mask of anger locked over his normally soft, smiling face. "Mom doesn't need it, and now that we have the room…"

The increasing distance between them threatened to break her heart in two. Didn't he know what this was doing to her, knowing he was leaving forever? Couldn't he feel what he was doing to her heart? Struggling to keep the tears in their rightful place, she yanked in a breath.

"Well, I'd better let you get back home. I'm sure Eve will be wondering what's taking you so long." Melody turned to her car and fumbled with the latch. Tears flooded her vision, blurring everything but the memories. Why did she have to be so fat and ugly? Why could guys like A.J. never notice her? Door open although she had no idea how, she dropped into the seat of her car, hoping she could get away without completely humiliating herself in front of him.

"I guess I'll see you later then," he said, standing mid-sidewalk.

She tried to smile as she waved. Then as if her life depended on it, she spun into the street. Brushing, wiping, and swiping at the tears, she fought to get them to stop even as her heart crumpled over them. A.J. Knight, the one decent guy who ever looked her direction, was gone, lost in the arms of a woman Melody could never have competed with even on her best day.

In her own driveway, Melody jumped out, slammed the car door, and raced inside. She didn't need A.J. Not if he could be that heartless. She started through the kitchen and only at the door to the living room did she remember she hadn't eaten since lunch. Defiantly she pushed on through and kept walking. If only skinny models had a chance, then her only option was to become one.

Four

"Don't even think about it! There's plenty of room." The blonde walking with Blaine up the stairs sounded just like Farin. From half-a-flight back Melody had no trouble making out their words or the flirty tone. "We're just going for the weekend. We'll be back by Monday. I swear."

"I'm busy, Lana," Blaine said, and at that moment his gaze swung backward down the steps as they turned at the landing. He saw her and did a double take. In the next instant, he looked as if she was his long lost accountant come back to tell him he'd won the lottery. "Melody! I didn't see you there. Wow. What are you doing here?" He stopped, which stopped Lana too as he waited for Melody to join them.

She was sure her face registered every question in her consciousness. Pushing a strand of hair behind her ear, she shifted her Biology book to the other hand. "Oh, hi. Um. I was... I'm going to class." Putting her hand on her book just as she reached where they stood, she smiled at him. "What're you doing?"

The fact that Lana was shooting daggers at her with her eyes did nothing to calm her nerves. She swallowed but kept her gaze on him, still trying to understand the situation.

"I can't believe I haven't seen you around. Have you been going to class all semester?" he asked as if he really was glad to see her.

The yes lodged in her throat, so she just nodded. The question of if he noticed her because of the four pounds she'd lost crossed her mind, but she beat that back to focus on more important things. "I graduate next Spring if I can get through biology."

"Ugh biology ate my lunch," Blaine said as if he had no clue the gorgeous blonde at his other elbow was getting more and more annoyed by the moment. "Who do you have?"

"Dr. McDonald."

"Oh, you poor thing." Blaine arched his back and threw his gaze to the ceiling. "You have my sympathies." Then he stopped. "Listen. Why don't you give me your number, and I can let you see my old tests? I know he gives different ones each time, but at least then you'd have something to study off of."

The suggestion was so out-of-the-blue, Melody knew she must be dreaming. "Oh. Uh. You don't have to."

Blaine smiled that mind-mushing smile. "I knew I kept them for some reason."

Lana glanced at her watch as Melody searched for a free piece of paper to write her number.

"I think I'll just meet you up there," Lana finally said, and Melody heard the annoyance.

Barely turning to her, Blaine smiled. "That's cool. I'll see ya in a few."

With a not-so-kind look, Lana flounced off. The second she was gone Melody could have sworn she saw Blaine sigh with relief. However, that made no sense at all, so she quickened her search for the pen. "I'm sorry."

"Na. It's cool." He leaned against the beige-tiled wall as other students jostled up the steps behind them.

Finally she found a pen and a small slip of paper. In her best handwriting, she transferred her number. Giving it to him, she let her gaze fall to their feet. "You really don't have to though."

"No biggie." He looked at the paper and then stuffed the number in the pocket of his charcoal slacks and glanced up the stairs. "Well, I'd better get. Don't want to be late."

"Yeah. Me too." She hugged her books closer to her. They climbed the second half of the stairs, and it became clear Blaine was stopping before her. "I'll see you later."

"Later."

And with that, she left him standing on the second floor, watching her climb out of sight.

Blaine wasn't particularly proud of using Melody to get out of Lana's crosshairs, but it was too convenient not to. However, after class he made sure to watch lest Melody find him and do something that could ruin everything like follow him to his car. At the green Toyota, he glanced around to make sure no one he knew was watching. Quickly he jumped in and pumped the pedal. This was always the most dangerous time of all. If anyone ever saw, if anyone ever suspected… It's why he parked in the parking lot half a mile away that was reserved for latecomers and idiots. It's also why he parked on the other side of the mall and walked around it every day to work.

Once again, he coaxed Lillian to life and spun out into traffic. Thankfully the darkness blinded most of the world. In the safe anonymity of traffic, Blaine allowed himself to relax. He settled back into the seat and let his mind wander through the maze that was his life.

December and he would no longer have to live this double life. He would get a job at some architectural firm, get himself a real apartment, somehow find a way to take care of Dylan and get him through school too. This whole eighty-six hour day thing would be a distant memory. As he drove, he remembered the little slip of paper in his pocket. At a stoplight, he fished around and found it. Three lights down he picked it up and examined it.

Melody Todd. Interesting. He'd known her almost a year, but he'd never even thought to ask her last name. He wondered then what else he didn't know about her. The traffic moved forward, and he joined it only momentarily forgetting he was driving. He thought about their previous couple of meetings. She was cordial but not fawning. Not like Farin or Lana. Just why, he couldn't quite reach but he felt it nonetheless.

Because it was safe and had nothing to do with him or his crushing existence, he let his mind wind through the questions about her. What was she taking in school? How close was she to graduating? How had she come to be at Anderson Community College? The thought of actually calling her drifted through him. It wouldn't hurt. Then again, it wouldn't make anything any less complicated either. With that thought he flipped the slip of paper to the dashboard and pulled onto his street.

He wouldn't call her. He knew it, and he hoped she did too.

Melody pushed back at the thoughts of the overwhelming hunger gnawing at her. Blaine Donovan had spoken to her, asked for her number even. That couldn't be a coincidence. Her strategy was working. Forty more pounds or so, and maybe all the Blaine's of the world would be falling at her feet. It wasn't a given, but the chance meeting on the stairs had given her more hope than she'd had in months.

Thursday, she hoped. Each ring of the phone while she was studying made her heart jump. But it was never him. Once it was Deana from math class wanting to know if she wanted to go to the bars with some of them on Saturday. She declined. After all, by Saturday she might well have a date with a great guy, and she didn't want to have to share him.

Friday was more of the same except that a creeping feeling of "he isn't going to call" had begun whispering in the back of her mind. She chose to ignore it, and because it was rather quiet, that wasn't too hard.

By Saturday at work, she snapped at three people, and Nathan had to tell her to cool it. Hope still reigned, but it was losing the battle.

As she studied for the biology test on Monday night at the kitchen table, she glanced at the clock every so often. Why wasn't he calling? Had something horrible happened? Some accident? Some emergency? That was stupid and lame, but it was the only way she could think of to keep the real reason he wasn't calling from her heart.

Tuesday was a blur of hoping and giving up, hoping but knowing. When she pulled up to school on Wednesday, however, hope was losing the fight badly. She got out and dodged and weaved her way across the highway. If she could just see him, get a glimpse of him, see if his leg was in a cast up to his neck or something, anything that might explain that what she knew wasn't real.

At the drinking fountain on the first floor, she caught sight of him striding in the door. He had his glasses on, which was a whole new look for him in her eyes—more sophisticated and suave. But there was no cast, not even an obvious limp. Instead he strode right to the staircase and started up. Feeling stupid but having no better plan, she scooted to the staircase which spiraled up the other direction in a mirror to the one he was on. Carefully she climbed, catching glimpses of him just above her on the opposite side.

Sage button-down shirt, pressed just right. Charcoal pants. It was when she caught a glimpse of his shoes that her heart turned over and tears invaded her heart. She wondered if he even thought about what it would be like to run into her again or if he even cared enough to be embarrassed if he did. Would he even remember he had gotten her number? Probably not.

One thing was for sure in the whole stinking mess. She was sure to fail biology now.

Blaine didn't breathe a full breath until he reached the second floor. He had some lame excuse about going out of town ready in case he saw her, but he hated lying—especially to nice people like Melody. She didn't deserve to get mixed up in his off-kilter life. It was far better for her to stay as far away as possible. That's what he would've done if he'd had a choice.

That thought dogged him through the evening and all the way home where he found his mother passed out in a heap on the couch. Dylan was on the floor next to her, holding her hand. His little eyes closed in sleep that was anything but peaceful. With a sigh that really wasn't, Blaine put his backpack on the table and went into guardian mode. He picked up Dylan and had to fight to stay standing under the weight and length of his little brother who was becoming anything but little.

Down the darkened hallway, he weaved being careful not to clunk Dylan's head on the walls or the doorjamb. The kid had obviously had a tough enough night without giving him an additional headache. At the bed, Blaine worked the covers backward with his knee and then lay Dylan down. Blaine pulled the blankets up, stood back, and shook his head. They had to get out of here.

Thursday night, Melody never even noticed the phone ring until her mother called to her.

"Melody!"

"Coming!" she answered, flipping the book closed. With any

luck she wouldn't make it back to finish the reading anyway. In the living room, she flopped on the couch. "Hello?"

"Melody?" the soft female voice asked.

"Yes?" The last thing she wanted was to have the telemarketers on her trail.

"Oh, good. I'm glad I caught you. Hmm… This is Lisa Taylor, Jeff's wife?"

Confusion slid into and around Melody. Lisa Taylor? She didn't know a… "Oh. Lisa." Dread slithered through the confusion. "Eve's friend."

"Yeah. That's me." Lisa laughed happily, but nothing in Melody reciprocated the feeling. "Listen, we're going to have a little housewarming party for A.J. and Eve on Saturday night. We were hoping you could come."

To a housewarming party for that traitor? "Oh. I don't know. I might be scheduled to work." She wasn't, but she could arrange it if necessary.

"Can't you get off?" Lisa asked. "I know it would mean so much to A.J. if you were there."

Yeah, right.

"Really," Lisa said when the pause lasted too long. "Please, Melody. We'd love it if you came."

Not one piece of her wanted to say yes, but she couldn't say no. Cutting off every possibility of ever seeing him again would surely kill her. "Okay."

"Yeah?"

"Yeah. I'll come."

"Great." Lisa quickly gave her directions and said great three more times before it was time to sign off. "Well, I guess we'll see you about seven on Saturday. Oh, and Melody. You can bring a date if you want."

What Melody said after that, she had no clue because every synapse in her brain was homed to that one word—date.

"Hey, sorry to call you at work," the male voice on the other end of the Harmon's phone line when Blaine was paged at four o'clock on Friday. "This is Jeff, Eve's friend. Listen, I won't keep you long, but we're having a little party…"

For twelve hours since he'd hung up the phone, Blaine had considered calling Melody. It wouldn't be a crime exactly, but after his previous behavior, she had every right to ram the phone down his throat, and he knew it. So he didn't call. Instead he called Peyton.

Five

It was a desperation tactic pure and simple. Sure, the logic behind it was there even if the sanity was a little thin. Melody couldn't show up dateless nor could she not show up—although that option had crossed her mind more than once. So she had done the next to the last worst thing. She called Bobby.

Bobby Wilson was more redneck-ladder-climbing-ghetto-dweller than up-and-coming anything. And truthfully, his time away at College Station hadn't done much to improve the situation. He showed up in his big, old, beat-up white Chevy pickup with pipes that could be heard in Dallas. The fact that she had been the one to call him was not lost on Melody nor presumably on Bobby either.

"Well, look what the cat dragged in," he said by way of greeting when she got into his pickup at her curb. Letting him come to the door and get her was a set-up to never hearing the end of it from her mother, and she knew it.

"Nice to see you, too," she said, fighting for the frost not to find her words or tone as she slammed the door behind her.

Keeping her gaze away from him, she waited for him to pull away so he wouldn't drag every neighbor to the windows to see what was going on. However, neither he nor the pickup moved. Finally, she looked over at him, and his long, slow, wicked smile took an eternity to make it from his eyes to his mouth.

"It's been a long time, Mel-o-dy." He ogled her up and down. "Time's not changed you much, I see."

Melody licked her lips as revulsion rose in her throat. She fought to slow the racing of her heart. "Yeah. It's been a while. Huh?"

The light blue eyes leered at her from beneath the pate of

closely cropped dark blond hair. "You don't have to sit all the way over there, you know?" One long arm ensconced in red plaid reached over to her. "You can come on over here like you actually like me."

Just get through this, her heart pleaded even as she made the journey from passenger's seat to middle. It's only one night.

Everyone with the exception of A.J. seemed cordial enough and almost happy to see Blaine. Eve squealed her excitement when he walked in the door, and that always made things better. However, she had a bevy of guests to entertain, so she couldn't very well stick to his side the entire night. Thus, he was in the corner, drinking a beer when he glanced toward the door and nearly spewed cold foam all over the new beige carpet.

The swallow of liquid burned all the way down to his gut. Blinking twice, he struggled to assure his mind that he was actually seeing what he thought he was seeing. Melody, looking awesome in a crystalline white scoop-neck shirt that clung in all the right places, stood next to a tall guy who wasn't exactly keeping a polite distance. Slowly Blaine lowered his glass as he gazed at her. Not up in the clip as it usually was, her soft, blonde hair cascaded down onto her shoulders, all one length, but flowing like he'd never noticed it do before. He let out a long, slow breath.

A determined blink brought his mind back to his own reality, and he shook his head, knowing he'd already blown any chance of ever being with her. Stupid. He was so stupid. The whole situation was stupid. Not only could he never be with her, there was no way he could keep up appearances as long as it would take to actually have a real shot with her. Of course he had no hope of a real shot with anyone at the moment.

"Hi, there," a slim brunette said suddenly standing at his elbow. "I'm Charlotte."

Blaine turned to her, not fully letting his attention get to her from Melody. "Hey."

"I saw you standing over here by yourself, and I thought maybe you'd like some company."

"Oh, sure."

Somehow Melody hadn't expected Blaine to be there. The whole Bobby thing was about getting to A.J., but if she could rub it in Blaine's face too, so much the better. He was standing in the corner with some lithe brunette she'd never seen. Either that meant he'd brought a date she knew nothing about or he was trolling for new conquests. Typical.

Turning on her charm, she wrapped her arm through Bobby's. He looked down at her in surprise and chomped his gum twice as a wicked glint went through his eyes. Putting his arm around her all the way down to her hip, he pulled her closer so he could whisper in her ear.

"Don't get too fresh. I might have to take you outside right now."

Melody wanted to hurl. Instead, knowing they were on display, she reached up and hit Bobby on the chest, leaving her hand there for the benefit of anyone watching. "You'd better watch it…"

"Well, well, look who it is." A.J. was suddenly standing right in front of them. His light blue shirt and soft brown eyes made her heart flip, but she kept up the act as if he was just some guy she once knew.

"Well, A.J. Knight as I live and breathe." Bobby took his hand away from Melody to shake A.J.'s hand. It was the least polite handshake she had ever seen.

"Bobby," A.J. said, barely keeping his disgust under the surface. "I didn't know you were back in town."

"Just got back a couple weeks ago." Bobby put his arm back around Melody, and it was all she could do not to cringe. "I hope you don't mind me just showing up like this, but Mel couldn't wait to hook up again."

The revulsion on A.J.'s face when his gaze went from Bobby to Melody was unmistakable. "Oh, really." He clamped a hard mask of stone over his face. "Well, we're glad you could come."

"Oh! Here. This is for you." Melody held out the little present to him.

A.J. took it, never looking very happy about any of it. "You didn't have to, but thanks." He took a step back. "Enjoy. I've got to go find Eve. We're running low on drinks."

"Oh, okay." If her heart could've hurt anymore, Melody didn't know how. It felt like someone had just yanked it out and stepped on it. "I'll see you later."

"Yeah. Later." The words were spat more than said.

Her gaze slipped to the carpet as deep ache crawled through her. However, before she had time to recover, Bobby leaned down, his breath hot on her ear and neck.

"Speaking of drinks. Let's go get something. I hope they have whiskey and not just beer."

Let's hope not. "Oh, I'm not really thirsty yet, but maybe later."

"You mind if I get something?"

She shrugged, smiled, and moved with him every step over to the drinks.

It had been half a night of listening to Ms. Fashion Wanna-Be while watching Melody with Mr. Show-off himself from across the room. Every move the guy made screamed JERK. Still Melody hung on his every word, smiled at him like he was Superman, and generally made sure to blast that they were together on a loud speaker. It was beginning to make Blaine seriously ill. He needed air or at least a break.

"If you'll excuse me," Blaine said, wanting with everything in him to get away from the brunette what's her name who had attached herself to his side sometime before time began. They'd been talking for almost two hours, and he still didn't know her name. He didn't care. She was like all the rest of them—aggressive and obnoxious with her high titter of laughter and one-track-minded womanly wiles. It made him sick.

The only thing worse was the show going on across the room. He tried not to watch as he turned at the wall and stalked down the hallway to find the bathroom. In truth what he most wanted was to make a clean get-away, but he couldn't be rude to Eve—even if he wanted to ditch everyone else.

It was at the very end of the hall, right at the cusp of the bathroom threshold that he heard the voices. He would've dismissed them except the mention of her name yanked his full attention that direction.

"…I don't care if Melody did bring him. I don't want that jerk in my house." A.J. paced across the small opening of the door beyond, and Blaine cowered into the darkened bathroom instinctively.

They couldn't see him. He hadn't turned on the light, and the hallway was dark. But still, he didn't think eavesdropping out in the open was the best way to make a great impression either.

"She's a big girl," Eve said, moving so that her silhouette was visible outlined by the soft lights of the master bedroom. "What's so bad about him anyway?"

"He about killed her once. I'm not going to stand around and watch him do it again."

Blaine sensed movement toward the door, and he ducked into the bathroom just as the door down the hall swung open. Flattening against the bathroom wall, he left the door open enough to be able to hear. A.J. plowed down the hallway with Eve right behind him. They stopped on the other side of the bathroom threshold.

"A.J., come on. Tonight was supposed to be special." She stopped him by grabbing his elbow and swinging him around. "Lisa and Jeff knocked themselves out to make this nice for us. Please, please, don't ruin it."

The pleading in Eve's voice was so desperate, it wafted over Blaine's heart as well.

"Please." She moved toward A.J., and Blaine let his gaze fall to the darkness. It was such a private moment between the two of them, how could he not? "I know you think the world of Melody, and I love you for that. I know you want to protect her, but please don't cause a scene tonight. Tomorrow you can call her and let her know how you feel."

"What? Am I supposed to just let him have a wide open shot at her tonight?"

Eve backed up from the intensity of his voice. "Maybe… Maybe, we could… I don't know. Do something so she doesn't go home with Bobby, but with someone else."

"Like who? Except for Dante who's like 12 years older than her…"

"Maybe Blaine. He's here too."

A huge whoosh of air went into Blaine's lungs and clung there.

"Blaine? Spoiled little rich jerk Blaine? Oh, yeah. Like that's an improvement."

Eve softened. She really was trying. "Come on, A.J. Blaine's a nice guy. You should give him a chance."

It was like forever passed before either of them spoke again. There wasn't a fiber of Blaine that had moved, and his muscles had begun to atrophy. Yet how could he move? Not only would they know he had heard everything, A.J.'s already dim view of him would surely be set in concrete from then on.

"Fine," A.J. spat. "Fine. I won't say anything tonight. I'll call her tomorrow."

The breath Eve breathed coupled with the soft kiss she put on A.J.'s cheek about did Blaine in. A.J. Knight didn't deserve her. He wondered at that moment if any man did. With that they moved on down the hall. Long after they were gone, quietly, slowly Blaine closed the door and counted to 70 before he turned on the light.

When he did, the first thing he saw was his reflection in the mirror over the double sinks. He wanted A.J. not to be right. He would've fought it with his fists had he had the chance. But looking into his own eyes, what did he really see? A guy who was living a flagrant lie and flaunting a life he could only dream of living. With a shake of his head, he dropped his gaze and gave up trying to figure it out. There was no answer. Not a good one anyway. So it was better to forget it, and move on.

"Oh, come on, loosen up a little," Bobby said, holding the glass of Coke mixed generously with whiskey out to Melody. "It's not going to kill you. You haven't even had one all night."

"I really…" Melody suspected it would taste as awful as it looked; however, he was standing there holding it, and making a scene wasn't her idea of smart. "Okay. Thanks," she said with a forced smile.

"To being back." Bobby held up his glass, and Melody clinked it although they were both in fact plastic.

They both took a long drink. The foul tasting concoction burned all the way down Melody's throat. "Huh." She let out a breath of disgust. It was the worst thing she'd ever tasted.

"Melody!" The co-owner of the new house said happily coming over to her, and blinking back the stinging liquid, Melody turned to her. Dressed in a slinky black sheath, Eve looked runway ready. She extended her hands and pulled Melody into a quick hug that almost spilled Melody's drink. "I haven't even gotten to talk to you all night."

Oh, God, please get me out of here! Melody begged as she backed up and gave Eve that same plastic smile she'd given everyone else all night long. "Hi, Eve. Nice party." She took another sip, fighting to act normal, but this drink was as bad as the first. It was all she could do to catch her breath.

"And who's your friend?" Eve turned slightly and held her hand out to Bobby. "I don't think we've met."

"This is Bobby… Wilson." Melody put her hand on Bobby's back to push him in front of her. "He's my… date." Again, wishing she could disappear, she took another sip and glanced around the room, noting that brunette girl was now talking with someone else. Blaine didn't seem to be anywhere. Not that she cared. She searched for somewhere else to look, somewhere else to focus on as she took another sip. Ugh. Anything had to be better than this—the drink or the situation.

Eve beamed a hundred-watt smile on Bobby. "Oh, well, Bobby. It's so nice to meet you. We're so happy you came."

"Yeah, well…" Bobby had that look of a man who'd just fallen into the charms of a beautiful woman—sloppy and delirious.

A moment passed. Melody waited for someone to say something. When no one did, she cleared her throat. "Hmm. Well. I'm just going to run to the restroom right quick while you two get to know each other a little better."

Bobby never took his gaze off Eve. "Okay. If you're sure."

Melody rolled her eyes. "Yes. I'm sure." She shook her head, sighed, and turned down the hallway. On her way, she took another drink of the awful-tasting stuff. "Blech." It was getting worse with every sip.

At that moment the door to the bathroom opened and out stepped Blaine, nearly crashing right into her. "Oh!" He jumped back. "Mel! I'm sorry. I didn't see you there."

Either the drink or the humiliation was getting to her. Swaying, she barely caught her balance. "Yeah, there's a lot of that going around."

His cheerfulness fell like it had been pushed off a cliff. "Huh?"

She shook her head and lifted her chin. "Never mind. Hi, Blaine. How are you?" Knowing it was the way to look coy and casual, she lifted the glass to her lips and took another drink. "I was surprised to see you tonight, but then again, you're such the social butterfly, why should I be surprised, right?" She took another sip.

The longer he stood there, the more uncomfortable he looked. "Listen, Mel. I wanted to say I'm sorry for not getting back to you with the notes. I…"

The strength of the drink was really starting to cloud her judgment. All she wanted to do was escape into the bathroom and let the tears fall for real. But at the moment, he was both blocking the door and standing just a few inches from her in a darkened hallway. Neither of which were helping the aberrant, disjointed signals spinning in her head. She fought not to sway although it wasn't easy. "Yeah, well. That's not important. You were just being nice, right? It's okay. I get it."

Concern and hurt crossed his face. "No, Mel. I… I meant to… I just…"

She threw her head back, which caused her equilibrium to swirl dangerously. "Hey, Blaine. Come on. We're not kids here. We both know you had no intention of calling me although why you wanted my number in the first place is beyond me."

Standing there, he gazed at her, searching for something to say, but there was nothing to say. When the truth steps in, it's really hard to lie around it.

"Umm, listen, I hate to be rude," she said, pulling herself to standing although she hadn't really moved, "but I really need to use the little girl's room."

"Wha…?" He looked around. "Oh, sure. Of course. I'm sorry." He moved from the doorway but stood and watched her go in. "I really am sorry, Melody."

She turned a sad, spinning smile on him. "Yeah, aren't we all?" And with that she closed the door.

Blaine closed his eyes to the ache shooting through him. She was hurt, and she was furious. That much was obvious. And she had every right to be. With a sigh to settle what a real jerk he'd been, he turned back for the festivities in the living room although he didn't feel much like partying.

The sobs seemed to come from middle earth, and as Melody sat on the closed white porcelain lid, she was powerless to stop them. Gasping for air, she fought to get them to stop even as she leaned heavily on the wall, but they marched forward like an invading army, dripping over her lashes and falling onto her hands that tried to stop them. How could she be so stupid? How could she have thought that bringing Bobby would change anything? How could she think the six pounds she had shed would change anything? They hadn't, and they never would.

To everyone else, she was still fat, ugly Melody Todd, and she always would be.

Six

When Melody finally stumbled out of the bathroom, she forgot her drink which was just as well. It had done what it was supposed to do in spades. Her entire body felt like it was on a giant rubber band, swinging and swaying, under no direct control from her at all. She reached out and touched the wall to steady herself. It didn't help.

Sounds, spinning like a funhouse, spiraled at her from the light dancing at the end of the hallway. She raked in ragged breath after ragged breath, trying to stop the spinning. Her heart raced although she couldn't quite tell why. Pulling her eyes open through the haze that surrounded everything, she concentrated on walking. It took every effort she could muster.

For ten minutes, Blaine had been watching the hook-up across the room. Bobby and Fashion Girl. Blaine's gaze kept going nervously to the large opening that led to the hallway. At some point Melody was going to come back and see them together. He wanted to do something to stop that from happening, but he couldn't think what. Then before he'd worked all the way through that question, the two of them headed for the door and left.

He checked his watch. A frown formed on the end of the numbers. She'd been in there an awfully long time. Maybe someone should go check on her. At that moment his gaze snagged on movement at the doorway, and his breath froze in his chest.

Blotchy skin, eyes puffy from the tears, swaying like a soft breeze might knock her down, Melody stood there—if it could be called standing. First instinct said get over there, but Jeff Taylor, one of A.J.'s friends noticed her first. He stepped up to her, concern etched all over his face.

Time stood absolutely still. And then, like a rag doll falling from a shelf, she pitched forward right into Jeff's arms. Jeff caught her as someone standing close to them screamed in surprise.

"What…? Mel…?" A.J. rushed past Blaine to get to her.

Chaos erupted as party-goers morphed simultaneously into rescue and panic modes.

Lifting her gently, Jeff turned. "Clear the couch!" he ordered as he carried her limp body over to it. Guests scattered. The coffee table presented only a mild problem. Eve appeared with a pillow, and Jeff laid Melody on it gently. In seconds the coffee table was across the room courtesy of two big burly firemen.

A.J. and Jeff knelt next to her, talking softly. Blaine couldn't keep his gaze from her pale skin. Even her hair looked ill. He couldn't move. Not a muscle, not a nerve. Fear gripped him in its icy tentacles.

"Mel, baby. Come on, sweetheart. Talk to me. It's A.J." He was taking vital signs even as he spoke. "Come on, girl. Wake up."

"What happened?" Eve asked in fear from the other side of the room. Her arms were clamped around her middle. "I just saw her. I just talked to her. She was fine."

It was then that Blaine remembered the drink. It was impossible to know, but he had to try. He raced through the room, pushing through the gawking onlookers. He ran down the hall to the bathroom where he flipped on the light. Sure enough it was right there. He grabbed it and hurried back down the hallway, careful not to spill it on himself. Walking right up to the couch, he held it out to the two men kneeling there. "She was drinking this."

Looking up at him with a concerned but questioning gaze, Jeff took the little punch glass and sniffed it. Then he looked at the contents and frowned deeper. "Roofies."

"What?" A.J. leaned closer and peered in the glass. "Oh, you've got to be kidding me." He turned his full attention back to Melody and started shaking her gently. "Mel. Come on. Come on, girl. Wake up. Say something. Talk to me. Mel, come on. Please."

"Call 911," Jeff commanded, handing the glass back to Blaine.

"What?" His brain wasn't processing all of the information coming into it.

Jeff took one serious-as-death look at him. "Call 911. Now!"

Disoriented and terror-stricken, Blaine made for the kitchen wondering how and where he might find a phone. By the time he got there, however, he met the large goateed fireman coming the other way. "They're on their way."

"… on their…" Nothing was making any sense to Blaine. Roofies? Melody? How? Why? Then A.J.'s words from the hallway rang in his head. He almost killed her once… What did that mean? He turned back for the living room, the questions swirling in his brain just as it ran into one solid answer.

Around the couch stood a circle of concerned faces, each silent, watching, praying, hoping, but disbelieving. Blaine looked at them. The feelings of their panic-stricken faces seared to the insides of him.

"Come on, Mel. Come on," A.J. pleaded at the couch.

"Where did Bobby go?" Blaine asked, sidling up to Eve.

She shook her head in incomprehension. "I don't know." Then wide-eyed, she looked at him. "You don't think…"

"He probably gave her the drink. Who else could it be?"

"But why…?" Her gaze fell to the floor, and he knew a recording of A.J.'s words screamed through her mind. "Did you…? Do you know him?"

"No." Unfortunately or he'd already be on his way to clobber the guy. A.J. was right. He was a snake. Anger flowed through Blaine, hot and acerbic as he looked at Melody on the couch. Why had she come with that jerk anyway? A sick feeling crawled through his gut.

The wail of the siren outside snapped those thoughts in two. There were more pressing matters at the moment. Two EMTs came in and got right to work.

"We're with the fire department," Jeff said. "We think she ingested roofies. We've got…" He looked around. "Where's that glass?"

Blaine grabbed it up and handed it to him.

"This is what she was drinking." He pointed to it. "See the flecks at the top?"

The EMT nodded. He spoke into his radio, and they went

back to get the stretcher. It was all Blaine could do to keep himself back. They knew what they were doing. He didn't. Besides, it wasn't his place, but he couldn't help but wish it was.

"You know, it could be hours before she wakes up," Jeff said as he sat down next to Blaine in the waiting area. "You really don't have to stay."

"I know, but I kind of feel responsible." Blaine pulled himself forward—torn between staying with her to make sure she was all right and going home to make sure home was all right. "I wish I would've known what was going on when I talked to her before. She kept drinking that junk all while she talked to me. I should've stopped her."

Jeff shook his head. He was nice for an older guy. "You can't put that on yourself. You couldn't have known."

Swiping at the moisture and fatigue under his eye, Blaine clamped a frown on his face. "Still. I should've." He stretched out his legs and leaned back against the wall, closing his eyes against everything that had happened. How much of his stupidity had caused her to go out with Bobby in the first place? How had she talked herself into that being okay anyway?

The doors to the ER swung open, and A.J. strode out. He walked right up to Jeff who stood. Blaine stood too although warily and hanging back as much as possible.

A.J. planted his hand on his hip and glanced back at the doors. "They pumped her stomach."

The pause came and stayed, lasting far too long.

"And…?" Jeff asked, glancing at Blaine, clearly wondering how he would keep the two guys standing if the news was as bad as it was sounding.

"The alcohol and drugs were all they found. She hadn't eaten in like who knows how long. The stuff went right into her bloodstream." A.J. spun and put his hands on his head. "That stupid, son of a…"

"Hey, whoa, calm down." Jeff laid a hand on A.J.'s shoulder. "Punching walls isn't going to help Melody or anybody else."

That only brought pain in place of the anger to A.J.'s face.

Jeff exhaled. "What else did they say?"

"The worst is over, they think, although she came awfully

close to going into respiratory failure." Kicking the chair, A.J. spun and sat down. He put his hand to his head and shoved it through his hair.

As much as Blaine hated the guy, it was hard not to feel sorry for him. He obviously cared for Melody a lot. "Did they…?" Blaine cleared his throat. "Did they find Wilson?"

"On his way back into Houston with Charlotte." A.J. sighed, stood up, and paced three steps to the window which twinkled with late night lights. "Thank God she's all right."

Blaine knew it really wasn't his fault, but the guilt hounded him anyway. "I'm really sorry, A.J. If I would've known…"

Worried, sad, scared eyes came up to lock with his. The fire in them melted. "Nah, man. It wasn't your fault. Mel's just too darn trusting. Always has been."

"This wasn't her fault," Jeff said, jumping instantly to her defense. "Jerks like Wilson need to get what's coming to them."

"Yeah," A.J. said. "Well, I'd like to dish some of that out myself."

"You and me both, brother," Jeff said. "You and me both."

Breathing. It was the first thing Melody was aware of. Breathing and a deep, bone-numbing heaviness. She fought to open her eyelids, but they just rolled up and right back down. The breaths went out only. They didn't seem to be coming in at all. With effort she turned her head, but the movement made everything swim. Sick and so tired she could hardly think, she fought not to drift back out.

The fog was so thick, she couldn't really hear or see anything. Fear began to creep over her, climbing through her, sweeping what was left of her breath away. What was happening? Where was she, and why couldn't she wake up?

"Hey, there, gorgeous." The voice was right above her, inches from her, and yet she couldn't see it. Instead it reverberated through her skull. "You really had us worried there for awhile."

"Huh…" She tried to talk, but nothing sensible came out. In fact, nothing sensible was making it from her brain either. She fought not to make it so. The only thing she could grasp at was how much everything hurt. That and how scared she was. And how tired. She tried to push herself up in case wherever this was wasn't safe. "Uh…"

"No. Now you stay right there. You're fine. You're safe. It's A.J., and I won't let anything happen to you."

"A…" The J was there somewhere, too, but she forgot it. She squeezed her eyes closed against the incredible pain and dullness shooting through her head.

"Shh. You just rest. Take your time. It's okay."

There was so much more she wanted to ask, to say, but just like that it was all gone, and the darkness took over once again.

From across the room Blaine watched them. A.J. was so good with her, so steady. Jeff too. They were amazing. He had frozen to the spot the moment trouble struck. He hadn't even been able to even make one simple phone call. How useless was that?

A.J. straightened from the bed. "She's asleep again. I think I'll go call Eve, let them know she woke up."

Never moving from his spot, Blaine nodded. Jeff had stayed in the waiting room, and A.J. stepped out there as well. Seconds, minutes, years passed as Blaine stood, gazing at the pale face, the closed eyes, the fall of blonde hair. How had he ever been so blind as to not see her? The memory of her walking into the party earlier played through his mind. Yes, he had to be an absolute idiot not to notice.

With a glance at the door to make sure A.J. wasn't on his way back in, Blaine gathered his courage and walked the ten steps to the side of the bed. When he got there, what to do next escaped him. What he wouldn't have given to have the nerves of steel of the other two. Carefully he reached out and touched the back of her hand that had an IV stuck on top of it. He hated needles. He hated hospitals. But he wasn't going to let that stop him.

"Hey, Mel." He let out a long breath. "Umm…" This was impossible. What was he supposed to say? Dropping so that he was more leaning on the bed than standing next to it, he slid his hand under hers and closed his eyes. For a long moment the words were nowhere in his brain. Then like the sun breaking over the horizon at dawn, they came. "God, please be with Melody. Please. She needs You, Lord. We all do. Please guide her back to us. Please, Lord. She needs You."

There was a softness beside her now, a haze but it was a gentle haze. She reached for the only name she could remember. "A.J.?"

The haze seemed to move although she couldn't tell quite how. "Hey, Mel. No, it's not A.J. It's Blaine."

"Blaine?" She tried to locate that name in her head. Where was it? It must've fallen to the dark floor along with all the other memories. "What…?"

"Shh. You're all right. Just rest."

"But…"

"Did she wake up again?" Another presence, on the other side of the bed.

Melody turned her head that direction, but the movement sent her swirling.

"It's okay, Mel," the second presence said. "It's okay. I'm here. I won't let anything bad happen to you. I swear."

It was then that Melody realized something bad must've happened. What was it? A car wreck? A freak accident? She tried to remember but found only an inky blackness.

"Just rest," he said again. And she did.

"How long will she be like this?" Blaine asked quietly over the now-sleeping Melody.

A.J. glanced up, and there was disgust in his eyes. "With roofies it can last like eight hours. Not like this but before she's really awake again. But that's not the main concern now."

Nothing in him wanted to ask the question. "How's that?"

This glance up wasn't any friendlier. "Sometimes there's short term memory loss. It can last a couple days."

It took everything for Blaine to fight off the shakiness in him. "But… it's not permanent, right?"

A.J. shook his head. "No. But it can be pretty scary."

Blaine let his gaze drop back to her face. Although he didn't say them out loud, the prayers started once more.

Melody was full awake now, but the swirling continued. She wasn't at all steady, nor did anything make sense. A.J. was there though. He never left her side. The only time he did, she went into a panic attack, and he was summoned again quickly. That other guy was there too. Blaine, Blake, Brian. Something like that. He never left either although she couldn't quite pinpoint why.

"Time to get you home, missy." The large black nurse dragged the wheelchair into the room and right up to the bed. "We got your discharge papers signed, and this nice young man has agreed to be your escort."

She was glad to see the nurse refer to A.J. rather than the sullen, unshaven guy who stood in the corner. Why was he here again? She fought with her memory to piece everything together as A.J. helped her from the bed to the wheelchair. The party clothes she had obviously chosen for this strange occasion felt better than the threadbare gown from before. Still, it all seemed somewhat surreal.

"You good?" A.J. leaned down to her ear.

Melody nodded, trying not to move too much. And with that the little caravan went out to the elevator, down to the lobby, and out the sweeping double doors. The wind was warm and humid, and Melody tried to get it into a category. Too warm for February. Too cool for July. What month was it again? She hated feeling like everyone was looking at her and wondering why she couldn't remember such simple things.

At the curb, they helped her out of the wheelchair and into a tall, silver SUV that she didn't remember ever having seen. She wanted to ask but decided they would think she was crazy if she did. In the vehicle, she latched her seatbelt while a short conversation passed between A.J. and the strange guy. Melody tried not to look, not to stare, not to notice them glancing at her. There was something so familiar about him. What was it?

Then A.J. hopped in the other side. "Ready?" He looked tired, very tired.

Still not trusting herself, Melody simply nodded.

Blaine hated the blank look in her eyes. The sparkle was gone, replaced with a fear and a wariness he'd never seen. It unnerved him. The guys said it would fade, that her memory would come back in a day or two, but Blaine had no way of knowing if that was true or not. He carefully pulled out behind the SUV and followed it into traffic. He'd only been to her house twice, and he didn't want to get lost.

As he drove, he thought through all that had happened, and he raked his fingers through his hair in frustration. He wondered how she was really feeling, and he wished with everything in him that he could be up there, with her, in that SUV. It was a wish too great to be hoped for. "God, please, please help her through this."

"Oh good, you're home," her mother met them at the curb. "How are you, Sweetheart? A.J. called me. He told me what happened. Are you all right?"

The questions came at her like bullets from an AK-47, and Melody blinked into the force of them. She was glad when A.J. appeared to help her into the house.

"She's still a little woozy," he explained. "And she may not remember much for awhile. It's what that stuff does."

"I still can't believe it. Bobby Wilson? Margaret's son? How could he do something like this?"

They were now at the door, and her mother opened it, the string of words never so much as slowing down.

"I hope they lock him up and throw away the key, doing this to an innocent young woman. It's just terrible. Why would he do something like this?"

The room was starting to spin again, and Melody held onto A.J. to keep from toppling over.

"You okay?" he asked, and she could see even in her present state the worry etched on his face.

"Yeah," she rasped. "I just want to sit down."

"Okay. We're almost there." At the couch he sat her down gently, and it was only when he stepped back that she realized the strange guy had followed them in.

Ripping her gaze from him in embarrassment, she pulled in a jagged breath. "I think I'll be okay now. Thanks for bringing me home."

A.J. nodded then bent down and gave her a hug. "Let me know if you need anything. Okay?"

She nodded because that was all she could think to do. What would be really nice was to lean over, stop fighting, and go to sleep.

"Umm, could we talk, in there?" A.J. asked her mother, and

the two of them left the room.

It was like being under a microscope with no way to get out. She knew he was watching her, but she didn't have the presence of mind to know what to do about that. He stepped over and sat on the coffee table right in front of her. In the next second her hands were cradled in his, and his gaze drilled into hers. She looked up but couldn't quite figure out why anyone would look at her like that.

"You take care of yourself, okay?" he asked. Worry bled through the words. "If you need anything… anything, let me know. Got it?" He reached up and brushed a strand of hair off her forehead.

She nodded, kind of. He had nice eyes. They were kind and concerned. She liked those eyes.

"You get some rest. I'll be praying for you." And with that he stood, leaned over and kissed the top of her head. This whole thing was so confusing. There was the question of how she got in this state and why they were being so nice to her. Then there was the question of who this guy was and why he was acting like she might die at any moment. It was all one big swirl meant only to keep her guessing.

A.J. and her mother walked back in, talking quietly. Then A.J. addressed the guy with the nice eyes. "We'd better go and let her get some rest."

"Oh." He glanced back down at her. Standing right in front of her, he looked like a giant. "Okay."

"Thanks for getting her home okay, you two." Her mother followed them to the door, and then they were gone.

Melody wanted to understand something about what had just happened, but at that moment sleep took precedence. She started to lie over onto the couch cushions.

"Oh, no, you don't," her mother said, pulling her back up. "You're going straight to bed, young lady. I'll make you a cheese sandwich and bring it up to you."

There was no fight left anywhere in her, so Melody complied like a docile lamb.

"But you're sure she's going to be okay?" Blaine asked, glancing back at the house with worry.

"Yeah." A.J. strode to the silver SUV. "Give her a day or two, and she'll be the same old Melody." He yanked the door open and crawled inside. "See ya."

"Later," Blaine said, wishing he could go back up to that door without A.J. doing what his gaze said he'd like to. The same old Melody? He wondered if that was even possible in his eyes anymore.

"I don't know," Eve said the following morning as they sat in the break room, her latte never even having been touched. "I'm so worried about him. This really rocked his world."

Blaine sat in the break room, trying to comfort Eve who was alternately trying to comfort him. "How's that?"

The look on her face was at once distracted and concerned. "He came home last night and pounded on those drums until I thought I was going to go insane. He wouldn't talk to me at all. I don't know. It scares me, I guess."

"He wouldn't…" Blaine couldn't even get the right words out. "He wouldn't hurt you, would he?"

Surprise jumped to Eve's face. "Hurt me? A.J.? No. No way. But he's so angry. I just don't know how to fix that."

Concern for her drifted through Blaine. "Well, maybe it's not something to fix. Maybe it's something to let him work through in his own time. Us guys don't like to feel out of control, especially with people we love. Maybe he just needs a little time to get this behind him, and all will be right with the world again."

Eve considered that a long moment. Then she looked at him with anxiety in her soft eyes. "She was really bad, huh?"

The question felt like an arrow stab straight through the heart, and without knowing it was coming, he'd stupidly lowered his shield. He nodded slowly. "Yeah. She was."

Her sigh was soft. "I just don't understand why Melody would go out with someone who would do something like that to her. I mean, A.J. said…" The words trailed off.

But Blaine needed to know. "A.J. said…?"

A conflict of interest battled in her face. Finally she exhaled long and hard. "A.J. said Bobby hurt her before. I don't know what that meant exactly, but I can't figure out why she would go out with him again if that's true."

Blaine was battling the same questions. "I don't know. I guess some girls like the living on the wild side thing. I can't explain it, but I know it happens. Like dating the guy on the motorcycle who treats them like crap, and they all follow him around like little lost puppy dogs. Or the women who keep going back to men who beat the living snot out of them for sport." He let the words trail off. He had to. They were hitting way too close to home.

A moment and Eve looked at her watch. "Time to hit the bricks." She stood, and when Blaine stood too, she gave him a quick hug. "Thanks. I needed that talk."

"Anytime."

When he got home at nine, Blaine cleared the table and did two rounds of dishes. They hadn't been done in a week. His brain slid through everything—work, school, home, the party, A.J., Eve, Melody… How could one life get so complicated? It was a question he had no answer for.

Seven

Melody hadn't gone to work. She wanted to, but her mom was adamant that she needed one more day of rest. Truthfully, she was glad. The pieces had begun falling back in place, and most of them were disturbing if not downright frightening. The "what ifs" crowded through her like late afternoon traffic headed out of Houston. What if she hadn't been with friends? What if Bobby's plan, whatever that was, had worked? What if he had gotten her out of that house because she was sick before anybody realized what was going on?

None of the possibilities that crept through her mind did anything but send shivers up her back and cause fear to permeate her being. Then there were the even worse thoughts, like what had she said to Blaine when she met him in the hallway. Like the memories of a ghost she remembered talking to him, and she remembered he wasn't particularly happy when he left. But what had she said? And why had he accompanied her home that day A.J. came?

As she made herself a piece of toast, she tried to sort through that. He had his own car. A.J. didn't need a ride. So why did Blaine come? The phone rang, and she answered it because she was the only one home. "Hello?"

"Melody." The word was more a statement than a question.

"Yes?"

"Oh, good. I was hoping you'd be there. This is Eve."

Melody squelched the sigh but not the eye roll. "Oh, hi, Eve. What's up?"

"Well, I… I mean, we were wondering how you're doing."

Like she wanted to go through this with Eve. Where was A.J.

anyway? "I'm fine."

"Really?"

"Yeah. All better." Melody nodded as if confirming the fact. Okay, so the fact that she was holding onto the cabinet to keep her standing made that more a lie than the truth, but she wasn't going to tell Ms. Perfection that. "So what's going on?"

"Oh, well… A.J. and I were just wondering if you might want to come over Friday. Just so… I mean… well, we didn't get to talk much the other night."

Needing a distraction, Melody bit into the toast and chewed. Yeah, she noticed. "I don't know. I'm kinda busy this week." Now that was an outright lie, but what in the world did she want to go to A.J.'s place for? So he could really rub her face in it? Or so he could chew her out? Neither sounded appealing.

"We'd really like to see you. You can bring someone if you like."

Yeah, because that worked out so well the first time.

Saying no was the most logical thing to do, but it felt so awful to say it. "Can I think about it?"

"Oh. S-sure. I'll just give you our number." Eve transferred the number that Melody dutifully wrote down. "We'll grill out. A.J. got a new grill he's just itching to use."

Melody smiled in spite of feeling punched. A.J. had been so nice to her throughout the whole knocked-off-her-feet thing. How could she be mean to him now? "I'll get back with you."

"Okay." Eve was silent for a moment. "And Melody? I'm really glad you're okay."

"Thanks." When Melody hung up the phone she looked at it for a long moment. She would say yes, eventually. She knew it as much as they didn't. Then as she stood there, the phone jangled again to life, and she jumped at the sound. In less than a second she had it up again. "Hello?"

"Hi." It was a salesman. He sounded breathless and hurried. "Umm, I'm sorry to bother you, Mrs. Todd. This is Blaine Donovan. Melody's… Well, I'm a friend of Melody's. Is she there?"

Maybe it was the sound of his voice or the sheer shock that he'd called. Whatever it was, Melody could get no words to come out. She had to swallow twice to get the bite of toast down her throat. "Oh. Uh. Blaine. Hi. This… This is… Melody."

"Oh, Mel. I'm sorry. It didn't sound like you."

She tried to think of something to say, but the memory of standing in A.J.'s hallway and the questions of what she had said the last time they talked were making that impossible.

"Mel? Are you there?"

"Uh, yeah. I'm here." Shakily she reached for a chair and lowered herself onto it. Fighting to get the words to line up, she scrunched her face together. "Um, did you need something?"

There was a pause as the questions raced around and around the track in her brain.

"No. I mean. I was just… I was wondering how you are."

As much as she tried not to, she loved that voice. It was at once strong and gentle. Still, letting her thoughts go there was not wise. "Yeah, I'm better." She put her hand to her head, slid her fingers into her hair until her temple dropped into her palm, and rested there. Suddenly, she just wanted a long nap. "How are you?" Lame, but she didn't really want to talk about how stupid she had been.

"Worried about you."

That did funny things to her heart. "I'm fine, Blaine. Really."

Another pause. The pauses were doing strange things to her growling stomach.

"So would you object to me seeing that for myself?" he finally asked.

"For your… Why?"

"Because I want to. Can I come over? We could go out and get a hamburger or something. Unless you've already eaten that is. Then we could just go to the park or something."

He sounded so nervous. So un-Blaine like.

She forced herself to sit up. "I'm fine. Really. You don't have to…"

"Mel." The way he said her name stopped her. "I want to, okay?"

"O… Okay. I guess." She looked down at her clothes—frumpy, wrinkled T-shirt, old sweatpants. Fashionable and together she was not. "Can you give me a little bit?"

"How's an hour?"

How about 90? With barely a sigh, she said, "Okay."

Why she had agreed to this, Melody couldn't tell. She had absolutely nothing to wear. Her clothes were more Wal-Mart knock-offs than Armani originals. Somewhere between having nothing to wear and what in the world would he want to see her for, she spent the next hour freaking out. When the doorbell rang only 45 minutes later, freak out hit its zenith. Surely not. She wasn't even ready. She didn't even have make-up on yet!

But the doorbell rang again, and knowing she was the only one in the house, she treaded down the stairs to get it. One glance out the window told her it was as bad as she had feared. "Hm." As quickly as possible, she tried to make herself presentable, but it was a useless endeavor. With a swing, she yanked the door opened and tried to smile and act like she had gorgeous guys show up on her front porch all the time. It was a losing battle. "Hi."

The brightness of her greeting was met only by the seriousness of his. "Hi." His gaze swept the length of her, and she squirmed wishing she'd had a lot more time to put herself together.

Breathing past the surging of her heart, she smiled and stepped back. "Come on in." As she backed up, she watched him come into her house that only then did she realize must be pathetic and horrible compared with his. She backed right into the little table in the entryway, knocking the leprechaun knick-knack over. At the last possible second, she grabbed it up, willed her heart to calm down, and set the little green guy down with shaking hands.

"Um, I'm sorry. I'm not quite ready yet." She turned and hurried into the living room, looking around, and seeing absolutely everything that was hideous about the place. "Um, here's the remote. You can have a seat and watch some TV if you want."

He held his hands up, even as he looked only at her. "That's okay. I'm not real big on TV."

"Oh. Okay." She dropped the remote to the table. "Well, then…" Pointing to the stairs, she took a step toward them. "I'll just…"

That gaze, his gaze. It unnerved her to the core.

"Take your time."

With that, Melody turned and raced up the stairs, her pleasantly faded jeans and slingback brown heels were the last Blaine saw of her. He hoped she wouldn't change the sleeveless white wraparound shirt. It was cute. He was glad the dazed, blank look in her eyes was gone, but the sparkle still hadn't returned. Or maybe it was simply hidden by the wariness that was now there. Pushing those thoughts to the side, he walked around the cozy living room, feeling the familiness of it wrap around him. It was done in gold and orange tones. Out of fashion maybe, but nice just the same. He walked to the little shelves holding the pictures and picked one up.

It was Melody. He was sure of it. She was precious in her little diaper and T-shirt atop the little red tricycle. Her halo of white-blonde curls shone in the bright sunshine. A smile drifted to his face as the safety and predictability of her life slid over him. She was lucky. The noise behind him made him set the picture back onto the shelf carefully.

"Oh. Please don't look at those. They're horrible."

When he turned, horrible was nowhere to be seen. He was glad the little picture was already back on the shelf, or he might have dropped it. "I'm sorry. I was just looking."

And looking was what he was doing now. She hadn't changed the wrap shirt, but she had added a touch of make-up and a turquoise belt that peeked out between the shirt and the jeans. Her hands were dug in the back pockets of her jeans, and her face was all nerves and timidity. "Ready?"

Blaine could hardly think straight enough to say it. "When you are."

Quickly she wrote a short note to her mom—so she wouldn't worry. He watched her, his heart softening at the sight and the thought. He was glad she had someone to worry about her. That was important.

When that was accomplished, they locked the front door and walked out to the curb. At the car, that wasn't technically his car, Blaine opened the door hoping Peyton wouldn't make good on his threat to get rid of it now that he'd bought a BMW. Just how Blaine might explain the absence of "his" car to everyone who knew about it was beyond him. However, there were far more pressing matters than the stupid car to worry about right then. He crawled in and made sure she was all right. She was although she wasn't looking at him.

Looking both ways and in all the mirrors, he pulled into traffic. He caught the sigh she let out. When he glanced at her,

her gaze was out the window.

"It's been awhile, huh?" he asked, referring to the last times she was in this car.

"Yeah. At least that was better than the first time. I can't believe you ever even talked to me after that." Her gaze dropped to her hands. "Thanks for that, and for the other night."

"I…"

"No. Blaine." She cut him off by turning to him abruptly. Something in him said he should be looking at her when she said this rather than driving, but the distinct possibility of wrecking his friend's mega-bucks car kept him from it. "Really. I want to thank you." The breath was good for both of them. "That whole thing the other night… I know you… Well, I wanted to say thanks and I'm sorry… for whatever I said."

He did glance over at her then. "What you said? What did you say?"

Squeezing her eyes closed, Melody fought the pain that slashed across her face. "That's just it. I don't even know what I said. Something stupid, that's all I know."

Blaine wasn't following at all. He drove to the first burger and ice cream joint he came to and pulled in. He didn't want to have this conversation fighting Houston traffic. Pulling into a parking spot, he put the car into park and shut it off. A breath to settle his heart, and he turned to her. "Look, Mel. You didn't say anything stupid. Believe me. It was nothing you didn't have every right to say."

Horror crossed through her eyes, and she let her gaze drop to her hands. "I'm sorry. I… wasn't really… thinking all that straight."

A dull knife carved through his heart at the thought of how terrifying that must've been. By the look of her it still was. "What do you say we get something to eat? We can talk about this later."

Her head went up and down although her gaze never really came up to his. Vowing to make her forget all about Saturday, he got out and came around to her side just as she got out of the car. She didn't really look at him, more mumbled the thanks, and let him close the door. This was all so awkward. He wanted to reach over and guide her to the door, but that was presumptuous. This wasn't, after all, a real date. She didn't even like him. Still, she deserved better than having a jerk around who wasn't even a gentleman.

At the door, he snuck around and opened it for her. Surprise went through her glance, but she stepped in front of him and into the muted-colored room. The sunshine and humidity from outside gave way to the air-conditioned atmosphere of the brown and beige establishment. Blaine moved a half-step and guided her forward without ever so much as touching her. A step and then a few more as she looked at the overhead menu, and he looked at her trying not to look like he was.

Her eyes were a light, sparkling blue, perfectly proportioned to the long blonde hair that fell past her shoulders. They weren't slender shoulders, but he liked them just the same.

"Order whatever you want," he said, remembering the report of alcohol and drugs being the only things in her stomach.

"Oh, um." She glanced at him and then back to the menu. "I'll just have the side salad. No dressing."

He looked at her in concern and confusion. "That's all? You don't want a burger or a chicken sandwich? They have really good chicken sandwiches."

"No. That's okay." Her arms were wound around her middle. "And I'll just have water."

Blaine seriously thought about arguing, but the guy was ready to take their order, so he relayed the information being sure to get a large fries in case she wanted some. "That's it." He reached into his wallet just as she held out a bill. He caught sight of it and shook his head. "No, that's okay. I can get it."

"You don't have to buy mine."

"Mel," he said as exasperation crawled up him. "I've got this."

She scrunched her face in displeasure but put the money back in her pocket. "Fine."

Her disagreeable off-handedness was starting to make him think she meant it. He collected the food and angled their paths over to a little table by the window. At least if this turned out to be as bad as it was going, they could always opt for watching the traffic. Blaine set the food off the little tray, went to put it back, and get some ketchup. By the time he got back, she had her salad open and was tossing it with her plastic fork.

Wordlessly, he unwrapped his hamburger and set the fries between them, just in case. He picked up a fry, realizing the hamburger would have to wait until he got the conversation going again. That wouldn't be easy as her head was down, her concentration on her salad only.

"So, how's school going?" It was desperate, but what was there to talk about that wasn't a mess between them at the moment?

She glanced up, and he caught sight of the dotting of freckles across her nose. They were cute. "Okay I guess. I've got 12 hours this semester. I'll probably take summer school just 'cause what else am I going to do?" She shrugged and took a small bite of her salad.

Blaine had used the opportunity to take a bite of his burger. He slurped his Dr. Pepper quickly. "What's your major?"

"Management. But that was like the least worst option. I think I might like buying or something like that, but I needed to get something going. I'm a little behind the curve."

"Ugh. I hear you there." He took another sip. "I'm almost 27. You'd think I'd be a grandfather by now."

For the first time since they'd left her house, Melody smiled a half-smile. "You look like a gramps."

He angled his drink at her. "Hey, watch it. That was for your ears only."

"Oh, sorry." She ducked her head. "Gramps."

The smile had a will of its own as it came from his heart to his mouth. "Very funny."

"So what's your major?"

Between the bite and the drink, it took him a minute. "Architectural Design."

"Architecture? Wow." Her face came up full and beautiful then. "That must be so interesting."

He nodded. "It's cool. I like doing the models."

"I bet. So you design buildings then?"

"Yeah, I want to… someday."

"Someday." She pushed back in the chair, her gaze not really doing more than staying glued to her salad. "That always sounds so good but so very far away."

Gently he looked at her. "So what does your someday look like?"

Her gaze flashed up but then dropped. "Oh, you know. House, husband, kids, dog."

"Inside or outside?"

The look on her face was at once surprised and interested. "Outside." She wrinkled her pert nose. "Definitely outside. I'm not into hair and stuff all over everything."

He nodded. "And these kids, you're planning to have… what? Five, six?"

She laughed as he took a bite of the hamburger. "Two or three. Four tops." Her hand, which had nice long fingers with rounded but not overly long fingernails, lifted her drink to her mouth. "So what about your someday?"

Stretching, he sat back in the chair, narrowing his gaze at her. "House, wife, two kids. One boy. One girl. A decent size place where my sheltie could run and play."

"A sheltie?" She picked up her drink. "Those are nice."

He nodded. "I think so."

"So, this sheltie is something you have now…?"

His drink clunked to the table. "Uh, no. Right now. Well, let's just say right now my place doesn't mix well with pets."

"Ah," she said as if she understood.

He noticed then that her salad was barely touched although his sandwich was almost gone. "I'm sorry. Did you want something else?" Nodding to her salad, he surveyed her.

"What?" A moment and she realized what he was saying. "Oh, uh, no. I'm just not very hungry."

Blaine eyed her up and down. "You just ate?"

"Oh, well… No. I mean, yeah. I mean, I'm just not very hungry."

He wanted to argue, but she was crawling into her shell again, so he quickly switched tactics. "Well, that's okay. I just…" With everything in him, he wanted to ask, but he couldn't find the right words. "So, have you talked to A.J. and Eve?"

That question made her drop her fork to the table, reach for her cup, and take a long drink as she looked out at the traffic. Worry crawled through him as he watched her. Lovely. Another sore subject. Were there any that weren't sore where she was concerned?

"I'm sorry," he said, spinning his burger around the paper wrapper, his appetite gone.

Without really moving, she shook her head. "It's okay." She set the drink down, but never lifted her gaze from it. "I just… It's just…" Her gaze came up to his, and there was so much written there, he couldn't read it all. Stamped across all of it was a hurt that made his own heart ache. Her gaze slid back out to the traffic beyond. "She called me today. Just before you did."

"Oh, really? Eve?" he asked, fighting desperately to sound nonchalant as he picked up his drink. There was so much about the crisscrossing of their relationships that had never made any sense to him.

"Yeah." Melancholy thoughts drifted over her face. She exhaled slowly. "She wants me to come over Friday night."

He waited for more, but that seemed to be all she was willing to offer. "And that's a problem?"

She glanced at him and pursed her lips. "It is when you're me."

Blaine had never wanted to be so close to anyone. Everything about her drew him into her world. He watched her, seeing the pain, hearing it in her voice, and wanting at all costs to make it go away. "Why?"

That non-nod was back. The fact that she was fighting not to cry seared through him. "They don't know what it's like… seeing them, like that."

Understanding dropped like bombshells around him. "Together?"

She nodded, squashing her lips together to keep the emotion from overflowing.

"So you've been friends with A.J. a long time then?"

"Since we were kids."

"And you went together?" He knew it was shaky ground, but he needed to know.

"No. Well, kind of, but it never really worked out." She shrugged and let her finger go up and down the condensation on her cup.

He let his head fall to the side to be able to see her face. "But you wanted it to?" His heart fell at the look in her eyes. It was at once sad, defeated, and accepting.

"I was never perfect enough for him." Her smile really wasn't one. "He liked the pretty girls in school, the cheerleader types."

His gaze never left her face. "You're pretty."

She sniffed at that one. "Yeah. Uh-huh. That's why the only guys I can get to go out with me are low-life creeps."

Bobby. The name went straight through him like the hot tip of a sword. He leaned back, trying to appear casual. "So, what's up with that anyway? Are you and Bobby going together now?" He prayed that her answer would be a decided no.

What he got instead was a mere shake of her head. "We did. At one time. In high school. He just came back into town a couple weeks ago."

They were getting much closer to answers he desperately needed. "And the party?"

Loneliness and hurt crowded across her face. "I didn't want to go alone." When she looked up, her eyes pleaded for him to understand. Then her gaze shifted and fell back to the table. "Plus, I knew A.J. would be mad if I brought Bobby."

Well, that worked. "Why did you want to make A.J. mad?"

There was a barely sigh. "To get him back…"

A piece clicked into place. "For hurting you."

Again she nodded. He admired her courage at saying it if not her tactics at doing it.

"Does he know how much you're hurting over him and Eve?"

Melody shook her head very slowly. "He knows I've never liked her, but I've never really told him why."

"Don't you think he deserves the truth?"

She shrugged. "It wouldn't change anything. They're married. He loves her. Not me. End of story." She sighed. "Besides it's pointless anyway. It's not like he'd ever seriously go out with someone like me anyway, even if he wasn't married."

"Why not?"

Her eyebrows arched like he was an idiot for even asking the question. "Look at me. I'm not exactly anybody's idea of Miss Perfect."

Okay, so she wasn't rail thin or drop dead gorgeous. That didn't mean she had no attractive qualities. "Perfection is highly overrated."

"Huh. Tell that to the guys out there." She took a drink, and Blaine couldn't help but think the guys out there had some screws loose if they were so stuck up as to not give her a real chance. "Take you for example."

Horror punched into his chest as her steel hard gaze found his face.

She surveyed him with cold contempt. "You're rich, good-looking, all the girls flock to being around you."

Somehow none of that sounded like a compliment.

"Why would someone like you want to spend any time hanging around me?"

Defensiveness slipped into his spirit. "Oh yeah? Then why are we out having hamburgers and salad on a Monday night for no reason?"

She nailed him with those hazy blue eyes. "I don't know, Blaine. Why are we?" Laying her hands on the table, she leaned forward just a bit. "My guess is because you feel sorry for me, and you wanted to make sure I wasn't going to die on you. Well, you know what? I don't need your pity. I'm a big girl, and I can take care of myself."

"Yeah, like Saturday night, I guess." He didn't know why but the challenge in her voice brought out the daggers in his.

"I…" A barrage of terrified tears jumped to her eyes, and she collapsed backward away from him. Her gaze stayed on her fingernails on the table. "That was different."

Knowing it was stupid, he pursued. "Why?"

The swallow and breath took her whole effort. "It just was." She paused, and he waited. "I really never thought he would stoop so low as to do something like that. I know that sounds stupid now, but I never thought he would actually hurt me."

A.J.'s words which were never far away echoed again in Blaine's head. "You were very lucky. You know that, right?" Blaine looked at her, waiting for her to answer in the affirmative. "Mel?"

Her gaze came up to his and then fell. "I just wanted to go out, have a good time with some friends, maybe even flaunt that I had a date a little. I never expected him to…"

Silence fell between them.

He didn't want to ask, but he had to know. "And now?"

"Now?"

"If he calls…"

She laughed at that. "He's not going to call."

"Yeah, but if he does. You're not going to go out with him again, right?" Why wouldn't she answer a simple question? Panic slid into him when she said nothing. "Melody, you wouldn't go out with him again, right?"

Her gaze drifted out past the tables, away from him. "We'd better get home. I've got some studying to do." She stood and headed to the trash.

"Wha…?" He scrambled up after her, grabbing trash as he went. Barely getting it dumped before she made it to the door, he followed her out. "Mel. Are you serious? You would go out with Bobby again after what he did to you?" Blaine was with her step-for-step all the way to the car, but he was following only, nowhere near leading. "Mel. Hey."

At the edge of the car, he caught hold of her elbow.

With one jerk, she whirled so quickly, her hair spun in the breeze around her. "Look, I'm not stupid, okay? Bobby's a jerk. I get that. But I also know it's only that type of guy who ever asks me out. It's the ones who take you to the bar and want to take you home because it would be fun, the ones who take you to a dance and leave you there because they can have more fun with their friends than they are having with you. Those are the kinds of guys I can get to go out with me. And to tell you the honest truth, it's better to be out on a date with a guy who can't stand you than to be sitting at home playing Mouseball until your eyes bleed."

Her gaze challenged him to argue.

"You're serious." He tried not to sound incredulous that she could think so little of herself.

The intensity on her face crumbled, but she ducked before he could see any real tears. "I want to go home."

Blaine let go of her elbow, sighed, scratched the side of his ear, and then nodded. What choice did he have? He stepped over to the Carrera, hating himself for it. She was willing to throw herself at guys who would trash her, but she didn't seem to want to give him a second glance. Why was that? He asked the question again as she got in without looking at him. What he wouldn't give to be able to just be as honest with her as she was with him. He couldn't imagine admitting to anyone what she'd just admitted to him.

Carefully he opened the driver door and got in. Her head was down, her gaze on her hands. The desire to just tell her everything was nearly overwhelming, but how could he do that? It would ruin everything. She would tell A.J. who would certainly tell Eve who would probably tell the rest of the universe and then some. Burying all of it, he turned and started the car.

"I'm sorry," Melody said so softly he barely heard. "I don't know why I said that. It's just this whole thing with A.J. came up, and I'm still not feeling real good, and I don't know if I should just call and tell them no, or try to find somebody to go with me…" She shook her head and sniffed.

Glancing over at her once he was in traffic, Blaine knew for a fact she was crying. Every few seconds she would reach up and wipe her eye although she tried not to be obvious about it.

"Tell you what," he finally said, being able to take the breaking of her heart no longer. "What do you say I go with you on Friday?"

Panic flashed from her blotchy gaze.

"Just as friends," he said quickly, lest she get the wrong idea.

Her gaze left his again, and he silently begged her to accept the offer—anything, anything to keep her from going out with Bobby the Druggie again.

"Are you sure?" The pieces of her heart were evident in the crack of her voice.

"Definitely."

Eight

Melody knew it was childish, but on Wednesday at school, she went to the other end of the building to get to the third floor. Sure they were going out on Friday, but it wasn't a real date. Friends. Isn't that what he said? It was what they all said—eventually. But she couldn't take being compared to Lana-What's her name with the suede skirts and the non-existent waist.

True the last three days she was down another pound, but she still couldn't compete with the Lanas of the world, and she knew it. In Biology her thoughts wandered everywhere they weren't supposed to. It was becoming increasingly difficult to concentrate on anything these days. She ticked off her to-do list for the following day and added a trip to the gym to the list. It had been nearly a week, and the last thing she needed was to start gaining again because she was lazy.

At the end of class, she hauled herself up and out of the chair, pulling her backpack up and grunting with the effort. If she could just get rid of this headache. She wished she'd thought to put some aspirin in her backpack. She needed to start doing that. It was obvious the headaches weren't going away on their own. As she crossed past the staircase, she wondered if he was down there. It was a sure bet that he looked like a million bucks. He always did.

She looked down at her own T-shirt and jeans and sighed. One more reason to know that going out with him would never work. Still it would be nice to see him—just to assure herself he wasn't some apparition she had dreamed up.

Blaine had looked for her up and down each hallway and around the turns of the staircase up and down. He wondered if she hadn't come and what that might mean. Was she still feeling ill from the weekend? Would it be wrong to call and check on her when he got home? It would be nice to at least know she was okay.

As he walked to his little beat up car and worked the lock that was sticking more and more every time he used it, Blaine let himself wonder what it would be like to really date her. You know, if he could and all. Not that dating her was a possibility. First of all, she obviously thought he was an obnoxious rich jerk, which would have been funny if it wasn't so ridiculous. Then there was the whole how could he pull off keeping the secret of his real life from her. Not to mention the actual time commitment involved in going to school, taking care of Dylan, working, and trying to keep home from completely falling apart. He didn't exactly have scads of free time for something as frivolous as a girlfriend.

The thoughts boomeranged through his brain, back and forth, back and forth all the way home. They were still knocking up and down his synapses when he got to the front door. It was then that his senses kicked in. Something wasn't right. What he couldn't tell, but the feeling crept over him. The sound of his mother's scream confirmed the worst of the nightmares he'd fought to keep at bay for so long. Fear and protectiveness leaped through him like a hungry lion, and he yanked open the door, knowing the real-life nightmares had caught up with them once again.

"I said, 'Get out!'" his mother screamed hysterically as she stood there in the kitchen with a knife in her shaking hand. Dylan cowered just behind her in the doorway.

One look told Blaine the hulk of a man standing between him and his family was the same man he'd had more than one run-in with. However, any surprise of an entrance he might have made was destroyed by the squeak of the door when he opened it.

Jerking around, the tattooed, muscle-bound man he'd never called Stepdad glared at him through beady, dark, drug-laden eyes. "What're you looking at, punk?"

Blaine let his backpack slide to the floor as fear and courage battled for control. With his stepdad's focus split, Blaine looked over at his mother. "Call 911, Ma."

Her gaze said she wanted at all costs not to do that.

"Now!" Adrenaline gushed into his veins like Niagara, and his senses all homed in on how to survive until the cops showed up. Reaching down slowly, he grabbed the handle of the broom that always stood by the stove by the doorway.

"Don't do it, Elaine." His step dad turned on his ex-wife who slid down the wall toward the phone. "I said, 'Don't do it.'"

"Hey, Dave," Blaine said, drawing his stepfather's attention back at him. With all his might he swung the broom and caught Dave just above the beltline.

The oaff of the broom hitting the man's middle resounded through the room. Barely doubling, his stepdad straightened slowly, menacingly. His beady eyes now filled with fury and hate. Blaine had taken his one shot, but holding the broom as if it would do any more good, he stood his ground in the doorway.

"We need the police. Hurry." His mother's panic-stricken voice shrieked through his nerves as he stood face-to-face with death itself. She started through the address.

Dave, angered by the hit and the disobedience, whirled around and stomped over to his ex-wife. Ripping the phone from her hand, he slung it into the wall with a crash. Who was screaming now, it was hard to really tell. All of them and no one at the same time. Blaine's gaze caught on his younger brother's terrified face, and for one second he prayed for the safety of them all. Then instinct kicked in. He dropped the broom, grabbed the chair from next to the table, swung it and brought it down with a whack across Dave's broad back.

The big man who had just taken hold of his mother stumbled forward but didn't fall. Instead, he let go of his prey and turned instead on his former stepson, wild-eyed and livid. "I thought your mama taught you better manners than that, boy." He grabbed the chair from Blaine's grasp and slung it between them into the wall. "Well, since she didn't, it looks like it's up to me."

The ominous hulk advanced on him, and the cabinet was what finally stopped Blaine from going through the wall to get away. He knew what was coming. It wouldn't be the first time, but it might well be the last. He only hoped he could hold Dave's attention until the cops showed up. Two feet away the booze on Dave's breath made Blaine woozy.

"You rotten little mama's boy." Each word was spit like a wad of chewing tobacco right in Blaine's face. "Well, I guess I'm going to have to teach you a lesson. Looks like you forgot the last one."

The first punch landed squarely in his gut, and Blaine doubled over the fist, fighting to stay conscious. Swarms of memories swam through the pain. He gasped for air, finding none. Squeezing his eyes closed to keep himself upright, he straightened still gasping for air that wasn't there.

"Not so tough when you're fighting with your bare hands. Huh?" Dave took hold of Blaine's shoulders and slammed him over into the stove.

"Dave, stop! Please! Please! I'll give you the money! I swear I will! Don't hurt him!"

In the haze of mind-numbing pain, Blaine knew the screams were coming from somewhere, but they were difficult to really hear for the intense ringing in his ears. He could feel the blood coming back up his throat. Retching bile and blood choked him, and he coughed trying to keep them down.

"You think you're so smart." Another punch landed on the left side of his head as a sound permeated the air around him. Was it sirens or angels? He couldn't tell. "I'll show you just how smart you are, pretty boy."

With the last of his strength and still doubled over, Blaine launched himself into the middle of the man who had no reason not to send him to the hospital or heaven right then and there. They toppled backward, crashing over the table and chairs. On the floor on the other side, Dave came out on top, leering at him with hatred so deep it could've been a reflection of the pit of hell. Fists, knees, feet. They all found their mark as Blaine did the only thing he could—curl into a ball to ward them off. The sheer noise was enough to make his head crack.

"Police! Open up! Police! Freeze! Now!" Shouts came from every direction at once. "That's it! That's it! Stand up! Put your hands on your head!"

Light burst onto the scene just as everything went black.

"C'mon. C'mon back to us, son."

"Ugh! Oh!" Pain reverberated through every cavity of Blaine's entire body as a cough came choking up. The harder he tried to stay awake, the worse it became. Still he couldn't just give in to it. There was too much riding on him not. He pushed back at the blue clad figure shining a headache-inducing light into his eyes. "Ugh! Don't do that."

Struggling, and only with the help of the figure, he pulled himself to sitting and crawled the two feet over to the wall. At least there he had something to lean against. He wiped his hand across his face, feeling the sticky ooze that clung to the side of his head. He pulled his hand back and looked at it. Blood. Yes, it was blood. He nodded as if to explain that to himself and then let his elbow fall against his knee, spent.

"We need to take you in, sir. We've got the gurney."

However, Blaine waved them off, pulled his hand across his mouth which felt as sticky as his temple. "I'm fine." He still wasn't really breathing, more exhaling through the words. He put his hand up to the bridge of his nose and pushed upward. "Really. I don't need a doctor."

"Son, you took a pretty good beating there. We really need to take you in and get you checked out."

With no strength left anywhere in him, Blaine grabbed a chair and struggled up onto it. He had to convince them. There was no other choice. "I'm fine, guys. Really. Nothing a little peroxide won't fix."

His attention caught on his mother's thin frame standing with one of the police officers on the other side of the kitchen. Strange, he hadn't realized she was that thin. He wondered if it was just the way the light seemed or maybe it was the pale cotton housedress she wore. The blackness swirled around him again, but he fought it off. Somehow he had to stay upright. They couldn't afford a hospital visit.

When he stood, only half of him went up. He clasped his arm over his stomach and ribs. How he got across the kitchen was a mystery because the only thing keeping him from passing out was willpower. "Did you tell them about the restraining order?"

"Oh, Blaine. My God. Look at you." His mother put her hands on his face. The pity and fear in her eyes rang through his soul.

"We took it out three months ago," Blaine said, realizing if he found a way to take charge of the situation, he might be able to forget about the severe pain shooting into his body like knives. Still, he grimaced with each movement.

"So this isn't the first time?" the police officer asked as he wrote something in his book.

"Uh, no, Sir." Blaine tried to straighten, but that was asking far too much. "But it's never been this bad."

"Our divorce is supposed to be finalized the first part of May," his mother supplied.

"And he's angry about that?"

The flash of pleading apology his mother sent his way confirmed Blaine's worst fear. Dave wasn't just some guy his mom had been stupid enough to marry. He was also her connection to the drugs that she had sworn she was no longer on. "I guess so."

"So there's nothing else? Nothing you want to put in the report?"

For one, single second the thought of telling the man everything he wanted to know flashed through Blaine. But his mother's eyes wouldn't let him. He let his gaze fall. What else could he say? "No."

The cut on his temple wasn't all that bad. It was the rest of him that felt like it'd gone through a wine press. On Friday night, Blaine did what he could to cover up the remaining nicks and bruises on his face, tried to brush his hair down and over the cut, which didn't really work, made sure his ribs were wrapped as tightly as he could get them, took Dylan to the babysitter's, and headed for Peyton's. The maid let him in the mansion's palatial front door and led him all the way around and out to the pool in the back.

"Well, well, look who's back," Peyton said, gazing up from his seat on the lounge chair. He looked up at Blaine preparing for a more targeted barb when suddenly he stopped. His face sank in concern. "What happened to you?"

Blaine hated his friend knowing how far they had fallen. He hated everything about the whole situation. Living four doors down from this very house seemed a million years in the past. "Oh, you know. Can't stay out of trouble too long." He eased himself onto the empty lounge chair just to Peyton's right, fighting not to groan, but it wasn't easy.

Tanned, blond, with feathered hair and chiseled features, Peyton was the embodiment of Houston prosperous. Of course that had more to do with his father's oil wells and land deals than anything Peyton himself had ever done. With the rest of the world Peyton was less than deep, but ever since Blaine came to his aid when the six kids in elementary school were planning to beat him up, Peyton'd had a soft spot where Blaine was concerned. He sat up and inspected Blaine closer. "What's up with this?" He reached out to touch the cut, which was far more visible than Blaine wanted it to be. He ducked away, turning sideways in embarrassment.

"A fight at a bar. Wednesday." He lifted his chin, clenching his teeth through the lie. "Me and some buddies were kicking back with a few cold ones. This jerk came over and started making trouble. You know how it is…"

Peyton knew very well. Together they'd seen their share of stupidity growing up. It was half the fun of being rich. Peyton had never really asked about the new circumstances in Blaine's life. It was easier to pretend nothing had ever changed. But at that moment, Blaine saw the look of complete comprehension in his friend's face, and he pleaded with fate not to let him ask. Calm understanding slid over the questions in Peyton's brown eyes. He laid back down on the lounge chair. "Well, I hope you're not planning on finding more action tonight in my car. I just had it washed, you know."

Settling himself back onto the lounge chair, Peyton resumed soaking in the late afternoon sun. It really wasn't warm enough to sunbathe yet, but Blaine knew Peyton liked the picture it made. If nothing else, Peyton knew about images. He knew how to make them and how to protect them. That's why Blaine had come to Peyton in the first place. Peyton understood.

"No way, dude." Blaine laughed, pulling himself forward to stop the pain that caused. He shifted, hoping that would help. It didn't. "One gnarly fight's enough to last me for awhile. Melody and I are just going to hang out with some friends." The second her name was out of his mouth, he wanted to yank it back. Great!

"Mel-o-dy. Hmmm." Peyton drilled him with his gaze. "You're going to have to bring her around sometime. Introduce us. Show her off a little."

"Oh, I don't…"

"I know." Peyton snapped his fingers, bringing him upright. "Next Saturday. Daphne's having her summer kick-off party."

The very idea drilled through Blaine. "I don't…"

"C'mon, man. Just cause your dad's a jerk doesn't mean you have to ditch your friends."

There were so many things wrong with that statement, it was impossible to find a place to begin. He looked out across the sparkling pool. "So, do I get the car or not?"

Peyton sighed and angled his face up to the sun. "Of course. But bring it back in one piece."

"You got it."

Melody was determined not be late for this date, so determined, she'd been ready for a full thirty minutes before the doorbell rang. She jumped from the couch and raced to the entryway. "I got it." Her happiness had just made it all the way to her face when she swung the door open.

His head was down, his gaze on the sidewalk behind the dark sunglasses. Her first thought was gorgeous. Then he looked up at her. Happiness plummeted into horror.

"Blaine. What…?"

He never moved, and the smile was barely there. "Hey."

Stunned, Melody swallowed, trying to remember what she should do next. She stepped backward. The sight of his handsome face marred by dried cuts and bruises sliced through her. "Are you okay? What happened?"

There was an apology written in every move he made. "I should've called and told you. It's just…"

"No. No. That's okay." Waves of worry crashed over her as she watched him wince in pain when he stepped up the stair and through the door. "What happened?"

"It was dumb. I got in a fight, at a bar, defending a friend of mine." Carefully he reached up and removed the sunglasses.

Sick horror surged through her. "Blaine." Without really thinking about it, she stepped toward him and touched the blood-red scab just over his temple. Thinking was becoming a real issue. Her gaze fell to his face although he wasn't looking at her. "We don't have to go. It's not worth…"

"No." The sharpness of the word stopped her. "It's okay. Really. It's better than it looks." His eyes pleaded with her to believe him.

She didn't want to, and really she didn't. But what choice did she have? Pushing the fall of hair out of her eyes, she wrenched her gaze from him. "Okay. If you're sure…"

He nodded.

"Then I guess we'd better get going."

Gratefulness wafted almost to his smile as he turned to head back to the car. He replaced the sunglasses, which did only a passable job of covering anything.

Melody knew he wanted her to act normal, as if he didn't look like he'd just gone ten rounds in the ring with Mohammed Ali, but it wasn't easy. It was five minutes of utter silence in the car before she could take it no more. "Do you have any CD's or anything?"

"CD's?" His glance was at once surprised but then fell back into nonchalance. "Oh, umm. I think there might be some in the glove box."

Wishing she'd had far more practice at being on an actual, actual date, Melody reached for the latch. However, it didn't pop open. She tried again. "I think it's stuck." She wound her head down trying to see what was wrong with it.

"Maybe it's locked."

She waited a full ten seconds for him to tell her how to open it. "And… what's the trick to unlocking it?"

"Huh?" He glanced at her. "How should I… Oh. Uh. I don't…" He reached across her and jiggled it. It didn't even consider giving. After one more try, he resumed his position behind the wheel. "Huh. I don't know."

Melody narrowed her gaze at him in confusion. "You don't know how to open the glove box?" She reached for it and tried again. "And how long have you had this car?"

"Oh. Uh. Couple years." He slammed on the brakes to avoid hitting the little white SUV in front of them.

"A couple of years and you haven't opened your glove box?" She worked the latch sideways and then up and down, but it stuck and held fast.

He shrugged, focused now solely on traffic. "I never really had a reason to use it."

That stopped her, and she glanced at him. "But I thought you said the CD's were in here."

"Oh, uh. Yeah. They were." He turned into the lane to the left of them, a move which sent her careening into her door.

She barely caught herself, and it was difficult to think, balance, and survey him all at the same time. "So are they in there or not?"

There was a glance, well, part of one, but for the most part he kept his gaze glued to the traffic beyond. Melody couldn't be at all sure what just happened, but one thing was clear—whatever it was, he didn't want to talk about it. With talking out of the question, she reached over and touched the stereo power button. At least they could listen to the radio. Instantly the car was filled with window-shattering sound. It pounded through her, resetting her heart's rhythm.

She slammed her hands against her ears as she fought to figure out how to turn it down to a normal, sane level. Scrambling, she turned every knob she came to, and how there could be that many on one simple radio she had no idea. Then his hand was scrambling with hers, bumping into her as it too searched for the magic knob that would make the pounding drumbeat stop.

One flick of one of their efforts, and they were once again plunged into silence. Melody closed her eyes and then peeled them up from their resting place. "Wow. That was loud." She put her finger in her ear and shook her head. "Do you always listen to your music at ear-splitting levels?"

"No. I didn't… I mean. Somebody must've messed with it when I took it to get it cleaned." He still wasn't looking at her. At all.

The understanding of what a blundering dunce she was came over her, and she squeezed her eyes closed to pull some piece of not-hopeless back to her. She wanted to apologize, but that seemed lame. What was she going to do? Apologize for roping him into this nightmare? She should. Honestly. As bad as this was going, there wasn't much hope for the rest of the night. However, she couldn't find the words, so she sat back in the seat, kept her hands on her lap and her big mouth closed the rest of the trip.

By the time they got to A.J. and Eve's Blaine knew Melody had to know everything about what a phony he really was. After all, who owns a car for two years but doesn't know how to turn the stereo down? Who owns a car and has no idea where the CD's are, or doesn't even know how to open the glove box? Her silence screamed how surely she was onto him, and no matter how hard he tried, he could come up with no way to smooth things over and make them go back to how they were before things started spiraling so far out of control.

The only good thing was that Dylan was with Mrs. Rodriguez tonight, so at least Blaine didn't have to worry about that. However, as they ambled together up the walk toward the little beige house, the understanding of who he was about to see hit him full-on. He'd taken the last couple of days off work so no one would know. But judging by Melody's initial reaction, Eve not noticing was a pretty long stretch.

As Melody rang the doorbell, he stood behind her, wishing for his own sake he hadn't come but standing there and not running for hers. She deserved someone who would treat her like a princess, someone who looked at her with longing and love, someone far removed from all the frogs she'd so obviously kissed in her lifetime. And then before he could get another thought into words, one of those frogs—maybe the biggest of all—suddenly stood there, opening the door.

"Hey! You made it!" A.J. held out his arms to Melody who slipped into them for a quick hug. Strange how that made Blaine want to smack the guy. Couldn't he see what he was doing to her by holding out the bait of his friendship only to throw that she could never be with him up into her face again and again?

At that moment, arms still around Melody A.J.'s gaze caught on Blaine, and anger flashed through his eyes. He stepped backward, out of the hug. "I didn't know you were bringing someone."

Melody turned to Blaine as if she'd forgotten he was there. However, in the next second, she laced her arm through his and smiled up at A.J. "Eve said it was okay. I hope you don't mind."

When Blaine looked at her, his heart did an odd tap-dance. True, she really was beautiful in her own way, but more than that, he could see the farce of how hard she was trying to make A.J. understand what he'd missed out on. With nearly no effort, he turned on the smooth jets, thankful for all those way-cool parties with the super rich crowd who couldn't care less about anything deeper than who was driving what, and who happened to be with whom.

"I hope you don't mind," Blaine said, knowing just how much she wanted A.J. to eat his heart out and just how much A.J. hated him. Both might well work to her advantage tonight. He pulled his arm out of hers and laid it over her shoulders. "How could I say no to an invitation like this?" His gaze locked on Melody's surprised one, and completely into character, he leaned over and brushed the edge of her ear with his lips, pushing the pain in his ribs from his consciousness.

She giggled in surprise and delight, pushing at him but not really hard enough to get him to move.

When he came up for air, he looked at her long and lovingly. It wasn't hard. A.J.'s movement at the door broke the spell, and when he glanced up, one look at A.J. told him they had hit the target square.

"Yeah. Well, why don't y'all come on in? No use standing out here on the porch all night." A.J. stepped in and let the two of them, still arm-in-arm cross in front of him. Blaine had no trouble noticing the look of disgust plastered all over his host's face. Yes, this could work out very much in Melody's favor.

They hadn't gone six steps into the house when Eve came into the living room from the kitchen. One look and she stopped cold. Blaine's arm was still around Melody, and he wasn't at all sure what of the whole situation surprised Eve the most.

"Oh. I… didn't… Hi, Melody." Eve ripped her gaze away from Blaine and placed it on Melody. "We're so glad you decided to join us."

He felt Melody's instant nervousness as she squirmed next to him.

"You did say it was all right to bring someone, right?"

When Blaine looked at her, his heart softened toward her. She really was trying, and she really was hurting. That much was clear to anyone who took the time to look.

"Of course. Of course." Eve strode over to them. "I was just a little surprised. That's all. I thought…" Her words trailed off as her gaze slid over Blaine's face. "They said you'd been sick."

That brought Blaine back from acting land. His gaze fell to their feet as he shifted just slightly away from Melody. "Yeah, well."

Eve surveyed him carefully—the cut, the bruises. Her gaze questioned him with no words.

"I got into a little barroom thing the other night. Some idiot broke a bottle over my friend's head." He shrugged. "I'll live." It was strange how the lies came easier and easier each time he retold them.

"That's a heckuva souvenir you got there," A.J. said, and there was an edge to the tone.

Again Blaine shrugged. "Hey. You play. You pay. Know what I'm saying?"

A.J. scrutinized him up and down. "Yeah. I sure do."

"Well," Melody said, knowing that Blaine didn't want everyone standing around playing doctor all night.

"Oh, come on in," Eve said, motioning to the sofa. "Please, have a seat."

Melody followed Blaine. She didn't have much choice as he still had her collared. At the beige couch, she saw him wince as he sat. Instantly she scooted far enough away that she wouldn't be pressed up against his ribs. He hadn't said they hurt, but she could tell they did. However, once down, he replaced his arm over her shoulders. First instinct was to question it, but she knew why he was doing it, and as absurd as it was, she didn't want to stop him. For this one night, they would pretend to be totally in love.

In a stupid way, it felt better than all the reality she'd ever lived had.

Dinner was great—chicken something with an orange glaze and three vegetables to go with it although he noted with some concern how very little Melody had eaten. Nonetheless, by the time Eve brought out dessert, Blaine was stuffed. He held up his hands and waved them. "No thanks. I've got to let this settle first." Leaning back carefully in his chair, he jumped at the stab of pain. It was strange how certain movements he could never quite predict hurt so much.

Instantly Melody's gaze was on him and her hand was on his knee. "You okay?" It was whispered, barely loud enough to make the gap from her to him, but the concern in her eyes said it all.

"Yeah. I'm fine." Gamely, he put his arm around her and pulled her over onto his shoulder. The screaming of his ribs nearly did him in, but he smiled just the same at A.J. "So, I hear you're a poker player."

A.J.'s attention was focused in on Melody, and he had to shake himself to get back to the conversation. "What…? Oh, yeah. Some." He reached over and grabbed his tea. It was clear to Blaine how flustered he was, and inwardly Blaine smiled at that. "Just some of the guys from the fire department and me."

Blaine reached for his own drink, which turned out to be much more painful than it looked. "Jeff and Gabe?"

"Mostly. We play some Thursdays. You should come."

Even if it was possible, he wouldn't have come because there was no sincerity to that invitation at all. "Oh, no can do. I work Thursdays." He glanced over at Eve who had resumed her chair. "Well, most of them anyway."

The soft rubbing of Melody's hand on his thigh snagged his attention, and he looked at her. It really was fun to be with her—even if it wasn't for real. His smile didn't have to be faked. It came without any help. The middle of him surged into his chest, and his breath caught. Then he came crashing back to reality. He jerked his gaze over to them. One sat doe-eyed, the other horrified. "What do you say we go relax a bit in the living room?"

At that, they all jumped into motion. Eve stood and grabbed three plates. Instantly Blaine felt bad for making the suggestion. He should've just sat and let them make the suggestion. However, it was too late for that. "Oh, here, let us help you with those." He reached for the plates in Eve's hands as she came abreast of him.

"It's okay. I've got them. Really. Y'all go on."

He hesitated, unsure of protocol in this situation.

"Go on," A.J. said. "I'll help Eve. We'll be there in a sec."

Melody stood behind him with her hands in the pockets of her white jeans. He glanced back at her and smiled. "Well, if you're sure." Reaching for her hand, he took it out of her pocket and pulled her slowly with him. They went out of the kitchen nook, through the little hallway, and back into the living room.

At the couch, he noticed that Melody once again let him sit before she lowered herself carefully onto the couch. The concern in her eyes was deep. "Are you sure you're okay? We really don't have to stay if…"

Softly he smiled. "I'm okay. Really. Now would you relax?" To prove his point, he reached over and pulled her next to him. After only a single shift, he found comfortable and settled in. It was truly amazing how nice this felt even with bruised up ribs and hosts who were anything but abundantly happy to have them—not to even mention that it was all for show.

For a single moment he caught the angry whispers in the kitchen, and he hoped Melody hadn't heard them. Then A.J. strode into the room and over to the recliner. He turned on the television, flipped to the Astros game, and turned it all the way down. The Astros. Baseball. At least A.J. had some smarts to him.

A.J. picked up a little card off the end table and read it absently. "So, you go out a lot then?"

"Hm. Out?" Blaine shifted, not knowing if the question was for him or Melody, but sensing by the tone it was directed at him.

"Yeah, you know. Partying?" A.J.'s gaze drilled into him.

"Oh. Uh. No. Not really."

Eve's entrance jerked his gaze to her, but he hadn't finished the answer, so reluctantly, he turned back to A.J.

"It was just… me and some friends after work the other night. No big deal until Godzilla showed up."

"I thought they said you got sick Thursday," Eve said, and Blaine's attention snapped over to her.

"Oh, well. Yeah. I did. I mean it happened Wednesday night."

Not being able to catch onto the spiraling of life around him, Blaine felt Melody tense. However, he didn't have enough brain cells to really attend to why.

He laughed, trying to throw them all off the scent, but the breath pinched across his ribs. The wince was impossible to hide, and he shifted before pulling a fake smile to his face. "Some idiot decided we looked like good target practice. I guess he was right." Blaine looked at Melody who was staring at him with a look he couldn't quite read. Out of desperation, he glanced up at the television just as the Astros turned a double play. "Wow! Did you see that? What a throw."

The night seemed endless. They were like oil and water—two couples with so little in common, the only thing they had in common was having nothing in common. By the time ten o'clock rolled around, Melody could take the tedium no longer. It wasn't that they weren't trying to be nice. It was that they were having to try much too hard.

"Well, I really need to get home." She yawned for emphasis.

Scooting to the edge of the sofa as gently as she could, she ran her thumb under her nose. It was itching from something—air freshener, a spice in the chicken, the company—something.

"Do you really have to go so soon?" Eve asked, and there was an acknowledgement in the tone of just how badly the night had gone.

Blaine followed Melody off the couch albeit slowly, and she stepped to the side to give him as much room as possible. He was doing an admirable job covering just how much pain he was in, but she could see it in his eyes with each move he made. She sighed, knowing she shouldn't have made him come. Calling and canceling. It's what she had wanted to do. Now she realized with clarity, it was what she should've done.

Her gaze only asked him if he was okay, and guilt ran through her at the depth of the ache in his eyes. He smiled, but it was work. With her gaze, she pleaded with him to be all right. Not really thinking about it, she reached over for him—comfort or support or something like that. She wasn't really sure any more.

"Well, take care driving home." A.J. stood from his chair and reached over to shake Blaine's hand.

Melody couldn't look at him. She was too disappointed, too humiliated that he would treat anyone with as much disrespect as he had Blaine.

"I guess we'll see y'all later," A.J. said, retracting his hand.

Yeah. Much, much later.

"Drive carefully." Eve met them at the entryway as they headed out.

"Take care," Melody said, sensing this would be the last time in her life that she would see them. She didn't fit into their world, and she wondered if she ever had. She walked to the car with Blaine right beside her. He had been so kind all night, acting like he really liked her. It wasn't hard to figure out why. At the car, he opened the door for her, and she slid in. Ache sliced through her as she glanced back up at the porch where A.J. and Eve stood.

Her gaze dropped as Blaine got in. Life would never be like that for her, and hot tears stung her eyes at that thought. As he pulled away from the curb, she sniffed back the tears, wishing everything about her whole life was so, so different.

They drove only to the end of the block before she looked over at Blaine, sweet Blaine who had put his own comfort and peace aside to help her out… again. She didn't deserve him even as a friend. "Thanks."

In surprise he glanced over at her. "For what?"

"For acting like you like me."

This glance held more concern. "I do like you."

"Yeah." There was a small laugh. "But not like that. Not the arm around the shoulders, like-like kind of thing." She shook her head trying not to cry. "Still it was nice to pretend for awhile."

Blaine's gaze was less on the traffic than on her. "Why do you do that?"

She looked over at him, his face alternately illuminated and then darkened by the lights outside. "What?"

"You act like nobody would ever really be interested in you. Do you really think that's true?"

How he could even ask was beyond her. "I've had six dates in the last year. Four were with you, one was with A.J., and one was with… Bobby. I don't exactly see eligible guys knocking down my door. Do you?"

He considered that. "I took this psychology class last year, and they said that we attract what we believe about ourselves." He paused. "Not that I believe all that stuff or anything, but maybe if you stopped running yourself down about stuff, maybe more guys would see how fun you really are."

She laughed. "Fun? Yeah. There's a word." Her gaze fell to her hands swathed in the darkness at her lap.

"What? You are fun. I had fun tonight."

"Yeah, it was a barrel of laughs trying to make sure everybody didn't kill each other."

"That wasn't about you. That was about them." Then inexplicably, he reached over and took her hand. The gesture filled her entire body with warmth, and when she looked at him, he was looking back. "You're a cool person, Melody. You don't give yourself enough credit for that. Nobody gets to see it because you're so scared to show them because you put on this mask that's not real."

She retrieved her hand as she shook her head. "They don't want to know the real me. They already can't stand the fake me. What makes you think they'd fall head over heels for something even worse?"

"How do you know it's worse? Maybe it's the mask they

don't like."

The thought went through her mind and spun there for a moment. "All I know is A.J. has his life now, and I have mine—what's left of it anyway. That much was pretty clear tonight. We used to be able to talk about anything and everything. Now when he looks at me, all I see is the disappointment. I hate that."

"I don't think that was about you." He glanced her direction before retraining his gaze on the street outside. "I think it was more about who you were with."

"Yeah, he was thrilled about that, huh?" Melody considered that and then looked over at him. "Well, I don't care what A.J. thinks. I think you're an awesome guy. He just doesn't know you like I do."

The smile that came to Blaine's lips was at once grateful and sad. "Oh, yeah. I'm such a catch."

That stopped her. "Well, of course you're a great catch. Look around you. You've got a fabulous car, great clothes, a good job. You're working on the college thing. Besides all that, you're not too hard on the eyes."

"Dents and all," he said with a laugh.

Her smile was real this time. "Dents and all." They were getting close to her neighborhood, and for the second time that night, Melody had the distinct feeling that a guy who would be in her heart forever was about to say good-bye forever. Her gaze dropped to her lap. "Just so you know, I'll never regret spending the time we have together. I've had more fun with you than with anyone I've ever been with… well, you know, not that we were together-together or anything, but…"

His gaze was soft. "Me, too."

At her house Blaine got out, helped her from her side, and walked her to her door. The only thing he regretted was that he didn't have the guts to hold her hand. But they weren't on display anymore. There was no reason to pretend out here with only the ambient light and the stars to see.

"Thanks again, for coming," she said, and he hated how appreciative she had to be about him taking a few hours out of his life to hang out with her.

"I enjoyed it." He caught the question in her eyes. "Really."

Right at the bottom of the first step, she stopped and turned, swinging her hair over her shoulder. "Well, be good. And no more bar fights. Okay?" Her smile was so sincere it tugged on his heart.

Suddenly Blaine was caught in it and in the feeling of being with her. What made him do it, he would never be able to say, but at that moment it seemed the most natural thing in the world to do. He leaned toward her, and their lips touched. The simple kiss swept all sanity from him. He had expected soft and nice—like every other girl he'd ever kissed. He didn't expect it to feel like electricity all the way through to his toes.

It was like falling through a giant black hole with nothing to grab onto. Flailing emotionally, he realized only after he'd deepened the kiss what message she had to be getting from this—either that he was a jerk who wanted more like the rest of them, or that he was worse, telling her he wasn't interested and then making her feel like he was.

At that thought, Blaine jerked back. He ran the back of his thumb under his bottom lip. His breathing was uneven and hard. He blinked, desperately trying to find reality. What he should say, what he should do? Nothing was coming to him as he stood there staring at her. All he wanted to do was to lean in for another kiss, grab hold of her and never let go. However, there were so many reasons that could never work, he couldn't count them all.

"Well, goodnight," she said shakily. Emotions upon emotions traveled over her features as she backed away from him. Then with a snap, she broke the connection and raced up the stairs. In the next heartbeat she was gone.

With a slow close of his eyes to question where his sanity had gone, Blaine turned back for the car. When he got to it, all he wanted to do was kick the thing. If there was just some way to be honest with her, to go back to the beginning, to the moment he had panicked when Eve asked him out, to not get the car, to not start down this stupid road of lies. If…. It was a big word.

Nine

All day Saturday Melody had been on a loop of questions with no answers. Why had he kissed her like that? Why had he kissed her at all? After all, they had talked about the fact that he had no interest in her… like that anyway. And then he went and kissed her like he did. Or maybe that was how he kissed everybody. She thought about asking Farin, but one look at her slick smile and the doe-eyes she was making at the cute guy buying tennis shoes struck that idea off the list.

No, Blaine Donovan had no real interest in her, and letting herself believe he might was a great way to go through a heartache she wanted no part of. It was that thought alone which had gotten her through an entire afternoon of reshelving shoes, but even that thought evaporated when she turned onto her street at 7 and saw A.J.'s new silver SUV sitting in her driveway.

Oh, no. You've got to be kidding me. Keep driving, Mel. Just keep driving. What good can possibly come from stopping? Anger swelled inside her followed closely by solid resolve as she pulled up next to the curb. He wasn't her babysitter. He wasn't her parent. After last night, he was hardly even her friend. She got out just as he came out the front door, and every horrid emotion she'd been running from slithered right over her.

"I'll be sure to tell her," he said to her mother who stood in the door behind him. His wave stopped mid-path when he turned and saw Melody getting out of the car.

"Oh, good," her mother called. "You made it, Sweetheart. Look who stopped by."

Melody didn't so much as acknowledge the statement. She went around and popped her trunk and hauled out her purse and backpack. Knowing she would have to go up there sooner or later, she defiantly chose later, choosing instead to rummage and gather up stuff she'd been collecting for a month. A minute, two, and she heard her mother say goodnight. He was coming. She knew it. She could feel it. Hands full, she stood just as A.J. stepped up to the little car.

"Done?" he asked. She shrugged as he reached for the trunk lid and slammed it. Then he planted his hands on his hips, blocking her path to the sidewalk. His gaze went straight into her. "Listen, I think we need to talk."

"About what?" But her attention snagged on the sweater that was falling out of the pile in her hand. She swung it trying to get it back into her control. It didn't work.

"About you and these guys you are choosing to date."

The tiny laugh jumped from her. "What're you my guardian? I'm a big girl, A.J. I can take care of myself." Annoyance tromped over her when the sweater slipped a little closer to the ground.

Without asking, A.J. reached down, retrieved it, and piled it on top. "You've got to know I'm worried about you, Mel. I can't help it. I am. First Bobby and now this guy… Blaine. You've got to know this isn't smart."

"You don't know anything about Blaine. He's a nice guy."

"He's an arrogant, selfish jerk. That's plain from a 100 yards away. What I can't figure out is why you can't see it."

"You just don't know him."

"I don't have to. Remember when we were in school how the jocks treated everybody like they were dirt on somebody's shoes. That's the way this guy is. He thinks he's better than everybody else. And what's up with this bar fight thing? Do you really want to go out with somebody who thinks a good time is going out and getting smashed up at a bar?"

"He didn't start the fight."

"But he didn't walk away either."

"And your point is?"

"My point is you deserve better, Mel. These guys are serious trouble. How can you not see that?"

She felt something else slip from her grasp, and she struggled not to drop everything right there on the asphalt. "Yeah? Well, that's just too bad because I like Blaine, and he likes me, and there's not really anything you can do about that." It was all a lie, of course, but she didn't care. She would not give him the satisfaction of telling him they had no intention of seeing each other again. "Now if you'll excuse me." She yanked whatever it was back up to her and swung it all to the side to mount the curb.

"Mel, come on. You don't have to be like this."

On that she turned on her toe to face him. "I don't have to be like this? I'm not the one who changed. I'm not the one who fell in love and got married and moved off."

It wasn't fair how cute he looked in his backward cap and blue and white jersey. "Come on, Mel. That's not fair. What did you think? I'd live out here forever? Did you think I'd never get married, never have a life?"

She didn't know what she'd thought, but what she did know at this moment was that she hurt. Badly. "I've got to go."

"Think about what I said," he called after her.

When she got to the front door, what she had hoped would be a clean getaway became a wreck of yanking and pushing and throwing things into the house. How dare he come over here and start lecturing her on who she could and couldn't date? How dare he be so condescending and hurtful toward Blaine? Blaine. Who had gone out of his way to come and see her when she was sick? That was a whole lot more than A.J. ever thought about doing. Did he come and visit? No. Even his wife had to call because he was too busy or couldn't be bothered. Such a great friend he thought he was. Yeah, right. Well, he could stay busy for all she cared. She had no desire to see A.J. Knight ever again. That was just all there was to it.

For four days Melody had been spinning in the inexplicable caldron of guys and their intentions. She had finally come to the judicious decision that none of them could be trusted and that they all had a duplicitous agenda. Bobby, Blaine, A.J.—they were all the same. They used you for the time it worked for them, and then just like that, you were a nobody again.

Blaine hadn't called. Not that she expected him to. But that kiss on the front porch had been enough to make one small part of her hope. By Tuesday she had killed that one small part. She hated herself for being taken in by his sweet talk and charms. He was a snake just like all of them. In fact, the kiss was probably just a warm up for him to see how far she would go with him. After all, they'd been out a few times by now, and true to form, he expected a little something in return.

She hated him. She really did. She hated all of them, for no other reason than they were guys and they were jerks. On Wednesday she went up the center stairs and caught sight of Blaine talking with Lana What's Her Name on the mirror staircase. Melody could've thrown up. Those two deserved each other. She kept climbing.

"I promise, Blaine. It'll be lots of us. It's Karlie's birthday. She said to tell everybody," Lana said. Her long blonde hair was pulled back from her chisel-angled face. The straight nose, the preppy clothes, they spoke of high expectations of life.

"I don't know. I'm working until 9 Friday."

"Perfect." That perky voice and bounce were so fake. "We can meet over at Bar Houston about ten." She lowered her lashes at him. "You know, it's so nice to have a friend to be able to ask out. I hate going by myself."

"I thought you said there'd be lots of people."

"Oh, there will be, but I hate being odd man out. So you'll go then?"

"I guess."

By the time class was over, Melody's whole spirit was wrapped tightly around fury at the whole male population. The pop quiz Professor Warner sprang on them didn't help at all. When she went down the stairs trying not to look for Blaine, her brain started again around the endless loop of why he had ever agreed to go with her in the first place. Face it. Even twelve pounds couldn't make that much of a difference. The thought of stopping for a big cheeseburger and fries on the way home stabbed into her. As she pushed out into the deepening night, she debated the thought. No one would know. More to the point, no one would even care.

They hadn't noticed up to now, why should they start now?

It was movement to the far right of the far parking lot that caught her eye first. She glanced that direction not even really paying attention, but a snap of recognition stopped her. Slowing, she crossed next to a car parked in one of the center spots. Her gaze drilled through the darkness at the figure standing across the way. It was Blaine. She was sure of it.

But he wasn't standing next to the little gold sports car. Instead, he was working diligently to get the door to a horrible little green something or other open. His project sat atop the trunk. Melody sank closer to her shield, hoping he wouldn't turn around and see her. What in the world was he doing anyway? Surely he wouldn't be breaking into someone else's car. Not out here in the open like this. Her heart lodged in her throat at the implications of what she was seeing.

Besides, what would he want to break into that car for? It didn't look like it even ran. It wasn't like he was going to steal the thing. At that moment the car door he was working with came open, and he glanced around the parking lot. Ducking farther, she managed not to be seen. He quickly stowed the project in the back, got in, and after one unsuccessful try, finally got the car started. The headlights slashed through the darkness, and then sliced across the parking lot before he pulled out into traffic.

Melody kept her safe hiding spot, ducking so he definitely wouldn't see her as he drove away. When he was gone, she stood, staring after him. Did that make any sense at all? If it did, she couldn't find it.

After work Friday, Blaine seriously considered not going to Bar Houston. Lana would be mad, that was a given. But surely he could come up with something plausible. Something so she would give him a break about not showing up. Then again, there was that final project he'd been roped into being her partner for. He had to find a way to quit sitting next to her.

With a sigh, he realized that not showing up could adversely affect his grade not to mention his future. So he turned in the direction of Bar Houston as he exited the mall parking lot. He would put in a little face time, make her happy, and then beg off with some excuse about another party or something. When the lie of his real life had become so draining, he couldn't really tell, but for now, it was a necessary evil. They didn't know, and they wouldn't. It was too important to his future. When he graduated, he would need contacts, good contacts, maybe even an internship.

Lana's family was well-connected. Her father owned one of

the largest design offices in Southeast Texas. It wasn't that he wanted to use her for that connection, but he certainly didn't want to do anything to jeopardize it either.

As he neared the bar, he loosened his tie and then took it off altogether. Stuffy and stodgy was not the dress code at Bar Houston. Upwardly mobile. Yes. Stuffed suit. No. He flipped the tie into the side seat and unbuttoned the top button of his dress shirt. He wondered how Dylan was doing at Mrs. Rodriguez's. The thought of calling and checking crossed his mind, but he had no way of doing that. He'd just have to trust that things were fine.

Three blocks from the bar, he found an out-of-the way office building parking garage and pulled into it. There was no reason to get Peyton's car tonight. This would work just fine. He slipped out of the car and hurried down the darkened streets. The thumping of the music and the noise of the crowd was unmistakable. He so remembered when he and Peyton had snuck in with Peyton's friends' IDs. Strange how that seemed like a lifetime ago.

At the line, he attached himself to the end and looked at his watch. 10:15. He wondered if she was already inside. Probably. He looked for her half-heartedly in line but gave up. There were too many people and not enough interest to sustain the search. The line moved surprisingly quickly, and in no time he was in the midst of the crowd inside. The thumping music thundered through his body.

When the headache had started, he didn't know, but he was pretty sure the music wasn't helping. He angled his steps over to the rounded booths. That's where most of the groups usually met up. Hand in pocket, he searched through the haze, wondering if he might indeed not find her and be able to have a reason to go home. A couple stepped out in front of him from one of the tables, and he ducked to the side. "Excuse me."

"Sorry."

It was only when he looked up that the horror of the situation flooded over him. His glance behind A.J. who stood in front of him took in Eve. "Oh, hi." Blaine swallowed, wishing he'd heeded the whispering of his spirit to not come.

"Hey, Blaine," Eve said, holding out her hand with a slight glance at her husband. "I didn't expect to see you here."

He shook her hand and then watched it drop back between her and A.J. "Yeah. Uh. Some friends of mine asked me…"

"Blaine! Honey! Good. You made it. Finally. I've been looking everywhere for you." How, why…. he didn't know, but suddenly Lana practically smashed into him. He caught her so she didn't fall right over him, and in the next second her arms were around him—one around his waist, the other scrawled up his chest and to his neck. One whiff told him she'd been drinking and a memory of the last time he was with her when she was drinking snaked through him.

He tried to corral her ardor, but it didn't work very well. "Lana. Umm… I'd like you to meet my… Well. This is Eve and A.J." He was vaguely aware that he should know and recognize the others sitting at their table, but putting logical names with faces was impossible at that moment. He fought to look calm and cool even as Lana gazed up at him with that dull, loopy smile which wasn't helping at all. "So are you all out celebrating?" He glanced at the others at their table.

"Just out," Eve said, her gaze going to Lana every other second. There was a long pause filled only by the music. "Well, it was nice to see you."

"Yeah, you too." He looked down at Lana and tried to find an appropriate smile for the situation. "Well, we'd better go. Y'all have fun."

"Y'all too," Eve said.

It was not lost on Blaine that A.J. looked like he'd just eaten a vat of uncooked octopus. Turning with Lana still hanging on him, Blaine beat it for another spot.

"They seem nice," she said in that sickly sweet voice that raked right over his nerves.

"Yeah." His mood which had been less than enthusiastic prior to now, dropped all the way to sullen and snarky as they joined her friends. At odd moments he tried to be the cool, super-fun guy those at Lana's table had seen on other occasions, but the truth was, he just couldn't get there tonight. It felt way too much like an act, and the truth was, he was getting really sick of acting.

Every-so-often on his way to or back from the dance floor, he glanced over to their table. There were six of them although he was having trouble remembering the others' names. One was Jeff. He thought. Yeah. That sounded right. Gabe? That seemed right too, but the two women, he couldn't find those names no matter how hard he tried. Back at his own table, his gaze went across the way to Eve's table but was jerked back to his own by Lana and her thousand ways to convince a guy she was serious.

"Hey!" he said just before midnight as her hand drifted a bit high up on his thigh. He turned and looked at her. "C'mon, Lan. We talked about this. We're just friends, remember?"

She pouted her disappointment. "But I thought…"

"It's not happening. Okay? I've told you that. I like you. I do, but not like that."

A seductive smile spread to her lips. "Like what then? Like this?" She slithered over him, drawing his mouth to hers.

Backing up, he would've gone through the wall to get away from her. He pushed her backward. "Hey! Seriously. It's not happening. Okay? Not tonight. Not ever."

She crossed her arms over her ample chest. "Then what good was asking you?"

He was wondering the same thing.

"Hey, dude," Peyton drawled through the phone the next evening. "I was just wondering if you were still coming to Daphne's tonight. It's going to be off the chain."

"Oh, can't," Blaine said, scraping the molded contents of a bowl into the trash. "I just went out last night with some friends."

"What? Two nights in a row too much for an old man like you?"

The disgusting mold of the next pot in the sink stuck like glue to the side of it. He shouldered the phone and scraped harder. "I've got a lot to do here. I haven't been home in what seems like ages."

"You sound like my mother."

"Hey. Your mom's cool."

"You, my friend, are getting older by the minute. I thought you were bringing Melanie."

"Melody. And no, you said I should bring her. I never actually agreed."

"What? You two too good for us?"

"No." He stacked that pan with the others to the left of the sink. Now he knew for certain, he should've begged off last night's anaconda fight to do the dishes. Lana wouldn't have understood, but it would've been so much more productive than living through four hours of an all-out nightmare. "It's just I've really got a lot to do tonight. Finals are coming up, and I've got this final project I need to be working on, and…"

"Uh-oh. I hear them. Do you hear them? Those tiny violins. Aren't they cute?" Peyton paused. "Well, if you're just going to bail on us again, then…"

"I'm not bailing. Okay, I am. But for a good reason."

There was another pause before Peyton tsked his tongue. "You are seriously scaring me, my brother."

"Next time," Blaine said, not meaning a word of it.

"I'm going to hold you to that."

Something told Blaine that was more a threat than a promise.

Melody was elbow-deep in Biology notes when her mother called from downstairs. "Mel, phone!"

Phone? On Saturday night at 9:30? It could only be one person, and that person she did not want to talk to. Reluctantly she tramped down the stairs to the kitchen where she grabbed the phone and plopped into a kitchen chair. "Hello."

"Hey, there. What're you up to?"

A smile slid to her face at the sound of Blaine's voice. "Not much. What're you up to?" Thank goodness it wasn't A.J. like she'd assumed.

"Being bored."

"Bored? What's up with that? I figured a popular guy like you would have a thousand parties to go to on the weekend."

"Nah. One invite but I didn't really want to go."

"Oh, yeah? Why not?"

The sigh came through loud and clear. "Been there. Done that. Got the T-shirt. Besides it sounded like much more fun to call you."

"Ah, yes. I'm such scintillating company. I would much prefer me to the Houston glitteratzi as well."

He laughed, which should've been hurtful, but strangely it didn't feel that way. "So how's your week been?"

For one moment she thought about mentioning the little green car, but it all still seemed too strange so she didn't. "Pretty much just work and school."

"You ready for finals?"

"Trying to be. Biology's going to eat my lunch though."

"Ugh. There's a disgusting thought."

Melody laughed out right. "You've got a point there." She took a breath. "No, it's the whole systems thing. What systems belong to which organism. That gives me fits."

"Well, why don't you let me help you? I've still got my notes from last semester here. I could quiz you or something."

That struck her as odd. "Why would you do that?"

"Because I'm bored, remember?"

Two hours later when Blaine hung up, he couldn't help but be happy he had called. Somehow spending time with her even over the phone had a way of lifting his whole spirit. He went into the living room where he found Dylan asleep on the floor. Guilt swept through him. He should've been spending his free time with his little brother not calling up girls he had no chance with anyway.

With that thought dogging him, he pulled the child to his feet and walked him step-for-step to his room. He vowed to spend more time with the child once school was over. He would have a week or two before intercession and summer school. Surely there was something fun they could do. However, as he went to his room to get ready for bed, his thoughts turned once again from Dylan to Melody. The smile came unbidden.

Although it made no sense and he might have no chance with her, for this moment, all he wanted was to be with her. Life would have to sort everything else out after that.

All week long Melody fantasized about what it would be like to see him again on Wednesday. She had this whole scenario of meeting him at the stairs and him sweeping her off her feet running on loop in her brain. What she didn't plan at all on was making it halfway up the first set of steps and hearing his name right behind her.

"You and Blaine were looking awful tight Friday night," the voice said, but obviously not to Melody. Her steps slowed, and she recalibrated her hearing to behind her.

"Yeah, well…" Lana laughed a flighty little laugh that made Melody want to throw up. "You know Blaine. He doesn't really have time for pleasantries."

"So this final project thing might not end with the project then?"

"We haven't really set anything official yet or anything."

"But that's just a matter of time, right?"

Lana's giggle confirmed all the doubts Melody had done her best to bury. Suddenly her feet felt like lead and her heart did too. She kept climbing even as the two girls peeled off for their own class on the second floor. What kind of a game was he playing anyway? Clearly he had gone out with Lana on Friday and done who-knew-what afterward. So why had he called her on Saturday? And what was a call really worth on balance with going out and going back to someone's place?

Frustrated with herself, she stomped into Biology. When would she ever learn?

Blaine looked for Melody everywhere after class on Wednesday. He'd wanted to be early to have a chance to talk, but there was a catastrophe of Sopheclean proportions in the men's wear department, and he'd barely made it to class at all. Hustling out of the room the second the class broke, Blaine was all the way to stairs before he heard his project partner calling his name. "Blaine!"

He closed his eyes in frustration. Why did she have to sound like a bleating sheep?

"Blaine!" She caught up with him at the cusp of the staircase. "What are you running away for, silly? I've got this final layout for the project. I thought we could go over it tonight." Her lashes angled up to him. "Unless you want to get together sometime later this week."

"What? No. Uh. Now is… fine." He glanced around once more and then reluctantly leaned toward her, wishing with everything in him that she would hurry this along. "What do you got?"

The word humiliation came nowhere close when Melody had made one flight of stairs and come face-to-face with the true reality of her situation. Together, they stood at the top of the stairs not trying to hide anything. He stood there, leaning over Lana who was looking up at him with adoring, fawn-like eyes. It was sickening. With one jerk, Melody spun around, slung her backpack to her shoulder and strode off down the hallway in the opposite direction. Blaine Donovan had made a fool of her for the last time.

Students streaming by them was the first indication Blaine had that the classes above had finished. He glanced up from the plans Lana was showing him, and his gaze jumped from face to face, searching for hers. Then he caught sight of her striding the other way down the hall. He tried to decide why. Did she park that way? Was she going to the Student Union or the library? However, at the double doors, she hit the door so hard it cracked back into the brick wall on the other side.

And he knew. Either someone had told her, which was a distinct possibility or she had seen him with Lana—or both. He glanced down at his project partner who was gazing at him with a look that no one could mistake. "Listen, I'll just take this and get back to you." He snatched up the paper and folded it in two.

"But we've only got two weeks to finish this, and I really want an A on this project, Blaine."

"Yeah, so do I, but I don't really have time right now." He stuffed the paper in his backpack and looked back at the vacant door down the hallway. She was gone. There was no hope of catching her now. However, that didn't stop him from trying. He took off in that direction. "I'll call you… sometime."

She was left only to call after him. "Don't forget."

Hot fury burned through Melody. What an idiot she was. And to think, she had thought he might actually be interested in her. What a joke. What a bunch of hooey. Blaine Donovan was interested in one person and only one person. And that person was definitely not her. She only wished she had figured that out before her heart got smashed to smithereens in the process. It took one yank to have her car door open. Slinging her stuff in, she jumped in and fired it up. Never again. She wouldn't give him another chance to make her believe his lies. That's what everything that came out of his mouth was—lies.

A.J. was right. And she hated Blaine even more for making her think that. Well, Lana could have him. They were perfect for each other. Let them all go on and live their happy lives. She didn't need them—any of them. She would be much, much better off going on with her life as if she'd never heard the names A.J., Eve, and most especially Blaine.

Running, Blaine nearly knocked over a knot of students headed out to the parking lots. "Sorry," he called to them, never really slowing down. His feet pounded the pavement. His backpack whacked into his hip as he ran through the first lot, searching, before fighting traffic to the second lot. Only when he was there and had surveyed it twice did he accept the fact that once again, he had messed up. Once again he had hurt her. Great. Just fabulous.

Melody was furious with him, and she had every right to be. In fact, if he liked her at all, he should let her go, let her be. It wasn't fair to keep dragging her into his miserable life. What was that saying? Misery shared is doubled? It was something like that. As he stalked over to the little green Toyota, his thoughts drifted to his parents. His original parents, before the divorce that changed everything about everything. That had certainly been true for them.

The lock stuck as it always did nowadays. He worked it, jiggled it, pleaded with it, and finally kicked the door out of utter frustration with his whole depressing life. "I'm sorry," he said instantly feeling stupid for his outburst. What did kicking the door help anyway? Nothing. Nothing would help. He should get used to it and move on. It was the only thing that made any sense.

Nothing had gone any better for 12 straight hours. Blaine woke up late, dumped coffee on the only clean shirt he had, got Dylan to school late, which meant a trip to the principal's office, which made him even later for work. He missed two commissions when the customers up and decided to try a different store for no reason he could really see. By the time he made it to the break room at 12:05 to start lunch, he was convinced the day could get no worse. And then it did.

"Looks like you're back to normal," Eve said suddenly standing right next to him at the beverage dispenser.

"Huh. That would be nice," he said so contemptuously, it caused her to stare at him. He closed his eyes, shook his head, and sighed. "I'm sorry. It hasn't been a great day."

"Too much bar-hopping I guess." There was ice in her tone, ice he'd never heard there before.

"What's that supposed to mean?" He took his sandwich and water over to the table and sat down in a heap.

She followed him, sat down primly, and shrugged, looking right at him. "Seems to me you've been partying a lot lately, sowing the wild oats and all that."

The condescension in her voice brought out the defensiveness in his. "Sowing the wild oats, huh? That's original." Who was she to question what he did or didn't do with his life anyway? She was only a friend and barely that.

For the longest moment of his life she sat surveying him. Her gaze crawled into his nervous system and tingled there. "So what's the story with you and Melody anyway?"

"Me and Melody?" What business was that of hers? "What do you care?"

Eve pulled herself forward slightly. "Well, for one, Melody is a friend of mine, and I don't like seeing her jerked around. For another, she is like a little sister to A.J., and you toying with her is not going over so well in my household."

Blaine snorted at that. "And that gives you the right to run her life… or mine?"

A piece of the condescension melted away. "Look, Blaine. I just don't want to see her hurt, that's all."

"And you think I do?"

"Well, if you're going together like it looked at my house the other night, I can't see how going out partying with some other bimbo the next weekend makes much sense. Unless…"

Her pause got his attention, and he looked up. "Unless what?"

The look she gave him was at once compassionate and judgmental. "Unless you're the scumbag A.J. says you are. Then it makes complete sense."

Honestly he couldn't care a wit what A.J. thought, but the fact that he was trashing Blaine to every girl who mattered at all to him didn't sit well. "Well, it doesn't matter anyway."

"How's that?"

"Me and Mel." The words hurt like fire to say. "We're just friends. There's nothing going on between us."

That didn't ease her concern. "And the other night at our house?"

The ache over the whole mess spun in turmoil in his heart. "Look, I know she deserves better. She doesn't need an albatross like me hanging around her neck."

True compassion took over. "You're not an albatross."

Anger and disappointment with himself crowded through his thoughts. "Oh yeah? A minute ago I was a scumbag."

Eve heaved a sigh and scrunched her face slowly scrutinizing him. "You know. I just can't figure you out sometimes. One minute you're this nice guy that I really like being around, and then all of a sudden you're this arrogant jerk who has a real attitude problem. What's up with that?"

"Sometimes the real me just comes out. I guess I can't help myself."

Her gaze narrowed even further. "And which one is the real you?"

The question slammed him into a brick wall. He stared at his glass, not drinking, not really even seeing it. "I don't know."

It was a long moment before she continued. "For what it's worth, I think the nice guy fits you much better, but I think you're scared to be him."

"Why would I be scared of that?"

"I don't know. Why would you?"

Pain tore through him so deep it felt like it ripped the middle of him apart. "Because being a jerk is so much easier."

"Why?" Her voice was soft, and she laid her hand on the table, gazing at him. "Blaine, you're really selling yourself so short here. That jerk thing only pushes people away and hurts everybody. It's no way to live."

Breathing through the ache was becoming impossible.

"Look, I know how hard you try to impress everybody."

A co-worker from shoes strode into the break room and over to the coffee machine. Eve sat back, watching both Blaine and the woman. In minutes she was gone, and Eve sat forward once more. "From what I see, you've got a real choice to make here."

"Oh, yeah? What's that?"

"Who you're going to be and how you're going to live your life. Trying to be both at the same time only means you're neither. You really need to take some time to figure out what's important." Her gaze stayed so soft it caressed his bruised and wounded spirit. "That's what growing up's about—figuring out what's really important and pegging your life and your actions to that."

Growing up. He would be 27 in three days. He'd kind of figured the growing up part was over. "And that works?"

"Better than anything else I've ever found."

Later, as he walked to his car Blaine thought about Eve's words. Figure out what's really important and peg your life and your actions to that. Figure out what's really important… What's really important… The words slid through his mind, snagging and holding at odd moments as he walked all the way around the perimeter of the mall to the little knot of cars around the lonely tree. He'd been parking here almost since he'd gotten the job. It was part of not letting anyone know what his life was really like.

He thought about Eve and sighed with the thought. She didn't even know the real him, not really. She knew what she had seen, but what she had seen was part of the mask, not the man. Blaine got in the car, loosened the tie, and reached for the starter. Lillian didn't even sputter. "Oh, no," he pleaded to the sky. "No. Come on. You can't be dead. Not now. Not today."

He hit the starter again, but it did no more good than the first time. With a deep sigh and small shake of his head, he climbed back out and went to the back to retrieve the jumper cables. Three cars down, a man walked to his car with his wife and three handfuls of bags in tow.

Blaine hated this. It was humiliating. "Uh, sir? Sir?"

The man looked up, clearly ready to make a break for it if the situation warranted.

"I'm sorry," Blaine said, stepping closer with the cables still in his hands. "My car won't start. Could you…?"

One look at the fear on the man's wife's face, and Blaine's heart fell. They weren't going to help him. Heck. He wouldn't help him. "That's okay," he said quickly. "I can go back in and get security." He started away.

"No," the man finally said, his voice deep and booming. "That's okay, son. Hook up them cables. I'll pull up next to you."

Thankfulness flooded through him twined generously with guilt. "I'm sorry. I know you're really busy. I really appreciate this." He quickly went around to his car, popped the hood, and worked the cables.

In mere moments the man was next to him. He opened the hood and got out, looking remarkably like some mountain. His stature was only enhanced by the yellow straw cowboy hat a top his head.

"I really appreciate this," Blaine said as he watched the man hook up the cars. A lie about why he was driving such a heap was poised on his lips. It would certainly make the out-of-control firing of his humiliation-quotient settle, but just as the words hit his brain to say, he stopped them. Which one are you going to be? Which one? He breathed through the question. Then, in that moment he made the decision. "This car is on its last legs. I'm just doing everything I can to get her one more mile down the road."

The man stood and smiled at Blaine. "I hear you there. We were married ten years before we could afford anything that didn't die every time we got in it."

Relief and hope flooded through Blaine as the man lifted and replaced his hat.

"Why don't you try it now?"

In one swift motion Blaine was behind the wheel. He breathed to settle the excitement and hit the starter. Lillian fired to life with no more effort than that. His smile spread through him. "Yes." He climbed out as the ticking sound Lillian had started making knocked in his ears. "Thank you so much, Sir. I really appreciate this."

The man removed the cables and handed them to Blaine who shook his hand in admiration. Oddly there wasn't contempt or condescension in the man's face, only respect. "You know a lot of young kids like you wouldn't be caught dead in a car like this. It's nice to see the younger generation recognizing that hard work will get you somewhere. Owning every nice thing out of the box doesn't build anything but debt and fear. It's no shame to drive something you can honestly afford, son." He lifted his hat again and smiled. "Remember that."

Blaine nodded, understanding more than the man could

possibly know. "I will. Thank you, Sir."

"You take care, son."

All the way home, Blaine had thought about the man and his words. It's no shame to drive something you can honestly afford. He thought about the mask Eve had talked about earlier. As he made the frozen pizza for supper, his thoughts turned to their current living conditions. His gaze went around the sparse, dirty kitchen. It wasn't 4114 Palermo. It wasn't even two steps out of hell, and yet, it was what he could afford.

When his parents divorced, he had understood enough to know about the debt his father left his mother to shoulder. A house they couldn't afford, two beautiful cars on lease that sucked them dry in months. He still remembered the day of the foreclosure sale. It was two days after the repo guy had shown up for the cars and three weeks before the bankruptcy. He thought it was the worst day of his life. Yet that was the day, the moment that for him, everything had changed. It was the moment he had accepted the fact that with his father gone, and it was up to him to make sure the family survived.

With his mother eight months pregnant, and their finances in shambles, he'd had to get a job. And it was a job he'd hung onto tenaciously for ten years. It wasn't glamorous, but it paid the bills for this place. As he looked around, he realized how much shame he'd been living under for ten long years. He'd made himself responsible for the fact that they couldn't live in the neighborhoods with pools and maid service. But the truth of the matter was, he had done his best.

It wasn't much, but it was a something.

He thought back to earlier in the parking lot. He'd taken the chance to be who he really was, and it had given him insight and hope such that he had never known before. With everything in him, he wanted to do that more, but just how to do that more was the real question.

As he went to work on the project, the question stayed on loop in his brain. And one name kept coming through with the answers he needed. Eve.

Ten

"Good morning, oh wise one," Blaine said, striding into the break room Saturday morning. He was scheduled for a full day shift, but for once in the longest time, he felt truly up to the task.

Eve hiked her eyebrows at him. "You sound happy."

"Huh. Wouldn't know why." He grabbed a cup of coffee and sat down next to her. "First, I have to say thanks for yesterday. I know you didn't have to be that honest with me, but I'm glad you were."

There was a small hopeful smile. "So you're not mad at me forever?"

"Mad? No." He spun the coffee and leaned forward. "Well, okay, I was, but let's just say I kind of got a sign that you were right." He glanced at her, and she looked intrigued. "So I'm kind of wondering what else you've got."

"What else?"

"Yeah. I mean how do you go about figuring out what's really important—like you said yesterday?"

She surveyed him for a long minute, then took a breath and lowered her gaze even further. It took a long minute for her to gather the courage to say the words that were making Blaine more nervous with each passing second. Finally she laid her wrists on the table and let her gaze fall to them. "Do you believe in God?"

"In... God?" The question pushed him backward. "Well, yeah. I guess so. I mean we used to go to church and stuff. Why?" He took a sip of coffee, watching her with trepidation.

"Well, in my experience," she said slowly, "figuring out what's important has been about learning what's important to God and then making those things important in my life and in how I live."

"O…kay. Explain that."

It seemed that she was going deeper into herself each time she tried to answer. "Well, like honesty. Honesty is important to God, so making it important in my life has given me the chance to have conversations like this. It's not that I ask for them or that I seek them out. They just show up. And then I can take the peace I've found and help somebody else find it too."

Blaine was nodding, not so much because he understood but because he was absorbing what she was saying.

"I can't explain it exactly," Eve said, her gaze bouncing only intermittently from her fingernails to him. "But the more I get in line with what God says is important, the more peace I have and the more peace I can help others get to."

"And you figure out what God thinks is important how?"

Eve's gaze chanced up to the clock, and she stood quickly. "Time to get cracking."

He followed her up. "You didn't answer my question."

"I will."

Thinking was becoming truly annoying. No matter how hard Melody tried not to think about Blaine and Lana standing there together, the thoughts were going nowhere. It was frustrating because when she pulled her Biology book out to study, she thought about him. When she went to work, she thought about him, there with Dylan and then with Farin. That thought was even more infuriating.

Farin was now going with some guy named Caleb. He showed up, called, and generally hung on Farin's every move and word. They were sickening. It didn't help that Farin made a point of sharing the intimate details of every date they had during lunch break, or afternoon break, or any other time she happened to be around.

Like Melody really wanted to hear about that. She was still going to the gym and eating next to nothing, but the pounds were stubborn, and they were wearing her willpower out. It would've been different if she could have seen any progress either in her body or in her love life, but both seemed stuck on perpetual hopelessness.

On Tuesday night, she was an hour from closing when a guy walked in. "Hi, there. I'm looking for some work boots."

"Okay," Melody said from her position at the counter. "They

are over there in the very back."

"Thanks," he said and ambled in the direction she had indicated.

Going through the pre-closing checklist, she restocked the bags at the front and went to straighten the purses.

"Melody," Nathan said from behind her.

She turned slightly. "Yeah?"

"Listen, I've got to run get something for Nancy. Tomorrow's our anniversary, and I've got nothing. Do you mind closing up? I really don't think we're going to have a flood of customers in the next hour."

"Oh, okay. Sure."

"Awesome. I knew I could count on you." And with that, he went to the back.

It was several more minutes of straightening when she realized the man was back with a box in hand.

"Are you ready, sir?"

"Found something." He held up the box, his dark hair brushing his shoulders when he did so.

Melody smiled as she walked to the cash register. However, once there, the center of her chest squeezed shut as she took a real look at him. Haggard and sun-hardened, his blue plaid shirt looked at least a size too big. She punched her code into the register and opened the shoe box. Pulling the first boot up, she checked the size and ran the tag remover over the little gray piece of plastic to remove it. It was only when she pulled the second boot up that she knew she had a problem.

Worry coursed through her as she retrieved the first boot and rechecked the size. They were, in fact, different. She ran through her options, but none of them were very good. "Um, I'm sorry, sir. These sizes are different."

"Huh?"

"The sizes are different. This one's a ten. This one's an eleven."

"Is that a problem?" He leaned on the counter with both elbows to see what she was showing him. His dark eyes struck a chord of fear in her.

"Well, we can't sell two different sizes. It makes it impossible to sell the other pair."

"Oh, well." He straightened with a nice smile. "I'm sorry. I didn't realize that would be a problem."

"Yeah, well." She checked the box and put only the correct boot in it. "It's company policy. You can go back and get the match of either one if you want."

He seemed to consider that. "You know, maybe I don't need them boots as much as I thought."

It was strange that although he gave her no indication of anything other than being a nice guy, it was all she could to do maintain her composure. "I'm really sorry, Sir."

"No. Don't worry about it. I'll just…" He pointed to the door, and she nodded, feeling absurdly glad he was leaving and wishing he would already.

"Have a good evening."

His smile slid through her. "Oh, I will."

She watched him walk all the way out to his pick-up truck, get in, and drive away. Breathing, she checked her watch. Half an hour to go. She wished she hadn't told Nathan he could leave. Something about the man in the pick-up truck gave her the creeps.

After ten agonizing minutes of alternately checking the front windows and telling herself she was being ridiculous, the jingle of the front doors brought Melody's attention to it. Utter terror smashed into her when she glanced around the shelf where she was straightening shoes. There wasn't another customer in the store, and very few even out on the sidewalks. Pulling "just be cool" to her, she stepped around the shelving. "Oh, hello, sir. Is there something else?"

The man with the dark eyes and long hair stood gazing at her. "I just wanted to come back and say I'm sorry about before, with them boots. I shouldn't have tried to pull that one on ya."

"Oh, well, that's all right." Her hand straightened the shelf of shoe boxes automatically. She tried to look unfazed and nonchalant, but her heart was pounding like a speaker about to blow. "Don't worry about it. It happens a lot."

"I know." He started toward her, which hammered her heart even harder. "But you seem like such a nice young thing. I'd hate to think I put you in an awkward position."

"Oh, no. No, you didn't. It's okay."

He ambled to her closer and closer. "Well, I don't want you

getting in trouble over me being stupid."

The fact that she was behind the shelving and not in view of anyone outside got her feet moving. Melody hurried to the front counter, crossing past him but far enough away to avoid a reach if he tried something. He followed her. She could feel it. At the front counter, she felt only barely safer. Licking her parched lips, she bent down and pulled the box of shoelaces up to sort them. "Umm, is there something else?"

Without ever taking his gaze off of her, he leaned onto the counter between them. "You sure are nice." His glance took in the nametag pinned to her chest. "Melody." His gaze came back up to her face. "That's a nice name. I guess you're really into music."

"Music? Oh, no. Not really." Her hands were shaking, and she fought to simultaneously get them to stop and to think through the situation. What if he didn't leave? What was the best way out of this situation?

"So you're not into that hip-hop crap all the kids are into these days then?"

"Oh, umm, no. Don't listen to much of that." The shoelaces were done. She set them to the side and turned to him, forcing her voice to sound normal. "Um, did you want to try on something different? Some other kind of boots or something?"

"Nah." His smile slithered through her. "I've just been out driving all day and thought I'd stop and talk with this nice salesgirl I met awhile ago. You don't mind, do you?"

What was the correct answer to that? "Uh, no." She looked around the store seeing all the things that needed done but they all would necessitate her leaving the window, and leaving that window could be deadly. "But I'm about to close, and I really need to be getting home."

"Oh." He straightened. "Well, that's okay. Maybe I can just stick around and walk you to your car."

The Bible Eve had given Blaine lay in the passenger's seat as he drove home on Tuesday night. He smiled again that she had done that. She didn't have to. He could've bought his own. Some second hand bookstore had to have one. Yet here was this one. Nice. New. A gift from a friend. It was strange what a small shift of events had done for his head and for his heart. Being honest.

One moment of just being who he really was, and life had altered itself around that decision, realigning itself around that one simple act.

His gaze went out the window as it normally did on this trek home. Galaxy Shoes in neon letters shown out in the fading light. He wondered if Melody was there. There was no telling what her schedule was. He'd never bothered to ask, but the Bible called to his soul. Be honest. This is a place to start.

Glancing at the clock, he knew it was closing time. She probably wasn't there anyway. He redirected his gaze to the street in front of him. Don't drive on by. Stop, Blaine. Talk to her. This is living what's important. Doing what needs to be done in the moment you think about it. Rationally it made no sense, but his heart wasn't listening to rational any more. She deserved better than he had treated her. True, she probably didn't ever want to see him again. But if he was going to start being honest, this was one place that would have to be addressed. Sighing at the absurdity of the action, he spun Lillian into the strip mall parking lot.

"I'm sorry, sir," Melody said, forcing herself not to panic. "It's time for me to close."

"What's this sir business? You can call me Cal."

"Umm, Cal." She walked to the front doors, knowing he wasn't leaving, but not knowing how to summon help. "Really. I need to lock up now."

The look in his eyes struck fear into the center of her. Breathing hurt.

"I told you I could help. I'd hate for you to be here all by yourself. The city's a dangerous place, you know. Especially at night. You don't know what crazies might be out there."

She didn't know about out there, but she was pretty sure in here wasn't very safe. "I appreciate it, but I can't let customers stay in here while I lock up. It's policy, you know."

His grin was at once frightening and friendly. "But we were just getting to know each other. Surely that's not a crime, is it?" The moment his hand touched her arm, sheer terror clutched her.

Not wanting to rile him, she fought not to shake him off. "Really. You need to go now."

"You don't really want me to go. Now do you?" He was

inches from her and closing fast.

The front door came open so suddenly, Melody hadn't even realized anyone was on the other side of it. Her gaze jerked to it as the overwhelming fear cascaded over her. "Blaine." It wasn't really a question or a statement. More a cry for help.

"What do you think you're doing?" Blaine demanded, staring holes through Cal who dropped her arm and backed up a step.

"Shop's closed, Buddy," Cal said, menacingly. "Melody was just about to lock up for the night."

She couldn't get even a single word out through the fear. Her gaze locked with Blaine's and without saying anything, she told him everything.

His gaze turned to Cal, a look of solid resolve etched on his face. "It's time for the lady to lock up. That means it's time for you to go."

"I was going to walk her to her car," Cal countered.

"Yeah, I'm sure." He glanced at her. "Mel, do you know the number for mall security?"

"Se…cur… Uh, yeah." Stumbling through the terror jamming all the rational signals in her brain, Melody barely got the words into the air as she stared at him, not really comprehending anything.

"Good," Blaine said, staring only at Cal. "Call it."

"Call… O… Okay." She turned for the counter, wondering how it had gotten so very far away.

Cal waited one more second, ready to call Blaine's bluff, but the younger man never so much as blinked. Finally Cal backed away, circling Blaine toward the door. "Hey, man. No need. I'm outta here." He slid past Blaine and pushed out the door. "I'll see you later, Melody."

When she turned, it was all she could do not to faint. It was as if the whole world had narrowed to that one face, that one second. And then he was gone.

Blaine grabbed the shiny silver door handle. "Get the keys, Mel. Lock the door."

But she couldn't move. Tears, fear, horror, and shock mixed, spinning her world into the depths of nothingness.

"Mel!" Blaine commanded. "Keys. Now."

Shaking her head and swallowing hard, she pulled the keys from her pocket and stepped to his side. The lock clicked just as

Cal drove away in the pick-up. Every scenario that could've happened had Blaine not picked that moment to show up plummeted through her consciousness. "Oh, my…! What…? Why…?"

Tears jumped through the breaths she wasn't taking, and she collapsed into them just as Blaine's arms came around her. Moans and sobs were all she could get out as she clung to him. Strong and solid, he held her, stroking her hair and shushing her sobs.

After time no longer mattered anymore, she pulled back and wiped her eyes.

Serious, overwhelming concern streamed from his eyes. He didn't let go of her, instead he put his hands on her shoulders. "You okay?"

She nodded, but there was no belief anywhere behind it. Sniffing back the tears, she forced air into her lungs as her gaze went back out the window. He was gone, but it was impossible not to see him still standing there. Terror ripped through her. "I've got to get home. Mom's going to be panicking."

Someone was panicking, but it wasn't her mother. Still, she had to find a way to get it together so he wouldn't know how totally freaked out she was.

Timidly, she looked up at him. "I… Um, could you wait?"

Soft compassion drifted into his eyes. "As long as you need."

When they walked together into the parking lot some thirty minutes later, Blaine sensed her checking, glancing around, looking for him—Cal, the idiot who had scared her out of her mind. He wished he knew how to calm her, but there wasn't much he could do.

"Um… I…" The sparkle and fun were gone from her eyes. "Would you…? I mean, I know it's out of your way and everything."

He reached over and put his arm around her protectively. "Do you want me to follow you home?"

The nodding was three quick movements. "I'm sorry. That guy just…"

Resolve to protect her from all the Cal's of the world rose in him. "Hey." He turned to her, stopping in the middle of the near-empty lot. Lowering his gaze to look at her, he settled the feelings with a breath. "I've got your back, okay? I'm not going to let anything happen."

Her gaze held his for only a moment, and then it fell to her feet as she nodded again. Carefully he turned her to her car where he took the keys from her shaking hands. If there was a way he could've driven her home, he would have, but that was a logistical nightmare. Then just before he closed her door, he remembered.

"Umm, I'm in my…" He pointed across the lot at the little green car.

She took one look, and whatever he'd expected to happen, didn't. Instead she only nodded.

He didn't want to make the next request, but he had no choice. "Make sure I get it started, k?"

Again she nodded. He hated that. He wanted words, actual, actual words, but she had said so few of them, he knew that wasn't going to happen any time soon. He closed her door and jogged over to his car. The questions of how easily she'd accepted the car crowded into him, but he pushed them down. Take care of her now. The rest can wait.

He got the door opened with only two yanks, jumped behind the wheel, and saying a prayer hit the starter. It cranked and then started up. "Thank You, God," he said to the car ceiling. Quickly he backed out and watched her do the same.

The traffic was relatively light, and all the way to her house, he said prayer after prayer for her and thanking God that he'd heeded that voice in his head. He was determined not to go down the road of what if he hadn't. That was too horrible to contemplate. "Dear Lord, I know You don't know me too well, but please be with Melody. She needs You, Lord. She's terrified right now. That guy is an idiot. Help her drive safely, Lord. Please…"

The drive home was a haze of red taillights and inky black darkness. Her hands shook so badly, Melody had to sit on one to get it to stop. The breaths came in gasps, and she fought the tears the entire trip. Every third second she glanced in her mirror to make sure Blaine was still there. He was. Those little headlights stayed right there.

By the time she pulled to the curb of her house, her breathing had almost returned to normal although she had a pounding headache. She killed the engine and grabbed her purse off the seat. She'd just stood from the car when the little headlights blinked off behind her. In less than ten seconds, he was at her side.

Instead of peppering her with questions and his concern, after one compassionate look, he chose to simply turn with her. Six steps and he put his arm around her. Melody knew all about his history and why she should tell him to get lost, but the truth was, right then, she needed him, and he was here. Feeling the relief and gratefulness for that simple fact, she laid her head on his shoulder. Together, they walked into the front yard where the little bench swing stood.

It wasn't a plan, but her feet angled them over to it, and he followed as if he knew that's where they were headed. At the swing he sat down, steadied it for her, and collected her into his arms when she sat. Shock gave way to fatigue, and she closed her eyes, letting the horror and the what ifs drop away.

For his part, Blaine simply pushed the swing slowly with his toe. Neither moved beyond that. It was strange to her how comfortable this felt, like he wasn't embarrassed to be sitting in a front yard that wasn't even watered properly. The little sprinkler sat out front. The top arm of it leaned like an abandoned see-saw. The house was less than spectacular. They didn't even have a swimming pool or a maid or six TV sets. And yet, he was here, holding her as if that made perfect sense.

One small part of her wanted to ask, to voice every question and concern in her, but the rest of her simply wanted to believe that somehow this could actually be happening. As absurd and ridiculous as that sounded, it was all she wanted from this moment.

She never asked, never so much as broached the subject of his ugly car and how he'd come to show up for no reason at just the right moment. That was okay with Blaine. Somehow in the silence, surrounded only by the soft hum of traffic, he didn't want to think about any of that, only that she was here and she was safe. He laid his head over on hers and closed his eyes.

He liked how she smelled—all flowers and spices. It fit her. The soft fall of golden blonde hair caressed his cheek, and he let it with no qualms. She wasn't moving, so neither would he.

How long they sat like that, he didn't really know, but after late evening turned into night, she sighed and pulled up from his embrace. His arms immediately felt empty. Instead of letting her go, he let his hand drop so that it rubbed up and down her back. She leaned forward, putting her elbows on her knees and arching her back into his touch. A moment and she flipped her hair back with both hands and turned to look at him.

"Thank you."

His smile was soft and compassionate. "You're welcome." As she stood, his gaze followed her up.

She stood there on the lawn, three feet in front of him and stretched. He still liked the way her periwinkle polo shirt looked on her—even in the dim light. Pert nose, shiny but tired eyes, she looked at him, and for all the words that should have been there, he could find none of them.

"You need to get home," she said, her gaze never leaving his face.

Blaine stood and stepped toward her. His hands came up to cup around her arms, and he lowered his gaze at her. "Are you going to be all right?"

She let her head go back slowly as if contemplating which way to move it, then slowly it came forward. The next three short nods came just faster. "Yeah."

With that, it was time to leave. He knew it, but nothing in him wanted to. "Will I see you tomorrow night—at school?"

Her smile was barely there and then grew slightly. "Yeah."

Although it's all he wanted to do, kissing her now would be wrong. She'd just been through a terrible experience, and to take advantage of a vulnerable moment like this was a move reserved for scumbags and jerks. Both of which he'd decided never to be again. It wasn't easy when he pulled her to him for one more hug to not seal his concern for her with a kiss, but he pulled away and gazed at her seriously. "You would tell me if you weren't okay, right?"

This smile was brighter, and a spark of the light in her eyes came fired to life. "Yes. I would tell you."

"Good because I'm here, and I care. Okay?"

Gazing at him, she nodded.

"K. Just so we're clear on that."

Clear on that. Melody had thought about those words a million times. The fact that he was her friend was abundantly clear. What wasn't as clear was what she should do with these feelings of wanting him to hold her forever. Friends didn't do that kind of thing after all. Friends get together for drinks and to watch baseball games. Friends don't kiss in the moonlight and whisper sweet nothings in each others' ear. But those were the things she wanted to do with Blaine. How she would ever pretend they weren't was beyond her.

When she crawled into bed, fear from earlier tried to get in, but she shut it out with the memory of him, holding her. That memory would be with her forever.

Eleven

"I got my part done," Lana said as she walked up to Blaine on the first floor the minute he stepped into the building.

He'd been looking for Melody ever since he made it onto campus, but she didn't seem to be anywhere. He wondered if she just dropped from the sky in time for class—considering he never saw her until she was on the stairs. Not likely but it did make him chuckle.

"Oh, yeah," he said, digging in his notebook. "So did I. It wasn't nearly as hard as I thought. The draft turned out awesome."

Comparing notes, they started up the stairs.

Every fantasy Melody had allowed herself to have since he'd walked off the night before crashed into a million pieces the second she saw them together. He said he'd see her tonight, but seeing him like this—deep in conversation with Miss Perfection—made her stomach turn. She chose the opposite staircase and climbed slowly through the descending students. He didn't want to talk to her. He just said that. He was a nice guy. Nice guys said things they didn't mean just so you would think they were nice.

However, just as her foot hit the second floor, her gaze found his waiting for her. He was leaning against the far wall, and Lana was nowhere to be seen. Melody's gaze fell in embarrassment. She didn't want to look like she was looking for him, which of course she had been.

"Hey." He raised his chin in acknowledgement.

Melody clutched her books to her chest as she took the few steps over to where he stood. "Hey." She could think of nothing else.

He reached out to rub her arm. "You doing okay?"

There was a short fast nod. "Trying."

He hesitated as his hand dropped. "Will you wait for me after class?"

It wasn't what she had expected, but she couldn't get the no out. "Sure."

"I'll meet you on the first floor. Don't leave. Okay?"

"I won't."

Melody spent the final Biology class not reviewing the material but previewing the coming conversation. What did he want to talk to her about? The night before? The state of their relationship—whatever that was? All the pieces that fit nowhere in this incomprehensible puzzle? The possibilities were endless.

"That's it. The final will be Monday night at 7," the professor said, and with that, students stood and gathered their belongings.

Melody gathered hers too, slowly. She arched her purse up onto her shoulder, grabbed her backpack and books and followed the crowd out. At the stairs she took extra care not to miss one. In the state her mind was in, that was a distinct possibility. At the bottom floor she found him sitting on the simple, little wooden bench facing the stairs. He stood the second he saw her, swinging his backpack to his shoulder as he did so.

The walk over to her seemed like it took an eternity, but when he was there, she had no idea what came next.

"Um, can we walk?" he asked, sounding extremely uncertain.

"Sure." She turned her steps to the outside door and pushed out into the warm humidity of the Houston, Texas evening.

Instead of heading straight out to the parking lot, Blaine turned them up the opposite walk, deeper into campus. Melody followed, questioning the move only in her heart. He was quiet until they had left the hubbub of the departing students behind.

When he glanced over at her, she had no idea what he was about to say.

"I owe you an apology," he finally said slowly.

Instantly her head jerked to the side. "An apology? Blaine…"

"No." He held up his hand. "Please. Just let me say this."

She took a step. "O… kay."

He walked three more steps and then ran his hand up, over,

and through his hair, spiking it unnaturally. When his hand came down, he rested it on the strap of the backpack across his shoulder. "I haven't exactly been honest with you."

Somehow she had suspected that, but she kept walking and said nothing.

"That car… the Carrera. The one I've been coming to get you in like when I took you over to A.J. and Eve's?" He took a breath. "It's not mine."

She sucked in a rough patch of air as her head tilted on the admission.

"It's my friend Peyton's. He lets me borrow it… sometimes."

With difficulty, she digested that information, spinning it through her mind, fighting to get it to make some sense.

"My car is the little green hatchback I was driving last night. It's not great, but it gets me where I need to go."

They walked another six steps before Melody looked at him. "Why? Why would you lie like that?"

Blaine took two steps and exhaled hard. "Because I didn't want to be poor. I didn't want Eve to think I was poor, so last year when she asked me out to the amusement park, I panicked and asked Peyton to borrow his. Then the whole thing with you happened, and…"

As she absorbed that news, a thought that truly made her sick hit her. "Wait. You mean I got sick in Peyton's car?" Humiliation rained through her. Great now everyone would know what a total loser she was.

"No, don't sweat it. I cleaned it up before I brought it back. He never knew a thing."

That should've made her feel better, but it really didn't. "So then you're not some mondo-rich kid from million dollar mansions and poolside parties?"

The question pulled him down onto the stone statue in the middle of the square. Head down he gazed only at his shoes. "No."

Which explained the car, except for one small detail. Melody knew enough about the lifestyles of the rich and famous to know they didn't just go around loaning out their cars. "I don't get it. If you're not rich, then how did you talk Peyton into…?"

His gaze came up, and in it, there was a plea for understanding and a desperate sadness that swept her heart away. "My dad left us when I was 17. He was a lawyer, a big time partner in a law firm. He ran off with his secretary. Left me and my mom who was eight months pregnant at the time to clean up the mess he'd made." Blaine leaned back against the horse statue's leg. "And let me tell you, it was one gigantic mess.

"We were in debt up to our eyeballs, the house, the cars, the stuff. Being a lawyer, he knew how to set up his escape so we'd be left holding the bag for it all. He did a good job of it too." Blaine leaned over and put his elbows on his knees. His backpack slid to the ground, and he reached down only to prop it on his ankle. "That first couple of months was hell. The bank repo'ed our cars. Then they came for the house. Mom had Dylan in the midst of utter chaos, and by the time it was all over we were in a dumpy little dive we could hardly afford on Mom's part time paycheck."

He pulled in a long breath and let it go in a whoosh. "So I went to work. I dropped out of school three months before graduation and did what I had to do."

That slammed her backward. "You didn't graduate?"

Slowly he rubbed his hands together. "I got my GED." He shrugged. "It was something. Five years later I went back to school." He pointed up at the Admin building looming in the night. It was still dotted with a few lights. "Community college. They'll take anybody."

That didn't sound like much of a compliment to her, but she brushed it aside. Listening, understanding was too important. "And your mom?"

This breath was harder, more sarcastic. "She really fell apart. Before I knew it, her money was disappearing before it ever made it into our account. I couldn't figure it out until she started bringing Dave around."

Somehow, even with all he had told her, she had no clue who Dave was. "And Dave is…?"

The look on Blaine's face was full of contempt and hate. "My stepfather. 'Cept he was never much of a father at all." He glanced over at her with a look she couldn't read. "Dave wasn't just my mom's husband. He was her dealer."

Although she tried not to, Melody felt her eyes go wide. "Drugs?"

Blaine didn't look at all pleased, but then he shook his head and shrugged. "She needed an escape from the rotten life she'd fallen into. He gave it to her. It was that simple."

Fear punched into her chest. "And now?"

His look was disbelieving. It seemed he'd expected her to run screaming for the exits not to sit there and listen and ask questions. "Now…" He paused so long, she was sure her heart quit beating. "You know that fight I got into the other night?"

Somehow this wasn't where she thought they were going. "Yeah?"

He nodded three times without really moving, more trying to get the words out. "Well, it didn't happen at a bar."

"It didn't…?" Pieces she didn't like at all fell into a puzzle she didn't really want to see. "Your stepfather beat you up?"

"Ex-stepfather. But yeah. He showed up looking for money Mom apparently owed him."

"Did she?"

"Owe him?"

Melody nodded, and Blaine sat back.

"Oh, I'm sure she did. It's not like she's off the stuff. She's just not married to the jerk anymore."

Horrific scenarios began to wind through her mind. Each worse than the last. "Did he… I mean was this the first time he's… hurt you?"

Blaine's eyelids fell half closed. He thought about the question for a long minute, and then he shook his head. Her heart cracked in half for the strength of the man sitting next to her. Never in her wildest imagination would she ever have thought she would be hearing this story from him. This wasn't paradise she had always pictured him in. It was a nightmare.

"What about Dylan?" The question was more of a plea for something to be all right in this picture.

"He was there the other night. It's one of the reasons I got it so bad. I had to, or Dave might have gone after Mom or Dylan."

At that moment, Blaine Donovan was her hero times ten. She had never met anyone who would willing step in between a person he loved and real danger. The scene of him standing between her and Cal the night before wafted through her consciousness, and she was even more grateful than she had been then.

Sitting down next to him, she gently laid her head on his chest as he leaned back against the statue. Each move she made was more a question than a statement until she was down, listening to his heartbeat through the soft, starched shirt. Somehow she hadn't been grateful enough for that heartbeat until this very minute.

Her hand rested on his chest, and after only a minute, his came down and rubbed slowly up and down her shoulder. They sat like that as time slid by. Finally she arched her gaze up to his face.

"Why didn't you tell me?" Guilt for every time he'd gone out of his way for her went through her heart.

It took two breaths for him to answer. "I didn't know how."

With that, she picked her head all the way up, turned it, and rested her chin atop her knuckles. "Never again, okay?"

His gaze drifted down to meet hers.

"I'm serious," she said, holding his gaze with hers. "I'm here for you, okay? Good or bad. Right or wrong. No matter what. I'm here."

There was the softest gratefulness she'd ever seen in his smile and his eyes. A moment and then he yanked himself up, pulling up all the way. She straightened too and then backed up, trying to figure out where he was going. Before she got too far, his hand came up to cup her chin, and she fell into his gaze, unable to look away.

Then, gently, slowly he came toward her. This time she knew what was coming. This time she closed her eyes, feeling how safe it seemed and knowing how dangerous it was. This time she wasn't kissing some rich, arrogant jerk who was sure to break her heart. This time she was kissing a man she could fall really hard for, so hard, she might never find her way back.

His lips brushed hers, and for that moment, Melody had no desire to even care about anything other than him. A touch and his lips left only to brush hers again with a soft caress that relaxed everything in her. He smelled like sweet pine needles and musk. The combination of which was enough to make her swimmy headed. That, and he was asking again and again with his kisses how this could be happening, how he could be here with her in the moonlight, their backpacks on the ground long forgotten.

She didn't know, and she didn't care. She was here, and for this moment, that's all that mattered.

When he broke the kiss and pulled back, everything in her wanted to grab him and never let go. His hand still caressed the side of her face, and she never wanted it to leave. Life couldn't get any better, and if she let him go now, she might never get him back. After all, it had happened before.

"So, now what?" she asked, opening her eyes as trepidation she didn't want to feel laced the question.

He looked at her, measuring her thoughts with his eyes. "I don't know. What do you want?"

The question yanked doubts up by the dozen. "I don't know. I guess we could… go back to your place?" Her own suggestion snapped through her as she realized in light of what he'd just told her that was probably a very bad suggestion. "Unless that would be too weird for you. I mean… I don't want you to feel like I'm judging you or anything. I'm not. I just…" The words wound around to the admission she'd never really wanted to let any guy know. "Um, I've never really done this kind of thing before."

Blaine's ardor plummeted with his gaze and his hand. "Mel." He leaned forward and ever-so-slightly away from her. "Listen, don't take this wrong. Okay? But I don't want to sleep with you."

A dull knife plunged right through her. She wanted to slap him. Hard. If he didn't want to sleep with her, then what in the world did he kiss her like that for? "Oh. Yeah. I understand." Fighting the tears this time was impossible. They came too fast and too unexpectedly. What was she thinking? How many times had he said they were just friends? Besides what would a good-looking guy like him want her for?

"No, Mel." He turned to her and took her hands in his. "That's not…" He let out the breath in a whoosh. "That's not what I meant. I meant I don't want to sleep with you right now, this minute, tonight. That doesn't mean I don't ever want to sleep with you." He exhaled slowly. "This whole being honest with somebody thing is so new to me. I don't want to mess it up by moving too fast and making mistakes I'm going to regret."

Ugh. This was getting worse. He could see it written all over her face. Gently Blaine reached up and cupped her chin in his hand. "Mel. Hey. Look at me."

After a moment her gaze, wary and sad, came up to his.

"You are a beautiful, kind, wonderful person. You deserve better than some jerk who talks a good game to get you in the sack. If this is real, if we're real, then there's no need to rush into anything… as much as I want to."

Tears of hopeful skepticism came to her eyes. "You do?"

The small laugh jumped to his heart. "Of course I do. What do you think I am, stupid?"

She let her face be held by his hand.

"Come on. Look at you. You're beautiful and desirable. You're funny and kind and sweet. What guy in his right mind wouldn't sweep you off your feet and carry you off to his castle? But I want this to be right. You deserve for it to be right."

Her head came up then, and her gaze locked on his. He had never seen the raw hope, the pleading for someone to see her, to believe in her that he found there. It was then that he vowed to do everything in his power to protect that hope and to never let it die.

"You are too special for me to play games with. I don't know where this is going, and I'll tell you right now, I'll probably make more mistakes than right moves. But I don't want being with you to be based on anything but what's best for both of us. Okay?"

She gazed at him and finally smiled. "Okay."

The smile that spread through him started at the bursting of his heart and ended by spreading across his face. He nodded and then pulled her back to him. It wasn't hard to know what he wanted. What was less sure was how he would ever live up to all he'd just said.

Melody crawled into bed much later than normal, still feeling what it was like to be in his arms, still feeling what it was like to be let into his world. It was a far different world than she had expected, and yet what mattered most was how he was obviously handling a desperate, horrible situation. She rolled over thinking about Dylan. Where had the boy been all those nights Blaine had been with her? At home with his mother? That wasn't a settling thought. She vowed to ask the next time she talked with him. And with that thought, she fell asleep.

The feeling Blaine awoke with on Thursday was one he had never felt. It was at once peaceful and hopeful. Yes, as he looked around his tiny room, he hadn't physically moved, but he was different than he had been even only the day before. The memory of talking with Melody drifted over him, and he arched an arm behind his head to savor it for one more minute.

It was then that he remembered it was in fact his birthday. He smiled at that. How appropriate. 27. A new person. A new life. And he was determined to get this one right.

He turned his head to the little wooden nightstand and caught sight of the Bible he'd laid there the night before. Never would he have considered himself a Jesus Freak, but something about the little book called to his spirit. He lifted it, pulled himself upright, and grabbed his glasses. Maybe this would be a good way to start out the new year.

However, he'd never taken Bible Study, and he had no idea how to read the Bible. So he simply flipped it open, ran his finger down the page, and started reading.

Lord, you have probed me, you know me: you know when I sit and stand; you understand my thoughts from afar. My travels and my rest you mark; with all my ways you are familiar. Even before a word is on my tongue, Lord, you know it all. Behind and before you encircle me and rest your hand upon me. Such knowledge is beyond me, far too lofty for me to reach.

Where can I hide from your spirit? From your presence, where can I flee? If I ascend to the heavens, you are there; if I lie down in Sheol, you are there too. If I fly with the wings of dawn and alight beyond the sea, Even there your hand will guide me, your right hand hold me fast. If I say, "Surely darkness shall hide me, and night shall be light"—Darkness is not dark for you, and night shines as the day. Darkness and light are but one.

You formed my inmost being; you knit me in my mother's womb. I praise you, so wonderfully you made me; wonderful are your works! My very self you knew; my bones were not hidden from you, When I was being made in secret, fashioned as in the depths of the earth. Your eyes foresaw my actions; in your book all are written down; my days were shaped before one came to be.

How precious to me are your designs, O God; how vast the sum of them! Were I to count, they would outnumber the sands; to finish, I would need eternity. If only you would destroy the wicked, O God, and the bloodthirsty would depart from me! Deceitfully they invoke your name; your foes swear faithless oaths. Do I not hate, Lord, those who hate you? Those who rise against you, do I not loathe? With fierce hatred I hate them, enemies I count as my own.

Probe me, God, know my heart; try me, know my concerns. See if my way is crooked, then lead me in the ancient paths.

Blaine let his head thump back against the headboard. Know my heart, know my concerns. See if I'm crooked, then lead me in your paths. It seemed an answer to his own prayers. He needed a lot of guidance if he was to find the path God seemed to be calling him to. He glanced at the clock. Time to start a new life.

"Okay. I know it's not a real cake," Eve said, sitting down next to Blaine in the break room and sliding a cupcake with swirly icing on it over to him. "But it's the thought that counts, right?"

Skepticism pulled his eyebrows up when he looked over at her. "What's this for?"

"Your birthday, silly. You didn't think I would forget, did you?"

He lifted the cupcake, surveying it slowly. "Nice. What did this cost? Eighty-five cents in the vending machine?"

"Ninety," she said with a smile, "but who's counting?"

Blaine laughed. "So do I get it all, or am I sharing?"

Eve shrugged. "It's yours. You can do what you want."

With a smile, he broke it in half and handed her part. He held his up. "To growing up."

Her smile spoke of her being proud of him. "And every good thing that comes with it."

On Friday night Blaine dialed Melody's number. They hadn't talked since Wednesday. As the phone rang, he wondered if she would be different now that she knew.

"Hello?"

He loved that voice. "Hello, there. I'm looking for Melody Todd. She just won a special prize from our prize department."

"Oh, really? What special prize is that? I don't remember signing up for such a thing."

By the tone of her voice, Blaine knew she knew exactly who it was. It was nearly impossible not to laugh. "Well, it goes something like this. I want to see you, and I'm willing to beg if necessary."

"That's my prize? Seeing you or seeing you beg?"

Then he really did laugh. "Your choice."

"Can I choose all of the above?"

"I was hoping you'd say that. How about a burger? I can meet you there in thirty minutes."

There was a long pause. At first he thought she must not have heard, then he thought the phone had gone dead, finally the fact that something was wrong traced through him. "Mel?"

"Uh, yeah. Listen, Blaine, I know this is going to sound weird, and it's probably none of my business if so just tell me."

His heart hit his shoes. She was about to break up with him. However, he steeled the hurt already crowding through him. "Mel, whatever it is, just say it."

"Well, I got to thinking the other night. When you go out, what happens to Dylan? Does he stay home with your mom or what?"

Blaine had to let the air out of his lungs slowly. He hated being judged, hated feeling like his life was under a microscope because he knew all the flaws someone looking would find the moment they started looking. "Well, most of the time I take him over to a neighbor's house unless whatever I'm doing is after work or school. Then he stays here."

This pause was shorter but still evident. "And that's smart?"

Defensiveness crowded in on him. What was he supposed to do? Not have a life at all? Take Dylan everywhere he went? He reined his anger in with difficulty. "Look, I'm doing the best I can. I'm not exactly in a position to…"

"No, hey. Blaine. I'm not trying to make you feel bad. I just don't want us going out and putting Dylan in danger. That's all."

The disbelief followed by relief was almost overwhelming. However, he still saw no real way to fix the situation. "So, what? Do you want to bring him with us on our date? That doesn't sound very romantic."

"I think…" She took a breath. "I think we're going to have to face the fact that the way we date is going to be a lot different than most couples. We're not going to be able to just take off and go bar hopping like other people."

"But…"

"No. Now, listen to me. You've got responsibilities. I see that, and I'm okay with it. But you're not going to neglect those responsibilities because of me. Got it?"

"You're serious."

"Yes. I am."

She was, and somehow after getting past how bizarre this all seemed, it made Blaine feel lighter than he ever had before.

"Okay. Then I'm bringing Dylan?"

"Yes, sir. You certainly are."

At the burger joint, Melody pulled up in her not-too-bad little white car. She scanned the parking lot but didn't see him. Her heart surged at both thoughts—that of seeing him and of what if he didn't show. If he didn't, it wouldn't be the first time she'd been stood up, but something told her this one would hurt more than the others. A soft smile came to her heart and lips when the little green Toyota rounded the corner and drove up into the parking spot next to hers.

She surveyed the car and caught sight of Dylan. It wasn't easy to keep her trepidation over the situation in check. Could she really do this? Could she date somebody who had so many conflicting responsibilities and obstacles standing between them? Settling the thought that she would do her best, she watched as Blaine rolled down his window, reached through, and opened the door. It was odd seeing so many things wrong in his life.

When he stood from the car, it was impossible not to stare. The T-shirt he wore was white but for the navy collar and sleeve edges. She'd seen him in a lot of things, but never, ever jeans and a T-shirt. And these jeans weren't designer either. They weren't even knock-offs. Truthfully they looked more like hand-me-downs from the local thrift shop. It was everything she could do not to stare at him in total shock.

"Hi," he said, smiling brightly and removing the only part of his outfit that looked like the Blaine she had known to this moment—the sunglasses she'd thought were Ray Ban but knew now must've come from the supermarket.

"Hi." She hated how seeing him like this was affecting her. It was like meeting someone she'd never met before, and that feeling twisted around her lungs, holding her air in a giant fist.

He went around the car and helped the child from the other side. By the time they made it back to the sidewalk, Melody was gulping her fear, desperately trying to look normal although she had no clue what that was anymore. When they came back around, Blaine smiled at her. "Hey, there."

"Hey," she said, her gaze dropping from his to the little boy. He was cute. Slicked back black hair and thin tanned face—he stood just behind Blaine.

If she was going to do this, she was going to do it right. She reached down to the child. "Hi, Dylan. I'm Melody."

Only the child's gaze went up to her. She smiled anyway and reached out to touch his shoulder. It was smaller than she'd even realized. Straightening, it was hard to hide her nervousness.

"You ready?" Blaine asked, clearly sensing her unease.

She put a tight smile on her face. "Yeah."

With that Blaine watched her turn and walk to the door. Her jeans weren't overly tight, but they showed off the curve of her hips a little too much for the well-being of his sanity. She had obviously put effort into her attire and hair. He hadn't. As he caught the door on her swing, his stomach knotted. The last thing he wanted to do was to make her question going out with him. But the truth was, jeans and a T-shirt was much more his true style than the suits he wore every day of his life.

Still, he felt underdressed, way underdressed. Concentrating on breathing because he couldn't go back and make a different clothing choice, he stepped up behind her. Being this close always did freaky things to him, but this time it felt like plugging into a 220 outlet. His gaze slid from the board down to her shoulder and the fall of hair. What he wouldn't give to have the guts to reach out and touch it, to touch her, to throw caution to the wind and find a way to be with her. Instead he cleared his throat and forced his gaze back up to the menu. "What sounds good?"

Her glance at him held surprise. "I think I'll just have a salad."

He laughed. "You're going to turn into a rabbit." But he smiled and started forward.

However, she reached out and stopped him. "Blaine."

With that, they were mere inches from one another. The pull to her was unmistakable.

"I'll get mine. Okay?" she said softly as she glanced at the guy waiting to take their order.

All his gaze wanted to do was to focus on her lips. Those lips that had been so soft and sweet under his. "Um, I can get it. It's cool."

Her blue eyes filled with compassion. "No. Okay? It's fine. I can pay for my own."

Looking at her, with everything about her scrambling his thought processes, he couldn't find the words to argue. "Okay."

She stepped forward, and he breathed in the snapping of the spell. If this kept up, they'd be eloping and on their honeymoon by midnight.

Melody got her food, not even bothering with the dressing. She hadn't eaten in hours, and her stomach growled in protest, not to even mention the headache which never left these days, but she was fighting a weight plateau that wouldn't budge. In fact, she'd somehow managed to gain a pound in the past two days, and that was worrying her more than she wanted to admit. However, she pushed all of that to the back of her mind as the two handsome Donovan brothers approached her table.

She slid around on the hard yellow plastic of the booth, trying to get comfortable and anchored her gaze to the salad. It seemed safer that way.

"Looks like we waited out the crowd," Blaine said as he helped Dylan in. He set about getting ketchup and the burgers all laid out for both of them. It was strange to see him acting so much like a father, and wanting not to stare, Melody let her gaze bounce across the restaurant.

"What crowd?"

He shook the fries out of the container and retrieved his arms to work on his own supper. "Exactly. Most of the time this place is a madhouse on Fridays. But it's not so bad after 8:30 or 9." He seemed to be in perpetual motion, and Melody couldn't help but see how immensely different he was like this. It did nothing for her own nerves.

"Oh." She took a small bite of salad, tasting how tired she was of the leafy green stuff. For healthy food, salads sure got old.

"I guess you're getting ready for finals Monday." He took a quick drink of his soda.

"Trying. I'm going to be so glad when this semester is over."

Picking up the burger, he turned it around. "You're taking

intercession or just summer?"

"Just summer. I don't think I'd make it through intercession."

He nodded hard as he chewed. He seemed to be in a hurry although she couldn't quite tell why. "I've got an intercession. Art History. It's one of those basics I never found time for anywhere else."

"And you're taking summer school?"

"Twelve hours. I'm ready to get this show on the road, you know? Twenty-seven is way too old to be rummaging around community college."

Melody forked through three more lettuce leaves. "And then what?"

"There's a drafting thing at Lana's Dad's company. An internship." The words slammed to a stop, and he looked up in concern. "Not that I'll take that, but it's an option."

Lana. Lovely. Melody tried to stuff that down with the next bite of spinach leaves. "But that's what you want to do? Drafting."

"I'd love to do actual architectural stuff, but at this rate I'll be a hundred before I get that accomplished." He picked up a French fry and spun it in his fingers. "I'm hoping wherever I land, they will like me so much that they'll pay for me to take more classes. I'm tired of this struggling to do all of it myself—work, school, paying for school." He took a breath. "I don't know. I figure, get to December and then worry about that part."

She ate a little more of her salad and took a long drink of her large water. Water. It was the main staple of her diet these days.

Blaine's gaze fell beside him. "You want more fries, buddy?"

The little head shook side to side.

"He looks tired," Melody said, watching the little eyelids slide down and rest for moments on end.

"End of school. He's only got three more weeks, but that time change thing gets him every year."

"I hear you there, Dylan," she said, taking another sip. "I hate new time. Give me November any day."

Blaine's soft almond-colored gaze swung up to her. "November? Really? You don't like summer?"

She wrinkled her nose. "Too hot and sticky. I'm a fair-weather kind of girl."

For the first time his smile lost the nervousness. "I thought you were the one who couldn't wait to go out boating last year."

"Ugh." The cup hit the table with a thud. "Don't remind me. That was horrible."

His smile fell. "Why? What was so bad about it?"

"Well, for one, I felt like we were crashing the party, and two, the swimsuit thing is not my idea of wow fun."

Confusion traced over him as he leaned back, pulling Dylan to him. "Why's that? You looked great that day."

Melody lifted her chin skeptically. "Yeah, and you need your eyes examined."

"What? You did."

"Uh-huh." She didn't want to pursue this track, so she quickly found another. "Besides I can't hot dog as well as some people."

His smiling gaze fell from her face. "Yeah, I was a little over-the-top, huh?"

"Just a little," she said, knowing they both knew it was an understatement. She took a sip of her water. "It's okay. I know it's a guy thing."

The middle of his eyebrows drew together. "How's that?"

"You know peacocks fan their feathers. Guys show off." She shrugged. "Same thing."

"And girls don't?"

Shaking her head, she thought about the question. "It's not the same."

"Oh, yeah? Why not?"

"Because girls are more subtle about it. They dress up, put on make-up, and hope you notice. Guys will get in your face to get you to notice them—especially if you look like a model and dress like you're on the Victoria Secret runway."

His gaze fell even more. "You didn't have a skimpy suit. As I recall it was a one-piece turquoise with ribbing stuff down the front. It was nice." He took another drink as her gaze fell.

She heaved a sigh. "I wasn't talking about me."

Confusion went over him. "Then who…?" Understanding coursed across his face as his gaze fell. "Eve."

Melody hated this topic, and somehow they always came back to it.

Carefully Blaine shifted in the booth. "Is she really that bad?"

Acknowledging how far down on the scale she was compared with Eve was difficult. "No."

That the word was a lie wasn't hard to see. Blaine surveyed her. It was impossible to miss how sad she was when she talked about things like this. "Well, I think you were beautiful. I know I sure noticed."

A light pink tint fanned across her cheeks. Her gaze went down to the child now sleeping next to him. "I should let you get home."

Blaine didn't want to go. He wanted to sit here all night and just talk, but that would have to wait for another time. "You're probably right. As much as I'm going to hate summer, he's ready for it."

The statement seemed to stop her. "Why are you going to hate summer?"

He hadn't really thought about the comment when he made it, but now he was stuck with either a lie or the truth—neither of which he liked. Pulling the child up, he searched for a way to word it so it wouldn't sound awful. "No school means options I really hate. Either it's day care which is way too expensive. Mrs. Rodriguez who's great for a night or two here or there, but her husband smokes, and it's not the best place during the day either. Or leaving him at home all day." Blaine shook his head. "I just hate thinking about it."

"Oh." Somehow he was getting used to that compassionate look she had when the topic turned to Dylan. "Yeah, I can see how that would be tough."

After a few more moments of silence, they exited the booth and started for the door, where she pushed it open and held it for him. The child, once so small, now ran from his shoulder to his knees. Carrying him was getting more and more difficult every time he did it. Very soon it would be out of the question entirely. At the car, he got the door open, put the boy in the passenger's seat, and locked him in. Then Blaine stood, shut the door, and met her at the sidewalk.

He could stand it no longer. Reaching down, his fingers found hers and locked there. The electricity surged into his heart bringing peace with it. "So, I'll see you Monday?"

"Mon…?" Her gaze was locked on his, questioning and nervous. "Oh, finals. Yeah. Monday."

Carefully he moved toward her, closing the gap between them. A touch of her lips was like setting himself on fire. The kiss relaxed everything from his shoulders to his toes while simultaneously awakening everything as well. What he wouldn't give to be going home with her right now. His fingers came up to brush her hair back and slide across her neck. The feeling ripped new desire from the center of him. His hand left hers and wrapped her waist, pulling her to him.

She relaxed into his arms. He felt it, and that pulled head-spinning passion into him. The door to the restaurant came open, and voices filled the night around them. He let her go so quickly, she almost fell backward. However, he grabbed her into an embrace at the last possible second.

"I love you," he whispered because nothing else would do the feeling justice.

Her grip around his waist tightened. Then he released her enough to kiss her forehead.

"You be good, okay?" he said lightly.

"I'll try."

All the way home and for the next two weeks, when Melody recalled the moment, what she most remembered was how intensely wonderful it was to be in his arms and to hear those words. They were precious and so very rare in her life that she held them close to her heart. Maybe the moment wasn't even as great as the memory, but it didn't matter. He had given her a gift no one else ever had, and for that alone, he had stolen a place in her heart that no one else could ever have again.

Blaine chose not to share his newfound love with Eve. There were too many ways that could blow up in his face. Still, they talked about God nearly every day that both of them were at work. Sometimes it was simple things like how nice it was to live with honesty, sometimes deeper concerns like what God thinks about divorce and even separation. He found out Eve had been in the church since she was a little girl and that it was her faith and A.J.'s love that had gotten her through the loss of her first husband, Dustin.

It was odd that Blaine had never known about that part of her life, but then he hadn't really known her all that well back then. Truthfully, he hadn't known her much at all prior to her asking him to the amusement part, but now he was glad she'd taken that small leap of faith. He wondered as May wound to a close how different his life would've been had she not taken it.

If not for that request, he never would've met Melody, and this new feeling of wanting only to get closer to God would never have come into his life. He had yet to broach the subject with Melody. There was no telling what she would do if he mentioned how much he talked with Eve for one, and for two, he had no clue where she stood on the concept of God.

Nonetheless, he and his Bible were quickly getting acquainted. Psalm 139, that first one he had read on his birthday had become a good friend. He practically had it memorized. But by now he had other favorites—some suggested by Eve, others he had found on his own. They were all comforting, speaking about how God had a plan for his life, how life wasn't all on his shoulders, and how God's grace could lift him out of the muck and mire of his life.

For a month, he'd been praying feverishly for an answer to his new biggest question—what to do about Dylan. He found himself once again voicing the worry over burgers and salad to Melody who had heard the same conundrum without complaint for straight three weeks. It was their special Friday night together although Blaine was beginning to wonder just how special these were. How many nights could burgers be considered a proper date? However, he was immensely glad albeit surprised that Melody wasn't getting angry about them. After all, most of the girls he'd gone out with would've been at least annoyed by now, but Melody didn't seem bothered by the venue at all. In fact, other things were worrying her much more than that.

"You know, I was thinking the other day. You never told me what you'd decided to do when school gets out," she said as she tossed her salad more than ate it.

Blaine's gaze traced up from his burger. "Intercession?"

"No. Dylan's school. Have you decided if you're doing day care or what?"

"Oh." His gaze fell back to the burger and then over to the little dark-haired boy who sat munching on fries. "I haven't decided yet." The question twisted his chest. He wished there was some simple answer he was somehow not seeing.

The tossing slowed. "Well, I was thinking. My first two summer school classes are online, and in July I'm only taking one…"

He wasn't following what Dylan's situation had to do with her school schedule. "Yeah?"

She shrugged. "Well, if I took on babysitting, I might be able to only work nights or weekends at the store."

A second of incomprehension and then concern drove right through him. "Oh, Mel, I can't ask you to do that. This isn't your problem."

Her gaze hit him solid. "And…?"

Skeptically he narrowed his eyebrows. "And what?"

"And whatever other lame excuse you're going to try." She leaned forward on the table. "Look, you might as well get them out now because I've thought about this, and it could really work."

"Mel," he said slowly as he laughed but only slightly, "look, I appreciate the offer, really, but you need your job…"

"I'm not saying I would do it for free. What do you pay Mrs. Rodriguez?"

"Less than you make."

"But I'll be home anyway. I got a scholarship and a grant for the summer. I was planning on cutting back some at the store anyway. Plus, I'll be home taking the classes, and if you have to, you can always let Mrs. Rodriguez fill in."

His jeans suddenly felt welded to his legs. He stretched and pushed them down. "Mel."

"What?" Her blue eyes were filled with stubbornness. She glanced down at Dylan. "Look, I care about what happens to him as much as you do. I don't want him pawned off on people who don't really care. He deserves better than that. You know it, and I know it. Plus, I'm available. What could it hurt?"

"But…" Blaine could hardly get all the way through the thought. The arrangement might be really great, but what if it didn't work between them, what if they ended up hating each other by the end of the summer? Where would that leave Dylan?

She leaned back and pushed her fingers through her hair. "Just think about it. Okay? You don't have to tell me right now."

His gaze finally fell to the table. "Okay."

Despite the tenuous way they'd left the Dylan issue, Melody had no arguments when Blaine took her hand on the way out of the restaurant. She loved these times, these simple moments, holding hands, talking about the present and the future. The more she got to know him, the more in love with him she fell. And when he kissed her at the cars, it was like being reawakened to what life could be.

She drove home, a soft prayer on her lips. "God, let him see that Dylan and I could have a great summer together."

Twelve

"How's intercession?" Melody asked over the phone the next Tuesday. It was the 28th of May. Only two days until school was out for the summer, and still he hadn't really made up his mind about the whole babysitting thing. She was trying to let him decide on his own, but it wasn't easy.

"Stressful. My final's in three days, and I haven't even started studying for it yet."

"Oh, well, then maybe I should let you go."

"No!" The word was sharp, like a cry of someone who's fallen off a cliff. "Sanity right now would be a very good thing."

Her? Sanity? She laughed. "Funny. I never thought of myself as the sane one in this relationship."

"Are you kidding? Without you, I'd probably taken a rocket ship to the moon by now."

"Rocket ship to the moon, huh? That could be interesting." The smile that lit her heart every time she got the chance to spend time with him spread through her. "How's Dylan?"

"Ugh. Ready to get out. They cleaned their desks with shaving cream today. Don't ask. I think the teacher's got issues."

Melody let that drift into oblivion. "How's your mom?"

His sigh was hard. "Out. She left awhile ago for who knows where."

What could she say? Nothing would make his situation more livable. She wanted to ask again about the younger Donovan brother, but she was starting to sound like a broken record. "How's work?"

"Not bad actually. I talked to Eve today. She was telling me about this young adult group they have at her church. It sounded kinda cool, but I have no idea where I would fit that in."

Just what about that statement was the worst, Melody had no

idea. Eve. Church. Young adult group. She'd never been big on church. As far as she could tell, it was a waste of a perfectly good hour of sleep on Sunday. Still, she liked how it lifted his voice. Nothing else seemed to. Nonetheless, she couldn't keep the trepidation from her voice. "So are you going to join?"

Even asking hurt. If he joined the church group, it was a pretty certain bet that he'd find some sweet young adult with a 20 inch waist and a 15 pound Bible. Melody had neither. She ran her fingers through her hair that felt like dead weeds. Six strands came out with the motion, and she lifted them up to examine them. That had been happening a lot lately. At this rate she'd be bald by summer.

She reached over and flicked the hair into the trashcan.

"No, I just don't have the time right now, but I'd love to join a Bible study somewhere." He paused. "You probably think the religion stuff is stupid, but I don't know… it's really not so bad when you give it a chance."

He could give it a chance for the both of them. Even Blaine Donovan wouldn't talk her into becoming a Bible freak. She decided to change the subject.

"So have you decided about Dylan on Monday? I'm talking to Nathan tomorrow about my summer schedule." Her voice had lost much of the patience and some of the kindness. Truth was, she was tired. With two successive clunks, she slipped off the shoes she'd had on since 7 that morning. Something to eat and a shower sounded like a very good idea.

Again he sighed. "I went by the day care place today. It was a mad house. They've got little babies through twelve-year-olds, and I don't know which were worse. I just hate the thought of leaving him in that chaos all day."

"How much is it a week?"

"One-sixty a week—no matter if he comes or not."

She waited for him to decide in her favor.

"I don't know. There's just not a good answer."

The barb went through her, slicing every tender spot there. She ran her fingers through her hair again and came out with another five strands. Frowning, she reached over and dropped them in the trash. Maybe she needed a different kind of shampoo or conditioner. The ones she was using certainly weren't doing the trick anymore.

"Were you really serious?" Blaine finally asked, and she sat forward at the worry in his voice.

"Do you think I would've offered if I wasn't serious?"

"Well, I don't know." A moment and he sighed. "Maybe we could try it for a week, and see how it goes. But if it's not working for you for any reason…"

"You sure don't have much faith in me, do you?"

"I just don't want to overload you. Taking care of a kid is a lot of work."

She smiled. "How about you let me worry about that?"

And so, Monday morning Blaine found himself walking a rather reluctant Dylan up her sidewalk. He still had his doubts about whether this was a good idea, but the truth was his heart simply wouldn't let him take any of the other options.

"Good morning," Blaine said when Melody opened the door, looking shower-fresh. With minimal make-up, the freckles across her nose were clear. "Hope we're not too early."

"No. Not at all. Come on in." She stepped back and let them through the opening.

Blaine walked all the way into the living room. He still liked this house. It was cozy and warm, and the thought that Dylan would be spending time here with her made much of the trepidation slide away. "Here's his backpack. I put microwave mac and cheese in it. There's some toys and an extra shirt." He handed it to her and watched as she examined the contents. "I get off about five, so I should be back here by 5:30. If you need me, call Harmon's and have them page the men's department."

She nodded and then looked up at him. "We'll be fine." Her gaze fell to Dylan, and she held her hand out to him. "Won't we, bud?"

Looking back and forth between them, Dylan took her hand and stepped to her side. Blaine stood looking at them, trying to find the courage to leave them here like this. "If you need anything…"

"We'll call." Melody nodded and then her smile drifted to her eyes. "We'll be fine, Blaine. We promise."

"Well, okay. If you're sure."

"We're sure."

Melody stood at the door watching Blaine drive away. Then she shut the door and turned to Dylan who looked half asleep. "How about some breakfast? What do you like?"

His gaze up at her was dark and slightly frightened.

"C'mon." She held her hand out for him. "Let's go see what we've got."

Slowly his small hand came up into hers. She didn't know how much God would even care to hear, but she breathed a quick prayer anyway. Somehow she had to make this work—good intentions only in this situation wouldn't be enough, and she knew it.

All morning long Blaine thought about calling. It was driving him crazy. He shouldn't have agreed to this. Of course, he would be worried about Dylan no matter where he left him, but this was more stress than he had bargained for.

"Looks good," Eve said, striding into the break room at just after noon.

Blaine looked down at the tuna sandwich he hadn't so much as tasted. "You have very low standards."

She grabbed her lunch from the refrigerator and brought it to the table. Putting her apple to one side, she looked at him. "So, how's it going? Did you survive intercession?"

"Ugh. Barely. I think I squeaked by with a B—by the hand of God, I assure you."

"He's pretty good about stuff like that."

Blaine bit into a chip. "No kidding."

"So you're off for what then—a week?"

"No such luck. My online opened this morning, and my in-school starts tomorrow night. Tuesday and Thursday through July."

"Wow. Nothing like a killer schedule."

He shook his head. "You have no idea." His thoughts went again to Melody who had insisted that she keep Dylan until Blaine was out of class on Tuesdays and Thursdays as well. It was crazy. She didn't know what she'd agreed to.

"You're awfully far away," Eve said, gazing at him. "What's going on?"

He hadn't told her for fear of all the repercussions it could cause. Shaking his head, he let his gaze fall to his barely touched sandwich. After a moment his gaze came up to hers. "If I tell you something, do you promise not to tell A.J.?"

Concern crowded her features. "Why?"

"Because it's about Mel, and I know he'll flip out and think I'm the worst person on the planet if he knows."

Concern layered over the previous concern. "Why? What's going on?"

With a small breath to settle the decision to tell her, Blaine let it all out. Well, most of it anyway. He skipped the part about his crummy living conditions and his mother. That part was just too hard to admit. But he told her about Dylan and the day care situation and Melody and how he wished there was another option but he couldn't find it.

Eve never flinched, just sat, listening.

When he finished, Blaine looked at her. "Do you think I'm making a mistake?"

She gathered her words carefully. "I think that you… are very, very lucky. Melody is a wonderful person, very sweet and caring. I know she and I didn't hit it off right away, but I know by the stories A.J.'s told me that you're not going to find a more loyal friend. I think God gave you this solution, and you should trust Him that He has a plan."

Blaine nodded. "I've been reading about that a lot. Jeremiah 29:11 and all that."

"It's true." Her gaze fell to her perfectly manicured nails. "Sometimes it might not feel like it, but it's true."

For some odd reason, Blaine felt the need to ask who they were talking about, but he beat that thought back. It wasn't like she was in great need of faith to follow God's plan. What did Eve have to doubt God's love and wisdom over now? She was married to the second love of her life, and their lives were perfect. He brushed the feeling to the side. "I'll try to remember that."

"What do you say? How does going to the park for a picnic sound?" Melody asked Dylan who had been playing quietly on the floor with his tiny trucks and cars.

He looked up at her, and a feeling that could only be

described as love gushed through her.

"How about it? We can make peanut butter and jelly for you and iced tea for me." She put her hand down to him, and after only a moment's hesitation, he reached up and put his hand in hers.

The day had been perfect but for how quiet Dylan was. That worried her. He'd never said more than ten words altogether in her presence anyway, but somehow she'd assumed when it was just the two of them, he'd be more talkative. She was wrong. Desperate to break through the wall around him, she glanced at him as she gazed up at the sky.

"Let's see what shapes the clouds are today," she said, lying back on the denim patchwork quilt spread across the soft blanket of grass. It took her a moment to get comfortable; however, he didn't really move. Hoping she could get some response, she looked up at the clouds drifting lazily by. "Look." She pointed up at one. "It's an elephant."

A second and a half and Dylan followed her finger upward until his eyes narrowed in skepticism.

"Don't you see it? See, there's the trunk, and there's the big ears. See?"

"It looks like a cat."

"Wh…? A cat?" She ratcheted her shoulders around. "Where?"

Carefully Dylan lay down next to her and pointed up. "See its ears are kinda pointed and its long tail."

"Tail? That's the elephant's trunk!"

"Nah. Elephant's aren't that skinny."

"Maybe he's on a diet."

Dylan scrunched his nose and shook his head. "Elephant's don't go on diets. Only girls do that."

The comment intrigued her. "Oh, yeah. How do you know that?"

"All the girls in my class," he said as if it was exasperating. "They want to look like the girls in the magazines at the store."

"And that's a bad thing?"

He shrugged. "I think you should look the way you look, not the way everyone else does."

It sounded so simple and so heartfelt, Melody wanted to hug him.

"Oh, look! It's a boat."

Melody looked where he was pointing. "See, I told you. You are good at this game."

It wasn't hard to see the smile on his face when she looked over. He really was a cute little kid.

The memory of her watching as he got out of the car, having to roll the window down to open the door, drifted relentlessly over Blaine even as he drove home with Dylan. It had been a long day, and he had more to do once he got home. However, nodding off was not in question as Dylan was intent on telling him every single thing they did all day.

"And then we went to the park, and Melody found this thing in the clouds. She thought it was an elephant, but it wasn't. It was a cat. And then I found this giant head with a mouth and a nose and an eye. She never could see it, so she finally gave up and said I was the winner."

Blaine glanced over. "So you like Melody then?"

"Uh-huh. We made peanut butter and jelly sandwiches, and she let me lick the knife. But it was okay it was one of those not-dangerous kind. Tomorrow she said we're going to go play on a playground she knows about. She said there's a tunnel thing that we can crawl in that goes under some water."

Soft gratefulness brushed Blaine's heart. He was going to have to thank her. In nine years he'd never seen Dylan quite like this.

By Friday when Melody got to the burger joint with Dylan, her love for the child was set. She watched as he ran across the restaurant to Blaine to show his big brother the masterpiece they'd spent most of the afternoon coloring. It wasn't elaborate, but it wasn't bad either. She sauntered over to the table where Blaine already had their food.

"Hey," he said, looking up at her with soft appreciation.

Her hand was tucked in her back pocket, and pushing up on it, she arched her shoulder and smiled shyly. "Hey. Sorry we're late.

We had to stop for gas."

"Not a problem. I hope you wanted salad. I took a shot." He turned it around for her.

"We went out to the park today and fed the ducks," Dylan said, chomping into his burger like a ravenous lion. He took a drink. "You should've seen them. They were like quacking and honking, and one about got me but Melody shooed it away."

"Honking?" Blaine asked skeptically as she sat down.

Melody shrugged as she stuck her fork in the salad. "There were a couple of geese. Quite the gathering, I assure you."

"So ducks, geese, and the park all in one week? However will you top yourself next week?" Blaine's gaze was at once appreciative and teasing. "Dylan's not going to ever want to go back to school."

The thought that had been floating in her brain for three days sifted again into her consciousness. She glanced over at Dylan and decided it wouldn't hurt to at least start the conversation. "I was thinking about taking him to the library on Monday. I've got some research to do there, and maybe he can check out some books."

Instantly the protest jumped to Blaine's eyes.

She held up her hand. "On my card. On my card. And the books would stay at my house, so they wouldn't get lost. But he says he doesn't like to read much."

A fog of quiet guilt drifted over Blaine's face. "They wanted him to read every night from school, but we didn't always get that done."

It wasn't hard to see why. She knew enough of Blaine's schedule to know he hardly made it home in time to do his own work, much less monitor his brother's.

She took a tiny sip of water to settle the first suggestion. Then she plunged ahead. "I figured as much." Setting the glass down, she paused a mere moment. "I was also thinking about getting some flashcards for addition and subtraction."

This time the concern drained all the way down Blaine's face. "Why?"

Melody shrugged. "I used to babysit for a girl a couple summers ago. She was about Dylan's age, and she could rattle off the answers to stuff like nobody's business." She glanced at Dylan, measuring her words for his ears carefully. "I want Dylan to be able to do that in the fall."

A moment and then another as Blaine played with the French fry under his finger. "I don't…" He glanced up at her and then let his gaze fall. It slid over to Dylan and then back to his cup. "I mean… I'm pretty stretched for babysitting as it is…"

Suddenly Melody caught his meaning. "No! Oh, no. I didn't mean you had to pay for them. We could make them on my computer for all that's worth. I just meant… Well, I wanted to make sure it was all right with you if I worked with him like that a little bit."

The explanation didn't really do much to ease his tension. "I hate to ask you to do that. You're already doing so much."

But she only smiled. "Dylan's a great kid. We're just looking for good, productive things to keep us busy. Isn't that right, Bud?"

His mouth stuffed with hamburger and fries, Dylan nodded enthusiastically.

Blaine's eyes said thank you in a million ways. "Did I ever tell you that you are a Godsend?"

Despite the reference, she smiled. "I'm trying."

"And she's teaching him math, and they're reading together like hours and hours every day," Blaine said in marked admiration to Eve three weeks later as they sat in the break room at noon. "And Dylan just loves her. She's all he talks about. Melody did this, and Melody said that. Now I'm getting worried about what happens when he has to go back to school."

Eve's dark eyes surveyed him.

"What?" he asked defensively, sensing that his rendition had somehow revealed things he wasn't sure he was ready for anyone to see.

"You," she said simply. "It's nice to see you so happy and carefree."

"Carefree?" He snorted. "I wish. I've got summer finals coming up, and I'm scheduled for a double shift tomorrow…"

She shook her head. "No. I didn't mean work and school. I mean deeper than that. You aren't afraid like you used to be."

"Oh, trust me, there's still plenty of fear to go around." Then he stopped and really listened to his heart. "But I know Dylan is taken care of. I know he's with someone who loves him as much as I do. That takes some of the pressure off."

Nodding, she smiled. "I can tell."

He paused a moment not really realizing there was one. Then his gaze went up to her. "So how about you? How's things at newlywed central?" It wasn't that he wanted to hear play-by-play about her life with A.J., but he sensed it was rude to never even ask.

Rather than answering, Eve let out a long, slow breath and corkscrewed her face as if she might burst into tears. The battle continued as he watched in gathering concern.

Finally, Blaine sat up, leaning forward as he put his hand on her wrist. "Hey." He lowered his gaze trying to snag hers. "What's up?"

She said nothing for a long moment and then shook her head. "I'm still not pregnant."

That pulled his hand off hers. "And that's a problem?"

"Well, we wanted kids right away. We've both wanted a big family, and with me getting older all the time, we didn't want to wait." When she looked at him, there were tears lining her lashes. "But for some reason, it's just not happening." She shook her head and ran her fingers under her eyes. "I don't know. A.J.'s trying to be okay about it, but I know he's worried too."

Man, this really wasn't his place except that she was his friend and she was obviously hurting. "Well, have you… been to a doctor or something to see?"

She shrugged, flashed an ironic smile, and then set her jaw. "My annual checked out. No problems. Nothing they can see that's wrong."

With everything in him, Blaine did not want to be in this conversation for so many reasons he couldn't name them all. "What about A.J.? Has he been...?" This was impossible. If he was A.J., the last thing he'd want to do was to go to some doctor to be told there was something wrong with him that would break her heart.

"He's scheduled for the Friday after July 4th, but…"

"You don't think he'll go?"

Her gaze jumped to his. "Oh, no. I know he'll go. It's just…"

Blaine nodded. He understood her unspoken words perfectly. "Well, I can't say that I know it will do any good, but I can say some prayers…"

When she looked at him, the tears were there again.

He stood and pulled her up into his arms where she laid her head on his shoulder. Gently he stroked her hair. "It's going to be okay."

After a moment she pulled back, and his gaze caught hers.

"Okay?" he asked, leveling his gaze at her.

"Okay," she finally said and started to let go of him. Then she jerked him back. "Please don't tell anybody, okay? I don't think A.J. wants anybody to know."

It tore his heart out to see her so sad and scared. "I won't."

Melody had quietly dropped out of her second semester summer school class. It was scheduled to start on Monday, four days after July 4, but she wouldn't be there. Blaine had never brought up the question that the second summer session was about to start and what was she going to do about that, so she didn't either. They saw each other when he dropped Dylan off and again when he picked him up, and on Friday nights, they saw each other for a couple hours at the burger place. Beyond that, she knew he was terribly busy.

He had to be. Working full time and full time summer school would kill an elephant. There were days he looked particularly stressed, days he showed up so tired she knew he hadn't gotten much sleep at all. She wished she could do more, but what could she do that she wasn't already? When she first dropped the class, she told herself she could sign up for an online something, but there weren't any of those she needed. So in the end, she decided that a couple weeks off to just watch Dylan wouldn't kill her.

The decision had sounded so perfectly logical she never thought anyone would even question it, and with that, she forgot about it. On Tuesday July second, Blaine showed up looking dog-tired at almost ten-thirty at night, long after the sun had gone down. His last final was now finished, but he looked far from enthusiastic about that.

"Wow. You look beat," she said as she gathered Dylan's things.

"Huh, that's one way to say it." He leaned against the wall separating the entry from the living room.

Worry crashed into her. "Are you going to be okay to drive?"

"Yeah." He nodded, looking like he might fall asleep at any

moment. "How was he today?"

"Awesome as usual. He's a great kid." She wanted to tell him more, but now was not the time.

Without really looking at anything, Blaine took the stuff from her grasp, stood to head for the door, and then remembered something. "Oh, yeah." He turned back and almost ran into her. "Eve invited us for the fourth. That lake house thing we went to last year."

Like a porcupine, Melody's self-preservation quills went up. He hadn't talked about Eve in what seemed like forever. Somehow Melody had hoped they were no longer conversing. "Oh?" She glanced down at Dylan, whose hair she was stroking. "What're you going to do about…?" She didn't want to ask in front of the child.

Blaine's eyelids fell closed, and he yanked them open. "Oh, Eve said he's welcome. Jeff and Lisa's little Alex will be there. Maybe they can play."

Rats. She wanted that to be a good excuse not to go.

"Unless you don't want to go," he said slowly, clearly unsure he was even still awake by that point.

Yes! That was it. She didn't want to go. But how could she say that? They were more her friends than his, and not wanting to go would certainly dredge up hurtful feelings somewhere. "No, that's fine. We can go. What time?"

"Uh, we're supposed to be there about 11:30 for lunch on Thursday."

The smile she plastered onto her face hurt. "Sounds great."

Thirteen

"Hey! Hey! Look who made it!" Gabe, the tall, goateed fireman Melody had met only a few times called when they stepped up the deck steps on Thursday. He held his hand out to Blaine who shook it. "Nice y'all could make it."

"Thanks for inviting us," Blaine said. He was in his swim trunks and a light T-shirt, which was great for the sticky weather of the day. For a solid week it had been hot, unbearably hot in fact even for the summer months. Melody could feel her hair gluing to her neck each second she was out in it. She felt like a barnacle on a boat, walking behind Blaine who seemed far more in place than she felt.

"And who do we have here?" Gabe asked, gazing at Dylan.

"This is my brother, Dylan." Blaine pulled the child in front of him. "This is Gabe. He's a fireman."

Dylan's eyes went wide. "In a real fire truck?"

Gabe laughed. "Yep, in a real fire truck."

"Cool!" The admiration from the child was obvious.

Picking up the drink from the deck railing, Gabe took a quick sip. "I think the others are inside." He stepped back over to the grill that was sizzling and popping on the far side of the deck. "Unless you want to help me cook."

Blaine looked at him for a moment. "I think we'll go grab something to drink first."

The smile Gabe had was teasing and understanding. "Smart man."

Dreading going into that house with everything in her, Melody followed the two of them. It was unbelievable how incredibly hard it was just to breathe. Although it was a beautiful day—blue skies, just the right amount of breeze blowing off the lake—the fact that she might in fact suffocate was never far from her mind. At the door, Blaine opened it for her. As gentlemanly as that should have seemed, it felt more like he was feeding her to the lions. She clutched her purse and her duffle bag and stepped in front of him.

"Hey! They're here!" Eve said as though their appearance was akin to the Royal Couple arriving. She dropped the tongs of the salad she was tossing and went over to them. The closer she got, the less Melody was breathing until her head was pounding with the lack of oxygen. "We're so glad you came." Eve hugged first Blaine and then Melody, who arched one arm under the one Eve offered.

There was nothing especially affectionate about the hug. Pretense more than anything else. Then Eve stepped back and bent down to Dylan.

"Wow, aren't you a handsome one?" Eve reached out and straightened the child's collar. Melody wanted to knock her across the room, but she stifled the desire. "You look so much like your big brother."

It was then that Melody felt the little body hovering closer and closer to her. She smiled and bent down to him. "Dylan, this is Eve, Blaine's friend." So she wasn't as gracious as she should've been. She felt like she deserved at least an E for effort. "Can you tell her, 'Hi'?"

"Hi." The syllable was anything but loud.

"Uh, where are the others?" Blaine asked, surveying the empty kitchen.

"Oh, the guys went into town to get some more barbeque sauce."

Blaine nodded. "Then I think I'll just head out and help Gabe."

Eve shrugged. "Suit yourself."

He turned and started out the door.

"Oh! Melody. Blaine. I didn't hear you come in." Lisa strode in the other side of the room—if it could be called striding. Eight months pregnant it was more like waddling.

"And now I'm going out," Blaine said. He looked at Dylan. "You going with me or staying with Mel?"

The child considered. Then his hand came up into Melody's. "I'll stay."

She smiled down at him. How could she not? She looked up at Blaine. "Go on. We'll be fine."

He took her at her word and left. Once he was gone, however, she questioned whether she could, in fact, pull this off. Eve had gone back to the salad, and Melody felt more out of place than before. However, at that moment a little boy with curly black hair toddled in.

"Wow!" Melody said. "Is that Alex?" She forgot her need to remain aloof from the situation. "He's adorable." When she walked over, Dylan followed, drawn by the chubby toddler with the slobbery hands. Melody sat down on the tile floor next to the smaller boy. "Oh, you are precious. I can't believe how much you've grown." She pulled Dylan around her and sat him on her lap. "Dylan, this is Alex."

"Hi, Alex." Dylan held out his hand, but the child just stared at him.

"There are some toys in the living room," Lisa said, "if you want to go in there. We brought some blocks and some trains."

"Cool." That was all Dylan needed. "Come on, Alex." With not much more coaxing, they were gone.

It took effort for Melody to pull herself off the floor. "Ugh." She brushed her jean shorts off. "Man, I'm not as young as I used to be."

"Tell me about it," Lisa said. "I wouldn't even attempt that anymore."

Melody smiled. "Well, yeah, but you have an excuse."

"Some excuse. I'm starting to feel like a beached whale. I can hardly get out of chairs anymore." She put some bologna in a bowl and scooped a heap of noodles with it. "Remind me again that this is worth it."

Melody fell into the dream world Lisa was living. "Worth it? How can you even ask that? You've got the cutest little guy on the planet and another one on the way." She reached over and snagged a carrot off the vegetable tray. "I'd call that seriously worth it."

From the other side of the room, Ashley strode in. She always looked wholesome. Not so much runway ready, more house mom of the year ready. Only at that moment did Melody question it that she'd never even heard her or Gabe talk about their kids. A thought slid through her. Lisa and Jeff always brought Alex on these outings, seeing that it was somehow Ashley and Gabe's place, wasn't it curious that they didn't bring their own kids? Unless…

"The reinforcements have arrived!" A.J. called as he and Jeff strode in from the front entryway. Then his gaze snagged out in the living room. "Who's the kid?"

Melody wanted to crawl under the table, and she physically shrank back against the cabinet.

"That's Blaine's brother, Dylan," Eve said, and there was a strain to her voice. "I told you they were bringing him."

"Oh." A.J.'s gaze slid over to Melody and held. "Yeah. I forgot." His normal buoyancy disappeared into sullenness. "Hey, Mel."

"Hey." She wrapped her arms over her middle, wishing they hadn't bothered to come.

A thick fog of awkwardness descended on the kitchen.

"Well, we'll just get this barbeque sauce out to Gabe," Jeff said, sidling up to Lisa for a touch and a small kiss. His gaze fell to the bowl, and he looked at it skeptically. "Looks wonderful. I think I'll stick to the steak."

"Haha." She laughed with no mirth as she angled her nose up to him.

He pecked the bridge of her nose, turned, and flipped the sauce bottle in the air. "Are the beans and potato salad ready?"

Ashley opened one pan and then another. "Yep. Let us know when the meat is."

The two of them went out the back door onto the deck, and Melody let out a breath of relief, hoping Blaine would stay on his best behavior.

"No, seriously," Gabe said as he sat on the lawn chair next to the one Blaine occupied. The clouds drifted lazily by as the popping and sizzling steak continued its hunger-inducing performance on the grill. "The Astros have a real shot at the pennant this year. The Padres are fading, and if Rivers can keep pitching like he has been, they'll be strong down the stretch."

"That's true, but Hampton's out for the season, and that guy they pulled up from Triple-A is just barely holding on." Never had Blaine been so thankful for the two lunkheads who worked in the

Casual Men's Department right next to him. It wasn't that he didn't like baseball, but he didn't have time to follow it like they did. Every day it was a play-by-play of the previous day's game, or the game just prior to that if the Astros hadn't played since then. But it was nice to be armed with some information to sound minimally intelligent now.

"Oh, now there's trouble," Jeff said, coming out the door and tossing the bottle to Gabe who barely caught it. Jeff put out his hand. "Hey, Blaine. How's it going?"

"Not too shabby." Blaine stood and shook the older man's hand. "How about yourself?"

"More of the same except I got moved up to driver last week."

"Really? Congrats. One of Houston's finest and all of that." Blaine tipped the bottle of beer he'd been holding up, feeling the comparison with his own life next to theirs. It was not a comparison he fared well in at all. With everything in him he wanted to spin some wonderful story about going to the Caribbean or Cozumel earlier in the summer, but he beat that thought back. What had Melody said about peacocks? Well, sometimes it wasn't the females but the males a guy was trying to impress with that stuff.

His gaze snagged on the guy standing with no smile at all behind Jeff. Pulling in the animosity, Blaine reached around Jeff to A.J. "A.J."

Looking like he might either throw up or pitch Blaine off the dock, A.J. shook his hand. "Blaine."

There was a long moment after that in which no one really said anything. Finally Blaine took a long drink of his beer that attacked his head with its chill. Bottle in hand, Gabe stepped over to the grill and opened the hood. Flames shot up, licking through and around the meat resting on the racks.

"Whoa. Careful there," Blaine said. "We might have to call the fire department."

"Yeah. There would be a fun situation," Jeff said, retrieving a beer from the cooler. "I'd love to see Gabe explaining to the captain how he'd managed to torch his own deck."

"It wouldn't be the first bone-headed thing someone around here has done," Gabe shot back as he tamed the flames with a pistol-grip bottle of water.

"Hey, you watch it there." Jeff pointed the beer he'd just opened at his friend. "Those stories go both ways, you know."

Gabe nodded. "And therefore, I will be shutting up now."

Jeff tipped his bottle and nodded. "Smart man."

The door behind them swung open. "Are you guys ever going to get that meat done?" Ashley came out holding the biggest bowl of potato salad Blaine had ever seen.

"If Gabe isn't careful, we'll be having charcoal for lunch," Jeff said.

"And you won't be eating at all if you don't watch it." Gabe opened the barbeque bottle and licked his fingers when it went everywhere. "Do we have the brush somewhere?"

"Uh, up in the cabinet, I think," Ashley said.

"I'll get it," Jeff said, and Blaine wondered if he was simply smart enough to extract himself from a horribly awkward situation.

What to look at, what to say. Gabe seemed safe, so he ambled that way. He leaned on the railing. "I guess we're boating again this year?"

"Of course. You going again?"

"You got it. I haven't been water skiing in… Well, since last year."

"Really?" Gabe pinned him with a strange look. "I figured you went water skiing every weekend… the way you looked last year."

There was more to that statement, but before he had a chance to ask, Jeff returned followed by a gaggle of women and children. They poured out of the house, a mass of voices and laughter. Blaine picked Melody out without really trying. She was smiling, but he couldn't tell how much of that was real and how much was an act. She was far too good at the acting thing. He watched her, holding Alex and trailing behind Dylan. She would make a really good mother someday.

He shook his head at that thought. When his gaze caught Eve, following Melody, his heart and gaze fell. Although Melody had a smile, Eve looked like she was about to cry. It didn't take Einstein to know why. As he watched the scene, A.J. went to his wife and put his hand on her back. They exchanged the barest of tired, sad smiles with each other and then melted quietly back into the merriment. Blaine's heart hurt for them, and for the first time, looking at A.J., the animosity fell away.

With everything in him, he wanted to tell Melody who was

now seated at the picnic table with Alex on her lap and Dylan at her side. She gave Alex his sipper cup, and her gaze went over to Blaine. Her smile was in her eyes as much as on her lips, and he knew then that it wasn't an act. She really was genuinely happy. That lifted his own heart even from the quiet sadness that was only steps away from her.

"Who's hungry?" Gabe asked, arching the platter into the air with the meat sizzling on top of it.

"Who's not by now?" Ashley asked. "You are the slowest cook in the universe."

Gabe walked over to her, set the meat on the picnic table, and swept her into a kiss. "I may be the slowest, but I'm also the best looking."

Ashley laughed as he planted a serious one on her.

"I thought we brought Dylan's cap in," Melody said, rummaging through their stuff on the little guest bed. Each had changed, and now all were making final preparations for some time in the sun. "I don't see it in this bag anywhere."

"It's probably in the car," Blaine said, watching her. She really had become much more like a mother in the last month. "I'll run out and get it."

"K." She set about roping and twisting her hair up into a ponytail as she retook her position at the mirror on the dresser. "The keys are in my purse on the couch or the kitchen one of the two." With an annoyed look, she fanned her fingers out as strands of hair fell to the floor. "Jeez."

"Got it. Come on, Dylan." He started out with his brother. However, he had seen her, and the questions attacked him. His heart dove into the turmoil of why she was losing her hair and how he could be happy being with Melody while he knew Eve's heart was breaking. There were no good answers for any of it. At the couch, he picked up Mel's white purse. It was nothing special, not Prada or Gucci. Just quintessential Melody—practical and unassuming. Without really thinking about it, he unzipped the top and started his search.

However, the first thing his fingers met up with caused him to stop dead. He lifted the silver lined package out as the question went through his head. His gaze slid across the words, and the tenuous happiness he'd been clinging to fell into utter fear. Slim & Thin. Diet and Weight Loss Supplements. The middle of his heart fell to his shoes as life spun away from him. "Oh, Mel, what're you…?" He barely whispered the words and then swallowed even them when he heard the voices approaching.

"I don't think she was feeling good," Lisa said.

"She was so quiet at lunch. I hope there's nothing wrong." It was Ashley, and she sounded worried.

"Well, I know they've been trying, so maybe she has a reason to be sick." As one they broke into the living room, and Lisa pulled up short. "Oh! Blaine. I didn't know you were in here."

Quickly he stuffed the package back into the purse and dug out the keys without seeing them. "Not for long. We were headed out to the lake, but we seem to have lost Dylan's cap."

Across the room, Lisa sat down in the rocking chair and pulled Alex up to her. "Well, y'all have fun. Keep those guys under control for us."

"There's a tall order," Blaine said, trying to make a joke, but it hurt.

"No kidding," Ashley agreed, sitting in the wing-backed chair, pulling a magazine out.

"You're not going?" he asked, feeling like he shouldn't just leave.

Ashley shook her head. "Nope. I've been on a boat with Gabe. Too much for my nerves."

Blaine laughed and then hurried out with Dylan to get the cap. Sure enough, the silver SUV was nowhere to be seen. His heart fell further. He wished he could call them, ask, find out how she was, but that would never happen. So he quickly went to the little white car. Concerns pressed down from every direction, and he had no idea what to do about any of them.

The soft white swimsuit she'd bought on Saturday was more snug than she wanted it to be. Somehow Melody had convinced herself that by now she would've lost enough to make it fit a little better. She pulled the straps forward, trying to get it to stop digging into her shoulder blades, but it was hopeless. This plateau was worse than the last. The truth was, she'd finally resorted to pills last week. It wasn't great, but how else was she supposed to get down to her goal weight? Eating nothing and exercising obviously wasn't working.

She was proud of herself for not succumbing to the temptation of throwing up. It was ever-present, but so far, she'd vowed she would not do that again. Pulling the elastic around the back of her leg down, she took a side view in the mirror. Disgust with herself crowded over her. Next to Eve she was going to look like a walrus. If only there was a way to get out of going. But Dylan wanted to, and he had vowed not to go if she didn't.

Stuck and knowing it, she grabbed her sunscreen and plastered a smile on her face. What other choice did she have?

How he would ever not look like death warmed over, Blaine had no idea. When Melody walked out of the house to meet them on the deck, it was all he could do not to flip out at the risks she was taking with her health. She had to know the dangers of not eating and taking diet pills on top of it. But thinking back, what had she eaten for lunch? Not much.

His gaze slid down her frame, and he shook his head in disgust that she would think there was anything wrong with her. Somehow he had to tell her that, but at the moment they were being joined by the bopsy twins. Serious conversation of any sort would have to wait.

"Wow! Look at you, Mel!" Gabe said, appraising her. "Nice suit."

"Thanks." She seemed to squirm under the attention.

"You guys ready?" Gabe asked.

"Guess so," Blaine said, sincerely trying to sound excited but falling far, far short of that. He stood with Dylan as he sensed Melody taking a head count.

"Uh, where're A.J. and Eve?" she asked, anchoring her arms around herself.

"They took off," Jeff said. "Eve wasn't feeling great."

Blaine had to think that must be going around. He didn't feel so great either, and even Melody didn't look like she felt all that great anymore. Pushing everything else down, he stepped over to her. Carefully he leaned closer. "It'll be fun. I promise."

Her eyes questioned that, but she tried to smile.

The heat of the day, the sticky air, and her perpetual headache were not boding well for a marvelous day on the lake. Add to that the slight nausea, and Melody wondered if there was something rotten in the potato salad. There was no reason for Eve to get sick. It probably had to do with the two of them showing up. A.J. certainly hadn't looked at all pleased. Not that he ever did these days.

Melody seriously considered begging off going on the water. She certainly had enough reasons to use, but the guys looked so happy and excited, how could she worry them? Plus, Dylan was only being brave because she was. She couldn't disappoint him.

"Watch your step." Blaine took her hand and helped her onto the boat.

The rocking motion swarmed over her. Fighting to keep her balance, she grabbed the first seat and fell into it. This was going to be a study in acting like she'd never performed.

The whole afternoon, Blaine kept watch over her. Every so often he would see her sway slightly, and he wondered again about the pills. Each of the guys took their turns on the skis. Melody wouldn't even consider it, and Blaine let it go quickly. The last thing he wanted was her out on skis, not physically well. As the day slid into late day, he watched again as she brushed her hair back and flicked the strands that came out into the water.

He noticed without trying to how grasslike the hair across her hairline was. It didn't look healthy at all, and although she'd been in the sunlight all day, her face had a slightly gray hue to it. The more he looked, the more unnerved he became.

"Do you want to go out again?" Jeff asked Blaine from the front.

"Oh, I don't know. I'm kinda tired." He was liking having his arm around her, being able to soak up the sun together. Besides it was almost possible from this proximity to believe he could do something to protect her.

"Tired? Did that word just come out of his mouth?" Gabe asked, tooling the boat around the lake slowly. "I thought he was Superman."

"False advertising," Jeff said, shaking his head with a laugh.

Blaine sighed and pulled himself forward. "Fine. Just so you don't think I can't out-ski both of you with my eyes closed."

He felt Melody look up at him, and when he looked down at her, there was a soft pride in her eyes. It drilled into the middle of his soul. She knew everything about him, the good, the bad, and the really ugly, and yet she still looked at him like that. How that was possible, he had no idea.

"Don't have too much fun without me." He leaned down and laid his lips on hers. Pulling his hand up, lest she have any questions who he was hot dogging to impress this time, he laid it on her soft neck. She laughed softly, and he could hear the embarrassment. When he pulled back, he was only inches from her. "Don't go anywhere."

She laughed again.

Blaine flipped the skis out, jumped in the almost warm water, and swam around getting ready. When he got in position, one look took in Melody, her arm around Dylan's waist as they watched him, and his heart slid through his chest. The understanding that these were the types of experiences he'd always wanted to give Dylan but never had the resources cracked over him. He had to rake the breath over the swelling of his heart. Because of her, that kid was getting to see a life he'd never imagined he would ever be living, and so, Blaine realized, was he.

Picking his hand up, he waved. Gabe turned to drive. The motor accelerated, and with one jerk, Blaine was up and flying across the water. The wind whipped at him as he hopped one wave and headed for the other side of the boat. He waved to her, and both she and Dylan waved back. Their smiles were priceless. Maybe next year they could come again. Maybe by then things would be very different for all of them.

Where that thought came from, he had no idea, but as he tested it in his heart, he knew it to be true. This day would prove to be the turning point for all their lives. He was sure of it.

Fourteen

Seated around the little fire pit in the center of the deck, Melody snuggled in to Blaine's warmth. Dylan was asleep on the couch inside, and it would be time to leave very soon. However, right now, she was too enthralled with watching Gabe burn marshmallows "just so" to think about leaving. He was so easy-going and fun to be around. They had spent most of the day laughing at him.

"So, Melody," Gabe said, turning to offer her the latest charred just so marshmallow, "I guess you're burning the midnight oil with classes these days."

"Uh, no thanks," she said about the marshmallow.

"Suit yourself." He ate it himself, waiting for her answer.

"Yeah, well." The answer stuck in her throat as she sat up from her comfy place. "I took two classes online last session."

"Oh, really? What are you taking this session?"

It took effort not to choke. "I'm…" She cleared her throat and reached for her water under the chair. "The classes I wanted this session didn't work out like I thought they would." She fought not to think about Blaine sitting right there behind her listening.

"Man, you've got to hate it when that happens." Gabe glanced over at Blaine. "You want another one? I'll char it for you real good."

"Uh, no thanks. As wonderful as that sounds." However, he didn't make it sound good at all. His hand which had been drifting up and down her back for the better part of thirty minutes had snagged and stopped.

She wanted to look at him, but she didn't dare. Making like nothing at all had happened, she leaned back to him being careful not to look at him. "So, Lisa, when's your bundle of joy due?"

Across the deck, Lisa rubbed her hand over her belly. "First part of September."

"Which reminds me," Jeff said. "You all are coming to help us move the 14th, right?" He pulled his own marshmallow off the little wire, being the only one not trusting Gabe to cook his. Leaning back in his lounge chair next to Lisa, he popped it in his mouth and chewed around it.

"The 14th?" Gabe asked. "Oh, no can do. We're going for that family reunion thing in Dallas, remember? I asked off for it like six months ago."

"Are you kidding me?" Jeff straightened. "You said you didn't want to go to that, and you were going to…" His words stopped as his gaze traveled over to Ashley.

Her gaze went to Gabe. "I thought you said you couldn't wait to go."

Gabe ducked his head over the little wire he was holding. "Who wants another marshmallow?"

A slow awkwardness dropped over the group.

"Great," Jeff said. "That's the only weekend we've got. Now what're we going to do?"

"Maybe you could ask Dante and Hunter," Gabe offered.

"Yeah, if I want all my stuff broken. I talked to A.J., but he's iffy too. They've got some wedding to go to on Saturday night."

"I didn't know y'all were moving. I thought you loved that house," Ashley said to Lisa.

"We do, but with the baby coming, and I'm going to try to do a lot of my work from home now, we need at least one more bedroom and somewhere for my office too."

From behind Melody, Blaine shifted. "Well, I could help on Sunday if you don't get enough help Saturday."

All gazes swung over to them, and Melody felt on full display. She glanced back at him to see if he was serious. He certainly looked it.

"I could bring Dylan," he continued, shrugging. "We could make a day of it."

Gabe reached over and jabbed Blaine. "Dude, he's got a waterbed. Have you ever moved a waterbed?"

"We're having some of the big stuff professionally moved, thank you very much," Jeff said with a frown. "But of course that's only half the battle."

Melody wanted to look at Blaine, but this was between him and Jeff.

He shrugged beneath her. "You can count us in. Isn't that right, Mel?"

The question was like a swift, stiff, gale force wind. She blinked, shifted, looked at him in panic, and then collected herself. What was she thinking? A.J. and Eve wouldn't be there. Blaine would. "Sure. It sounds like fun."

"Me drive? You drive?" Melody asked as they exited the house after saying their good-byes.

"I can." At the back door, Blaine helped Dylan in and with the seatbelt latch. The child never really woke up. Too much water and sunshine.

In the car Melody handed the keys over and put her head back. All-in-all it hadn't been too awful. The four of them were nice, and with A.J. and Eve gone, the stress level was manageable. Blaine drove out to the Interstate in her car and turned south. Most sane people had headed back home hours earlier, so traffic wasn't too bad. Melody had just settled in for the hour-long drive when she felt Blaine's glance. Something about it made her alert systems flash on.

"So when were you going to tell me you dropped out of class?" he finally asked, glancing at her again before staring out the front window. He didn't sound at all happy.

The question and tone skittered across her heart. "Oh. Um, well, I didn't really drop out. I'm just taking a break."

This look wasn't any happier. "You weren't planning to take a break this summer."

Shrugging, she tried to deflect the question. "Yeah, well. Things happened."

"Like Dylan?" Every word he spoke sounded angrier and angrier.

She turned toward him. "Listen, Blaine. It's really not that big a deal. I'll pick up the hours in the fall."

Frustration scratched across his face. "I didn't want you to change your plans on account of us. I thought you knew that."

Anger snapped over her. "Is this about my schedule or your pride?"

A flash of irritation jumped at her. "What's that supposed to mean?"

"Look, I'm doing this for you and for Dylan. Why can't you be grateful about that?"

"Because I don't want special favors, that's why, and I also don't want to mess up your life over helping us."

How she could be in trouble for going out of her way to help was beyond Melody. "Wait. Wait. Hang on. I'm helping you out, and you're mad at me for that? What sense does that make?"

"I don't want you rearranging your life for us. What if we're not… What if…"

She almost asked what he was trying to say, and then the answer became clear. "What if it doesn't work out between us?"

He stared straight ahead, having no answer.

A moment to breathe and to get the words right. "Look, Blaine. I know things didn't work with your parents. My parents weren't much different, but I know one thing, when I get married, I don't want it to be about some piece of paper. I want to know that the person I'm with is my best friend and my teammate. I don't want it to be me and him living in the same house but living our own separate lives. I don't want to roll over at night and feel like I'm in the marriage all alone. That's what happened to my mom, and I saw how horrible that is.

"Maybe this is idealistic. Maybe it's impossible. But I want to be a team with my husband, and I want to be a team from the get-go. Not him better than me or worse than me, but equal partners who give and take and work things out for the good of the team."

"But how can you not going to school be what's good for the team? I don't want your life to be put on hold for mine."

A sigh and she knew the answer. "Look, I've been running for three years straight, trying to get the right education so some guy might consider going out with me." More truth began coming through her spirit. "I always thought I wanted to be in retail. I liked it better than I had liked anything before that. But this summer, being with Dylan, I'm beginning to think maybe there's something else out there for me, something I would like even more."

"What's that?" The animosity was gone from his eyes when he glanced at her.

"Well, I don't think I could handle teaching like a whole class, but I might really like being a teacher's aide. I really like working one-on-one with kids, and I'm good at it. Did you know Dylan has been working on division as well was multiplication? And he's good at it. And I don't really have a way to measure it, but I think his reading is getting better too."

This glance held more concern than anything. "So what're you saying? You're going to change your major?"

She shrugged. "I don't know yet, but I'm thinking about it. I don't have to decide anything right away. But my class for the summer was on marketing. If I took it and then decided that's not what I wanted, I would've wasted that time and money and not been able to help you out. This way, I can take a break and explore my options."

The pools of amber light swept over and under the car as they drove. She began to feel what it was to be with someone and be completely alone. He was in the car, but she couldn't tell if he thought she was completely insane for doing this or not.

"So this wasn't about doing it because of me?" he finally asked.

"Not entirely. No. Not that that didn't enter the equation because it did. Look, I see how important it is for you to get finished by December. Getting out will mean a big increase in your options, which I kind of hope means an increase in our options." She held up her hand. "Not that I mean we're anything more than dating. But I think practically speaking we need to put a toe in making decisions based on what's good for us, not just based on what's good for you or me."

He looked over at her with a look she couldn't read. "You're serious?"

That felt like a knife. Never had she felt like such a fool. Blaine had no intention of making plans with her. Her gaze fell. "I… was." A rock of stupidity went through her chest. "I'm sorry. You're not ready. I wasn't saying we had to, just that that's how I'm starting to…" She was making it worse. Finally she shook her head and let her gaze go out the world flying by her window. What an idiot she was. It was like she was screaming, Hey, chump, where's my ring? No wonder guys ran the other direction from her.

"Hey," he said softly. "Hey." Reaching over, he took her hand.

Her gaze followed. "I'm sorry."

"No." He closed his eyes for a fraction of a second. "I'm the one who should apologize. It's just. I never saw this coming." The breath was barely there. "I've never been as honest as I have been with you. You've gotta know that, but marriage? Even talking about it is a really big step for me. I mean I watched what my parents went through, and I don't know if… I don't know if it's worth that."

It wasn't hard to see how deep the hurt ran in his life. Melody corralled her feelings although it was difficult. "I'm not talking about going down to the church and signing the papers right now." Her voice was pleading, and she hated that. "I just meant this feels different than the guy calling up to see if I'm free on Saturday. I've never really had to navigate my life around someone else's before." As close as cracking in two as she had come only moments before, Melody realized it was time to go for broke. If he wanted out, now was the time to say it before she invested even more of her heart and soul in this relationship. "I never really felt like that was something that was needed until now."

Darkness had once again overtaken outside the car as they pulled onto her street and drove in silence to her house. His little green car sat along the curb. She had never acknowledged quite what that car did to her heart, but the truth was, if he were to drive off tonight and never come back, she had no idea how she would ever go back to life without him. Not even losing A.J. had hurt as much. She let her gaze fall from the car to her lap. Even thinking about it hurt.

Blaine parked the car and shut it off. All of life plunged into silence around them. He sat for the briefest moment and then turned to her. "I don't want to hurt you."

Oh, here we go. That's just a step away from 'I think we should just be friends.'

She closed her eyes, willing the cut to be quick and merciful.

"I saw what my mom went through," he continued so slowly she knew it would be anything but quick or merciful. "I won't lie to you. It's been hell on all of us. It's been ten years, and we're still not through it. I've never been able to figure out how Dad could do that to someone he loved, or said he loved." The words stopped, and Blaine shook his head. "I don't think I'll ever understand it. But what I do know is I can't do that to someone I love. The only problem is, I don't have a roadmap to tell me how not to. I don't want you to not go to school for me because if we don't work out, then I've messed up your life, but if we don't start making some decisions together, maybe that's how Mom and Dad went off track." He put his head on the headrest and pleaded with her in his eyes to answer the conundrum. "I don't know what to do."

All she could think was he hadn't actually said the words she thought he would. "This may not be the answer," she said softly, "but I think sometimes you've got to let your heart do the thinking too." She held him with her gaze only. "So what does your heart say?"

He exhaled sharply. "That I'd be crazy to let you go. That this is what I want more than anything, and everything else means nothing if I don't get this right." The words were there, but his soft brown eyes were so full of sadness and fear, it tore her heart to pieces.

"Then tell me what you're thinking about Dylan staying with me. Do you think that's working?" She'd never really asked outright, and this seemed as good a time as any.

Peace slid through his eyes as a smile jumped to his lips. "Are you kidding? He loves you. All I hear is what you're going to do tomorrow, what you did today, and how great you are." Then the smile fell slightly.

She sensed the shift in his mood but couldn't understand it. "And that's a bad thing?"

His gaze fell into the darkness below his hands. "Dylan's a great kid. He just doesn't know that things don't always work out."

At that, Melody heard what he was saying loud and clear. "You know, Dylan was telling me the other day about his life. He said he knew there were other kids who had more than he does, but that he has something they don't have—a brother who really loves him. He loves you, Blaine, and I think you really love him. Right?"

His face fell further into irritation and anger. "Of course."

"And you would never walk out on him, would you?"

"On Dylan?" The very thought seemed to horrify him. "No

way."

"But what if it gets hard? What if he gets on your last nerve someday? Would you walk out then?"

Blaine's face creased in disgust at the thought. "No. I'd find a way to make it work."

"Make it work, yes. But would you stop loving him?"

There were tears close. "No. I could never stop loving Dylan."

She let him with his thoughts for a moment. "Then you are capable of the type of love that stays—good or bad, no matter what."

His gaze slipped to hers. "What's your point?"

Slowly she shook her head. "No point. Just something to think about."

The stirring in the back brought both of their gazes to it. Dylan sat up rubbing his eyes. "Are we home?"

"No, buddy, but we're getting there."

Fifteen

Blaine's mind was a confusing swirl of contradictory and maddeningly incongruous thoughts. He liked Melody. He really did. He liked spending time with her. He trusted her like he'd never trusted anyone. And yet where exactly was that trust leading? She obviously had assumptions about its trajectory, but those assumptions scared him to death. There was the whole question of her schooling. In one way he understood and he was vaguely grateful somewhere deep, deep down below the fear of what she might expect in return.

And on top of everything, there was the question of what to do or say about the pills. He saw clearly now both her desire to lose weight and what it was doing to her. True, to him it was great to be thin, but thin in and of itself wasn't the point. The point was to be healthy, and she wasn't.

How she wasn't freaked out by the loss of hair and occasional unsteadiness, which he had also witnessed but not wholly understood until now was beyond him. And then there were the headaches Dylan had mentioned but Blaine had never really assigned importance to until now. However, was it his place to say anything about her life? That she wanted them to become more than friends was abundantly clear. What wasn't as clear was how close he wanted to get to finding out what happened after that.

On Friday he dropped Dylan off with very little conversation. He couldn't even look at her. Confusion reigned everything in him—every thought, every breath. By some ability other than his own, he made it to work, but the truth was, he was a stressed out mess.

Melody was tired but not that tired. She knew a brush-off when she saw one, and nothing about his actions spoke of the two of them going any further than they had. Sure, he'd said something along those lines on a couple of occasions, but it was clear some other part of him was in control at those times. Once again, she was stuck where she always ended up eventually—alone and confused.

She stepped on the scales in the bathroom. Drinking water like a sieve, she was constantly having to take pit stops. One look at the numbers and she growled low and menacingly. How was it possible to gain two pounds in one stinking day? It wasn't like she'd scarfed down a whole steak and a plate of potato salad, but was one little bite asking too much? Frustrated, she stepped off and swiped off the light. That was just about her luck these days. Fat, ugly, friendless, and alone. Yep, that was about the extent of her life.

"Oh, you're here," Blaine said when Eve walked in the break room at just after four. "You eat out for lunch?"

"Something like that." She swiped at the cups for coffee and knocked them over, scattering them across the tiles. "Crud." She put her hand to her forehead, beating back the pain that was etched all over her being. Frustration emanated out of her as she bent and yanked the cups from the floor.

"Hey." Blaine stood, swiped the cups up, and stacked several on the little cabinet. Then he stopped to look at her. "What's wrong?" Somehow in all of his own concerns, he'd forgotten all about hers. Why Melody would want to be more than friends with him when he wasn't even all that great at the friends thing was more than he could explain. Still, he reached out to Eve gently. "Hey."

She was crying now. Her was head down, her body quaking silently.

"Hey, no. Don't cry." He pulled her into his embrace. "Shhh." He couldn't help but think how much smaller and fragile she felt than Melody. It was as if they were the antithesis of each other. Moments passed during which he searched through his mental files of what to do in such situations. However, he came up empty.

"I'm sorry." She pulled out of his arms and grabbed three napkins for tissue. "I thought I could do this."

True worry crashed over him. "Do what?"

"This." Throwing her hands out to the side, she looked around the break room. "Work. Live." She blew her nose long and loud.

Now she was really scaring him. "Whoa, Eve. Where's this coming from?" He led her to the table. "Here. Sit down. You want some water?"

At the table she nodded pathetically, and he jumped into action. Although he'd always thought the hero cool, he knew with equal veracity that he could never fill the role. However, today, for this one moment, he stopped thinking about the right moves or the cool moves and just did it. In seconds he was sitting down, pushing the water over to her. That's when he remembered the absence of the silver SUV the day before.

"Are you still not feeling well?" he asked, staring at her, trying to figure out what was going on.

She glanced at him. "Depends. Physically or emotionally?"

"Both." A moment, and then horror enveloped him as he watched her crumble into the tears again. Not knowing what else in the world he could do, he reached over to her. She leaned toward him and let him hold her again. She seemed incapable of fighting it.

"Eve, come on, girl. You're scaring me. Say something. Talk to me. "

Quiet sobs gripped her, and Blaine simply held her not knowing what else to do.

After a few minutes, she pulled herself together again and sat back. Her gaze was only on her water. She dragged in a breath and sniffed back the tears that still shimmered on her lashes. "We went to the doctor today. They don't think we can have children without help."

Blaine's hand rubbed up and down her back. "Then you get help."

She shook her head slowly, sadly. "It's not that easy. It's really expensive, and insurance won't cover all of it."

He fought against the dwindling of her options. "What about adoption?"

The anguish washing her face made him wish he hadn't asked. "I don't know. I just… I wanted this so bad, and now…" The words trailed off.

It was something he'd known since his parents split. There are moments that being an adult really and totally stinks. What do you say? Are there words? If there were, he didn't know them. "How's A.J.?"

She shook her head. "Devastated. He's on call tonight, so I probably won't see him until tomorrow at least." Her fist came down hard on the table, making it jump. "This is so unfair. He would be such a great dad. Why would God do this to us?"

The quaking of her faith shook his own to the very core. He was so new to all of this having faith and trusting stuff he had no idea what to say to her much less what to say to himself. God, help. I'm out of my league here. "Is that why y'all left yesterday?"

It was like someone had hit the pause button. She sat staring straight ahead, and he knew both the answer and that he shouldn't have asked.

"It's so hard. Seeing them like that," Eve said like a hollowed out zombie. "I go, and I want to be happy for them, you know? But there's Alex and Lisa playing together, and I just can't help but think, 'Why not me, God? Why not her and not me?' I know that's selfish, but it's how I feel."

His heart hurt watching her struggling so hard. "I don't think that's selfish. I think you'd have to be the tin man not to feel something." He rummaged through his brain trying to find something comforting to say. It was like looking for hope in a pit of hell's flames. "You know, I don't know why God does stuff. I don't. I've been asking why about my parents' divorce for a lot of years, and I still don't have any answers. Sometimes I think knowing why would make a difference, and sometimes I know it really doesn't matter. They made their choices, and life followed.

"I can't explain it, but that colored me in ways I can't even explain. I want a family, but I don't. I want someone right here with me, and I don't. I don't know if the family thing or even the girlfriend thing will ever even happen for me, if I can ever have the guts to let it. Sometimes I think that's a good thing. Sometimes it scares me to death." He snorted and ran his thumb down the bridge of his nose. "I'm rambling." He dragged in a breath and let it out slowly. "I guess what I'm trying to say is I don't have any answers for you, but I do have a shoulder if you need one. And my ears are starting to work pretty good too."

Her smile was still sad but had taken on a grateful tinge when she looked up at him. She leaned over to him for a hug, and when he took her in his arms, he wanted with everything in him to make all things right in her world.

"I'm sorry," he whispered softly.

She nodded and sniffed. "I know."

That he was preoccupied was abundantly obvious when Blaine showed up at six-thirty. It was Friday. Normally they went out on Fridays. Tonight he didn't look like burger material, and Melody didn't feel like going through the motions if he had already let go. What could she say that she hadn't already?

"Monday?" he asked as Dylan headed for the front door.

Melody nodded, following him all the way to the door. She wanted to ask, to talk about this, to get it all out in the open. But she was afraid if she asked the question, she might have to hear the answer, and it was an answer she never wanted to hear. His soft green shirt looked touchingly inviting, but she fought the urge. She'd already pushed too far, pressed too hard, said too much. If she just hadn't…

A step down outside and he turned to her. At that moment there was no denying the soul-wrenching misery in his eyes. "Thanks, Mel."

Her heart broke for him, for them. They were words she'd wanted him to say, but not like this, not with him walking down her sidewalk away from her. "You're welcome."

For one second he paused, and then he turned and strode away with Dylan a half step ahead of him. Halfway down the sidewalk, he replaced his sunglasses, and she felt the distance growing between them. At the car when he looked back up at her, it was the old Blaine, cool, calculating, and in control. As much as she didn't want it to, what she felt most was acceptance of how utterly impossible it was for them to ever be together. Even if he got his life on solid ground again, it was a sure bet he would find some svelte honey in slinky clothes and heels up to her neck.

Melody closed the door and wished reality didn't have to hurt so much.

When the phone rang at 9:30, Blaine had the absurd hope that it was her. It wouldn't be. Not after the way he'd acted, but somehow the thought still went through his mind. "Hello?"

"Dude! What'd you do fall of the planet?" Peyton sounded mildly off-center which for 9:30 on a Friday night could easily be called right on schedule. "We missed you at Daphne's party."

Blaine pulled a chair over and sat down, trying to remember how long ago the party was. The truth was, he had no idea. "Yeah, I was kind of busy that night."

"Kind of busy? That's code for you found a better party, right?"

"Something like that." There was so much to be thankful for in their friendship, but at that moment, Blaine couldn't help but feel how far apart they had grown. It wasn't just the money. It was the direction their lives were headed, and for the first time ever, he almost felt glad about that. "So to what do I owe this phone call anyway?"

"Oh, hey, dude. I got an offer on the Carerra." Yeah, Peyton was getting more tipsy by the moment. A wail of music from a set of speakers pierced through the conversation. "Hey! Hey!" Peyton yelled so that Blaine had to pull the phone away from his ear to avoid getting his own eardrum blown. "Turn that thing down. Can't you see I'm on the phone?" He spat an expletive and then another for good measure and then returned to the conversation. "Sorry, dude. What was I…? Oh, yeah. The Carrera. I got an offer, but I told 'em I had to talk to you first."

It was strange how at one time this conversation would've driven nails of horror into Blaine. Now, it felt almost like releasing a bird from a cage. The opening of the cage took almost nothing. "Sell it. I'm not going to be needing it anymore."

"Really? Cause I thought… Awesome, Dude. Did you get you some wheels other than that horrible bucket of bolts you had that one time?"

There was no need to justify anything. "Thanks for letting me borrow it, Peyton," Blaine said, sensing this was the last conversation with this friend he would ever have. "But it's your car. You do whatever you want with it."

Blaine took Dylan to Mrs. Rodriguez's on Saturday and Sunday. With classes not starting until Monday, he used the weekend to accumulate some much needed hours. However, by Sunday night when he got home at nearly ten, he was wiped out—emotionally, physically, spiritually, mentally. How he would ever face the start of two classes in the morning, he had no idea.

He and Dylan walked into the house, which was terribly quiet and alarmingly dark. Blaine didn't like the sensations flowing through him at all.

"Where's Mama?" Dylan asked, and his fear screamed like a banshee. "I thought she would be home."

"Yeah, me too." Blaine made his way carefully into each and every room, reaching in to turn on the light first, preparing himself for what he might find. He'd always feared it would come down to her lying in a pool of blood, but he'd done his best to never let his head voice those thoughts until now. Room-by-room they made it all the way through the house to her bedroom.

"Go get washed up for bed," Blaine instructed Dylan. "I don't think she's here."

Dylan didn't look convinced, but he went to the bathroom anyway. When the water came on, Blaine closed his eyes, turned the light on, and praying the whole time, opened his eyes to examine the room. Nothing. Not a thing out of place. It looked as stark and miserable as always. The breath of relief was barely there. Knowing he was being silly either because of exhaustion or mental overload, he stepped in and checked both the closet and behind the bed. Still nothing.

The understanding that fear and fatigue were indeed getting the better of him went through him, and he shook his head at his own foolishness. Exhausted from everything, he met Dylan in the hallway and reached back and shut off the light. "You get on to bed. We've got to be on the road at six."

"K," Dylan said. A breath of a second, then he all-but dove into Blaine's arms. Not knowing what else to do, Blaine held him there. Could it be that Dylan was as scared as he himself was? *If he did something to get on your last nerve, would you still love him?* The words streaked into his consciousness, and he hugged the child extra tight. This couldn't be easy for him, and yet he was holding up remarkably well. Then suddenly he let go and without even looking at him, he headed for his room. "Good night."

"Night," Blaine said and watched his brother disappear into his room. Running his fingers through his hair, Blaine exhaled. Was it possible for everything to be a disaster and yet be exactly as you thought you had wanted it forever? And why did it seem that there were suddenly far more questions in his life than answers? He tried to think that thought through, but it only made him even more tired. "God, You're going to have to take over tonight. I can't do it. I'm done." With that, he went to his room and was asleep in minutes.

Two full days of shoes, customers, and hassles had convinced Melody she did not want to be in retail. She'd always thought it was a place she could move up, a place of movers and shakers and action, but watching Farin and Nathan battle about who hadn't ordered the right style of boot made her seriously reconsider that notion. In the face of everything, did the right style of anything really matter that much? Did it bring smiles to the faces of those who shopped there? Not really. They still looked stressed and unhappy even when they checked out, and headed out the door. In fact the more she really looked, the more miserable the majority of people looked.

It was a strange revelation that others weren't as content as she had once believed them to be, and that for the most part, she had been far happier than any of them this summer. Being with Dylan felt for the first time in a long time like the right path for her. She was excited to get up in the morning, excited to plan what they would do, and she loved every minute of being with him. All weekend, the prospect of Monday was what she focused on to get through the tedium of shoe sales. On Monday morning when they showed up, she smiled for real at his arrival.

"Hey, buster." She gathered him from his brother's arms into her own. "I missed you."

"We kind of had a late night last night," Blaine said, still not really looking at her as he dumped Dylan's things at the hallway entrance. "He might sleep a little while if you want to let him."

"Oh, okay." And she saw it then—the misery and exhaustion in Blaine's eyes. It was the same look she'd seen in the eyes of so many customers over the weekend. "Do you start classes today?"

He nodded, holding the breath in. "Seven-thirty and ten."

"And then you've got work?"

"Until seven."

Her own place in his life escaped from her consciousness, replaced by his position in hers. "You going to be able to handle all this?"

Surprise laced his eyes when he looked at her. "Yeah. I'll be fine."

Melody knew the iron hard quality of his determination and what that much determination could do to a fragile spirit. "Hey, be gentle with Blaine, okay? This little guy needs you in one piece." She tousled the little boy's hair as he pressed backward against her.

An understanding smile came to Blaine's face. "Okay." He heaved a sigh. "Well, I'd better go." He turned for the door. Just as he got there, she couldn't help it.

"Blaine."

He turned. "Yeah?"

"Don't worry about us. We're good. Okay?"

For one second the misery lifted from his eyes as he nodded. Then he opened the door and left.

She took a breath and looked down at the boy. "You want to take a little nap on the couch?"

"Yeah." He started in front of her to the couch.

At the couch, he lay down as she got him comfortable. It wasn't long, and he was again asleep. Melody sat down in the chair across the way and watched him. He was such a cute kid. Many of his features reminded her so much of his big brother's. Worry coursed through her at the thought of Blaine. He was struggling. That much was clear.

Her thoughts strayed to the times he'd talked about God and praying. Not that she really believed in all that stuff, but since he did, she figured it was worth a shot. She closed her eyes and let her thoughts go. "God, if You're up there, Blaine really needs You right now. He's got too much going on to handle it all himself, so if You could give him some help, I'd really appreciate it. Thanks."

Blaine couldn't tell how much was real and how much an act, but Eve seemed much better on Monday. He, however, was having heart issues of epic proportions. Melody had been so wonderful about everything—even his own idiocy in not knowing what he even wanted from their relationship, but what did that mean? That she was holding on or that she had let go? And which did he want? It was a conundrum no matter which way he went. They needed to talk, but how to accomplish that was an even greater problem that he simply had no more brain cells to work on.

"You look stressed," Eve said when she walked into the break room at four.

Blaine was hunched over his Modern Economics book, trying to make sense of anything written there. "Yeah? I wouldn't know why." He shook his head, realizing he should stop being so selfish and make sure she really was all right. Scooting a chair out, he waited for her to get her drink and sit. "How're you?"

There was a smile. "Better. We talked about it, and we went to church on Sunday." She nodded. "Better." Then her gaze swung to his. "Thanks for last week…"

He shrugged. "Oh, you know…"

"I was a mess."

"Not any more than usual," he said with a grin.

She punched him. "I'm serious. You were there when I really needed someone. Thanks for that."

He took in the compliment. "Hey, what are friends for, right?"

Leaning back, she took a drink. "So how are you and Melody? You looked pretty tight the other day at the lake."

His gaze dropped like it fell off a cliff. "Ugh. Let's not even go there."

With distress, her smile plummeted. "Oh, no."

"Oh, yes."

She looked even more concerned than he felt. "What happened?"

There was no reason to lie. She knew too much.

"Me. I'm the problem." He flipped the book shut with one swipe. "It's like I've got this button in me that starts screaming, 'Too close! Too close! Abort mission! Abort mission!' every time we take a half-step forward. "

Eve twisted her face into visible concern. "And Melody?"

He looked for the answer and found nothing. "I don't know. She acts like nothing's wrong, but I know she's hurt. I just don't know how to quit hurting her with my stupid need to not get hurt myself. Ugh. This is insane."

"Have you tried being honest with her about how scared you are?"

Blaine sat forward and scratched his ear. "Well, we haven't been out just the two of us in weeks and weeks. When we see each other, Dylan's always there." His gaze jumped to hers. "Not that that's a bad thing, but… It does make talking that much more difficult." The absence of answers stared him in the face. "I don't know. I give up. It's just too hard."

Eve surveyed him slowly. "Funny. I never took you for a quitter."

"Huh?" He looked at her, meeting the challenge of the words.

She shrugged and took a drink. "I just never pegged you for someone who gave up when the going got tough, but I guess I don't know everything."

Anger slashed through him, but he beat it back. "I'm not… Okay. I am on this, but come on. What else am I supposed to do?"

"Talk to her. Tell her how you feel—not just some of it, but all of it. How stressed you are, how scared you are, all of it."

"But what if she laughs in my face?"

Eve leveled her gaze at him. "Blaine. Do you really think she's going to laugh in your face?"

The answer was quiet. "No." Another protest rose in him. "But when are we going to have this conversation? When Dylan's sleeping in the backseat or in the booth at the burger place?"

Her gaze fell. "Well, you could bring him over to our place. We could watch him."

That thought sent him backward. "I couldn't ask you to do that. Not after everything…"

Compassionate and peaceful, her gaze took him in. "You know, Friday I might have agreed with you, but now, who knows? Maybe God set this up for a reason."

Blaine shook his head in honest awe. "You're something else, you know that?"

Eve lifted the bottle to her lips. "So I've been told."

The center of him was about to jump out of him and run as Blaine picked up Dylan later. He had no idea how he would ever explain this to her, but he had to ask.

"And the math paper we did today is in his backpack. We ate Chinese so the hamburger mac stuff is still in there, too," Melody said, digging and remembering, but clearly not planning to actually look at him.

As Blaine watched her, he let go of pushing her away. It wasn't hard to admit how grateful he was for everything she had done for him and for Dylan this summer. Giving only, expecting nothing in return, she was the embodiment of self-sacrificing love. He let out one more breath. "What're you doing Friday?"

Her head jerked up so fast, he was sure it wobbled a little. "Friday? I don't know. Why?"

"Well, I was thinking. We haven't had a proper date in awhile."

"Date?" Her eyes widened like saucers. "You mean you and me?"

He leaned in. "Well, I like your mom and all, but I think she's a little old for me."

Melody laughed but still looked wholly skeptical. "Uh, well, nothing that I know of. What do you have in mind?"

"Leave that up to me," he said, the mystery of the words making him wonder how he would pull off something great on his extremely limited budget of time and money.

Deep concern slid across her features. "What about Dylan?"

"I found a babysitter who's willing to watch him for a few hours."

"Mrs. Rodriguez?" she asked with worry. "Because he said…"

Blaine laughed. "It's not Mrs. Rodriguez. Come on, Mel. Trust me for once. I promise you won't regret it."

Looking like she'd just agreed to help him plunder the pyramids, she nodded. "Okay, but no funny business. Got it?"

He held his hands up with another laugh. "No funny business."

When Blaine and Dylan walked in on Wednesday night, the television was winking and blinking messages to the darkened house. Their mother hadn't been home for five days, and Blaine was beginning to wonder if they would ever see her again. However, when he got to the living room, all the nights of cleaning up after her came back with a snap. The sight pulled him down into the depths of anger and hurt.

"Get on to bed," he said to Dylan who stood on the threshold between the living room and kitchen assessing the life wrecked in front of them.

Bottles were everywhere, and there were needles on the end table. Blaine saw them almost reflexively. The sights and smells turned Blaine's stomach, which he remembered hadn't been fed in hours. However, even reeling, he sensed the child hadn't moved. He headed into the living room, trying to act unfazed. Over his shoulder as he picked up the bottles, he pulled up as much of his in-charge voice as possible. "I said, 'Get to bed.'"

"Is she… dead?" The voice was high, scared, terror-laden.

"No. She just passed out." The fury over the whole situation and his mother came out toward Dylan. "Now get to bed. We have to leave early tomorrow." He brushed past Dylan and threw the bottles in the trash with a crash that jolted both him and Dylan who still stood there.

"Are you sure she's not… dead?"

The tone of his voice was starting to remind Blaine of "I see dead people," and it was grating on his nerves. "She's not dead. Okay? She's just being stupid again. Now get on to bed. I'm not going to tell you again." Carefully he picked up two needles and carried them to the kitchen trash as well.

Dylan's eyes widened. "What's that?"

At the trash, Blaine's patience ran out. "Look at me. Are you in bed? No! I want you in bed… now!"

Still looking both terrified and horrified, Dylan slid down the wall toward his room. Blaine closed his eyes and dragged in air. He hated this. With everything in him, he hated this. No kid deserved to grow up like this. As he strode into the living room again, he made a decision. They were getting out. He couldn't help her anymore, and trying to was going to drag them all under. It wasn't what he wanted, but Dylan didn't need to be around broken bottles and needles and who knew what else. Tomorrow he would start looking for a new place.

When he walked by Dylan's bedroom after getting most of the living room clean, the door was cracked ever-so-slightly, and he heard the soft sobs. They snapped his heart right in two. Blaine looked up, trying to tell himself to just keep on walking. But he couldn't do that, not to the little boy who needed somebody so very much. Carefully, slowly, he pushed the door open. Huddled in the covers in the midst of darkness, the soft sobs filled the otherwise silent room.

Blaine stepped over to the bed and sat down. "Hey, buddy."

Instantly the sobs stopped, replaced by sniffles. "I'm sorry. I'm going to sleep."

His own harshness ripped through him. He reached over and rubbed his hand over the child's back. "I'm sorry I yelled at you before. I shouldn't have done that."

The sniffs continued. "I just… I think something bad's going to happen."

"No, hey. Nothing bad's going to happen. Okay? I won't let it."

"But what if… what if Dave comes back? What if he has a gun this time? What if he wants to kill us?"

Until that moment, Blaine had no idea that the same nightmare scenarios running through his own mind were also running through his brother's. Somehow he had hoped the child was too young to understand, but maybe he was just old enough to understand but not old enough to have any control over the situation at all. "Hey, come here."

And with that, Dylan was in his arms. "I'm scared, Blaine."

"I know." Blaine nodded as he buried his face into the child's shoulder. "I know. I'm going to get us out of here, okay? I promise."

The crash from the bathroom at half-past-dark-thirty brought Blaine out of a deep, disturbing dream. He couldn't remember all of it, but enough was clear to make the crash jolt him upright heart, body, and soul. Not really thinking clearly, he grabbed his glasses from the nightstand and the bat from next to the door. He opened the door, surveyed the situation, and stepped into the hallway where he found Dylan standing by his door.

Dylan rubbed his eyes. "What was that?"

"I don't know, but I'll take care of it. Just stay right there. Okay?" Stepping to the bathroom door, Blaine could hear his own heartbeat thudding in his chest, squeezing out the breaths. At the bathroom door, he stopped. "Mom?"

"Uhhh." The moan was beyond weak.

He pushed at the door and flipped on the light, revealing the horrific skeleton that had once been his mother. She was dressed only in a stained shirt and her underwear. For a second the horror of her emaciated frame and slack face hanging over the toilet slithered through him. Lowering the bat, he stepped in carefully. Glass lay everywhere, scattered among the plastic bottles that were still in one piece but were in a jumbled mess all over the floor. Red cough medicine dripped from the sink into a sickening pool to the floor.

He inched his way in. "Mom? What happened?"

"I…" And then she wretched.

How he kept his legs under him, Blaine would never know. What he did know in that moment was the flipping of the off-switch in his mind to thinking about anything. The robot he had learned to rely on kicked into gear as he went about cleaning up the mess she was relentlessly making of everything.

"I was trying to find some pills I had in there. Dave gave them to me," his mother said, wiping her mouth as Blaine picked up shards of dripping red glass. "Would you get them?"

"Pills? Pills? Mom! The last thing you need is more pills from Dave." He picked up three large portions of the glass and dumped them into the trash.

"No. It's not what you're thinking. It's not… Pills like aspirin pills." She was nodding off even as she said it. "I wouldn't take drugs, Blaine. I wouldn't. I told you I wouldn't."

Blaine snorted at her. "Is that where you've been all week? Out shooting up with Dave? Are you going to bring him back here, Ma? Is that your plan? So we can all be one big, happy family again?"

"No, Blaine, Baby." She reached for him. "It's not like that. I swear. He just wanted to talk… about the divorce. You have to believe me."

He dumped more trash into the garbage and then in all earnestness, he gave up. For ten years he'd been trying to clean up her messes, had been trying to make life good enough so she would want to live again. But all his efforts had been for naught. He hadn't saved her. He'd barely saved himself. However, at that moment he vowed he would save Dylan. No more excuses. No more justifications. They were leaving.

"We're moving out," he said, standing there looking at her. If he could've helped her, he would've moved heaven and earth to do it. But he couldn't. She and only she could make that decision. As he stood there, he finally faced that fact. "We'll be out by next week."

"Moving?" Hollow eyes, filled with only emptiness stared back at him. "How… Why…? You can't…"

He closed his eyes and gathered his courage. "I love you, Mom. I do. But you don't love yourself, and I can't help you if you don't want help. Where you're going, I don't want to follow, and I can't let Dylan go down that road either."

"But… Blaine." She couldn't get the words out as tears pooled in her eyes. "You're leaving?"

"Yeah, Mom. We're leaving." They were the hardest words he'd ever spoken.

"We're moving." Dylan sat at the counter in Melody's house on Friday morning, eating the last of the eggs. They needed to go to get groceries later. She'd already started making the list in her mind. However, in one second the list evaporated.

"Moving? What do you mean moving?"

"We're not going to live in our house anymore." He kept eating as if he wasn't setting off bombshells in her life and heart. "Blaine says I'll have to go to a new school." His little eyes looked up at her. "Do you think new schools are scary?"

"Scary?" she repeated, having great difficulty following the conversation. Then wise adult kicked in. "No, sweetheart. New schools are fun. You'll get to make all kinds of new friends. It'll be great. Just wait and see." She reached over and hugged him as her own feelings swirled in a confusing jumble inside her.

For the life of her, Melody couldn't decide what to wear. Everything was either too big or too awful. She'd vowed to go get new clothes at some point, but that hadn't happened. She put on the white wrap shirt she'd worn that first time they went to the burger joint. There were gaps in all the wrong places. One part of her was thrilled, the other was panicking.

He'd called this a date. A real date. At the time she thought that a good sign. Now she wasn't at all sure about that. Was he planning to tell her he was leaving? That they were leaving? The inside of her panged forward at that thought. Dylan was downstairs watching a cartoon. Melody tried to calm her rising panic at the thought of not ever seeing him again. Surely Blaine wouldn't do that to her, and yet that was exactly what he had warned her of in a thousand different ways, a thousand different times. Don't tie your life to ours, we could be gone tomorrow.

She was still trying to decide what it all meant when the doorbell rang. "Oh, no. I'm not ready for this."

The small bouquet of daisies in his hand was hardly steady. It looked more like the aftershocks of an earthquake as Blaine stood on her front porch waiting. He listened but heard nothing. Reaching up, he rang the doorbell again. His gaze traveled out to the curb where her white car sat. He hated the fact that they would have to take her car, and yet what choice did he have? Beginning to wonder where they were, he reached up again just as she swung the inside door open.

"Blaine?" The skepticism on her face rained through the word. "What…?"

"Hmm." He cleared his throat and straightened. "I thought you guys… Umm, I…" He looked down. "Oh, these are for you." Holding them out to her, he let his gaze fall to the concrete steps. Carefully he picked his gaze back up to her. "I wanted it to be a dozen roses, but…"

"They're beautiful, Blaine." She took the tiny bundle, and gazing first at it and then him, she shook her head. "Come on in."

He stepped into the house where he removed his sunglasses. "Sorry. I'm a little early. I got off a little sooner than I thought I would."

"Oh, that's okay," she said over her shoulder.

Following her into the living room, he found Dylan sitting Indian-style next to the couch, watching some animated something on the television. His heart snagged there. Once again he was struck by how much he wanted to be able to give Dylan this kind of life instead of the nightmare they were currently existing in. Not big. Not fancy. But safe and cozy and homey.

"I'll just put these in some water," Melody said, heading for the kitchen.

Blaine followed her, trying not to assess her physical health too critically as he did so. First things first. He needed to establish that he had some grounds to give his opinion. Then he was determined to get her to see this wasn't good for her or for them. From the table, he watched her search the cabinets. Finally she brought out a regular drinking glass.

"We don't get too many flowers around here." She set the flowers in it and fluffed them up a little. Then she took the bouquet to the sink where she ran water in the glass. Finished, she set it on the table. "Thank you."

"You're welcome." With everything in him, he wanted to kiss her. Right here. Right now. But once again, first things had to come first. "I guess we need to get Dylan packed up."

Melody nodded and started out in front of him. The electricity was almost physically overwhelming when she passed only inches from him. He slammed his eyes closed and swallowed hard to stop her proximity from overtaking his sanity. In the living room, she moved, gathering and straightening. "Time to go, bud."

"It's almost over though! Please!"

She was about to override the protest when Blaine stopped her.

"It's okay. We're not in a big hurry."

"Oh. Okay." It was clear from the confused look she gave him that she wanted to ask, but she didn't. For that, he was glad. There were simply too many things that would have to be explained if they ever got started.

When they headed north on the Interstate, Melody wondered again where they were going. It seemed to her that if he'd had this super-secret babysitter the whole time, it was odd that he hadn't ever mentioned her. The possibilities circled in her head like aircraft at high noon over Houston International. Wanting something to fill the awkward silence, she reached over to the holder above his head on the sun visor. It took only a few seconds to choose the CD.

She put it in the player, and finally, the silence didn't seem so loud.

"George Strait," Blaine said with a small smile. "Nice choice." And then he reached over and took her hand. Her heart leapt at the first touch of his fingers. They felt better than she remembered. Trying to push all the questions out of her head, she held his hand, for one moment believing and hoping that somehow it could all be all right.

Worry and fear crawled up Melody's gut as Blaine made the last turn. "You didn't tell me we were going to A.J. and Eve's." Unconsciously, she was pushing up and back in her seat as if trying to brace for a wreck. This wasn't at all what she had expected.

"We're not," Blaine said, glancing at her. "Only Dylan is."

"Only Dylan?" She glanced into the back. "He doesn't even know them. You're going to leave him with them, and he doesn't even know them?"

Blaine laughed softly. "Mel, relax. A.J. and Eve are nice people. He'll be in good hands."

Strange. If they were such good hands, then why did she feel like she was handing her first born to the devil?

Blaine walked the two of them up to the little house. He and Eve had prepared an entire Dylan game plan for the night—what to eat, what to watch, time for bed, the whole thing. So when he climbed the steps with Melody's hand in his and Dylan at his other side, there was only one small moment of utter terror after he'd rung the doorbell.

"Hi, guys!" Eve appeared, looking decidedly unfashionable in an over-sized T-shirt and Capri jeans that had strings instead of a hem. "Come on in." She pushed the door open. Her hair was up in some kind of clip, not looking as if she had even brushed it in a month. But when Blaine stepped past her, he caught the excited smile on her face. In the living room she guided them forward. "You can just put his stuff over there. Sorry, I'm a mess. I've been making cookies, and let's just say, they're not my forte."

Blaine laughed as he put Dylan's things down.

Eve went over and sat on the coffee table. "Hi, Dylan. I'm Eve. Remember me?"

He barely looked up. For one second Blaine panicked, maybe Melody was right. Dylan didn't even know these people—not really.

"Dylan," Melody said, letting go of Blaine's hand to bend down to the boy, "Eve is my friend. Remember? And she's Blaine's friend too. I'm sure you're going to have lots of fun at her house tonight." Melody looked over. "There's a DVD in his backpack. It's one of his favorites."

"Okay," Eve said as though she was taking mental notes.

"His pajamas are in there too."

At that moment there was a not-ignorable yipping sound accompanied almost instantly by a scratching noise on the back door.

"Oh, yeah. We got another little guy. A.J. brought him home from work yesterday." Eve opened the back door and in raced a mutt the color of mud. She tried to catch him but missed.

Dylan squealed at first as the little dog jumped at him, licking and sniffing in all-out glee. Eve shut the door and came over to the rescue.

"His name is Buster." She picked the little dog up, lifting her chin trying to get away from the dog's expressive ardor. "Buster, this is Dylan."

"Hi, Buster." Dylan put his hand out, and Buster jumped to lick it. Instantly Dylan jumped back and giggled.

"He's a little high-maintenance," Eve said, once again backing away from the dog's frantic attempts to show her how much he loved her. "Do you want to go outside and play with him? I'm sure he'd love to have somebody to run with."

"Sure." The saucer-like shape of Dylan's eyes made Blaine smile.

"Well, well. I thought I recognized that car," A.J. said, ducking in from the kitchen. A moment and he strode in dressed smartly in his EMT uniform. "Sorry I'm not dressed for the occasion."

"We're going to babysit while they go out," Eve said, standing and clearly expecting a firestorm.

"Out?" He sized up Blaine but withheld his assessment. He looked at Melody. "You're not working tonight?"

She dug her fingers into her back pocket. "Uh, not tonight. I've, uh, mostly been babysitting this summer." Her gaze went over to Blaine's, begging for help.

"Mel's been a real life-saver this summer." He put his arm around her, and this time there was no pretending to it. He admired her, and he was falling in love with her for real. There was no point in hiding it. His gaze turned to her and said as much. "I don't know what I would've done without her."

A.J.'s gaze registered extreme displeasure. "Babysitting? What about the store? What about school?"

Melody gazed only at Blaine, and her face held a soft smile of hope. "They're not going anywhere, but I sure am enjoying my summer."

There was a half a second of total awkwardness that neither Melody nor Blaine noticed.

"Hm. Well," Eve said, "you two better get going, or it will be time to be back."

Blaine was the first to break the connection, but he could tell Melody never really did. "I guess so. I'll just tell Dylan bye."

"I'll go with," Melody said, grabbing his hand. And they did.

When they were back in the car moments later, Melody had to force the air into her lungs. What was that anyway? Did the two of them just stand in A.J.'s house and act like they were together? She could've sworn they did, and she could've also sworn that it hadn't been an act.

"This feels weird," she whispered as they drove off.

He glanced at her. "What?"

"This. Being in a car with you and no Dylan. I don't think we've done this in like forever."

Blaine reached across the seat and pulled her fingers into his. "Forever's a long time." When he kissed them, Melody was pretty sure this wasn't an act, but she was no longer sure it wasn't a dream.

"This is probably all cold," Blaine said, realizing only then that the little paper bag he'd packed the food in was not about keeping anything the right temperature. He pulled the supermarket chicken out. "I wanted it to be all nice and everything. Not sure how well that's going to work."

The coleslaw was next in the little plastic container followed by the rolls and the salad. Sitting on the blanket he'd already spread out, Melody watched him skeptically.

"I know you don't eat much at the burger joint, but I thought…" Blaine laid it all out and pulled out the two paper plates and forks. Then he sat back looking at all of his efforts, realizing how pitiful they actually were. "This was really supposed to be more romantic. I had it all planned out in my head. I just…"

"It's fine, Blaine. Really. It's great. " Something in her voice indicated that it really was although how that was possible, he wasn't sure. "When did you do all of this anyway?"

"After work, well actually during work. I conned Jason into covering for me." Blaine took the two bottles of iced tea that was by now hot out of the bag. He spun the bottle to her. "Hot tea?"

She laughed. "You're crazy."

"Sorry," he said, deflating on the word. "This really looked so much better in my head."

Again she laughed. "Hey, don't worry about it. We're together. That's all that matters, right?" For a moment their gazes held, then she let hers drop. "I don't want more than the salad anyway."

Irritation surged in him. "Is that all you ever eat?"

She shrugged. "It's good for you."

"Not if it's all you ever eat." Although he was extremely frustrated, he reined his comments back in. This was going to be harder than he'd thought. "Don't you want something else too? Chicken at least?"

Seeming to shrink at the question, she shook her head. He wanted to argue so bad it was killing him, but he swallowed that and handed her a plate with only salad on it. Then he loaded his own. He had to find something else to talk about while they ate or they would both end up with indigestion.

"I got an A in one of my classes first summer, a C in the other, but they average out to a B." He ripped into his chicken. "How'd you do?"

"I got two B's. One was high, I think. One was low."

"So are you still thinking about changing your major?"

"I went in on Wednesday and got some papers. From what I can tell, I'm about 18 hours from being able to get a general, which would be great for a teaching assistant."

"What about teaching for real? Is that something you'd like to do?"

She took in a breath. "I don't know if I could handle that. A whole classroom? That's a lot of responsibility."

"Maybe you could do some substituting in the fall, see how

you like it."

"Hmm. I hadn't thought about that. I can't take all 18 hours then anyway. Maybe I could do like 9 and 9, and do some subbing." She took a bite of salad as she considered the idea. "That might work actually."

He took a bite of coleslaw just as she nailed him with her gaze.

"So, Dylan said something interesting today."

"Uh-oh."

She angled another bite at her mouth. "He said you're moving. So what's up with that?"

The bite went down the wrong path. He choked and grabbed for his tea. "Hmm. Yeah. Well. That was something I wanted to talk to you about."

Angling another bite at her mouth, she raised her eyebrows. "So talk."

He felt like he was on the witness stand. "Well, things have been pretty bad for awhile now, but well… It just feels like they're getting worse." He set his still-filled plate to the side and took another drink. "Mom left last weekend and didn't show back up until Wednesday. She's trashed again." His gaze left hers and slid out to the darkening sky somewhere out beyond the tall buildings and city lights. "I love her, you know? But I just… I don't know how to help her and keep Dylan safe, and it's getting to the point, I think I'm going to have to choose."

"Did Dave show up again?"

Blaine shook his head. "No, but she was with him."

"She told you that?"

"In one of her infamous moments of full-disclosure." A bug landed on his cole slaw, and he flicked it away. "Dylan's scared to death, and I just don't think it's fair to him to stay anymore."

Melody took a drink. "He's been saying that."

"What?"

"Nothing big. Just that he gets scared sometimes, and he's glad you're there. I think he's scared for your mom too."

He nodded. "So am I, but what do you do when somebody doesn't want your help? I've tried to get her to meetings and stuff, but she just won't go. She says she can quit, but she never does." The questions drifted through him for a moment and then he sighed. "So we're moving. I don't know when or where or how, but we can't stay there anymore."

"And what about your mom?"

The middle of him plunged off a cliff. "I don't know. I really don't."

They sat in silence for a long moment. Her salad was hot and not all that great, so Melody set it aside and took another drink. She let her gaze go up to the trees and into the deepening night beyond. "It's nice out here." Shaking her hair back, she leaned on one elbow and just let herself relax.

"It's nice being here with you," he said as his gaze went only to her.

"That's strange. I kind of thought you didn't want to be around me anymore." Why she kept being that honest with him, she had no idea, but it was almost like she was challenging him to break up with her. "After last week and all."

His gaze fell. "I'm sorry about that." The breath he let out was hard and guilt-ridden. "I'm such a dope."

"You're not…"

He held up his hand. "Let me finish." His gaze drilled into her. "Mel, I'm messed up. I am. I've known that for a long time now. At first it was because I had all the money in the world, and so I thought I was better than everyone else. Then I fell off that high horse, hard. It was like falling into a sewer and trying to figure out what direction you could go to get out of the crap. But everywhere I went, there was just more crap.

"I hated myself. I hated everybody else. I hated life and everything about it. It was awful. I blamed my dad and my mom and life and God. I wanted somebody to snap their fingers and put everything back the way it was, but nobody was doing that. I spent a lot of years really angry at the world for what it had done to me.

"I used that anger as an excuse to create this whole other life for myself. I was Blaine Donovan, ultra-rich jerk who jetted off to exotic destinations on a whim and had no problems in the world, except it was all a total lie. It wasn't until Eve pointed out that I was trying to be two different people that I really woke up to how stupid I was being. I finally had to take a real look at my life, so I could figure out what to keep and what to ditch. But as good as my intentions are even now, I'm still me. I still mess up on a pretty regular basis." His gaze found hers. "Like I did with you."

"Blaine…"

"No. I know I messed up, Mel. I know it. I can see it in your eyes when I can't tell you what's going on with me, when I freak because you want to make a decision that might help me out. I see how much I hurt you, but I just can't seem to stop. It's like life is swirling around me, and I can't figure out what the thing is that's going to fix it for everybody."

"You don't have to fix it for everybody. Just do your best, and be honest."

The words hung between them as the breeze wafted through the park.

"Be honest." He took a breath, seeming to consider that. "Well, okay. Letting you in scares me to death." He looked right at her, and she felt his words as much as she heard them. "Being me scares me to death too. I mean, who am I—really? Am I the guy who wears designer clothes to work, or the guy who cleans up his mother's vomit? Am I the guy who has the Lanas and the Farins of the world wanting to go out with me, or the guy who's so broke, he can add what he has in the bank on paper without a pencil? I've tried to figure it out, but it just doesn't make any logical sense no matter how hard I try. It's like I'm living two lives, and I don't really know how to be either one."

For a long moment, Melody said nothing. Then she moved to look at him ever so slightly. "Do you want to know who I think you are?" She waited, and when there was no answer, she continued. "I think you're a really awesome guy who has more on his shoulders than anybody can possibly handle alone. You're trying to be everything to everybody, but there comes a point when that doesn't work. You have to figure out what's most important to you and be that."

He laughed. "Now you sound like Eve."

"Well," she took a breath, "maybe Eve's onto something. You know, I think this has less to do with who the world thinks you are and more to do with who you think you are. Who are you, Blaine? Who do you want to be?"

He shook his head and let out a breath. "I want to be the guy that stands up for what's right. I want to do it right because that's the way it's supposed to be, and so people might think I'm worth something."

"Worth something?" Melody shook her head. "Blaine, you are worth something. Don't you see that? You are kind and gentle and so good with Dylan it brings me to tears sometimes. I love that about you, but you act like it's something to be ashamed of, like you have to make everybody believe you are someone you're not to be 'worth something' as you say."

"But that's what the world expects. To take charge. Get in there and do it. They don't give medals for caring, you know."

"Well, maybe they should. Maybe they've got it all wrong. Maybe caring is more important than all the money and education and accomplishments that you can string together." Melody took a breath and looked at him with open love. "You are a good person, Blaine. You are. You work yourself into the ground to make things better for your family and for everybody around you. You show up early, work late, put your all into every project you take on, and still you don't think you're doing enough." It was like she could suddenly see all the way to the middle of him. "You know, I could be wrong about this, but I think you've gotten really good at being your own worst enemy. I think you need to learn to give yourself a break."

"That's easy for you to say. How do I let Dylan down like that? How do I not do everything I'm doing?"

Even she had to admit that it was hard to see the way out of needing to do everything. "I don't know. Maybe you don't, but maybe it's worth taking a look at it to see if you can. The money thing. Surely there are grants for students like you, scholarships, something."

"I've started the paperwork before, but it takes forever."

"Okay. So you let me help."

"Mel, I can't…"

"See that's what I'm talking about. Somebody offers to help, and you instantly shut them off with 'I can't.' 'I can't let you do that.' 'I can't ask you to help.' What is that? Huh, Blaine? Is it pride or something else?"

Truthfully Blaine had no answer for that question. All he knew was that asking for help sent him into spasms of feeling like a total failure such that even actually failing didn't do.

Because he'd been working on being truthful, he took a breath and shared what was in his heart although it felt like dangling over a cliff with no rope. "It's so hard for me to ask somebody for help."

"Why?"

This was so hard, hard to go deep, hard to admit what he'd never even admitted to himself. "Because it feels like it makes me a terrible failure, like everybody's looking at me and whispering what a failure I am. I feel like they will find out what I already know."

"What's that?"

"That I'm not good enough. That I'm not smart enough or strong enough to really do it. That I'm a waste of good space." He reached down and wrapped his hands over his ankles.

"That's why you act like you're better than everybody?" she asked softly. "Because you feel worse?"

Although it took more than a moment, he finally nodded. "I figure if I con them into believing I'm that guy, maybe they'll believe it and never have to get to know the real me."

"Which is who?"

His gaze came up to hers. "Somebody's who's scared to death and wants to do the right thing but doesn't have a clue what that is or how to do it."

"Oh, man. Welcome to the club." Melody shook her head and laughed softly. "I feel like that every minute of my life."

"And that doesn't bother you?"

It took a moment to answer. "Well, yeah, it bothers me… sometimes it bothers me a lot. I look around at the Eves of the world, and I think, 'What am I missing here? Why does life just fall into place for them, and it just doesn't for me no matter how hard I try?'"

The question sliced through Blaine like a double-edged sword. Sitting there, being honest with him, Melody couldn't know the spirit-searing heartache Eve had been through in the past week. As he listened, he began to see something he'd never really noticed before. Underneath the veneer of who they presented themselves to be, there were a lot of similarities to people down deep. They all had dreams and desires. Conversely they all had fears and guilt, things they would change, and things they would do everything in the world to get to do over.

Sitting here in front of him was not Melody, a traveler who happened to cross paths with his, but a soul, a spirit with a story, a distinct but still similar story. That story shaped her, made her who she was, just as every other person had their own story. Yes, there was the outside package, but that wasn't the whole story.

He thought about Eve—beautiful to a fault and yet broken and hurting underneath. His thoughts went to A.J., and although nothing in him wanted to admit it, the truth was staring at him too hard to dismiss it. As he went, person by person through those in his life, he saw their desperate attempts to hide the hurt and fear with… what? Everything. Clothes. Shoes. Money. Cars. Education. Position. Status. And down the other spectrum drugs, alcohol, anger, violence, selfishness. As he thought about it, he realized that it was the same disease just with different symptoms.

"Where'd you go?" Melody asked, and he felt her gaze.

His gaze swept through hers. "Have you thought any more about the God thing?" It seemed so central to everything because that piece was the one on which his life had begun to turn, and he wanted to share that with her.

"Well, since we're being honest." She smiled at him. "I prayed the other day. I don't know if I did it right or anything, but I felt so bad for you that day you came in. And that morning I prayed for you. Actually I just kind of talked to God, but it was the first time I've ever really done that."

His heart swelled toward her. "And how did it feel?"

She considered the question. "Good. Peaceful. Like there was really Somebody there listening."

Blaine nodded. "I've been reading my Bible, and it's the weirdest thing. It always talks about something I'm going through, no matter where I open it. I'm starting to think that it isn't a coincidence." He grew quiet and then spun and lay down on the blanket. The night had advanced in earnest and cool air had replaced hot. The second hand ticked off several seconds before she lay down shoulder-to-shoulder next to him.

The universe stretched above them. He had to ask the question because it was on his heart. "What would you think about going to church?"

His heart dangled on the end of that question for a long moment.

"With you?" she finally asked.

Letting his head fall to the side, he looked at her. "Yeah. What would you think about going to church with me?"

It took a breath to settle the thought. "Well, maybe I wouldn't say no."

They stayed like that then, side by side, just being together until both were stiff from the chill. Then together they packed up and drove to Eve's. There was much less tension, many fewer walls between them now.

Only a couple blocks from Eve's Melody looked over at him. "Isn't it weird to be for real?"

He glanced at her. "How do you mean?"

"I mean to be able to talk about something other than the weather and the latest CDs with somebody, to really be honest."

He smiled full-on. "Yeah, it's pretty cool."

"Yes, it is."

There was a softness about their new friendship as they walked up to Eve's. She came to the door before they'd even rung the bell. Even she looked different. Blaine couldn't explain it really, but it was like he was seeing the real in others rather than the façade now.

"Hey," he said softly following her into the living room as he kept careful hold of Melody's hand. "How was he?"

"Wonderful," Eve said.

In the living room, the sight completely stopped Blaine like a shot to the heart. On the couch lay A.J., his arm under Dylan's head, both asleep.

"They were watching the game," Eve explained as she got Dylan's bag. "I'm not sure which one fell asleep first."

Watching them, the older man protectively cradling the boy, the venom Blaine had felt toward A.J. slowly dissipated a molecule at a time. Maybe A.J. wasn't the horrible guy Blaine had made him out to be. Maybe just like Melody with Eve there really were things he didn't know about A.J., things that would make his animosity understandable.

It was a thought Blaine was still thinking Monday afternoon when Eve walked into the break room.

"Looks like talking went over well," she said, getting her water and sitting down.

"You could say that."

"What else could you say?" she asked, her smile coming through.

"Well, I could ask if you know a good church."

Her eyes shot open.

"No, not like that," he said with a laugh. "Don't go marrying us off just yet."

"Oh, man." She sat back and put her hand on her chest. "You scared me there for a minute."

"No. We talked about it, and we want to try church, but I have no idea how to even go about that."

"Well, I've got a few if you want to hear them."

"I'm listening."

Sixteen

Somehow when he'd asked the question, Blaine hadn't put the coming Sunday together with Sunday, the 14th—moving day. When Eve suggested they all go to church before showing up to move Jeff and Lisa, Blaine hadn't had the heart to decline. And so on Sunday morning, the three of them—Melody, Dylan, and he—pulled up at St. Mark's looking like three deer caught in headlights.

"Are you sure this is a good idea?" Melody asked, readjusting the scoop-necked blouse that was more scooped because there wasn't as much of her as when she'd obviously bought it. Twice he'd seen her pull hair out of her head, and he knew it was only a matter of time as to when he would ask now. But he would ask. They would talk. He knew that with no doubt.

"It'll be fine," he said with far more solidity than he felt. When they parked, he got out and ran around to get her. After a moment of readjusting, the three of them headed for the stairs.

"I feel out-of-place," she said, leaning in to him.

"And I don't?" he whispered back. That made her clutch his hand even harder. They had only barely made it through the doors when he caught sight of Eve waving at them from across the large gathering area. It was a moment more before he recognized A.J. standing next to her. No hat and in a suit he look radically different—kind of like the radical difference Blaine had been noticing in a lot of people these days.

They walked up, and Blaine offered his hand to a surprised A.J. "A.J."

"Blaine." A.J.'s gaze went from him to Melody, and there was a swirl of things in that look. "Mel." He started for her hand but the handshake ended in a short hug. "I'm glad you came."

When she stepped back, there was a soft smile on her face as she looked up at Blaine. "Blaine convinced me."

And for the very, very first time there was almost non-hatred when A.J. looked at him.

"Shall we?" Eve asked, and the little caravan started for the door.

Melody was serious about the feeling out of place thing. She did. Every inch of her did. Everyone else had on expensive clothes and heels she couldn't walk on in her dreams. Nothing about this felt even vaguely familiar, and it was feeling less so by the second. She followed A.J. into the bench, and Dylan and Blaine followed her. When she sat, the only thing she could think was, How in the world did I get here?

That thought was on loop through the first song and the piano music with the lady talking from the front. She snagged on a few words. Forgiveness. Joy. Salvation. But the meaning of the message went way over her head. She fought not to squirm. No wonder she didn't do this. The bench was hard, and the service was getting even longer than she'd expected. As she sat there, she decided, if Blaine wanted to do this in the future, he was going to have to do it alone because she wasn't coming back.

Another person got up and read some words. It made even less sense, and Melody fought the urge to look at her watch. The missed sleep over the last couple of nights began to encroach on her, and she stifled the yawn. She wondered how much longer the service would be, and she would've asked but figured that wouldn't go over very well.

"Good morning," the main preacher said, stepping to the podium.

"Good morning," the crowd responded, and as Melody looked out, she realized how many people there actually were. This wasn't some tiny, insignificant gathering. This was an actual crowd.

She sat up straighter, determined to listen if for no other reason than to be able to carry on a logical conversation later.

"What do you need to bring today to the cross?" the preacher asked. "We all have them—those things that need to be brought to the cross. Things that we've been through, things that have happened to us and to those we love that we don't understand. Things we're angry about or hurt over. You may think that looking at the person next to you, that they don't have anything to bring to the cross, but you would be wrong because we all have those things. Every single one of us.

"So what are your things? What things keep you in fear and bondage? What things do you not even want to tell your ceiling at night? What things keep you from experiencing God's love? What thoughts run through you on a daily basis—thoughts of inadequacy maybe, or failure or fear?"

Melody wanted to look over at Blaine. Surely he was as confused by how this preacher could've known what they talked about as she was. But she didn't have the chance.

"Maybe it's your station in life, your job, what you drive, what you wear. Maybe those are the things that chain you to believing you are not worth the Father's love. Or maybe it's something closer to your heart—a wayward child, a marriage that's in trouble, a dream that seems like it will never come true. Look in your heart. What is it that is tearing you apart? What is it that is keeping the wall between you and the love God has for you?

"The world comes up with a hundred and one of these things to convince us that God could never love us and that we shouldn't even love ourselves. We don't have a nice enough house, a pretty enough lawn, a big enough income. We don't look like the models in the magazines, or we don't lead exciting lives like the people on the screen—big or small.

"We know these things are gnawing at our souls, but instead of giving them to God, we rush around trying to be everything to everyone, never stopping long enough to consider what we are to God."

The words hit closer to the center of her heart with every round. Finally, Melody put her head down, fighting to breathe through them.

"The Bible talks about God's love for us. Here's what it says, 'There was a man who found a treasure in a field, and he immediately went and sold everything he owned and bought that field.' 'He went and sold everything he had, and he bought that field.' Do you think that man understood the unimaginable value of the treasure he had found? Sure he did. That's why he sold everything. He sold his cars and his house. He sold his clothes and his gym membership. He even sold that gold watch he'd gotten when he retired from the company. He went out and sold everything. Why? Because he had found something that he understood to be of even greater value, something immeasurably better than what he already had.

"And what is that treasure of immeasurable value that Jesus talks about in this parable? It's Him of course. Jesus Christ in His full glory and splendor, shining like gold. The one thing that happens when you really find Him is you are willing to give everything else away to hold onto Him.

"Ah, yes. True. But here's the amazing thing. Jesus was not only speaking about Himself. He was not just speaking of the treasure He is. He was also speaking about treasure you are." The preacher's words slowed and then stopped. He pointed at the crowd. However, Melody felt as if he was pointing only at her. She couldn't have looked away had she tried.

"Jesus Christ came one day to your field, and He found in you a priceless treasure. He looked at you and He said, 'Here. This is the treasure I am willing to give everything away to possess.' And then he did give everything away. He gave His very life to buy your field because of the immense treasure you hold."

He took a breath, gathered himself, took a half step backward. "And yet we still cling to these things that mean nothing whatsoever. Why? When today, right now, this minute, Jesus is asking you, 'What do you need to lay at the foot of the cross? What do you need to give to Me so you don't have to carry it anymore? What addiction? What fear? What is holding you back from Me and My love? Put it down, right here, at my feet, please. Put it down, and just let Me love you. Let Me hold you and show you what a treasure I think you are.'"

There was silence for a moment.

"I invite you to close your eyes and go deep inside. In your heart of hearts, look at Jesus as He holds His hands out to you to receive you in His embrace. In the silence of your heart, look at Jesus and say, 'Lord, today I give you those things that have kept me from You. I see now that You and only You bring real, lasting peace. I lay down my thoughts, my fears, my burdens. I lay them at the foot of Your cross. I lay my trials and all my dreams that haven't gone the way I'd hoped. God, I give them all to You now. I give You the times I have succeeded and the times I have failed. I give You the life I wanted and the life I'm living. Lord, I give them all to You, You Who love me beyond measure, Who bought and paid for me with Your own blood.

"'Jesus, I relinquish those things that are holding me back from loving You and those that are holding me back from letting You love me, today, right now.' Amen."

Tears dampened Melody's cheeks as she sniffed and said, "Amen." Her heart was heavy with all the preacher had said. Peace had felt so very far away for so very long. Was this why? Was it because she hadn't found the treasure hidden in a field? And even more, was it possible that He had been searching for her all this time as well? It was just too overwhelming to get her mind around.

As the service continued, she glanced over at Blaine who looked to be having as much trouble digesting everything as she was. "God," she prayed softly, "You and I both know that Blaine is a hidden treasure. Please, help him see that."

And then a whisper of a voice went through her heart, startling her with its clarity. And so are you, Melody. So are you.

"We'll meet you over at Jeff's," A.J. said as they all walked out to the parking lot afterward.

Blaine's hand was in Melody's for the simple fact that if it wasn't, he might not have been able to walk at all. She said something to confirm the plan, and together they walked out to her car. The fact that A.J. might see her car and start asking questions never even occurred to Blaine. He was much too overcome by the service.

When they got in the car, he still sat for longer than it normally took to prepare for a drive.

Melody glanced over at him, a question in her eyes and looking as shell-shocked as he felt. "If I didn't know any better, I would think that guy was at the park listening Friday night."

He felt the same way, but words still failed. Glancing in the back seat, he gauged his words carefully. "You're not going to believe this, but I just read that passage about the hidden treasure this week."

Her eyes widened. "Did you know… they were going to use it today?"

"How could I? I didn't even know we were coming until yesterday."

The implications of everything that was happening around them seemed incomprehensible. Blaine fought the shaking of his hand as he started the car and put it into drive. He reached onto the dash for his sunglasses, seeing next to nothing.

Could this really be a coincidence, or could it be something bigger, something more that he was just beginning to tap into but might never understand?

They had all changed from their Sunday clothes to moving clothes, and Melody was busy stuffing pillows into a giant box in the back bedroom when Eve walked in. Eve stood for a long moment gazing up at the wallpaper ringing the room. After a minute, Melody stopped to look up trying to see what she was looking at.

"It's too bad they can't take the teddy bear paper with them," Melody said because it was just too weird to stand there and say nothing. "It's so cute."

"Yeah," Eve said, and sadness dripped from her voice. She walked over and ran her hand slowly over the wall that was painted in several colors. It looked like it had been sponge painted or something.

The stuffing slowed as Melody watched Eve. There was something unsettling about how quiet she was. It was as if she was standing at a gravestone rather than next to the wall of a baby's room. Of course Melody knew about Eve's past, how she had lost her husband in a terrible accident. But what was bringing this sadness on now? Now when they really needed to be working or they would never get finished.

Melody picked up the comforter with the teddy bear on it and fanned it out to fold it. Because of its smooth surface, the comforter didn't want to cooperate and stay in the folds she was trying to put in it. "Ugh. No, don't do that." The edges slipped out of their places.

"Oh, sorry," Eve said, turning, and Melody saw her swipe her fingers under her eyes. "Here. Let me help."

As they folded the comforter, Melody watched Eve. Something was obviously bothering her, but there was no way it was Melody's place to ask. When the comforter was folded, the two of them stuffed it into the box on top of the pillows.

"It's a good thing they already got most of this, or we'd never make it," Melody said.

"No kidding. Kudos to the moving crew yesterday." Eve stepped back and sniffed.

Melody went over to the closet and opened it. Thankfully there was only a small shoe left in it. "Oops. Looks like they forgot something." She swiped it from the floor and held it up.

"Yeah, that's probably Alex's," Eve said, sounding like she was being strangled. "Just throw it in one of the boxes." She stood for one more second. "I'm going to go see what the guys are doing." And she left.

Not wanting to, Melody gazed after her. Strange. She was acting like this was her own house she was leaving not just the house of friends she happened to know. With a shrug Melody set about taping and labeling the box.

"Be careful with this one. It's dishes," Lisa said as Blaine came back to the kitchen for another load. He didn't even want to think what this would be like if they hadn't had most of it moved already. There was no table in the kitchen, no chairs either. Thus they had eaten lunch from bags on the floor.

"Got it," he said, lifting the box from the floor with ease. He took it outside and put it in the back of A.J.'s SUV. That's where they were trying to put the breakable stuff. On the way back in, he met up with Melody hefting a box twice her size. "Would you like some help with that?"

"I'll pay you," she said breathlessly.

With a smile he yanked the box up and started to the trailer. "This could get interesting."

"Haha." She turned and walked back in the house.

Blaine smiled. He loved teasing her. She had such a dry sense of humor although she caught his jokes, she didn't knock herself out to pretend he was hilarious. He set the box on the trailer.

"Help!" A.J. called from the door, and Blaine turned and raced to the porch. The top piece of the mirrored hutch wobbled dangerously until Blaine stabilized it. Picking up one end, he walked backward to the trailer.

"We need to get this secure. I don't want a lawsuit," Blaine said jokingly.

"Yeah. You and me both," A.J. said. Together they laid the thing up against one of the rails, and A.J. checked it to make sure it was secure. "Maybe we should put a blanket around this. I'd hate for it to get scratched."

"Oh, I saw Jeff put one in their car." Blaine headed for it.

"Figures Jeff would be moving the blankets and letting us do the heavy stuff."

Blaine retrieved the blanket and brought it back over. "From what I've seen, he's no dummy."

A.J. laughed a little and took one end of the blanket. "This is true. It's like he knew we couldn't come yesterday, so he plans this little job for today."

"I think they actually moved quite a bit yesterday. There really isn't much left."

Carefully A.J. secured the hutch that now resembled a green ghost to the railing. "Well, that's good to know." He dusted his hands off and looked at his watch. "It's after three. It's nearly an hour there, and then we've got to unload."

"Man, and I thought we were doing good." Blaine followed A.J. back to the house. They really were going to have to hurry.

They had just loaded the last two boxes—knickknacks from the kitchen. Lisa, Eve, and Melody were cleaning. Why, Blaine wasn't really sure. It wasn't their problem anymore, but it was like the Merry Maids had shown up in force.

"It's a woman thing," Jeff assured the two guys. "You should've seen how long Lisa cleaned on her apartment after we moved her out. I didn't think she'd ever get finished."

Melody was in the back vacuuming. It was the only movable appliance left in the house.

Jeff stood, assessing the situation for mere seconds. "Tell you what. Why don't y'all come in our car when you're finished? There's room for the vacuum in the back. That way we can head on and start unloading this stuff."

"Sounds good," Lisa said as she scrubbed on one spot harder than Blaine had ever done anything in his lifetime. "We'll be there in a little while."

Kissing his wife, Jeff nodded. "Don't clean too much."

"You know us," Eve said, wiping down the stove one last time.

Jeff laughed. "That's what I'm afraid of." He smiled at Lisa one more time. "Drive careful."

"You too."

The vacuum cleaner was still whirring somewhere in the house. Blaine wanted to go have that good-bye moment with Melody. It wasn't until he thought about Dylan that he found his excuse. "I'm just going to go tell Mel we're taking off."

"Don't take too long," Jeff said. "Hey, Dylan. Wanna ride shot gun? I'll let you program the GPS."

"Sure!"

At that very second, Blaine knew he was sunk. Trying not to think about it, he hurried back to the bedrooms. He found Melody sucking up a spider web in the corner.

"We're taking off," he verily shouted over the vacuum.

She spun like she'd been shot. "Wh…?" In annoyance, she hit the off button plunging the room into silence. "What?"

"I said, 'We're leaving.'" He pointed out the door. "The girls are staying to finish cleaning, but if we don't get this stuff unloaded, it's going to be midnight before anybody gets to bed."

"Oh." She looked genuinely disturbed.

"Don't worry. I'll leave your car. You won't have to ride with them."

"Oh," she said again, still not looking very happy about the situation. She raked her fingers across her hair and flicked the hair that came out with her fingers. "What about Dylan?"

Blaine swallowed the words. "He's already got shot gun with Jeff. Don't ask."

Concern traced through her eyes. "Will you be okay?"

He smiled and winked. "I'm always okay." Quickly he kissed her cheek. "I'd better get, or they're going to fire me."

"Okay. See ya." And he left her, standing over the vacuum in an empty room. It wasn't the best idea in the world, but the guys really did need his help. Trying not to think about leaving her there like that, he hustled out to the vehicles. Once outside, it took less than nothing to assess the seating arrangement.

"Hang on," he said to A.J. "Just let me grab my book."

A.J. nodded and angled the SUV with the little trailer on the back toward the white car. Thinking it could be the only thing to save his sanity, Blaine grabbed his Economics book out. If riding in the SUV got completely unbearable, at least he would have an excuse to do something other than talk.

Melody was finished vacuuming. The guys had been gone for quite awhile. She checked her watch, nearly 4:30. They would need to be going soon too. She started for the kitchen but stopped when she heard them talking.

"I know it's stupid," Eve said, and Melody heard the emotion in her voice. "But I about lost it earlier in Alex's room. Remember when A.J. and I came over to paint?"

"Remember it? I'm surprised the poor house survived."

"Yeah, but I just started thinking about how much has changed, about how much is changing, and how fast it's changing. I mean when I was a little girl, I had this whole idea of how my life would go. I'd go to college, meet some preppy guy. We'd get married and have babies, the whole nine yards. But today standing there in that room, I just thought how different it's all been than I thought it would be, you know? First Dustin, and now this… It's just…" There were tears now, not just emotion. "It's so different than I expected."

Lisa's voice had moved closer to Eve's. "You know I would fix this if I could."

Eve sniffed hard. "I know, but there's nothing anybody can do. It just is what it is, and I've got to find a way to deal with that and keep moving, but sometimes it's so hard."

"You know, I don't know if you know much about Ashley, Gabe's wife, but they went through this too. She had cancer years ago before they even met, and because of it, she can't have kids."

Again Eve sniffed, but this one sounded surprised. "I never knew that."

"They don't talk about it much. But she told me once how much it meant to her that Gabe would want to marry her even after he found out."

The sniffing continued. "Did they ever think about adopting?"

"I think they looked into it, but Ashley said her heart just wasn't in it at the time. That doesn't mean that they never will, but then she got into teaching, and I think that helps. She said the kids at school are like her own. She gives them the love she never got to give her own kids."

"But it's not the same."

"No. But that's just it. It never is. One person's experience is never the same as somebody else's. I think the point is to find a place you can give the love in your heart, and then you give it. If that's kids, great. If it's conventional, great. If not, then maybe God's got something else in mind."

"I just feel so bad for A.J."

Melody's heart snagged on the name, wondering what all this had to do with him.

"A.J.'s a great guy, and when you guys find the path God's calling you to, you'll see just how great he is."

The latch on the vacuum cleaner clicked, and Melody realized they'd probably heard it. Quickly she pushed the little red thing into the kitchen. "All done."

It took little to notice Eve wiping her eyes. It took everything to not react to it.

"Well," Lisa said, getting back to work, "I think we're almost done in here, too. Looks like it's time to get going."

A.J. glanced over at Blaine who had been trying to read without much luck for thirty minutes. Sunday afternoon traffic was pretty light for summer, and they were making good time. But no matter how hard he tried, his thoughts just wouldn't focus on macro-economic theories.

"Are you a business major?" A.J. asked.

"What?" Blaine's attention jerked up. Then he caught the look A.J. angled at his book. Blaine raised his eyebrows skeptically. "Economics? Uh, no. Least favorite subject. It's a prerequisite." He went back to the book.

"So you're still in school then?" There was a jab to that question.

"Yeah. I graduate in December. Architectural Design." Blaine bent his head to indicate he was reading—or trying to.

However, that seemed to interest A.J. "No kidding. Like

buildings and stuff?"

"Yeah, but I'll only get to do the drafting part for now, not much actual designing."

"Oh, why not?"

The money supply is tied to… "Because it's only a two year degree. You've got to have at least four to really get to design much of anything."

A.J. lifted his chin in understanding. "So why don't you get the four?"

Blaine exhaled hard. "Because at the rate I'm going, the two might kill me." Seeing he wasn't going to convince A.J. to quit talking, he took a breath and closed the book on his arm to keep his place. "I've been in school five years now. Because of work and other things, I couldn't really go full time."

"Oh, what other things?" Carefully A.J. changed lanes.

Life wrapped around Blaine's chest, choking the air out of him. "A lot of stuff. It just never really worked out for me to go full time."

A.J. nodded. "So you're not going to be working at Harmon's after December then?"

If Blaine didn't know better, he would've sworn A.J. sounded hopeful about that. "Depends if I can find something else that pays and has benefits. Nothing's really set in stone yet."

The sound of the tires on the pavement retook the conversation. After a minute, Blaine returned to his reading, but a thought went through him. He brushed it away and fought to concentrate. Scratching his head, he anchored his attention to the book, but it wasn't really working. One more futile attempt and he gave up. He glanced across the seat, measuring the question.

"Mind if I ask you something?"

"What's that?" A.J. barely glanced his direction.

"Well, you've known Mel for a long time. A lot longer than I have. And I was just wondering if you'd ever… well, has she ever talked about taking pills?"

"Pills?" The panic was instant and intense.

Blaine put up his hands. "No, I don't mean pills like drugs. I mean pills like, well, like diet pills." Why did he think this was a good idea? It wasn't. If he jumped out right now, maybe he wouldn't have to finish this conversation.

Although he looked like he wasn't really paying attention, A.J.

shifted in his seat. "Diet pills? Why do you ask that?"

Knowing it was fatal to continue, Blaine saw no other choice. "Well, that day we were out at the lake, I kind of found some in her purse. I know she's been dieting. There was that whole thing after the night she was with Bobby…"

A.J. slammed his fist into the steering wheel. "Cripes. I knew it. I knew he'd done it to her again."

Both confused and slightly afraid, Blaine stared at A.J. "Define 'again.'"

The glance was barely that. A.J.'s eyes grew darker and darker with each passing thought. "When we were in high school, that jerk asked her out our junior year. I told her going out with him was a really bad idea, but she wouldn't listen. He was always hanging around making these disgusting comments to her about how fat she was and how she was lucky to have him because most guys didn't date cows. It was disgusting. I tried everything I knew to get her to see what a jerk he was, but it didn't matter what I said or what I did, she just thought he was so wonderful, and if she just lost weight, she'd have a real chance with him."

The story faded, and Blaine fought with his heart not to jump to any horrible conclusions. "But she broke up with him, right?"

"More like he broke her. When she was beaten down to the point she completely hated herself, he told her he'd never really liked her and started going with Roxie Gallegos. Mel went into a real tailspin. She was sure he'd ditched her because of the weight thing. She started throwing up and doing really unhealthy things to lose weight. She just kept saying, 'If I just lose five more pounds, then he'll take me back. I can't lose him. He's the only one who's ever loved me.' It was horrible."

Ache for her broke over Blaine. He'd known, and yet he'd had no idea. "So this isn't a new thing then?"

When A.J. looked at him, the answer was clear. Slowly A.J. shook his head. "I wish."

Blaine considered that. He wondered how much if anything A.J. had noticed about her recent descent into dieting hell. Then another question overtook that one. "But why now? I mean there's Bobby, but she hasn't seen him since April, and I'm pretty sure that was just a one-time thing."

For the longest minute of his life, A.J. said nothing. Then he glanced to the passenger's seat. "You're serious?"

Heat flooded Blaine's whole body. This was about as serious as it got. "Yes, I'm serious. What's that supposed to mean?"

A.J. snorted. "It means I figured she was getting the same kind of crap from you."

"From me?" If Blaine could've cold-cocked the guy, he would have. "Why in the world would I do something like that?"

There was contempt written all over A.J.'s face. "Look at you. Money, cool, image-conscious. I'm sure every time she goes out with you, she's listening to you comparing her with all the hot girls you've bedded."

Blaine's fury reached a whole new level. "Now just where do you get off saying something like that? You don't know anything about me or my relationship with Mel."

"Well, I know you showed up at my house falling all over her, and then half-a-week later you were making out with some other hottie at the Bar Houston."

His anger fell into indignation and then boomeranged back into full-out anger. "I… That wasn't…" It took everything in him to rein in the rage. "For your information, Lana is a friend of mine. Yes, we used to go out. No, we're not going out anymore. She asked me out with a group of her friends. I went. I didn't know she was planning to throw herself at me."

"But you went out with another girl when you were seeing Melody."

"Yeah, I did, so sue me. We weren't serious or anything."

The anger etched on A.J.'s face. "You really don't get it, do you?"

"Get what?"

"That with Mel, it's always serious. She wants whatever guy she's with to be the one, and she's sure she's the problem in any relationship… even though she picks absolute jerks to go out with."

"Like you, I guess." It was a cheap shot, but Blaine was sick of getting beat up when it was A.J. who had hurt her more than any other guy she'd ever been with.

The shot hit its target square. "Me? What about me?"

"Oh, come on, A.J. Even you can't be that dumb. You've got to know she worships the ground you walk on. She was depressed for months when you got married, and getting married to Miss America probably didn't help her confidence in herself at all either.

Did you ever think about that?"

"But," A.J. stumbled on the word, "we weren't going together. We only dated like once."

"And…?"

The late day sun dipped farther and farther as A.J. searched for an answer. "And I told her kissing her was like kissing my sister." With that, A.J. let his head drop back against the headrest. "Oh, no." He closed his eyes, which Blaine did not take as the smartest move considering the traffic. When he opened his eyes again, A.J. shook his head. "This was about me."

"Yeah," Blaine said softly. "It was."

He let the understanding drain into A.J. There were some things that didn't need to be explained.

After minutes and minutes, A.J. glanced at him. "I feel like an idiot."

Well, there's a start. But Blaine said nothing.

"Did she…?" The pieces were clicking into place. "When she brought Bobby to the party…?"

"Yeah, it was to make you mad."

A moment and A.J. glanced at him. "And you?"

"Yeah," Blaine said, hating the word. "At first, but not anymore." The concern for her ripped through him, and his heart plunged with what she was doing to herself. "I'm really worried about her, A.J. She hasn't been eating anything. I mean like three bites of salad and some water. Her hair looks like seaweed, and I've seen her pull it out nearly by the fistful. She doesn't really talk about it, but I know she gets dizzy a lot, and Dylan's mentioned that she gets really bad headaches during the day."

"Have you asked her about it?" Now A.J. was concerned as well.

Blaine hated this answer, but he had to be honest. "No, I haven't."

"Why not?" They were back to A.J. being livid with a misstep by Blaine.

"Because I didn't know what to say!" Blaine exhaled slowly. "And I didn't know if it was my place to say anything. My track record with us hasn't been exactly stellar, and I didn't want to mess up again."

A.J. slid his fingers through his hair and then turned left into Jeff and Lisa's new neighborhood. "Well, we've got to say something. You know that, right?"

"We or me?" The question was barely there.

"Somebody."

The silver SUV with its little trailer pulled in behind Jeff's pickup and loaded flatbed. A.J. put it in park, and they watched Jeff get out ahead of them and stretch. He headed up to the garage and punched in a code, sending the garage door up on its track.

"I'm sorry about all of this," Blaine said, feeling the need to apologize for his part.

"Nah, man. It wasn't all your fault. I jumped to a lot of conclusions that weren't fair." A.J. sat, watching Jeff but not moving. "Thanks for telling me about this. I don't know what to do about it yet, but at least we're on the same page now."

Blaine nodded. "I really am worried about her."

"Yeah," A.J. said softly. "So am I."

Seventeen

The evening passed quickly. Once the girls showed up, the new house was a bee-hive of activity. A.J. and Blaine put up the microwave, and Melody was glad to see that for once they weren't at each other's throats. The drive and the required energy level of the exertion for the day were getting to her. Just before the pizza arrived, she went into the bathroom with four aspirins in her hand.

Three no longer made a dent in the headache. She downed them with a large gulp of water. When she came up for air, her gaze snagged on her own reflection. Her hair was getting much worse. She picked at it, and even the light touch was enough to break off a few more strands. With a frustrated sigh, she pitched them in the trash. Knowing there was nothing she could do about it now, she shut the lights off and went back to join the others.

The pizza had arrived, and she was so hungry, just the smell of it made her sick. Her throat started closing with every whiff, and throwing up was becoming a real possibility. However, she knew enough to know A.J. would suspect something if she said she didn't feel well. Somehow she had to get through dinner, eating enough to not let them know, but not so much that it made her sick. However, how she would ever do that was beyond her.

"I got breadsticks!" Jeff called over the four scavengers ripping the pizza apart at the table.

"Ugh. This is so good. I feel like I haven't eaten in a month," Eve said, biting into a piece of supreme dripping with cheese.

Melody stuck her fingers in the back pocket of her jeans and fought the nausea even as she tried not to watch. They can do that. Look at them. Eating like it doesn't even matter. It must be nice. Then her worst nightmare. Blaine stepped over to her, a plate of pepperoni pizza in hand.

"It's really good, Mel. Do you want me to get you a piece?"

"Oh, no. That's all right." Even the words were shaky. "Umm, I… got something on the drive over."

Eve's glance raked over her nerves. "But I thought you were behind us the whole way. Lisa kept checking the mirror to make sure we hadn't lost you."

How to breathe through the lies, Melody had no idea. "Oh, yeah. Well, I saved some of my sandwich from earlier. I ate it in my car."

Blaine didn't believe her. His look said that much.

"Come on, Mel," A.J. said, and his voice sounded strained. "At least have a breadstick."

The fact that everyone was now looking at her drove right through her. "Okay, fine. A breadstick." However, it was the one thing she knew. If you ever lose your willpower for one moment, you've lost the battle. She accepted the breadstick from A.J. and picked a small piece off just to show everybody that there was nothing to see here. They could move on with their lives.

Buttered and sprinkled with garlic, the breadstick made everything in her want to reverse course. Each bite was an all-out battle to get it down. But at least they were all talking again—to each other and not to her. However, she felt every glance Blaine sent her way. She sent a weak smile his direction, but it was clear he wasn't buying it.

With everything in her, she wanted to find a way to alter the conversation so that he wasn't focused on what she wasn't eating. "Oh, you know, Eve, I was going to ask you."

Eve's attention swung to her, and Melody swallowed hard.

"Umm, I was wondering what kind of shampoo you use. I mean your hair always looks so great, and mine is just getting eaten by the sun this summer."

"Oh, it's called Health & Shine. You can get it from any beauty supply place."

"Really?" Melody put a tiny piece of breadstick in her mouth. "You don't get it from Harmon's?"

Eve shook her head. "Theirs is way too expensive, and not nearly as good."

A breath, and Melody smiled. "Health & Shine. I'll have to try that."

When it was time to go, Blaine shepherded his bunch to the door. "Good luck getting everything set up."

"Hey, thanks for coming," Jeff said, clapping Blaine on the back. "We really appreciate it."

"Yeah, I would've never gotten the other place vacuumed without you," Lisa said. "You were a life-saver."

Beside him, Melody smiled. "Glad we could help. Well, we'd better get on the road. Blaine's got school in the morning."

When he turned, Blaine found A.J. standing there. Shaking hands, a serious message passed between them. Then A.J. stepped past him to Melody and gave her a hug that dragged Blaine's gaze to the ground.

A moment and another, and then A.J. stepped back, his gaze holding on Melody, his hands still on her arms. "You take care, okay?"

She smiled and nodded. "I will."

And then they extracted themselves from the evening. Blaine made sure to hold her hand down the steps and out to the car where he helped Dylan get in while Melody got herself in on the other side. Blaine got in, praying for the right words like he'd never prayed before. He pulled onto the street and pushed the play button on the CD player. With any luck, Dylan would fall asleep quickly.

Blaine looked in the rearview mirror. "Just lay your head down, buddy. It's going to be awhile."

The little eyelids were already drooping as the child nodded. He curled over on the seat, and Blaine waited two more songs before deciding the time had come.

"That preacher sure had some interesting things to say this morning, huh?" he said with a glance her direction.

She looked exhausted as she lay back on the headrest. "Man, that seems like eons ago."

He smiled over at her. "But it was really good, didn't you think? Especially the part about the things that keep you from feeling love."

Nodding, she simply let her head fall to the side so she could watch him. He felt it, the sweet, soft pride of her love of him. With everything in him, Blaine didn't want to destroy that although he was pretty sure his next words would.

He reached over and turned the music down. "Listen, Mel, I can't lie to you anymore. I found the pills, the other day when I was looking for your keys." The admission came out with a whoosh, and after a blink, her gaze fell from his face. He looked over at her. "I wasn't looking for them. I found them by accident."

Only silence came from her side, and he reached for her hand which gave nothing of a response.

"Come on. You're smarter than this. You've got to know this isn't healthy. I mean I know it isn't easy in this world with all the models and cover girls, but you've got to know that you're really beautiful just like you are."

If it was possible, she became even quieter, seeming to shrink completely to her side.

"Look, I don't know who you're trying to impress doing this, but you're scaring me. Okay? And A.J.'s not too thrilled about it either."

"A.J.?" The name snapped her out of her stupor. "What does he have to do with this?"

"Mel." Blaine looked over at her. "Look, I had to find out if this was something I should be worried about or not."

"You talked to A.J. about me?" Horror flashed through each word. "What gives you the right to do something like that?"

He could feel his grip on the relationship slipping. "I didn't know what else to do. I thought maybe he could tell me what to say and how to say it."

"So this was A.J.'s idea?"

"Yeah. Well, no. I mean it was both of our ideas. We just thought someone needed to say something. Come on, Mel, you've got to see how unhealthy this is. Not eating anything and taking pills on top of it? That can't be good for you."

This time when she retreated to her side, her demeanor was less sullen and more angry. She wrapped her arms around her middle and stared out into the night beyond.

"I'm not saying I don't understand," he continued, flailing for something that she would hear and accept. "I do, but this isn't the way to go about it."

She pushed her fingers through her hair. "I don't know what business is it of yours what I do or don't do. It's my body."

"Come on, Mel. You're the one who said we need to start making decisions together. Remember? I don't want to see you sick."

"I'm not sick."

"Then what's the deal with your hair coming out every time you touch it? And Dylan says you've been having headaches."

She threw her hands in the air. "Oh, great. Now you're grilling Dylan about this? Who else did you tell? Eve? Lisa? The Mormon Tabernacle Choir?"

Defensiveness crept into him. "No, I didn't tell them, but I would if I thought it would help."

Her mouth fell open as she stared at him. Then she shook her head, turned her gaze out her window, and put her knuckles to her mouth.

"Melody, come on. Don't be mad. You mean the world to me. You've gotta know that."

She spun. "Then lay off, okay? You don't know what it's like. You say you do, but you don't. You don't know what it's like to be made fun of, to be called 'Baby Fat' and 'Thunder Thighs.' You don't know what it's like to look in the mirror and hate everything about yourself. You don't know what it's like to want one slice of pizza but to know you can't have it because just looking at it will make you gain five pounds. You don't know what it's like to pass up every good thing you want to eat for a week and only lose maybe a pound—if you lose anything. Or to eat salad for a week and gain weight." She took a breath, but only a small one. "And don't tell me you do because you don't. You don't know what it's like, and you never will."

Blaine sat, absorbing how deeply frustrated she was. He understood that because he was frustrated too. "You're right. I don't know what that's like, but I do know what it's like to watch someone you love hurting themselves and knowing there's nothing you can do about it." He kept his gaze on the road only because there was no way he could look at her when he went into this deep, dark hole. "You know, I've watched my mother for ten years, drinking, taking drugs, and being with abusive guys who have beaten her senseless on more than one occasion. I've watched, and I've done everything I can think of to make her stop. I wish so bad I could do something to make her stop, to make her see what she's doing to herself. But she won't stop because she can't. Even if she wanted to anymore, she can't."

"That's different. I'm not on drugs."

"What do you call those pills in your purse?"

The silent anger was back.

"Mel, look, I'm not trying to lecture you, but you need to understand that I don't want to be with you because you've lost some weight or because you wear a certain size. I want to be with you because of you. I love you because of you. I love being around you. I love who I am when I'm with you. But watching you do this to yourself is killing me, and I don't know how to stop it other than saying, 'Please stop. Please.'"

Barely but he heard her breathing. He glanced at her.

"I didn't say anything before because I didn't want to risk losing what we've got. But then when I talked to A.J. today, I knew I couldn't not say anything anymore. You're too important to me. I don't want to lose you. I can't stand to think of my life without you."

For a second nothing. He drove, feeling helpless.

Then he heard the sniffle. When he looked over, she was crying. "Really?"

Wishing he could take her in his arms at that moment, he nodded. "Really. I love you so much, Melody. You've got to know that."

And then because the tears began sliding down her face for real, he pulled off the Interstate and onto a side street.

Instantly she sat up. "Why are we stopping?"

Blaine put the car in park and turned to gather her into his arms. "Because it's real hard to do this going 80." The closer she got to him, the closer he wanted her to be. When she was encircled in his arms, he tightened his grip. "I love you, Mel. I really do. I love you so much, and I hope you know that."

Her gaze came up to his, and she nodded with a soft smile. There was no reason in the world not to, and Blaine gave in to the tug of her spirit on his. Softly he dipped his head toward hers. And when their lips touched, he could've sworn he heard the angels singing.

For Melody the trip home could've lasted forever and she would not have complained. However, in no time they were pulling up to the curb at her house. As strange as it sounded, she felt different for the journey. She was still a little embarrassed that her hopeless attempts at losing weight had been so obvious, but at least he hadn't dumped her because she wasn't perfect. Not that it couldn't happen, but for tonight, it hadn't.

He put the car in park, sat for a second, and then turned to her. "I know you were mad about what I said before…"

"I'm not mad."

"You're not?"

She shook her head. "Embarrassed? Yes. Mad? No." Gently she reached across the seat to cradle his face with her hand. "How could I be mad at this face?"

His smile was amused and then shy. "I bet you say that to all the guys."

She laughed. "Yeah, all those wonderful, gorgeous guys who are just lined up at my doorstep."

The smile fell as he gazed into her eyes. "They should be."

Gratefulness for his life being in hers drifted through her. "I love you."

"Not half as much as I love you."

He reached for her, and after a tender kiss, she turned to lean into him. It was so peaceful to just relax there, completely protected and loved.

She hugged his arm to her tighter, shook her head, and let out a breath. "Can this really be for real?"

His lips brushed the top of her hair. "I sure hope so."

For four days Blaine had been searching the For Rent section of the newspaper. He was busy thinking through the ones that sounded promising when he turned onto his street on Thursday night. Dylan, thanks to a full day of roller skating in the park with Melody, was asleep in the seat next to him. He looked down at the child and smiled. He really was a wonderful kid.

In the next heartbeat as Blaine's gaze returned to the street, the flashing blue and red lights punctuating the night around him drove a knife of indescribable dread through his heart. Simultaneously accelerating and careening backward away from it all, he fought to judge in his head which house they were hovering around. He crept up the street closer and closer until he was almost on top of the house with all the lights. His house. Their house.

An ambulance stood off to the side. Horror arched through him. It took everything in him to get his hands to stop shaking enough to get car into park and the window down. He reached out and opened the door from the outside latch. He nearly fell into the street when the door gave way.

Stumbling and numb, he shut the door as quietly as possible and then raced up the front walk. He felt the curious stares of the neighbors from behind their curtains. They knew. They all did, and so did he. At the door he met up with a burly police officer who stepped into his path.

"Crime scene, son. You can't go in there."

"I'm…" Blaine struggled to peer over the man's shoulder, to get closer, to understand what was going on. "My mom…?"

"You live here?"

"Uh, yes. Yes, Sir." Still, he couldn't get a good look inside. What was going on? Why wouldn't they let him get to her? "Is she…? Is she okay?"

"Gunshot victim... female... deceased... possibly drug related," a nearby policeman said into the radio on his shoulder. "Ambulance on scene will transport the body to coroner's office."

The words spun through Blaine's fear and shell-shocked mind. "Deceased? What? No!"

Commotion at the door yanked their gazes that direction as two paramedics descended the steps with a gurney between them. No rational thoughts remained as Blaine pushed past the officer to get to the gurney.

However, the sheet covered all of the figure underneath, even the face. The steel contraption beneath was as cold as the sheet lying on it, and sanity jerked away from him.

"No! Mom? Mom!" The numbness in him crumpled into a sea of heartache and horror. "No! Mom? No! What happened? What happened to her?" Wild-eyed he grabbed for the figure on the gurney even as a policeman held him back, and with no other options, he looked at the EMTs for some explanation. "Tell me what happened. What happened to her?"

"Blaine?"

His own name pierced through the hysterical disbelief swirling inside him. He blinked hard, trying to get that face in the right slot. "A.J.?"

The shock took over then and the fight left him as two of them stood there, on the front walk of the house he had done absolutely everything to hide from every person who knew him. He had to get something out, ask some question, make some sense of something. "What… What happened? What happened to her, A.J.?"

A.J. looked at him, compassion and sadness flowing through his gaze. "I'm sorry. You're going to have to ask them." He nodded to the police officer now standing behind them.

"We've got to move," the other EMT said.

And with a push of the cold metal, they headed for the ambulance leaving Blaine swaying and alone on the sidewalk. "No! Oh, please! No!" He raked his fingers up through his hair, fighting to make some sense of what was happening even as the tears flooded his vision. The swinging of the red and blue lights around and around the scene only served to scramble his mind even further. Pushing all of that back, he forced himself to hold it together as he turned back for the officer.

"I need to know… I need to know what happened." He could hardly string the words together. "Please, sir. That was my mother. What happened to her? Please."

The officer consulted his notes. "The victim was your mother?"

"I… What? Yeah. I mean. Yeah." Blaine ran his fingers through his hair again, fighting the waves of sorrow and guilt. "She was here. I was working."

"Okay. Then we're going to need a statement," the officer said. "Where were you at approximately 9:15 this evening?"

"9:15? " The events began to swirl around him. How could this be happening? Not this. She didn't deserve this. He knew it was bad, but this? How could it have gotten this bad?

"Sir?" the officer said, lancing through the questions.

"Uh, oh." Blaine blinked slowly, trying to force his mind to think something other than questions. "I was… I was at work at Harmon's at the West Side Mall. I got off work at 9:30, and then I went to my friend's house to pick up…" His mind slid through the thought. "Dylan!" Without more than that, he turned and ran back for the car.

"Sir! Sir!" the officer called. He spoke quickly into the radio on his shoulder as he followed Blaine. "Sir?"

Skidding to a stop at the car, Blaine gazed in, feeling the entire world drop onto his shoulders. This was it, the moment he had hoped would never actually come. He was now totally and completely responsible for this child. Unbelievably Dylan was still asleep in the passenger's seat, and Blaine knew he would remember the ghostly blue and red lights illuminating his brother's fragile face forever.

"Sir?" the officer was now beside him. He followed Blaine's hollow, terrified gaze. "Who's the boy?"

"My… brother." Had there been anyone to catch him, he would've collapsed. However, there wasn't, so instead he leaned forward onto the car. He felt like throwing up. "How could she?"

"How could she what, son?"

Shaking his head in anger and hurt, Blaine knew there was no reason to lie anymore. Slowly he turned. Emptiness swallowed him up. There was nothing left. No reason to protect her anymore, no reason to cover for her. And with that thought the whole story came tumbling out.

Melody stood in the bathroom. All day it had been much harder to eat than she remembered. Every time she looked at food, reverse thrusters kicked into gear. She tried to eat an apple, but only got halfway through it before she thought she would be sick. For lunch she ate soup, which wasn't much better than the apple.

As she stood there, looking at the silver-lined package of pills in her hand, it felt like standing on a thin wire dangling over a deep canyon. Would giving up her weight loss attempts only make her even more miserable? She still remembered how lethargic and horrible she'd felt with the weight, but the truth was she didn't feel any better now. All she'd really done was traded one miserable for another.

Sure her clothes fit better, but her hair was a wreck as was her skin. She couldn't be sure, but she thought she didn't smell like she used to either. Standing there, holding the little silver packet of pills, her thoughts tracked back to Blaine. I'm not on drugs.

What do you call the pills in your purse?

Her gaze slid up to her reflection, and there was a hollowness in her eyes, a sick emptiness she didn't remember being there before. Maybe Blaine was right. Maybe this whole diet thing was a mistake. And if she wasn't addicted, then why was it so hard to just throw these things in the trash? She looked at them, feeling their tug on her soul.

You'll never be able to do it alone. If you quit now, you'll never look like the other girls. The battle in her spirit crescendoed to a deafening cacophony. Tears came to her eyes. She wanted so badly to be like everyone else—like the Eves and the Lanas of the world. Then her thoughts traced back over the sound of Eve's sad voice in the kitchen. Beautiful, thin, lovely Eve. Obviously there was something about her life that wasn't perfect, maybe more than one something.

Melody looked up at herself once more. Lay it down at the cross. Lay down what is keeping you from My love. Put your burden down and walk away from it. Closing her eyes even as her hand shook, she held out the packet over the trash. "This is it, God. I'm laying it down. I'm laying my burden with my weight down." Her fingers opened, and the package fell in a spiraling arc right into the garbage.

However, far from relief, utter terror ripped through her. What had she done? She couldn't do this on her own. She'd tried, and it hadn't worked. How would she ever be able to keep the weight off? How would she ever…?

"Melody?"

She sniffed and wiped the dampness from her cheeks. "Yeah, Mom?"

"A.J.'s on the phone, sweetheart."

"Oh, okay. Coming." She swiped at her eyes again, trying to get them to look less puffy and sad. Then she turned, brushed off the light, and ran to get the phone. As she headed down the stairs, she knew what this call would be about—him badgering her about the pills. She'd heard it all before, and nothing in her wanted to hear it again—especially now. She still couldn't believe Blaine had talked to A.J. about it. That still seemed so strange. She didn't even think they liked each other. At the phone she took a deep breath prepared to tell A.J. just what she thought of him meddling in her life again. "Hello?"

"Mel?" Something about the shaky way he said her name went straight into her like a knife.

Worry plunged on her. "Yeah?"

"Listen, I can't talk long, but something bad just happened at Blaine's place. I think you need to call him right now."

"What? Why? What happened?"

"I can't tell you any details, but call him. Okay?"

"O…kay."

Dylan was still asleep. Blaine had just finished giving his statement to the police. There was now a warrant out for Dave's arrest, for all the good that would do. The man was a menace and a chameleon. He had slipped out of more than one noose in his lifetime, and this one would surely be no different. The understanding that he had to get Dylan far away from the horror of this place sank into Blaine.

"Sir," an officer said, striding up. "There's a phone call inside the house."

The first officer looked at Blaine. Nothing in Blaine wanted to go back in that house. Nothing. But it would have to be done sooner or later. And sooner had shown up a lot sooner than he would've ever thought possible.

Finally Blaine nodded. "Will you watch Dylan?"

With a blink the officer consented.

Trying not to think, which really wasn't terribly hard, Blaine followed the younger officer down the walk and up the steps. Steeling his nerves, he stepped into the kitchen. A sweep and the thought that nothing seemed that out of the ordinary went through him. Then his gaze snagged on the living room, riveting there with sickening resolve. He closed his eyes, lest he see too much, yet he already had. Fighting to breathe, he went over by the kitchen wall, put his back to everything else, and picked up the phone. "This is Blaine."

"Blaine? What's going on? Are you okay? Is Dylan okay? What happened? Where are you?"

The center of him started shaking uncontrollably. "I'm… fine. Dylan's okay."

"What happened?"

How could he say those words? They didn't even seem real. He was shaking so badly, he thought he might start crying right there. "I… Um, can we come back to your house tonight? We can't stay here."

"Blaine. Why not? What happened?"

"Um, my mom is dead."

For Melody, there was simply no way to tell what to expect as she stood at her front door waiting for them. She tried to stop shaking. It didn't work. Her arms were wrapped around herself, trying to ward off the questions and the thoughts—horrible thoughts that wouldn't stop no matter how hard she tried to make them. When the little green Toyota pulled up to the curb outside, she yanked the door open and rushed out, oblivious to the seeping chill of the night air.

She got to him just as he got out of the car, and without words, she gathered him into her arms. He buried his head onto her shoulder and grabbed onto her like a man drowning.

"I'm so sorry," she whispered again and again because she knew nothing else to say. "I'm so sorry. Are you okay?"

He didn't say anything, didn't even seem to be breathing.

"Oh, dear Lord, how could this happen?" she asked, knowing just enough to know they'd been heading for this very wall for a long time. Still, somehow she had hoped just as surely as he had that it would never come.

When Blaine backed up and looked at her, not only was there overwhelming sadness in his tired eyes, but the shadow of whiskers covering his face was far darker than she'd ever seen it. He looked like he'd just come off a five-day drunk although she'd seen him only hours before.

Gently she took his face in her hands. "I'm so sorry, Blaine."

He nodded.

She gazed at him softly. "What do we need to do?"

He looked so close to tears, it ripped her heart out. Slowly he shook his head. "Can we get Dylan in and to bed?"

"Sure thing." And so as one, they went about doing what had to be done. Blaine got Dylan. Melody got their things. She followed them up the walk and then ran in front of them to get the door. Dylan wasn't even coherent as they got him to the couch, where the pillow and blanket were already in place. When the child was once again fast asleep, Blaine stood, looking at his brother, and then as she watched, the dam burst.

He exhaled hard, and Melody knew. She stepped over to him and gathered him once again into her arms. They stood like that, her holding him as minutes slipped into oblivion. They didn't matter anyway. The way it felt at the moment, the world might well have actually stopped around them.

Finally he pulled away and ran his hand down his face.

"Do you want something? To drink or to eat?" she asked, surveying him with no idea what to do next.

His gaze came up to hers, exhausted and empty. "A cheese sandwich sounds great."

Blaine sat at her table. He'd been in this house many times, but never had he sat at her table. Something told him that now he would always remember the first time he had. He watched her move around the kitchen, collecting things for him, and in the haze of everything else, he realize just how much he had come to love her. Describing it was impossible. She simply was the very best friend he'd ever had.

"All we had was Swiss cheese and white bread. It looks kind of anemic, but I hope it's not too bad." She set the plate in front of him and then gazed down at him with a worried look that hurt to see. "Do you want something to drink—water, juice, milk?"

"Uh, milk," he said barely getting the word out.

Melody nodded and went to the refrigerator. In moments she was back with the milk. She set it on the table and sat down in the chair next to his. Then she pointed to his sandwich. "Eat."

It was entirely possible that she would have to remind him to breathe before this night was over. Dutifully Blaine picked up the bread and bit into it. He didn't taste it at all. As he ate slowly, she simply sat and watched. When he was almost finished, she gazed at him softly.

"Do you want something else?"

He shook his head. "No, I'm good. Thanks." The last bite took an unbelievable amount of effort. True, bone-crushing exhaustion began to seep in. He yawned even as he tried to squelch it. When the yawn was gone, reality came back again, and he shook his head. "It's just so hard to believe. I sit here, and I think this has to be some bizarre nightmare I'm having. That I'm going to wake up, and I'll be back in our house on Palermo, and it was all just one big nightmare." The air whooshed from his lungs, dragging the anguish up with it. "What am I going to do?" Then an even worse thought hit him. "How am I ever going to tell Dylan?" Blaine crumpled forward into his hands. "This is going to kill him."

"Dylan knew it was bad," she said softly.

"Yeah, but this? This bad?" Anger leaped from him. "I should've done something to get her out of there. I knew Dave would come back. I knew he would."

"Blaine, you did everything you could have and then some."

"But I knew he was dangerous."

"And so did she. She made the choice to see him again. She did. Not you. You can't beat yourself up for her decisions."

"But I should've known not to leave her alone there."

A shadow slid across Melody's face. "Just be glad Dylan was here."

Blaine's head jerked up, and in the next second a dagger went through his heart at the thought of what might have been had Dylan not been with her. "Oh, my…" Once again he crumpled into tears. And once again she took him into her arms, finally kneeling on the ground in front of him as he sobbed onto her shoulder, quaking with the unimaginable grief.

They spent an hour in the kitchen, talking and crying. He told her some of the details although Melody was sure he might never even tell her all of them. Then it was clear how drained he was and how much he needed sleep. She took his hand and led him up the stairs to the bathroom.

"Get ready," she instructed at the threshold. "Take a shower, change, whatever. Take your time."

Gratefully his hand came up, and his fingers traced down the side of her face. "I love you. You know that?"

She laid her head into his hand. "I love you, too."

Then he went into the bathroom and closed the door. For the next twenty minutes she got things ready—an extra pillow from the linen closet, her bed, an extra blanket from the hallway, and her own palette on the floor of the living room. She knew without asking that Dylan might wake up sometime in the night and panic. Someone needed to be down there with him, and that someone was her. Then she went back upstairs just as Blaine was coming out of the bathroom, showered and exhausted.

Deep attraction surged through her when the fact that he was in glasses and his bathrobe went through her. He looked like those old English guys who sat in their studies and smoked pipes—except much more heart-stopping. "Um, I got my bed ready for you." Feeling like she might do something really stupid, she turned and started for her room.

"Mel…"

She just spun slightly and laughed at him. "Oh, come on. Don't be such a drama king. I'm sleeping downstairs with Dylan. Well, not with Dylan. On the floor by Dylan."

This time he looked truly exasperated. "Mel…"

Pointing at him, she took his hand and pulled him to her door. "No. Now, no arguing. Tonight you sleep. Tomorrow you can argue."

"But you're…"

"Being nice. I'm being nice. And it's okay. You'll live through it, I promise." At her door, she stopped and looked at him. Soft sorrow wafted over her heart. "I really am sorry."

He pursed his lips together and nodded. "I know."

A moment and she pushed him across the threshold. "Now get some sleep. If you need anything, you know where I'll be."

After only a step, he stopped and gazed at her. "Thank you, Melody. For everything."

It took a moment for her to get the words out. "You're welcome. Now get some sleep."

As he walked in and closed the door, she put her head down and said a quick prayer for him. She could only imagine how hard all of this was. As she headed downstairs, a thought hit her. In the living room she realized it was nearly two in the morning. Still, she knew them, and they would want to know.

After checking on Dylan, she went into the kitchen and picked up the phone. She pulled her mother's address book out and thumbed through it quickly. When she spotted it, she breathed a sigh of thanks that her mother was so adamant about writing down absolutely everybody's information.

Her hands shook as she dialed, and she had to force them to

settle enough to get the numbers in. When she put the receiver to her ear, she closed her eyes and willed her heart to stop racing. A ring. Two. She was probably going to get the answering machine.

"Hello?" The voice was groggy.

Instantly Melody wished she hadn't called. It was Eve, and considering A.J. might be working, it was highly possible she was there alone. This was horrible news to deliver to someone who's by themselves.

"Hello?" There was more fear this time. "Who is this?"

"Uh, Eve? Hi. This is Melody. Listen I'm sorry to call you so late."

"Melody? No, no. That's fine. What's going on?" She sounded fully awake now.

"Uh, Eve? Um, Blaine's mom got killed tonight."

"Blaine's…? Wh…? Melody, are you sure?"

"Yeah, him and Dylan are here at my house." She closed her eyes, again wishing she hadn't called. "I just wanted A.J. to know they're okay."

"A.J.? Why A.J.?"

The story circled her head. "He called earlier. I don't know how he found out. I don't know, but he called earlier, worried about Blaine. I just wanted to let him know they're okay."

"Oh. Okay." Eve paused. "How's Blaine?"

This exhale was hard and soul-draining. "Dealing."

"Yeah," Eve said softly. "Is there anything we can do?"

"Yeah, say some prayers. I'll let you know when I know anything."

"Okay." The line went silent. "Thanks, Melody. Thanks for letting me know."

"Sure."

When Melody curled up on the blankets in the living room floor minutes later, she couldn't believe she didn't just collapse from the exhaustion. However, for some odd reason sleep didn't come. Instead she lay awake for a long time, thinking and praying, for Dylan, for Blaine, for all of them.

Eighteen

As the sun peeked over the horizon none of Houston could see, a small figure prodded Melody awake.

"Melody? Melody? Wake up. Where's Blaine? Why didn't he come get me?"

She squeezed her eyes closed and scratched her forehead, knowing two things: she had not gotten nearly enough sleep and it was way too early for anyone to be waking her up. "Huh?"

"Where's Blaine? Why didn't he come get me?" The words were whispered but near frantic.

Slowly her eyes came open, and she looked around trying to get some part of her to latch onto reality enough so she would know where she was and what was going on. Then as she lay there, sights and images began to flood through her mind. The phone call. Blaine coming with Dylan. Blaine... Dylan... And then she came full awake.

"Oh, Dylan, sweetheart." Still blinking the sleep from her eyes, she sat up, feeling both the stiffness of her back and the pounding of her head. When she looked up, he stood there, a thin, spindly thing in his Spiderman pajamas and tousled hair. Instantly her heart went out to him. After today, his world would never again be the same. "Come here." She pulled him down to her side, knowing she couldn't lie but having no clue how to tell him the truth.

He sat down right next to her and scratched his head where his hair stuck up in an odd swoop. "Why didn't Blaine come and get me?"

The middle of her heart heaved, and she hugged him to her. "He did, sweetheart. He did come and get you." Leaning down, she kissed his hair. "But something happened and he brought you back."

"Why?"

Why? Why? The question dogged her as well. "Well, sweetheart, he needed somewhere for you to be safe, so he brought you back here."

"Safe? But I wanted to go home."

Oh, God, help! What do I say to him? "I know. I know. But Blaine's dealing with some things, and he needed a place for you to stay, so I said he could bring you here. Are you hungry?"

"Yeah." He scratched that spot again. "Do you have pancakes?"

She smiled the only smile she knew how to form. "Yeah. Let's go get some."

It was nearly 9:30 when Blaine woke up. His first thought was where was he. His second thought was why was he here. His third was a rush of remembering. Mom. The name cut through him like a hot sword as his eyes came wide open. Oh, no. This can't be for real. He rubbed his eyes and sighed, trying to choke back the tears. Somehow he had to keep it together. They were counting on him. Dylan… The thought brought up the image of the child sleeping in his car, the police lights swirling over his angelic face.

Exhausted to the point of not being able to force himself to move, Blaine somehow forced his feet out of the bed and onto the floor. Every drop of energy in him was gone. He ran his hand down his face, squeezing the ache down into his heart.

Knowing he had to, he reached for his glasses and put them on. It was only then that he really noticed the room. Her room. White and pink, it was the epitome of a girl's room. Funny. He'd never really considered her a girly-girl, not like this room indicated anyway. Pushing those thoughts aside to deal with more pressing matters, he reached over and pulled his navy bathrobe off the end of the bed. It was one of the few things he'd rescued from the house the night before. His heart jolted at the thought, and he exhaled hard.

He wouldn't think about those things now. He couldn't.

Although he was sure he looked atrocious, he needed to check on Dylan. His only hope was that his brother might still be asleep. Dumping the having to tell him on Melody seemed the height of weakness. Yet some small part of him hoped she'd already told him.

Wrapping the robe around himself, Blaine trudged down the stairs. It was so strange to be in her house like this. It felt very intimate in a way he couldn't quite explain. After all, he'd been with girls before, but never, ever like this, and this was much more intimidating. He heard the voices in the kitchen, and with one more breath he pushed the swinging door open.

Dylan looked up from his puzzle at the table. "Blaine!" In the next second his brother was in his arms. He bent and hugged him, having no idea what he knew and what he didn't. Then he glanced up, seeing her movement at the sink.

Melody turned, and her eyes were at once sad, knowing, and sympathetic. "See, I told you Blaine would be here."

"Did you see? Did you see?" Dylan asked in excitement. "I'm doing this puzzle with the horses."

"That's nice," Blaine said, barely seeing it. After only a moment's stop, he stepped over to Melody, and their embrace was like nothing he'd ever experienced. It was simply pure—no judgment, no lies. He held her to him, wanting it to never end.

When he finally released her, she pulled back and surveyed him. "How're you doing?"

He tried to smile but only half his smile went up. Once again it was time to get really serious. "Did you…?" He glanced at Dylan. "Does he know?"

Aching guilt went through her eyes. "No. I thought it was better if we told him together."

Blaine nodded both his understanding and his agreement. He reached down between them and took her hand. When he turned and saw the child sitting at the table, innocently putting the puzzle together, he had to take a breath. Dear Lord, I need some words here… Please. Together they walked to the table. "Hey, buddy. Can we talk to you a minute?"

Dylan looked up, and the light in his eyes flickered. "Sure."

Carefully Blaine sat down and pulled the child onto his lap. The breath did nothing to calm the chaos in his spirit. "Um, last night when we went home, something happened." It was then that Blaine felt her hands on his shoulders, and he looked up at her.

Silent support drifted from her gaze.

He returned to the task. "It was something really, really bad."

"Is Mom hurt?" Dylan asked clearly worried.

"Yeah, Mom got hurt. Dylan, Mom… died last night. She got mixed up in something really bad, and she just couldn't get out."

For a long moment there was no response.

"I want to see her."

The simple request tore through Blaine. "Well, I don't know if we can, buddy."

"I want to see her. I want to see Mom."

"I know that. I just… I don't know if they'll let us yet."

"But why can't I see her? I want to see her."

Blaine was losing control with every protest his brother made. Then he felt Melody move. She stepped around him and sat on her heels in front of Dylan. Leveling her gaze at him, she reached up and touched his arm.

"You loved your mom a lot, huh?"

Dylan was crying now. He wiped his eyes with his shirt sleeve.

"I know you did. Come here." And Melody pulled him into her embrace. For as little sense as any of it made, Blaine wrapped his arms around them as well. As one they cried for the loss of one life and the unknown of the one they now faced.

Eve and A.J. showed up at 10:15 just after Blaine had managed to get himself into something decent. He took one look at Eve and shook his head as he stepped into her arms. She just held him, allowing his grief to surface and overrun its banks once again. He wondered if he would ever again feel whole. When he let her go, he held his hand out to A.J. The handshake lasted only a second, and then A.J. pulled him into his embrace.

Something about that gesture tipped the scales on Blaine's equilibrium. With a hard pat on his back, A.J. let him go. It was obvious they wanted to say something, but it was equally obvious they had no idea what that something was. Eve's gaze slid past him to Dylan sitting on the couch, ostensibly watching a cartoon; however, Blaine less than anyone knew what he was thinking.

Eve laid her hand on Blaine's arm and stepped past him to his brother. On the couch, she simply sat and put her arm around the little boy's shoulder. Instantly he huddled into her. Blaine couldn't help but think they both knew just how deeply loss could ache.

"Have you called the police yet?" A.J. asked, wiping the bridge of his nose with his thumb. "I imagine they're going to do an autopsy."

Blaine nodded. "It's this morning. They think they'll release the body around four or so."

"And the funeral home?"

It occurred to Blaine how much more about this whole procedure A.J. probably knew. As for him, he felt as if he was stranded in a pitch-black room, bumping into things, thus bruising his spirit for all eternity. "I don't know. I've never really done this kind of thing before."

A.J. nodded as the doorbell rang.

"I'll get it," Melody said, striding in from the kitchen. When she had changed into the smoky sheath twined with white lace, he had no idea. In seconds there were voices, a few more seconds and Jeff and Lisa came around the corner. Upon seeing Blaine, Jeff held out his hand.

The sheer amount of love in the room was enough to bring him to his knees. When he had made such good friends, he had no idea.

By the time they left for the funeral home, they had an entire caravan—Blaine, Melody, and Dylan with Eve and A.J., Jeff and Lisa, and Gabe and Ashley. Blaine kept telling them they didn't all have to come, but truthfully he was glad they hadn't listened when they walked into the funeral home. He clutched Melody's hand tighter, hoping somehow she could keep him standing.

The funeral director offered his hand first to Blaine and then to each of the others in turn. Most of the rest of the evening passed in such a blur that Blaine hardly remembered it. He answered the questions, made the decisions that needed to be made. The few times that he stumbled someone was there to catch him, lift him up, and set him back right again.

All the actual arrangements were easy. Keep it simple. That's what he kept saying, "I don't know. Whatever's easiest. Keep it simple." If he said it once, he said it a hundred times. He tried to monitor Dylan, but that was difficult. Somehow though Eve had understood to take him under her wing, and she had done just that with remarkable ease and grace. Blaine was grateful for that. He knew he couldn't have done it.

And then they were leaving. They would be back the next afternoon for a brief service, and then interment. Interment. It was such a strange word. It kept running through his head as they drove back to Melody's place. He didn't even really know what it meant. As they drove, he put his hand on his mouth and gazed out at the late evening sky. Twenty-four hours.

Twenty-four little hours. Twenty-four hours ago he was adding up his commissions and wondering if they would be enough to afford a new apartment. And now, inexplicably he was here, driving home from a funeral home. A funeral home. That was another strange term. Home denoted a place you wanted to be, funeral did not. His brain relentlessly traced through every strange thing about this new existence, and there was so, so much strangeness there.

In no time they were back at Melody's. Time had become a strange thing too—measured in moments and lulls rather than seconds and minutes. He got out and helped Melody. She wrapped her arm through his as they waited for Dylan to disembark. And then as one, they walked into the house.

Where the food came from, Blaine wasn't at all sure. All he could ever tell was that Melody was somehow directing an army of volunteers. The women made dinner, they all ate, and then in a blink everything was cleaned. How she managed it all, he couldn't exactly tell because his mind was not on food or cleaning or anything even close to normal. And then as quickly as they had come, their friends headed out promising to be there the next morning.

Blaine shook their hands, hugged them, and told them thanks without ever really knowing he'd done anything. It was like there was this huge fog over his whole being that he wasn't at all sure would ever dissipate.

"I don't want to sleep by myself tonight," Dylan said when everyone else was gone.

Melody bent, putting her hand on his arm. "Why don't you sleep with Blaine up in my bed tonight?"

Something about that simple image, her so calm and caring as she dealt with Dylan, dragged up gratefulness Blaine had never known he possessed. Dylan nodded and headed up the stairs. A moment and Melody stepped over to his big brother who took her once again into his arms.

She put her hand on his chest, just over his heart. "How are you doing?"

Tiredly he nodded. "I'm okay. Thanks for all you did today."

Her gaze at him was full of soft admiration. "Hey, we're a team, remember?"

And he had no choice but to pull her to him again.

It truly was incredible that she could be so tired two nights in a row and yet have no hope of getting to sleep. As she lay on the couch, Melody's mind traced through her concern for Blaine and Dylan and finally about what tomorrow would bring. What must it be like to bury your mother? Over and over again, that thought went through her mind. How horrible that must be. In desperation, she finally got up and went to the kitchen. There was chamomile tea. It was supposed to help insomnia.

She was trying to be quiet, but when she heard the sound, she knew it hadn't worked as well as she would've liked. Surprise went through her when she turned to find it was her own mother who had stepped into the room.

"Can't sleep?" her mother asked. Only one other time had Melody seen her mother look so tired.

Melody shook her head as she stirred the tea. "I just keep thinking about what happened, about how Blaine goes on from this. I mean how that's even possible?"

Her mother sat at the table and waited for Melody to sit as well. There was something about the way her mother was looking at her that made Melody want to cry.

The smile on her mother's face was tight and sad. "None of us know. None of us. My mother died of a heart attack, and she had no idea. We had no idea. And then she was just gone."

"Boy," Melody said, "I barely even remember that. I was so young."

"It was a long time ago. That's how everything is. At the moment you think it will last forever and that that's all there will ever be, and then it's been a long time ago. I know. I've been there, more than once."

Melody sipped her tea. "How did you get through it?"

"Well, I cried a lot, and I got angry, and then I cried some more. But then life goes on, and you start dealing with today again rather than yesterday. You never forget, but somehow you start to remember a little less often."

"I don't know how Blaine is ever going to face this."

"Blaine's a strong, good young man. He is. And he will move on."

"But I don't know how to help him. I don't even know what to say sometimes."

"Sometimes you say more by just being there than you ever have to with words."

Melody nodded. That was certainly true for her this afternoon. The presence of her friends had made an awful day almost bearable.

"Just be there for him like you have been." Her mother reached over and patted her hand. "You'll see." She stood and pulled her ratty old supposed to be white but hadn't been in years robe around herself.

As she sat there looking at her mother, Melody realized how much she would miss that old robe someday. And something about that moment made her realize that there would in fact be a someday, a day when her own mother would be gone. The thought snagged her heart. At the door her mother turned, and Melody looked up again.

"I was proud of you today," her mother said. "Just so you know."

And then she walked out. Melody sat in that kitchen long, long after her mother had left. How many things had Blaine wanted to tell his mom, and now he would never get the chance? How many things had she not said to all those in her life who meant the very most to her?

Her gaze dropped to the simple cup, sitting on the table. Nobody knows the hour. Nobody.

Nineteen

When Blaine woke up, he looked over at Dylan who was still sleeping, and the enormity of his new life descended on him. "God," he whispered in his heart, "how am I ever going to do this? How can I raise Dylan by myself? I'm not ready to be a father. Why? Why did you have to take her? Why did she have to fall apart like that? Didn't she know how much I needed her, how much I still need her?"

And then he became aware that he was being watched. He let his head fall to the side where he found the little dark eyes gazing at him. There was no fear there, only peace. Blaine knew with one look that Dylan had forgotten.

"Hey, buddy. How'd you sleep?"

Dylan nodded still looking at him in a way that was making Blaine more concerned by the second.

"What's wrong?"

"I saw Mom."

The statement sent Blaine backward like a punch. "Dylan, Mom's…"

"I know, but I saw her. She was all dirty and sad at first, and then this angel came into the room. Mom looked at the angel, and as she stood there, all the bad stuff started like disappearing from her. And then she wasn't dirty anymore, and the angel put this really white robe on her, and Mom was happy again. She was happy, Blaine. She looked right at me, and she smiled. She's okay now."

"Dylan…" Blaine reached over to his brother.

"She's okay, Blaine. She's really okay. I know she is."

As he collected his brother in his arms, the only thing Blaine could think was he wished he could've been there to see it. "I know she is too."

There wasn't much of a service. The funeral director read something from what Blaine could only surmise was the Bible, and then a lady sang "Amazing Grace." He couldn't sing, so he just sat, holding onto Melody's hand. And then it was over. The graveyard wasn't much different. In no time it was all over, and they were leaving.

All day long, Melody kept watch over him and Dylan, and their friends kept watch over all of them. Back at Melody's house the mood was still quiet but not as somber as before. A.J. and Jeff dug into Melody's video games. From that point on, it was Dylan against whoever was the latest challenger. Blaine never played. He just sat back and watched Dylan and wondered.

He tried to think what tomorrow was, tried to remember even what day today was. It wasn't until Eve came and sat by him that he found a good clue.

She put her hand on his knee. "How're you doing?"

At first he tried to consider and reason out that question. Finally he just shrugged. "Okay, I guess."

Nodding, she looked over at him. "I talked to Melody before. We were wondering if you guys would like to come to church with us tomorrow." She held up her hands. "No pressure. I just…" Her gaze fell. "I just know how much that helped me when Dustin died."

For the first time since he'd learned about her loss, he had a real appreciation for the depth of her strength and her faith to find a way to keep going after her world fell apart. He nodded. "I think that would be a good idea."

And so the next morning, the three of them showed up once again at St. Mark's. Hand-in-hand they entered and found A.J. and Eve with little trouble. Every so often Melody glanced over at Blaine. She still didn't know what to say or how to say it, but like her mother had said, she was there, and she wasn't leaving.

They all exchanged greetings and then went in together. As Melody walked behind Eve, she suddenly sensed that something had changed. Exactly what that was she couldn't tell, but she no longer thought of the tall leggy woman with the long dark hair as an enemy. She was beginning to appreciate the looks that A.J. gave his wife, the way they clung together no matter the storm. Somehow her heart had come to no longer want him, but to want what they had—a love that was strong, a love that could withstand whatever the world threw at them.

She turned her gaze from them to Blaine, and with everything in her, she didn't want that with just anyone anymore. She wanted it with him, with Blaine Donovan. Her hero and her best friend. Feeling that to the depths of her soul, she squeezed his hand, and he looked at her in surprise. Gently she smiled, and his smile back was almost not sad. Had they been at the movies, she would've laid her head on his shoulder; however, that was a bit presumptuous sitting in the middle of a church.

So she simply let her gaze trace to the front as the service started. In her heart, she knew there was no telling today what part of the service might change how she saw everything about everything, but she was determined to be awake and alert when that moment came.

The only thing Blaine wanted to do was put his arm around her and hold her close. Of course that would've been awkward because his other arm was already around Dylan who was huddled up next to him. Still, he wanted to. He had come to want to protect her and love her as much as she had loved and protected him.

As the preacher stepped to the podium, Blaine shifted slightly. Strange how listening and learning had become so important in the last couple of months. Strange how before that he was trying only to get to the next minute in one piece. Now he was paying attention to the lessons of this one, this minute, and he had never known there were so many. He had learned so many this past week. His heart panged at the thought of his mother. This time last week she was alive. She was here, and she was alive. And now she wasn't.

It was hard to figure out why that was so hard to figure out. It just didn't feel right that she was somehow here then and gone now. It just didn't feel possible, and yet it was. It had to be because he knew it to be true. How it was true though, he still had no idea.

"A man sat up one night counting the grain in his barns," the preacher said. "He had his calculator there and his ledger. He added and re-added, and then he had a thought. 'I have had excellent years the last two years. What I need to do is to build bigger barns so that next year when I plant more, I will have more storage for the harvest.' So the next day he called his contractor. 'I want to tear down my barns and build three double their size.' 'Double?' the contractor asked. 'Whatever will you do with so much space?' 'Fill it, of course.'

"And so the contractor came, tore down the old barns, and began to build the new ones. As the barns were being built, the rich man set about his own work, double time. He added and re-added in his head just how much he would have to harvest to fill those barns, for why have them if he couldn't use them? The barns neared completion, and the harvest did as well. Then one night the rich man sat back looking out at the new barns and anticipating the coming harvest.

"His wife came in and told him she was lonely, but he brushed her off. There would be time for that when the barns were filled. His child came in for a goodnight hug and wanting him to read a story. The rich man rebuffed him also. Soon they would have money to buy many more books than any other child in the land, and he knew that then his child would really love him. So he told the child, 'Tomorrow. Later. Not right now.'

"The child went away sad, and the wife went to bed alone. And that night the rich man bent over his calculator and ledger and died."

Blaine shifted in his seat. He hadn't expected this. He hadn't read his Bible since before the world stopped spinning, before he'd turned on that street and everything in his life had changed, and worse, this story was brand new to him. He'd never heard it before that he could remember. However, now, the feeling that everyone else was staring right at him drilled into his consciousness. They must be for this was his story, his life.

"Now when the man died, his colleagues from the business world showed up, and the contractor showed up. They all praised the man for his success at raising and trading grain. They said what a success he had been, what a role model in how to operate a business. And his wife and his child listened to the words, thinking they wished he had been a little less successful to the outside world and a little more available in theirs.

"Everyone said how nice it was that they would be well taken care of because the rich man had prepared so well for his death. But had he? Had he prepared well for his death? This man, this wealthy, wealthy man had gone full-bore for the things of this earth—wealth, status, success. Building ever bigger, ever better, ever more. And yet, what did all that get him when he stood at the threshold of his eternity? What did he take with him? Did he take the barns? No. They still stood, not quite finished and still empty. Did he take the harvest? No. It was still in the field, now left for someone else to gather. Did he take the love he had given his wife and child and the love they had given him in return? Yes and that's all he took, although that was a pittance compared with what it could have been.

"Jesus calls this man a fool—not malicious, not devious, but certainly not a success. He called him a fool. Why? Because in pursuing the temporary, this man, this rich, rich man had squandered the eternal. He had squandered the truly important for the merely urgent. He got the point of life just backward—just as the world does. The world says that success is everything. But the Bible says, 'What profits a man if he gains the whole world but in the end he loses his own soul?'

"What profits a man if he gets the new account, climbs the ladder, gets the promotion at the expense of his family and his friends and his God? What profits a man if he gains everything but loses himself? You see, life is really pretty simple. It's just a whole series of decisions big and small. Decision after decision after decision. But do we ever ask where these decisions, these tiny in the minute decisions are leading us? Are they leading us anywhere we really want to go?

"Many of us approach our lives like a DC-10 bound for somewhere. We get on, and when we're in the air, the captain comes on the intercom. 'This is your captain speaking. We just flew over Hawaii. We are still over the ocean somewhere. We plan to keep flying until we see some land. Then we'll look for a lot of lights all bunched together, and if we have enough fuel, we will try to land there and figure out where we are at that point."

People laughed.

"Or we go the other direction and set all kinds of goals. I know people who would go into cardiac arrest if they lose their day planner. Why? Because they've completely lost sight of how to simply live in the moment. They treat life like one giant rush to one appointment after another. They have fallen for the lie that somehow by organizing every moment, they can somehow gain control over that which is not theirs to control. They set goal after goal after goal—for their work, their home, their families, their vacations even. When a friend calls, they try to get off the phone as quickly as possible because this call is messing up my carefully crafted schedule—I mean their carefully crafted schedule."

This round of laughter was a little more self-conscious, a little more nervous.

"Is it good to have some goals? Yes. If those goals are ultimately focused not on the temporary but on the eternal. As St. Paul reminds us in Second Corinthians, 'Therefore, we are not discouraged; rather, although our outer self is wasting away, our inner self is being renewed day by day. For this momentary light affliction is producing for us an eternal weight of glory beyond all comparison, as we look not to what is seen but to what is unseen; for what is seen is temporary, but what is unseen is eternal.'

"What he's saying is peg your life to the eternal, not to the temporary. Peg your life not to the barns and to the harvest but to the people you could love if you took the time, not to your success but to your soul. Not to goals and ambition but to love. Make the right things important in your life, and whether you have ten minutes or ten thousand days, you will know that you are in fact headed toward the right goal—not just floating around somewhere in the sky hoping to land in a good place before you run out of fuel."

The preacher paused. "Let us pray."

Blaine bowed his head as his heart pitched and arched in a hundred different directions. How long had he been focusing on the temporary? Forever? At the time he thought that's all there was, but looking at his mother's life as he did now, he realized that she hadn't taken a single thing with her. Not a single one. Not even him or Dylan. She had her soul, and that was it.

And one day he would only have his soul. He closed his eyes as the service continued, and although he knew he was making progress, he knew without a doubt how shriveled and pitiful his soul had become. It was cold, selfish, and hard. He had paid nearly no attention to it at all for 27 years, choosing instead to focus on the things that could get him somewhere in this life—

money, education, contacts. Now he didn't even want to think about those things. How much did they really matter anyway? Not much, if at all.

They couldn't hold him on a cold night. They couldn't comfort him and encourage him. They couldn't even make his life feel like it was worth living for more than fleeting moments at a time.

When his time came, he wouldn't take his car, his clothes, or his bank account. He would take his soul, and at the moment that was a very scary proposition. He vowed to ask Eve about it as soon as there was a chance. How to get his soul right, how to start living for the eternal rather than the temporary—it seemed so important now.

Before he knew it, the service was over, and the five of them were headed back out of the bench. Blaine looked at Melody, and strangely, she looked different to him. She looked older, more mature, and more like someone he wanted to spend his life with, rather than just some girl he happened to go out with once. His thoughts turned to his mother. He was still mad at her for so much, but for his soul's sake, he knew he had to find a way to let go of that. Love is what lasts. He'd read that in the Bible Eve gave him, and now he saw even that gift in a different light.

She wasn't trying to force something on him. She was showing him how to love by simply loving him. His attention came back to the room as he put his arm around Melody. They trekked out of the church together.

"So what're y'all up to now?" Eve asked, clearly measuring her words carefully.

"Back home I guess," Melody said, glancing at him for confirmation.

"Well, we're headed over to Lisa and Jeff's," A.J. said. "They said you're welcome to come if you want."

"Oh, I don't know," Melody said hesitating for him.

But Blaine knew now that the invitation was about their friendship. It was made out of love not obligation. It was amazing how different that felt. "We'd love to." He smiled at Melody when she looked at him questioningly.

"I wanna go with A.J.," Dylan said, pinballing between the four of them.

Blaine laughed and looked at them. He saw Eve's soft smile.

"Well, that's up to A.J."

One look and Blaine knew the answer.

However, A.J. put his hands up in front of his face as if to shield himself from the horror. "No! Not Dylan! Ahh! No! Please!"

Dylan took the bait and threw a flying tackle at A.J. who barely caught him.

Eve laughed. "I think that's a yes."

"Penny for your thoughts," Melody said as the two of them drove to Lisa and Jeff's.

"Oh, I don't know. I think you're going to have to spend more than that. I'm not sure a penny can do it justice."

Her gaze drifted from the passenger's seat over to his profile. "How's that?"

He took a breath to figure out where to even start. Then he reached over and took her hand. "Everything. It's just everything, you know? I mean I've lived 27 years. I thought I had it all figured out, and now I think I've completely missed the point of all of it. I've been so focused on my future—on what I'll be able to do when I'm out of school, what my life will be like in ten years, what I'll be able to buy, what I'll be able to own, who I'll be, how I'll be, who I'll know and who'll know me, so much so that I think I completely lost sight of everything that's really important… if I ever saw it at all."

She smiled softly. "You saw it. You did. It's not like all of that's been about you."

"Yeah, but too much of it was. Dang, Mel, do you know how many barns I've built, how many I've planned? I've been building them and building them and planning for more barns and more barns and more barns." He took a breath. "Sometimes I wonder if that's what my dad did, too, you know? If he was so focused on what he was building, that he had no time for us."

"He made a choice."

"Yeah, he did, and I'm afraid I'm making the same one." For a single moment he sat, thinking. "I don't want to make that choice. I don't. I saw my dad do it, and then, I watched Mom do it in a different way. I just don't want to get to the end and have nothing to show for it. You know? I mean look who came to

Mom's funeral—not her friends, mine."

"That must mean you're doing something right."

"That's what I mean. This is what I want. I want to go to church with you and then go to our friends' house. I want to be there for them like they were there for me. That feels so real to me right now."

Melody nodded. "It was weird today, in church, Eve smiled at me, and for the first time I was actually happy about that. I wasn't so stuck on comparing my life to hers and figuring out who was winning or losing. We just… were. That was nice."

"I really love it that Dylan likes hanging out with them. I think it's good for them and for him. Before, I would've been all panicked about 'What will they think? I don't want to intrude. I don't want them to think I can't handle it.' I was scared of everything."

She didn't say anything for second upon second. Then she let out a soft breath. "I threw the pills away."

His gaze snapped to hers. "What?"

"I did. I threw 'em away the other night. Pitched 'em in the trash."

He waited, but she said no more. "And…?"

"And, I don't know. It's still a struggle. I still don't want to have all that extra weight, but I know you're right. The way I was doing it isn't healthy. I guess I'm trying to figure out a happy medium—something healthy that I can live with."

Blaine nodded. "Maybe we could go out walking some night when I get off work or go roller skating. Dylan loved it the other day when y'all went."

"You mean when he went, all I did was try to keep up."

He laughed. "But still that sounds like fun, and it's not expensive. Like that night we went to the park. Okay, I don't recommend cold, greasy chicken, but that was fun."

"Yeah, it was."

He sat, lost in thought as the white stripes slid by them. "Have you thought any more about school and what you're going to do in the fall?"

She hesitated. "Well, I was kind of wondering what you were doing."

He glanced at her. "How's that?"

"Well, I'm assuming Dylan gets out of school at some point

during the day. What does he do after school?"

A flash of the image of the old house panged through him. "I don't know. I'll have to get our stuff out before the first." He shook his head. "I don't even know where we're going to go. But we can't stay there. I'd already decided that even before…" The thoughts swirled again. "I don't know."

Melody knew they had entered a different level but just how different she couldn't tell. Carefully she ventured out onto the fragile branch she hoped wouldn't snap. "Well, I was going to tell you. I saw a vacancy at an apartment complex not far from my house the other day—not that I was looking or anything. But a couple years ago when I thought about moving out, I looked at it. They have some nice efficiencies. They're small, but they were pretty reasonable." She shrugged. "I just thought maybe if you got something there, I could help out with Dylan when he goes back. I could pick him up from school or they could drop him off at my house. At least that way he wouldn't be home all evening by himself."

An odd look traced across Blaine's face. "You were serious about this team thing, weren't you?"

Her heart was soft and hopeful. "Yeah, I was."

He considered and then looked at her. "Well, maybe that's not such a bad idea. We do make a pretty good team if you hadn't noticed."

She smiled like a light bulb coming on. "Yeah, I'd kind of noticed that."

When they got to Lisa and Jeff's, A.J. and Eve were already there and inside. Melody met Blaine at the front of the vehicle, and for all the sadness of the week, today felt like a new start. He put his arm around her, and that felt so very right.

"You know what I think is awesome?" she asked as they walked together up the sidewalk slowly.

"What's that?"

"I love how being real with each other feels."

His gaze slid to her. "Oh, yeah?"

"Yeah, for a long time there I was trying so hard to impress you so you'd keep me around."

He nodded with a laugh. "And I was doing everything I could so you would never find out who I really was."

"We wasted so much time."

"Hey, we were learning," he said, hugging her to him. "I wouldn't call that wasted."

Her smile grew. "Me either."

They rang the doorbell, but Blaine couldn't keep his joy in. He turned and kissed the side of her head.

"What was that for?" she asked.

"For teaching me what it's like when it's for real."

The door snapped open bringing both gazes to it.

"Hey! You made it." Jeff called, seemingly to anyone who happened to be in the neighborhood.

"We did," Blaine said.

"Come on in." He pushed the door open so they could come in. "Everybody's in the kitchen."

Melody trailed Blaine although his hand never left hers. It was hard to explain how right simply holding her hand felt.

"Save some for us," he joked, walking in and seeing the crew seated around the table. Somehow that table looked bigger today than it had the week before.

"Hey! You made it," A.J. said, swinging his hand to shake Blaine's as if it had been hours. "Eve thought you got lost."

"I did not," she said as she put potatoes on Dylan's plate. "I had complete faith in you two."

"Uh-huh," A.J. retorted. "That's why you kept saying, 'Where'd they go? Are you sure Blaine knows how to get there?'"

The pout on Eve's face brought Blaine's heart up with a yank.

He pulled Melody in front of him. "Don't worry. I had my good luck charm with me. We weren't getting lost."

"Come on," Jeff said, indicating the other two chairs. "Have a seat."

Trying not to be obvious Blaine pulled Melody's chair out and waited for her to sit. "This looks incredible."

"Lisa," A.J. said, digging himself some more potatoes and gravy. "She's got skills."

Eve leaned over to him and patted his leg. "It's food. It's not hard to impress you, babe."

"Haha." A.J. lifted his chin to her as if he was offended, but she didn't let him be offended for long as she gave him a quick kiss and then tried to wipe the lipstick off.

"I'm sorry," she said, still wiping. "You married a mean wife."

"Amen to that," he said.

"Saying amen." Eve repositioned her napkin on her lap. "Should we say Grace?"

Melody joined hands with Blaine on one side and A.J. on the other. It felt weird to be between them and not feel like she was being pulled apart. Jeff offered a few words, everyone said amen, and life resumed. She had watched the melee for a few minutes when Blaine held the bowl of carrots up to her. Taking a breath, she felt him looking at her, and her gaze caught his. Slightly almost without moving, he nodded, and she smiled.

She accepted the carrots, looked at them, and her determination to do this the healthy way solidified. Scooping two spoonfuls onto her plate, she passed them on to A.J. That same look was on his face. Funny though, this time she didn't feel judged. Now she just felt loved. They cared. It was easier to put the potatoes on her plate and still easier to put the salad and the brisket.

When she started eating, she took it slow and let herself enjoy the food. The conversation flowed around her, and although twice she noticed Blaine watching her, she felt much less scrutinized than she had on her diet. It was a nice feeling to know he cared, not about her weight but about her health.

"So, Blaine," Jeff said, "what'd you say you were studying?"

Melody sensed Blaine freeze. She closed her eyes for a second, willing strength into him. Please, God, show him it's okay to be real.

"Uh, architectural design," he said slowly. "I'll graduate in December."

"Wow," Lisa said, cutting Alex's carrots into teeny-tiny bites. "That's a tough field."

There was a breath of a pause, and then Blaine nodded. "Well, I'll only have an associates, and it's only architecture, you know. It's not like the stuff you guys do." His gaze swept across Jeff and A.J. "It's not putting your life on the line or anything." He stabbed into a piece of meat, his gaze never really coming up again.

Her heart panged forward. She saw things, feelings on his face she'd only gotten glimpses of prior to that moment.

"Hey, don't knock where you're at," Jeff said, hefting a forkful of potatoes. "That job's important too. We rely a lot on the designers, a bad design can take a building down faster than a bad crew."

The middle of her heart lifted in gratitude for Jeff. Not only did he understand Blaine's pain, he was humble enough to find a reason to lift the younger man up. "I'd never thought about it like that," Melody said, and she really hadn't.

"Oh, yeah," Jeff said. "We like designers who think about more than coding a building, those who recognize how important safety is to those who work there and those first responders that might be called on something. Besides, if you weren't building the buildings, there'd be nothing for us to save."

Blaine's gaze came up from his food.

"And it's not like that's not a gift either," A.J. offered from the other side of her, and Melody almost fell off her chair she spun so fast. "Man, I couldn't get past Algebra."

She held up her fork. "I can vouch for that. I think Mrs. Nyugen passed him just so she wouldn't have to hear him whine anymore. 'I don't get this.'"

A.J. laughed. "You have a lot of room to talk. Seems to me I remember someone who always needed my help."

"Yeah? Well a lot of good that did me." Her laugh relaxed every piece of her—heart, body, and soul. Who knew this could actually be fun? She leaned back over to Blaine. "Hey, tell them about that guy. The one that came into Harmon's the other day."

"What? Oh, that one I was telling you about?"

"Yeah."

And with barely a breath Blaine launched into the story of the guy who wouldn't choose a coat but wouldn't leave. The more exasperated he became telling it, the harder everyone laughed until no one was even eating anymore.

"I bet he tried on that one coat like twenty-five times," Blaine said, coming completely out of his sullen shell. "'No. I want it tailored here,' he'd say. Hello! I can't change the style of the coat. What am I supposed to do, snap my fingers or rub some kind of tailor genie lamp?"

Melody looked at him horrified. "What? You're not magic?"

"Do I look like I'm magic?" he asked, skepticism raining through the question.

"Well, yeah, sometimes." She leaned in to kiss him as cat-calls, oohs and aahs sounded around the table.

When Blaine backed up, his ears were pink.

"Uh-oh," Jeff said, watching them with a huge Cheshire Cat grin.

"What uh-oh?" Lisa asked. "That was cute."

"That was not cute," A.J. said seriously. "That was the sound of the trap snapping shut."

Jeff pointed his fork at A.J. "You got that right."

Lisa's face fell into a frown. "You guys are so paranoid about us laying the traps for you to fall into."

"You don't?" Jeff asked, clearly sounding surprised. "As I recall, I was walking along minding my own business…"

"And what was I doing, ensnaring you in my evil web?" Lisa asked incredulously.

Jeff nodded. "Something like that." He looked over at Blaine. "Be afraid. Be very afraid."

Blaine laughed. "I'll try to remember that."

"Who's up for some dessert?" Lisa asked when the laughter died down.

Moans and groans plodded around the table.

"It's cheese cake."

Jeff shook his head at A.J. "You guys have got to stop coming over. I'm not going to be able to climb that ladder anymore if this keeps up."

"She's nesting," Eve said, patting Jeff on the wrist. "Just wait, when that little one gets here, she'll be too busy with round the clock feedings to worry about if you've eaten or not."

He looked at her and corkscrewed his face. "Isn't there some kind of happy medium there?"

"There is no such thing." A.J. shook his head. "Trust me on that one."

Lisa set the cheesecake right in the middle of the table, and panic swept through Melody. Sugar. Lots of it. The meal was delicious although she'd only eaten half of what everyone else had, but now how to get through this issue. If she said she didn't want any, A.J. was sure to give her that look. If she took some, wasn't that being unhealthy? Ugh. She hated these moments.

"I'm stuffed," Blaine said from next to her, "but that really looks good." He leaned over to her. "How about we split a piece?"

When Melody looked at him, her heart burst with gratitude. Without embarrassing her or calling attention to her, he'd taken the initiative to save her from the humiliation of the moment.

Lisa handed him the dish with the cheesecake and looked at Melody. "Are you sure you don't want some?"

"No, this is fine." But to Melody it was better than fine. It was the best fine she'd ever experienced. She took a small bite, and savoring wasn't even the word. It tasted like velvet Heaven. "Mmmm. Wow, Lisa, did you make this? It's incredible."

"I wish," Lisa said. "Eve brought it."

When Melody's gaze snapped over to Eve, she could've sworn she saw Eve shake her head as if deflecting the compliment. Eve's gaze fell to her own plate as she cut the tiniest sliver off. Softness wafted over Melody's spirit for this woman. She might have everything, but it was abundantly clear to Melody in that moment that Eve was as vulnerable as the rest of them. "This really is good, Eve. Did you make it from scratch?"

Never would Melody have been able to explain what she saw rush through Eve's dark gaze when she looked up. Surprise. Hope. Gratefulness. They were all there. "Yeah. It's my mom's recipe." And her gaze fell again.

It was at that moment that Melody realized how utterly unfair she had been to Eve. Eve had never done anything but be nice to her, and she had spent the better part of two years trashing every attempt Eve made at being friends. It was time that stopped.

"Well, it's awesome. If it's not some super family secret, I'd love to get the recipe from you sometime. Cheesecake is my mom's favorite, and she would love this."

Sincere happiness wafted through Eve's gaze this time when she looked at Melody, and a true connection was formed. "It's really easy. I can write it down for you if you want."

"That would be great." Melody met Eve's smile with one of her own. Two more bites and their cheesecake was gone. Another two minutes and so was everyone else's.

Blaine pushed the little plate away, sat back, and laid his arm over the back of her chair. "That was too good."

"You can say that again," A.J. said from her other side. "Now it's time for a nap and some baseball."

The women looked at him skeptically.

"In what order?" Eve asked.

"TV on, baseball found, lay down on the couch, zzzz." He put his hands out and his head back like he was sound asleep.

"See, I always said baseball is the most boring sport ever," Lisa said.

"Nope," Eve offered. "It cannot be worse than golf." She grabbed the spoon and set a serious look on her face. "'Tiger lines up the putt. It's a difficult lie…"

A.J. grabbed the spoon from her. "Like I ever even watch golf."

She grew indignant. "You did that one day, and when I came in and changed it you said…"

Both she and Lisa said simultaneously. "Hey, I was watching that."

"See what you have to look forward to," Eve said to Melody. "See, like this, they look so awake and alert, but you put a ring on their finger, and it's snooze city."

A ring? Where did that word come from? It sounded so… official. She wondered at that moment if he would ever give her a ring, if that could ever really be an actual possibility.

"And on that note," Jeff said, standing. He grabbed for dishes, and everyone else followed.

Blaine had never been around so much activity in all his life—save for the parties he only barely recalled. Even over the days of the funeral, it was the women who cooked and cleaned. Now he was part of the action as well, and it felt great. He laughed, he joked, he even kissed Melody twice on the sly. He was glad to see she was eating again, and he couldn't help but see the effect Dylan was having on Eve and A.J. It was like he was their surrogate child, and Blaine couldn't help but think he was as good for them as they were for him.

When the dishes were cleaned and everybody headed for the living room, he realized with a start that it was Sunday afternoon. Tomorrow, somehow he had to catch back onto the world—the world of work and school and problems so big he never wanted to think about them again. And one of the first staring at him was a mountain of homework. He was so behind, he would probably never catch up.

"What?" Melody asked, seeing the fun fall from his demeanor.

Blaine exhaled. He hated pulling her down with him.

"Blaine Donovan." She put her hands on her hips. "Don't you do that. What?"

He glanced toward the living room. "It's just… Well, I have a lot to read, and…"

An infinitesimal moment of interpretation, and she nodded. "Then we need to go."

However, he touched her arm. "I hate to make you go. You're having fun."

Her smile was soft. "We do what's good for the team, remember?"

Love, so tender it hurt, skidded across his heart. He pulled her into his arms and pulled in air and what it felt like to be loved. "You're awesome, you know that?"

"I'm only following your lead."

Twenty

Blaine had rented an apartment in the complex across from the one she had suggested. The efficiency was nice enough, but now there was the issue of fitting, moving, and dealing with five rooms of furniture and belongings. How he would fit it all in three little rooms was a complete mystery. When he started the project on the 21st it seemed doable. By the 24th even he had to admit he needed help.

There was the major issue of just walking into that house. Every single time he did, it killed his heart to remember how it had looked that horrible night. He tried not to remember. He had cleaned it as best he could, but there were still stains, still reminders, and he could do nothing about those. Then there was the physical issue of how to move all the stuff and where to move it to. He couldn't afford storage or movers. Moving it all himself across town especially with work, school, and Dylan seemed the other side of impossible. He'd measured the new space which he would take over on the first. It would fit the table, two beds and the living room chair. What he was going to do with everything else was beyond him.

As he stood in the living room on Wednesday night, dead tired from the day and gazing into the black hole of all he still had to get done, determination and willpower finally collapsed into "I can't do this." Dylan was staying the night at Melody's as he had every night since the Thursday that changed everything. That was a week ago, which was still hard to believe.

Walking into the kitchen and without even turning on the light, Blaine slid down the wall and dragged the phone down with him. He was too tired to even remember her number, so he let his heart dial it instead. When the digits were complete, he let his head thump back against the wall as he listened to her side ring. The boxes he'd managed to get hold of were stacked in the kitchen, looking like a mountain that threatened to avalanche right on top of him.

"Hello?"

It was impossible to say how much he had come to love that voice and how much he needed to hear it at that moment.

"Hey," he said, and the exhaustion and overwhelm permeated even that simple syllable.

"Uh-oh. Talk to me. What's going on?"

He heard the fear and the concern in her voice, but there was nothing he could do about that. There was nothing he could do about anything in his life at the moment. He shook his head, rolling it back and forth against the wall. "I can't do this."

"What's 'this'?"

"This." Boiling anger at his parents for throwing them to the wolves came up from the pit of him. "There's no way I can get all of this done by the first. There's just no way." He shook his head again, fighting the tears. Putting his face into his hand, he ran it the length of his face and let it stop on his chin. "I don't want to be here, Mel. I don't want to look at this place anymore. I've got homework to finish, a test on Monday I haven't even looked at yet. How am I supposed to get all of this done and go to work and take care of Dylan…"

"Blaine!" The name was a hard command. "Stop, okay? Slow down. Take a breath."

"What am I going to do, Melody? I don't even know what I'm doing anymore. How did I get here?"

This time she sounded as gentle as a summer breeze. "How you got there isn't as important as how you're going to get where you need to be. Listen. Let me make a couple phone calls. You don't have to do all of this by yourself. Okay?"

"But…"

"Blaine." It was another warning, another red flag that he was living in that miserable groove again. "I'm going to make a couple phone calls. Why don't you pack up your stuff for a couple days and come over here? There's no reason for you to stay in that place when I have a perfectly nice place for you to stay in right here."

"But I hate to put you out."

"You're seriously going to say that? After all we've been through? You're seriously going to worry about putting me out?"

How could he not? How could he impose on her and all those she would call after all they'd already done for him? They had lives of their own. They didn't have time to help him. In fact, they'd already gone way out of their way to help. Still, he knew she would shoot down any protest he put up. "No, I'm not going to say it."

"Good. Now put your stuff together and get over here. Have you eaten yet?"

Like there was time for such mundane things. "No."

She exhaled. "You'll be here in thirty?"

"There about."

"Good. Don't get lost."

He laughed just a little at that. "I won't."

It took 45, but who was counting? Melody had been on the phone since she'd hung up with him. Between that, cooking spaghetti, and watching Dylan, she wasn't at all sure she'd even noticed the time had passed. When the doorbell rang, she ran for it. Whipping it open, she smiled at him.

He looked worse than he sounded. "Hey."

"Hey," she said, tilting her head as she caressed him with her gaze. "Come on. I've got spaghetti for you."

It smelled wonderful. It tasted even better. Blaine would've thought that by now even his taste buds would be asleep, but he was wrong. However, the fuller his stomach got, the more tired pushed in on him.

"Wow, you look disasterized," she said, sitting at the other corner of the table with her drink and gazing at him with concern.

"That good huh?"

She absorbed that for a moment. "I called the guys. Jeff and Gabe can come tomorrow and Friday. A.J.'s off on Saturday. They all said just tell them what you need, and they're ready to help."

He ate a mushroom. "I don't even know what I need. There is so much stuff in that house, and there's no room for it in the apartment. What am I going to do with all that stuff?"

Melody considered that a minute and then stood. "Hang on." She left, and Blaine was so tired, he couldn't even wonder where she'd gone. In a few minutes she was back. She sat down again. "Mom says you can put some of it in the shed out back and the rest in the garage. Just the stuff you want to keep. The rest you can give away or sell."

There was a protest somewhere in the sea of exhaustion, but even he couldn't find it. He nodded. "That means I'm going to have to go through it and get it boxed up. When am I going to have time to do that?"

That stymied Melody for a moment. Even she seemed to be grasping the enormity of the situation. Finally she laid her hands on the table. "Tell you what. Why don't I go over tomorrow and help the guys box things up? Surely we can make a dent in it."

"But what about Dylan?" He was so tired and so stressed, it was everything he could do to beat back the tears.

"Lisa offered to keep him if we needed."

"Lisa?" he asked as if he'd never heard of her.

"She's working mostly from home these days so she can be with Alex. She said if we needed somewhere for Dylan, she could handle it."

Blaine exhaled and closed his eyes. "This is crazy."

"What do you have to finish tonight?"

That dragged him down even farther. "I'm supposed to read another ten pages, and I wanted to get my notes from Economics written out. But that ain't gonna happen."

"Let me do it."

He shook his head in complete exhaustion. "Mel…"

There was a pause as she surveyed him. "You know it's funny. I bet you would never believe me if I said it, but I think you're addicted to handling everything on your own."

"What?"

"Well, think about it. It's like me with the eating thing. I've taught myself that it's horrible if I eat, so when I look at food, my instant reaction is, 'No.' And it really doesn't matter how hungry I am or how long it's been since I've eaten. I watch you, and it's the same thing. Your instant answer to someone helping you is, 'No.'"

Maybe it was the exhaustion, maybe it was the grief that still clung to his heart, maybe it was the way he had lived for ten years finally crashing in on him. Whatever it was, Blaine was finding it impossible to find a reason she was wrong. "I hate relying on people. I hate owing them."

"Why is it owing? Do I owe you for rescuing me from the cheesecake the other day?"

It had to be the exhaustion because now he was totally not following. "Huh?"

"You know, when you said you were stuffed and we could share the cheesecake. You saved me from either having to take a whole piece out of guilt or refusing it altogether and knowing that everyone was looking at me. You rescued me."

Tiredly his eyebrows went up. "I just didn't want the whole thing."

"Yeah, and I just want to help. But because of the way we think about the cheesecake and the help, we automatically think our only option is to say, 'No.' It's not. Maybe it never has been. Maybe our thinking is what made it that way."

Now he knew he was too tired to follow this. "So you're doing my notes then?"

She smiled. "I'm going to do my best."

When Blaine laid down on the living room floor an hour later, tired pulled his eyelids down but not before he thanked God for letting her get sick at the amusement park that day. Never would he have thought he would be thankful for something so awful, but her getting sick was the best thing that ever happened to him. As he drifted off to sleep, he smiled at that bizarre thought.

"I think the most logical place to start is the kitchen," Melody said, desperately trying not to notice how truly horrible the neighborhood not to even mention the house was. The walls were dirty. The floor was dirty. The curtains were mere strings. Her heart hurt that the two of them had existed here for so long. They deserved so much better.

"Are we moving this to the new place?" Gabe asked, and even he had lost the lilt his voice always had. He sounded far more like the second-in-command lieutenant he now was at the fire station than she had ever heard him.

Melody nodded, opening the cabinet closest to the wall. "We might as well get started." However, she jumped a foot back when her gaze met up with a dead something that she could no longer tell what it was. "Ugh!"

Without question, Jeff stepped up behind her. "Why don't you start over by the dishwasher? That stuff's probably been used the most."

"O… okay." She backed up, feeling the bile come back up her throat as her chest squeezed out the air. God, help us get them out of here.

When he got to work at one, Blaine could stand it no longer. The thought of the task they were facing drove him to call. It rang and then rang again.

"Hello?" The voice was deep and could only belong to one big fireman he knew.

Blaine smiled in spite of the misgivings running through his head. "Hey, Gabe. This is Blaine. How's it going?"

"Oh. Good. But just so you know, you owe me double for making sure Jeff doesn't break anything."

"Hey now!" he heard Jeff's protest in the background. "I haven't broken anything."

"Well," Blaine said, trying to get his heart all right with this, "at least double of nothing is still nothing, right?"

Gabe laughed heartily. "This is true."

"Oh," Blaine said, hating to admit this, but he'd been thinking about it all morning. "Be careful when you open the far cabinet in the kitchen. There was something…"

"Yep. Melody found it about two hours ago. She screamed like a little girl."

"I did not!" Melody protested from somewhere else in the room.

Again Gabe laughed. "Hey! Fireman abuse! You know you need to learn to control your girlfriend."

Girlfriend. It was such a daunting word. Still, the sliding of his heart at the word made him know it was true. "Is she there?"

"Yeah, but she might not be if she keeps whacking me," Gabe said and then added an, "Ow!" for good measure.

The knot in Blaine's heart unwound. "Can I talk to her?"

"Sure. Here she is."

A moment. "Hello?"

If Blaine didn't know better, at that moment he wanted the word to be more than girlfriend. "Hey. How's it going?"

"Well, besides the dead animals and having to work with these two hon-yoks, everything's great. How are you?"

"Trying not to freak out too much." Gratefulness for everything she had done wafted into him. "Thanks for doing the notes. It's amazing. I can actually read your handwriting."

"See, I am good for something."

This smile was real. "Are you sure you guys are okay?"

"Okay?" she asked, and he heard the teasing. "Well, 'okay' might be stretching it a bit with these two."

"Hey!" This time it was Gabe's deep voice protesting.

Blaine laughed and then let the laugh fall away. "Yeah, but you're okay? You don't need anything?"

"You," she said softly. "But besides that I'm good."

She was getting better at that caressing his heart with her gentle teasing thing. It did things to him he hardly had the words to acknowledge. "I love you, you know that?"

"Hmm… seems like you've mentioned that once or twice before. Well, I'd better get back to work before these two destroy the place."

He wanted to ask, wanted to stay connected to her like this forever, but she was right. They had work to do and so did he. "I'll see you later?"

"I'm counting on it."

"How're things going at the house?" Eve asked when she sat down at the break table at four.

"Good." Blaine nodded. "I talked to Mel earlier. They're cleaning out the kitchen."

Eve nodded. "So how are you doing?"

He thought about that question and then rethought his thoughts. "You know I always thought this would be horrible. That I would die if any of you ever saw that house, but… I don't know. It's been… different than I expected."

"Different, in a good way?"

"Yeah, and that's totally weird to me. How is it possible that y'all can know every horrible thing about me and still talk to me like you like me?"

"Because we do like you. We like you. It has nothing to do with your stuff or your situation. You're a cool guy, Blaine. You always have been. You just never let yourself see that."

He breathed that in. "Yeah? Well, I think it has more to do with y'all than with me."

She tilted her head, making her long shiny dark hair drift down over her shoulder. "Mind explaining that?"

"Well." He spun his cup, sorting through all of the evidence. "You're not like everybody else. You don't judge—no matter how bad it is. I mean Melody found the mouse in the cabinet, and they were all just laughing and joking about it. I don't get that."

"Okay, first let me say, I'm very glad God chose to put me here talking to you rather than there dealing with the dead mouse, but what you're not seeing is this is how God sees you. He doesn't care about all the stuff, and I don't mean the mouse in the cabinet. I mean the junk in your soul, the fear, the hopelessness, the arrogance. He doesn't care about that because he only sees what's real. And what's real is that you are His child. His love isn't based on what you have or what you can do for Him or even on how you feel about Him. It's based on Him and His love for you, and that doesn't change. Ever."

"But to go and clean out somebody else's house when it's like that."

Eve nodded. "It takes love. Real love. Not the noun kind of love but the verb kind, the doing kind. Not the kind you give when it feels good but take away when it doesn't. Not the fast food, junk food kind of love—slick, prettily packaged, and empty. But real, no-matter-what love."

"But I don't know how you do that," he said, and in the depths of him he wanted to understand this. He needed to understand it because it felt so central to everything else. "How do you look at how horrible a life is and not run the other direction?"

She sat for a moment and then looked at him. "Remember the treasure in the field? That thing the pastor was talking about at church that one day?"

Blaine nodded, feeling like he would probably never forget that. "Yeah."

"Well, as you live with God, you begin to understand that

people have all this junk around them. They collect it. They hold onto it. They come to believe that it's them, but it's not. The junk is not what's real. What's real is the treasure, the priceless, valuable, precious treasure that each person carries inside themselves."

"Every person?"

"Every person. The trick is when you see the junk to know the treasure is there somewhere and to love them enough to be willing to dig. Knowing that, understanding that is what helps the guys go out and do the stuff they do to help people. It also makes it easier to forgive and to love. Everything becomes possible when you love like that."

"The verb kind."

"Yeah. The verb kind."

"Uh, Jeff," Melody said, shaking from the center of her as she stood at the threshold of the bathroom, her hand on the doorjamb lest she fall for the fear. "Could you come here?"

He looked back at her from where he was packing things. "Sure. What's up?"

She simply turned and walked slowly, in a daze, back into the bedroom at the end of the hallway. If she could've gotten the words out, she would've warned him. But where were the words? She walked over to the drawer that was still open. Her heartbeat thudded in her chest, sending what was left of her nerves scattering.

When he stepped up next to her, Jeff took one look at the gun lying atop the needles and bottles of stuff she didn't even want to ask about. As she had seen him do countless times that day, duty snapped on over everything else. "It's okay. Let me handle this."

Like she was going to argue with that.

From what she'd been able to glean, they had handled it. When the police car showed up half an hour later, she simply stayed in Blaine's room shaking but trying not to. To have a gun, in an unlocked bottom drawer where Dylan could find it… How could a mother even think about doing something like that?

When the voices receded down the hallway back toward the

kitchen, she couldn't keep up the act anymore. It was too much to hold. She sat down on the bed and let the weight of everything push her shoulders down, down, down until her elbows were on her knees and her head was bowed over them. "God, how did they live like this? He told me, he kept telling me, but I never imagined…"

"Hey." Jeff's voice was soft and concerned as he stood at the doorway.

Her head jerked up, and she swiped at the tears.

With a quiet, concerned smile on his face, he stepped over to her. "Come here." Gently he pulled her up from the bed and gathered her into his arms. The tears flowed freely then as he held her. "Shh."

"How could they live like this, Jeff? How could anyone?"

"We're gonna need…" Gabe's voice boomed into the room but stopped on the word and the sight. He stepped toward the two of them slowly. "Mel."

She heard the tender concern lacing his voice as well. She tried to pull away from Jeff, but he kept his hands on her arms as she swiped at her tears. "I'm sorry. I just…"

Gabe stepped over to her and put his hand on her back. At that moment, she was completely convinced that when they said "Houston's finest," people had no idea how true that was.

"Look. Be glad stuff like that still gets to you," Gabe said, tilting his gaze so he could look at her. "It worries me that it doesn't get to me as much anymore."

She was grateful for him, she was grateful for his words too. She was so grateful for them that she started crying again. "We are so lucky to have y'all."

As Jeff hugged her again, Gabe smiled at her. "Yep, and don't you ever forget it."

Why the sight of the boxes stacked in the kitchen and the empty, open cabinets surprised him so much, Blaine wasn't totally sure. He knew they were here. He knew they were working on it. But somehow he'd never really thought they would get this much done.

"Yeah!" Jeff yelled back down the hall. "I think the bed goes to…" He crested the wall and stopped like a horse being pulled up on the reins. "Oh, well, look who finally showed up. Good news, Gabe! Second shift is here!"

He set the box down and held out a hand, covered by a well-worn work glove. "Nice of you to join us."

Blaine shook Jeff's hand, seeing instantly that his present clothing choice was not going to be very practical for the situation. "Wow. You guys have gotten a lot done."

"We're down to the furniture." Jeff stood, wiping his forehead as Gabe came in. "Don't look now. Fresh reinforcements have arrived."

"Impressive," Gabe said, holding out his hand to shake Blaine's hand. "You got here just in time for supper break. Mel went out to pick something up."

It was truly amazing how one guy, not so much older than himself, could be so wise. As Blaine stood, in that minute, he realized he did want to be like them—not fighting fires, but learning to love as a verb just like they all did so easily.

"Oh," Jeff said, and his smile fell as he glanced out the open front door. "I need to tell you before Melody gets back. We found some things in the bottom drawer in your mom's room."

Blaine didn't like the sound of that, and he took a half step backward. "What kind of things?"

"Drug stuff," Gabe said, his voice falling another octave. "And a gun."

"A…" Horror streaked through him. "Are you… Are you sure? She never told me she had anything like that, not here." The revulsion snaked through him yanking up anger and pure abhorrence. "What was she thinking?"

Sitting down on one of the chairs in a heap, he shook his head at the crisscrossing of the horrific thoughts. Then one dominated the others, and he looked up at them. "You've gotta believe me. I had no idea."

Like two sequoias they stood there, judge and jury seemingly ready to pronounce sentence on him as the most rotten person in the whole world.

"We had the cops come confiscate it," Gabe said. "That seemed the easiest."

Blaine nodded. "Yeah. Yeah." The nodding became a shake. "I certainly don't want it."

Jeff glanced outside again. "You need to know. Melody found

the stuff. It really freaked her out."

Tons of guilt dropped on him like so many boulders. How would he ever face her again?

"Who's hungry?" Melody called as she pushed through the door into the house. There were even more boxes stacked in the kitchen if that was possible, and now in the living room there were the pieces of a bed as well.

"Well, it's about time," Gabe said. "What, did you do, go to China?"

"There was a wreck on the freeway. Traffic was crazy." She set the sacks on the table.

"Hey, Mel." Jeff came in, stepped over to the sink where he removed his gloves, and washed his hands. "It smells terrific."

"Yeah. I've been slaving over it for hours." She reached in and pulled out her grilled chicken sandwich. Choosing healthy was becoming easier the more she did it. She reached in and pulled out a burger. "Here's yours." That one went to Gabe. The next went to Jeff.

As it traded hands, she caught sight of Blaine leaning against the wall, watching her. He looked so much like he had that night getting burgers, it made her heart flip over. She really liked him in the jeans and T-shirt look. Of course, she liked him in the pressed slacks and button down too. It was becoming abundantly clear that she liked him no matter how he decided to show up. Shyly she stepped over to him and put her hands on his arms. "You made it."

His smile was cautious, wary. "Yeah."

"Cool. C'mon. I got you extra fries." And with barely a peck and a tug, she dragged him over to the table.

Twenty-One

When they were at her house later, Blaine waited until he heard her come down the stairs to check on them for the last time. She always did that, and he liked it more than he would ever tell anyone. At the couch, she pulled the blanket up over Dylan, stopped for a moment, and then turned to check on him.

"Hey," he said so no one other than her could hear.

"Hey." Her smile flitted over his heart. She stepped closer to him. "Shouldn't you be sleeping?"

"Shouldn't you?" He reached out for her hand, and she accepted the invitation. Carefully, she sat down next to him. It was these times, when it was just the two of them that Blaine looked forward to the most. He sat back against the footrest of the recliner and pulled her back next to him. No, "girlfriend" didn't do this justice.

A breath to settle the words. "Jeff told me about today."

"The mouse?" She laughed. "It wasn't as bad as he…"

"The gun."

The words stopped her, and her head fell forward slightly.

"It wasn't mine," he said as if she might think it was. "I didn't even know it was there. Gabe said by the set up, he thought she had probably started dealing too. They think maybe it was a deal gone bad that night."

Melody sat, simply nodding.

"I don't know." His embrace tightened around her. "All I know is I'm so glad Dylan wasn't there, and he wasn't there because of you."

She laid her head back, arching it over his shoulder so she could look at him. "Because of us."

A moment and he nodded. "Because of us." He heaved a sigh. "I'm sorry my life is such a train wreck."

"None of us are perfect."

"But it could be so much better."

"And it could be so much worse." She turned then to face him. "Don't you get it? I'm smart enough to know that stuff isn't you. C'mon. Give me a little credit."

"I know. I just… I just wish I could be the person you deserve. I hate dragging you through all of this."

"Hey." Her finger came under his chin and picked his gaze up to look at her. "This isn't about impressing somebody. It's life. You've got your mice in your cabinets, and I've got mine." She dropped his chin. "I think the important thing is we're being honest about them now. Don't discount that. This whole mess of a situation has forced us to stand together as a team. That's a good thing."

His gaze went to her of its own accord. "I still think you're crazy for wanting to team up with me."

"And you're not crazy for teaming with me?" She laughed. "Face it, we're both crazy, and it's okay. We're going to get through this… together."

He nodded and pulled her back to him. "Together."

By Saturday morning the fact that Blaine was still standing was more than Melody could fathom. The truth was, she was a centimeter from an utter breakdown from the strain and edging closer to it every second, so when he suggested that she sleep in a little and then take Dylan to Eve's, she gladly relented.

He, of course, was up with the sun. He only had a few last minute straggly things to finish up at the house, and then he was meeting A.J. to set up things at the new apartment, which had by some miracle come open earlier than he had thought. Melody considered it a miracle anyway. Then again, she considered a lot of things miracles these days.

She glanced into the other seat and smiled as she and Dylan headed north. Dylan was quite a trooper. "So are you excited about seeing the new place with your bed and everything all set up?"

"Yeah," he said, but it was soft and not very convincing.

Concern wafted over her. "What's wrong?"

His little gaze came over to her. "Do bad people live there—in the apartment?"

"Bad people?" She wasn't following, but she was concerned.

"Yeah," he said again quietly. "Mom said Dave lived in an apartment, but I couldn't go there with her because bad people lived there."

Melody's heart slid into her shoes. "Oh, honey." She reached over and gave him a hug. "This isn't that kind of apartment. It's really going to be nice. Really. You'll see."

He considered that a minute and then two. "Blaine said the school's so close I can walk there." His gaze came to hers again. "I don't want to walk there. What if there are bad guys on the way to school?"

That he had lived so long with the bad guys right outside and even inside his house and never gotten this scared was a testament to someone. Who, she wasn't quite sure. "Well, Blaine's going to take you to school every morning. And I'm going to come pick you up every afternoon."

His eyes widened. "You will? Every day?"

"Are you kidding me? I have to have my Dylan time. You know that. What would I do without this face?" She reached over and pinched his face between her thumb and finger. "Look at this face."

Dylan laughed as he pawed at her hand. "Stop that."

She glanced at him liking his laugh. "It's going to be okay. You'll see."

One last walk through. One last look at a life he was glad to be leaving far behind him. Blaine walked slowly, imprinting the memory on his heart for future reference. If he ever got the crazy thought of leaving Melody, he vowed to remember this moment. When he got to the living room, devoid of furniture and of life, he stopped. So many fights, so many nights, so many horrible memories, all leading to this moment.

"Mom, you'll never know how much I loved you," he whispered to the space around him. "I forgive you. I do. I know you were as lost as I was. But just so you know, I've made some really, really good friends. They're teaching me about real love, the verb kind. That's what I'm using now. The verb kind, the kind that loves you anyway. I know you're okay now, and I want you to know that we are too." He looked once more around the room, dragged in a breath, and let it go. "Bye, Mom. I love you."

"Well, look who we have here," Eve said, meeting them at the door and hugging Dylan on his way into her house. "Buster's out back."

Dylan raced to the kitchen. "Did you give him his bone yet?"

"Nope. I was waiting for you."

"Cool." He waited for the bone she took out of the cabinet and then raced outside.

Melody's heart went with him.

"He's such a great kid," Eve said, replacing the box.

"Yeah, he is."

She was about to say the words to make a graceful exit when Eve stepped over to the stove.

"Do you have a minute?" Eve asked, and Melody's fear shields flew up.

"Uh, yeah. I guess so."

Eve glanced at her as she picked up the little white kettle. "You want some tea? It's mango something or other."

How could she say no? "Sure." Carefully, Melody sat down at the table and waited for Eve who brought the two steaming cups over to her. She set one in front of Melody who mumbled her thanks.

When Eve sat down but didn't say anything right away, Melody seriously questioned her own sanity. Why hadn't she gotten out when she had the chance?

"I was just wondering how you think Blaine is doing with all of this. I mean I've talked to him at work and everything, but I know he's really good at putting up a good front when things get rough." She took a sip of her tea.

Melody considered the question. "Amazingly well, I think. I'd be under the bus having to deal with everything he is."

Eve nodded. "And you?"

A knife went through her heart at the kindness of this woman whom she had been nothing but rude to for reasons she now didn't even fully understand herself. "I'm just trying to be there for him, for them. It's hard sometimes."

Setting the cup on the table, Eve looked at her a long minute. "I heard about the gun. Lisa told me."

Melody now knew how Blaine felt. "It wasn't his."

"I know." Eve's gaze felt like it went right through her. "I also know how tough something like that is to find out. It had to be a shock."

Shock. Yeah. There was a good word for it. She'd gotten pretty used to being in shock's grip the past couple of weeks. "It's all been pretty intense. I try not to think about it too much so I can do what needs to be done. I try not to think too much about what living there had to have done to Blaine and to Dylan." The tears welled in her heart. "He told me on the way over here he's scared to move into the apartment because his mom told him he couldn't go with her to the apartment she was going because bad guys lived there."

Eve sighed and shook her head. "Ugh. Poor kid."

"Yeah, and I don't know how many other bad guys are living in his head either."

Slowly Eve nodded. "Been there." Then she laughed. "Heck, I'm still there."

Confusion twined through Melody. "What do you mean?"

Time slid into itself as Eve sat there staring at her cup. "When Dustin was alive, there was a time I wanted to know all about the bad guys living in his head—the fires, the lives he was out there saving, the lives he had lost. He wouldn't tell me." She glanced up. "Fireman's code and everything. It was hard. Then about the time I got my heart wrapped around that one, he got killed. I lived with some really bad guys in my head myself for quite awhile, and then A.J. showed up. At first I was really glad he wasn't a fireman. At least he wouldn't be running into burning buildings that might fall on him at any moment.

"But what I didn't bargain on were the bad guys living in his head—the lives he couldn't pull back from the edge, the times when he had to face un-faceable situations." She shook her head as her gaze stayed on her cup. "Some of them really get to him." Her glance up was only that. "Like last week. I'm not sure he's still recovered from realizing it was Blaine's mom in that house."

She sniffed. "And I'm not sure he ever will." There was the barest of pauses. "A.J.'s just like that. He cares so much, and he doesn't want anyone to be in pain—especially people he really cares about." Eve smiled at her. "But you already knew that."

If she didn't know before, Melody certainly did now. Somehow she had never put the phone call together with how he knew Blaine needed her that night. "So A.J. was there?"

Eve nodded slowly. "Yeah. I think that's why he didn't make it to help the last couple of days. I don't think he could face walking into that house again."

Compassion for her best friend gripped her heart. She looked at Eve, understanding far more than she ever had. "Thanks for telling me."

Again Eve nodded. "I just thought you should know."

The silver SUV was already parked in the lot in front of the new apartment. Although he was glad for the help, Blaine really had to question why God had sent this particular help. Yes, they seemed to be on near-speaking terms these days, but they were uneasy near-speaking terms at best. Steeling his nerves, he parked the green Toyota and climbed out. It was like facing Goliath head-on. He'd barely retrieved the last of his possessions from the car when he heard the door slam and the footsteps behind him.

"Need some help?" A.J. asked, striding up, backwards cap and North Carolina basketball jersey as usual. He almost looked happy to be there. Almost.

"Uh." The cord of the lamp Blaine was holding didn't exactly come out of the car with him. "Well, hmm… if I could get this stuff out without breaking something, that would be a start."

"Here." A.J. reached in and unsnagged the cord. "See. There you go." He wound the cord around the lamp, reached in and grabbed the box of cleaning supplies.

"I can get that little box if you'll hand it to me," Blaine said, pointing at the one on the far side. "And then we'll only have one more trip."

A.J. set the first box on the trunk, grabbed the second and handed it to Blaine, then retook the first one. "Lead on."

Blaine shut and locked the car, still mortified that A.J. had actually seen it, but he couldn't dwell on that now. There were far more pressing issues like how to come up with a way to not completely obliterate his chances with Melody for the next hour or so until she got here. He climbed the steps, willing his feet forward, went to the door, and unlocked it. On the other side, however, somehow he didn't at all remember them leaving this big of a mess when they left the night before.

"Wow. Nice place," A.J. said, and he almost sounded sincere as he put his box down with the rest of them.

Setting the box and the lamp he was carrying down, Blaine turned and surveyed his new life. It looked like the mountain of boxes had just thrown up all over his new living quarters. The boxes were everywhere. He put his hand up to his head, staring at the mess.

"So," A.J. said, "where do you want to start?"

Running his fingers through his hair, Blaine looked at the fork in the road ahead of him and chose the road that was getting easier and easier. "Would you believe I have no idea?" He looked at A.J. sheepishly and laughed. "The guys packed everything up. Melody decided what to send here and what to send to her mom's place. So I really have no idea what any of this is." His hand dropped back to his side.

A.J. nodded his understanding of the situation, looked at the project, and made some quick calculations. "Well, it won't do me any good to open boxes, I won't have a clue where anything goes. So why don't I carry and you direct? We'll see how that works."

It was as good a plan as any. They got to work. At first it was with minimal words. "Bathroom." "Kitchen." "Closet." But as the job continued, they both became more at ease with their respective rolls.

"This is a closet," Blaine said, handing it over to A.J. who took it and headed that direction. Blaine opened another box. "Man, I would never have gotten this done on my own. You know that?" He stood and handed the box to A.J. "Bathroom." Ripping the tape off the next one, he peered inside. "I'm telling you, those two are unbelievable. They should go into the moving business." He handed him the box. "Bathroom closet."

"Let me tell you, if you want two great guys on your team, those are the two to have," A.J. said. "I don't honestly know which one I respect more."

"I hear you there. Closet." He ripped into another box.

"That gun thing would've totally freaked me out, not to even mention if I'd had Mel there, but she said they just handled it. No questions asked." The box changed hands. "Kitchen."

A.J. headed that direction. "So you really didn't know she had it then?"

"I had no idea. I about passed out when they told me." He picked up another, and they had finally uncovered one wall. "Bathroom. I owe them more than I will ever be able to repay. That's for sure." He handed another box over. "Kitchen."

"So how's Mel holding up through all of this?"

"She's been a rock. I tell you what, she is really something special." Blaine handed two boxes over. "Bathroom closet." And he was at the end of those boxes as well. Amazingly the job was starting to look more and more manageable all the time. "Kitchen."

A.J. took the box as Blaine ripped into the next one.

"Oh, wait. This is kitchen too."

Without question A.J. turned, and Blaine put this box on top of the first.

"So how's she doing with the other thing?" A.J. asked.

"The eating?"

"Yeah." A.J. put those boxes on the kitchen cabinet and was back in mere moments.

"Better. She's really trying to eat healthy now, you know? Not overeat but not starve either. I think she sees what she was doing to herself which is great." The next box came in an arc from the floor to A.J. via Blaine. "Closet. It's weird, you know? I never saw myself with someone like her. She's so down-to-earth and just real. And it's so cool because I can be real with her too. Just me. I've never had that before." Another box got transferred. "Bathroom."

"So you're really serious about this then?"

Suddenly Blaine remembered who he was talking to. "Uh, well." He stood and scratched his ear, looking at the remaining boxes. There were so few left. Where did all the others go? "Yeah. I mean I can't imagine my life without her anymore, you know? She's just…" Words failed. He picked up a box. "Closet." Thinking through the statement, he could find no words. "I'd never really thought about marriage, not for me, you know? But then, Melody showed up, and it's nothing like I thought it would be, but somehow it's… better. And now…" He handed A.J. the second-to-last box. "I don't know."

Instead of turning with the box, A.J. stopped. "For what it's worth, I'm glad she found somebody like you."

Blaine snorted and picked up the last box. "What? A rich spoiled jerk who wasn't rich but just a spoiled jerk?"

For the second time in two weeks, he stood toe-to-toe with A.J. Knight. However, whatever he'd expected each time hadn't been there either one.

"I'm sorry about how I treated you… before," A.J. said only barely looking at him. "I judged you without really knowing anything."

Shrugging, Blaine started to step past his former nemesis. "It's not like I didn't give you every reason to hate me."

"And it's not like I gave you any reason to not totally blow me off either." A.J. took a long breath. "We were both wrong, but for Mel's sake, I want you to know I think you're the best thing that ever happened to her, and when the two of you stand up at that altar someday, I'll be in the front row cheering you both on."

It wasn't manly to let A.J. see the emotion, so Blaine ducked his head. After a moment to absorb it, he nodded. "I appreciate that." He looked up. "More than you know."

A.J.'s grin spread across his face. "What do you say we get this new place set up?"

Blaine nodded. "You got it."

When Melody walked in, she thought she must have the wrong apartment.

"Go long!" Blaine called from the back hallway. A flash of something streaked through the opening.

"And… touchdown!" A.J. hollered, doing a happy dance right out into the main room. However, the happy dance stopped cold the second he saw Melody. "Oh, hi, Mel. I didn't hear you come in."

"Yeah." Her eyebrows lifted, and she glanced down the hall. "I noticed. Uh, what's going on?"

"The movers," A.J. said, shaking his head. "We're trying to figure out a method to their madness."

Melody lifted her chin, still baffled. "Uh-huh." Before she got the next question out, Blaine strode in. Without so much as a hesitation, he stepped right up to her.

"Hey, Mel. I thought that sounded like my good luck charm." With a smile the size of the Grand Canyon, he swept her into his arms and kissed her soundly.

When she got to come back up for air, Melody looked from one of them to the other. "Have you two been sniffing paint or what?"

"No," A.J. said, stepping over to her. Blaine let her go, and A.J. wrapped her in his arms. "We're just glad to see you. Is that a crime?"

She hugged him, trying to catch back onto reality. "Well, no…"

"Good." A.J. pulled back from her. "'Cause I'd have to serve some serious time. Did you get Dylan to our place?"

Man, this felt weird. Bizarre. Unworldly. Kind of like falling into the Twilight Zone or the fourth dimension. "Yeah. I did." Then she remembered what Eve had told her, and the strangeness melted away. She looked right at A.J. "Oh, you know, I never told you thanks for calling me the other night."

His gaze fell from hers to his shoes. "Oh, it was no big deal."

"Yeah, it was." She looked back at Blaine. "And we both really appreciate it."

When A.J. looked at her, the goofiness was gone. Instead of words, he simply nodded. She hugged him again only this time she felt it like she never had before. Then she stepped back against Blaine, swiped at her eyes, and looked around the space.

"So, what're we standing around for? Let's get to work."

The next day the five of them once again sat in the pew. Melody, next to Blaine, his arm around her. Eve sat holding hands with A.J. and Dylan between the two couples. How it could all feel so right, Melody had no clue, but it did and for that she would forever be thankful. The preacher stepped to the podium.

"We all know about the miracles of Jesus—curing the blind man, making lepers whole, lifting the cripple from the mat his friends dropped from the ceiling. We've heard the stories, but there is an element that we often miss, an element that is central to the healing power of Jesus. In every one of these stories it was the touch of Jesus that changed things. It was Jesus taking the time to touch the broken, to see the blind man that nobody had seen begging for years, to stop, to notice, to help, to love, to touch another person, and by touching them to heal them. He healed their bodies, yes. But His touch healed so much more—their spirits and their lives.

"The touch of Jesus. It was a touch of great tenderness and hope and joy. It said to the person, 'I see you. You are special to me. I love you.' When Jesus touched people, they knew it because they were changed by it. Many ran into town proclaiming this man who had touched them, witnessing to His power. Look at the stories. Over and over again, Jesus touches someone, and their lives are never the same."

The preacher paused, shifting at the podium. "Does Jesus still touch people today?"

When the preacher paused again, Melody let her hand drifted across to Blaine's knee where his hand came over to cover hers. She looked up at him, and amazement was shining from his face.

"It depends," the preacher said slowly. "It depends on the decisions you and I make every day. When we stop to offer a word of encouragement or hope, that's Jesus, reaching out through us to a broken, blind, hurting soul. And that touch can still work miracles. It can still lift the lost lamb from the bramble and set it on the Savior's shoulders. It can still find the lost coin and call the neighbors to come and celebrate. It can be there, running toward the sinner who believed he was lost forever welcoming him home with loving arms and a long embrace.

"We all have that chance. We all have that commission. That is ultimately our call—to be Christ to each other, to reach out and touch others with the tenderness of Jesus. To love them, right where they are—without judgment or condemnation, but with love that is patient and kind, overflowing and abundant."

"The verb kind," Blaine whispered as if he were a zombie in a trance.

Melody glanced at him, but he didn't even seem to notice. Breathing through the tears, she returned her attention to the podium.

"The beauty of the touch of Jesus is that when it comes into our lives, we can't help but extend it to others. We want others—everyone we come into contact with—to share in this great mystery we have found. This mystery that changes ordinary water into the finest of wines—the best wine. That's what the touch of Jesus can do in a life.

"When our touch lifts someone else's burden and brings a light of hope back into their lives, then we are truly living our Christian calling. We are truly bringing His light and His life into this world. Imagine a world full of the gentle touch of Jesus. Imagine the lives that would be saved, the brokenness that might be healed, the unleashing of hope and love that would occur. The blind would truly see again, the lame would rise up off their mats and walk free forever.

"That is our legacy. That is our challenge. That is our commission… if we so choose. But it all starts with a choice. And that choice ultimately… is yours."

It was as if a bomb had exploded in his being. As Blaine led the others out, Melody barely got out of the bench before he wrapped her into his arms and kissed her head. They walked out to the parking lot, just holding each other. On the back steps, they stopped as first Dylan came up and then Eve and A.J. walking hand-in-hand.

"Jeff invited us," A.J. said. "But I think we'll just stop and pick something up—a couple buckets of chicken or something. Lisa's not feeling all that great."

"Oh," Melody said, still wrapped in Blaine's arm, "maybe we should just let y'all go then…"

"Are you kidding?" A.J. asked. "We'd probably be beheaded if we showed up without you three."

"Come on," Eve said. "Once that baby gets here, who knows how many more times we'll even get to do this?"

Blaine simply looked to Melody. He was so happy, it really didn't matter what they did.

"Well, maybe we can come for a little while, but we can't stay. Studious here has a test tomorrow."

"Studious? Or stud-ious?" Blaine's grin teased her unmercifully, and it worked beautifully. Her cheeks reddened nicely as her jaw dropped. "What? You were the one that said it." He pulled her even tighter to him.

"I want to go with A.J.," Dylan said.

"And Eve," Eve said as if she was hurt.

"And Eve," Dylan said, smiling sweetly.

"Much better," she said, pulling him over to her for a hug. She tousled his hair. "What do you say we let you pick out the dessert?"

"What?" Blaine asked in a mock pout. "No cheesecake?"

"Do you think I'm a factory or what?" Eve asked. "You only get cheesecake on really special occasions."

"Ah," Blaine responded as if he totally understood, which he didn't, but it didn't matter. Nothing mattered to his heart today. It was flying, and there was no reason to land now. "Okay. But you be good, Dylan. You listen to A.J."

"And Eve," Eve said.

Blaine laughed. "And Eve."

Feeling like her feet never so much as touched the pavement, Melody drifted with Blaine over to the little white car. She couldn't remember ever being so happy. At the car they got in, and he started it up.

"Does this ever seem completely unbelievable to you?" Blaine asked, glancing at her.

"What?"

"I don't know. Everything. I mean how did I go from barely scraping by, trying to do everything myself and failing miserably to feeling like I've got the best friends in the world, the girl of my dreams, and God's love to boot. How in the world did that happen?"

She smiled over at him. "I don't know, but aren't you glad it did?"

"Are you kidding? Truer words have never been spoken." He started out of the lot and headed into traffic. "I don't know about you, but I love coming to church here. I used to think church was a boring waste of time. I can't figure out how I had that so wrong before."

"I thought you were nuts the first time you said it. Did I want to go to church? Why would I want to go to church? But now, going, I just feel like Jesus is so speaking right to me. It's like I just want more and more and more. I want to know more about Him, to learn, to hear again and again how much He loves me. I can't explain why that makes such a difference, but it so does."

Blaine drove for several minutes. Then he looked over at her. "You ever think about what would've happened if…"

"If we didn't keep running into each other? If I hadn't called you to go with me because I wanted to get back at A.J.?"

"Yeah."

She put her head back and thought about how very far they had come. "Sometimes, but I so see now that God had a plan even in all the madness."

"It makes me want to trust Him all the more now."

"Yeah, it does me too."

He glanced at her again. "Do you think it gets any better than this?"

"Ugh. I wouldn't know how." Then she looked over at him. "But good or bad, I want it to be with you."

If he could've asked her at that moment, Blaine would have. His heart was there. His head was there. But his life wasn't quite. However, as he reached over, took her hand, and kissed it gently, he swore one day soon they would be together, not just as boyfriend and girlfriend, but as man and wife. For as scary as that had always felt before, the fear felt far more like excitement now.

He could do nothing less than marvel as they shared their hearts with each other all the way to Jeff and Lisa's. When they arrived, it was hard to fathom just how right this felt. These weren't her friends. They were his too. They had shown him in so many ways the touch of Jesus and the miracles that can happen when you dare to be for real with people.

When they stepped up to the door, Blaine reached out and rang the doorbell. Then he pulled her to him and kissed her head. She snuggled closer into his arms, hers wrapped tightly around him. It was just one more perfect moment to add to all the others.

Then the door popped open, and love once again welcomed them into its embrace.

Epilogue

"Oh, boy, don't look now! Here comes trouble! We've got company!" Gabe yelled to anyone within a five-mile radius as he stood on the deck over the spitting, hissing grill.

"Hey! Hey! Hey! We made it!" Blaine said, laughing as he helped Melody, his wife of four months, up the steps and onto the deck. They'd only known their new secret for three days, and already he was wild with worry and concern about every move she made. "Careful on that last step."

Dylan pushed past and rushed on ahead of them. "Guess what, Uncle Gabe, guess what! I get to go water skiing today!"

"Cool!" Gabe held up his hand for the child who was looking like less and less a child every day. Dylan hit it, still jumping up and down. Then Gabe held out his hand to Blaine. "Hey. Happy Fourth." Behind him, the hamburgers on the grill popped and spit loudly. "Mel."

"Hi there." She accepted the one-armed hug he gave her. "Are the girls inside?"

"They are," Gabe said, flipping a hamburger patty. "They're trying to figure out how to make some kind of jalapeño hot sauce. Consider yourself warned."

She bowed slightly. "Thank you, oh wise one."

"May the force be with you." Gabe did a hand out salute that had nothing to do with Star Wars.

Melody laughed. He was as crazy as ever. She left them tending the meat and pushed into the kitchen door where she found the three women just as Gabe had warned, standing over a blender, gazing at the green concoction therein. "Hi, guys."

All three gazes swung to her. "Mel! You made it!"

She had never felt more like a woman in an old hen's club than when she stepped into that kitchen, but she couldn't be upset by that. There was a rightness about it that wouldn't let her. Her life was no longer a single strand, it was now woven inextricably with the others represented by that gathering.

"Here, come taste this," Ashley said, holding up a chip with green something on it.

Dutifully Melody went over and accepted the chip. She bit gingerly into it, chewed, and considered. "Not bad. Maybe a little salty though."

"I told you," Lisa said. "It needs more sugar." She went about measuring more out.

"So how's our resident newlywed?" Eve asked, grabbing a chip sans the sauce.

"Ugh. Trying to get settled. You would not believe the boxes. I go to sleep at night, and all I see is boxes."

"Did Blaine ever get that bed put together, or are you still sleeping on the floor?" Eve asked.

"No, he got it up. We even got it on a wall that will work after only the fourth try."

They all laughed.

"Been there," Lisa said. She hit the puree button, and noise filled the kitchen.

Melody grabbed a chip and looked around the kitchen. "Where are Alex and Maddie?"

"The guys took them." Lisa stopped the blender, grabbed a chip, and dunked it in. "It's his turn to deal with them for awhile." She bit into the chip. "Yeah, that's much better."

In turn each woman tasted it and proclaimed it sufficiently edible. Melody's final mark of approval was for symbolic purposes only.

"Awesome." Ashley picked up the blender and dumped the contents into the waiting bowl. They'd just dug in when Jeff and A.J. came in from the front door, flanked and surrounded by two squealing children.

"Mommy! Mommy!" Alex ran to her, holding up a small red racecar. "Dad let me buy a car. Look isn't it cool?"

Lisa looked at Jeff and frowned.

He shrugged. "It was cool." Holding Maddie in one arm like the little featherweight she was, he put the groceries on the cabinet. "How could we pass up cool, Mom? Come on."

"Yeah," A.J. agreed. Then he spied the dip. "Food!"

Eve shook her head. "The more things change…"

"The more they stay the same," Melody finished, and they all laughed.

"Hey," A.J. protested around the chip already in his mouth. "I'm starving. I didn't eat breakfast."

"Oh, yeah?" Eve asked, grabbing a chip herself. "What were those two breakfast burritos you scarfed down on the way over here?"

"Snacks. Come on they were like this big." A.J. held his fingers three inches from each other. He grabbed another chip. "Hey, Mel. How's the new place?"

"Fantastic. You'll have to come see it sometime. We missed you moving, but Jeff and Gabe worked their usual magic."

"Yeah. I heard. We'll have to come over and see it sometime though. I hear it's great," he said, still chomping the chips like he was in fact starving.

The door snapped open, and Gabe peeked in. "Burgers are ready!"

Like a well-trained army, everybody grabbed something and headed outside.

Although Melody had begged off half of the annual water skiing adventure, it had been a great day—just relaxing with friends who really knew her, not having to impress anybody. It was excellent. The campfire in the little fire pit was slowly turning to embers as the hour hand arched up toward midnight. Around the fire, the couples sat soaking in the last of the warmth, no one wanting to leave just yet.

"Well," A.J. said, and all gazes drifted that direction.

Melody saw the tender look he gave to Eve as he sat up. Her heart melted at the picture they made. They were so right together, so good for each other. She was glad of that. A prayer of thanksgiving for them being in her life slid through her. She was lucky to count them as friends.

"We have some news," A.J. said, rubbing his hands together although he was still looking only at Eve.

At that not only gazes, but everyone's full attention went their direction as well.

A.J. turned to them but let his gaze fall to the wooden planks at their feet. "You all know we've been doing the doctor thing and testing thing. Well, we went in on Monday, and…" He glanced back at Eve, and there was no denying that look.

"There's a heartbeat," Eve said softly, picking her hand up to rub his arm tenderly.

"A…" Lisa asked, sitting up straight. "You're…? Are you serious? You're pregnant?" And then she was on her feet with Eve in her arms. "Oh, I'm so happy for you guys! That is… That is so awesome!"

Handshakes, hugs, tears, and congratulations flowed freely. It was as if the party was starting all over again.

"Man! It's been so hard not saying anything all day," A.J. said. "I thought I was going to keel over when Jeff asked me how things were going today at the store." He slapped Jeff in the stomach. "You really shouldn't do that to a person."

"Like I had a clue," Jeff said.

"And this is a new thing?" Gabe asked, rolling his eyes dramatically.

The whole group laughed.

It had nothing to do with duty, only with love when Melody stepped over to Eve and hugged her tightly. "Congratulations, girl. I know you are going to make a totally fantastic mom."

Eve was welling up now, some from the congratulations some from the happiness. "I just can't believe it sometimes. It doesn't even seem real."

"Oh, yeah? Wait until you can't see your feet anymore," Lisa said, wiping her own tears away. "Then it will seem very, very real."

Melody stepped back as Ashley stepped forward and pulled Eve into her embrace. "You're lucky, you know that?" She pulled back and her face was serious. "Don't ever forget that. Okay?"

Tears streamed down Eve's face. "I won't. I promise." And they hugged again.

Blaine stepped up behind Melody and entwined his fingers with hers. She looked at him as happiness and peace flooded through her whole being. He pulled her into his arms and kissed her head softly. "You want to tell them?"

Slowly she shook her head and looking at him, she whispered. "Not yet."

His smile took in only her gaze, and without saying a word, they agreed to keep the little secret that had made them both happier than they had ever been.

It was only later, driving home, that Blaine had the chance to ask her why she had decided not to tell them. "So, I've got to know why you didn't want to say anything tonight. Not that I mind. I kind of like the secrecy thing, but I'm curious."

Melody looked over at him, and love and peace flowed from her gaze. She shrugged. "Tonight was Eve's night. I'll have my night too sometime, and she'll be as happy for me then as I am for her right now."

Blaine nodded and then looked over at her. Once again he entwined his fingers with hers, lifted her hand, and kissed it. "Just so you know, Mrs. Donovan, I'm about as happy right now as I'm ever going to get."

"Me, too," she said as her whole heart opened to the possibilities life held out for them. "Me, too."

As they sped through the night, side-by-side, his hand in hers, Melody thought about the child now growing inside her. She laid her other hand there, sensing the tangible if not yet seen proof of just what's possible when you take a chance to be wholly, one-hundred percent for real. It was a chance she would always be glad she had found the courage to take.

Sneak Peek...
Coming February, 2013
from #1 Best Selling Christian Romance Author
Staci Stallings

ETERNITY

Chapter 1

It wasn't the best idea Aaron Foster had ever come up with, but he was desperate. It had been three months since "the break-up," and although he was still sure his heart would never recover, if he didn't find a roommate soon, his heart wouldn't be the only thing out on the street.

"Hello, you," Harmony Jordan said, throwing an arm around him and digging her chin into his shoulder as he stood next to the company bulletin board, notice in-hand, gathering up the courage to tack it up. "What ya doing?"

"Looking for a roommate."

Slowly Harmony's arm slid from his shoulder, and she crossed her arms, her long, sandy-colored hair sliding down almost to them. "Oh, yeah, I forgot, Bubbles moved out."

"Mandy," he said petulantly. "Her name is Mandy."

"Mandy, Brandy, Candy, Bubbles. Whatever. You know, you could do better than her."

He looked at her, set the square of his jaw, and shook his head. "Nope. Not anymore. I've given up on doing better."

Harmony cocked a disbelieving red eyebrow at him. "What's that supposed to mean?"

"It means, I'm taking myself out of the game." With renewed determination, he reached up and tacked the notice to the board. "I am officially single and proud of it."

"Yeah, right." She narrowed her hazel eyes at him without ever even glancing at the notice. "So, let me guess. Single, white male with medium-great apartment looking for roommate to split the rent. No smokers, druggies, or women need apply. 555-6472." She laughed as the annoyed look spread across his face. "Oh, yeah. And no pets either."

Their gazes locked as he tried to decide how much of her speech was teasing and how much was making fun of him. Her smile was maddening to the core.

"What?" he finally asked in frustration.

"Nothing." She shrugged as though the question and him were utterly beyond help. On her heel she turned and started away from him.

For two steps he followed her, and then he turned back to the board, ripped the notice off the wall, and looked at it. "Single, white male... " With one crunch he crumpled it into a tiny ball and threw it into the first available trashcan as he raced after her.

"What should I do then?" he asked, catching her just as she turned into her cubicle. "How else could I go about finding a roommate?"

She shrugged as her hands rifled through the papers on her desk. "You put the word out—to your friends, people you know. Ask them if they know someone who's looking."

"And that works?" he asked skeptically.

"That's how I met my last roommate. Best roommate I've ever had. She cooked, she cleaned, she even bought the groceries if I gave her the money."

"Hmm." He leaned onto her desk. "Sounds great. How can I... "

"You can't have her." Harmony, shorter in stature than him and much less sophisticated, continued to rifle through the papers strewn on her desk.

"Why not?"

"Because she got married six months ago that's why."

"Oh." He held out the papers in his own hands knowing he should be working. "Well, then, do you think...?"

"Sure," she said, looking up with a soft smile. "I'll ask around."

The papers fell back to his knee as he looked at her gratefully. "Man, I don't know what I'd do without you."

Two days later Harmony poked her head around the corner of Aaron's cubicle. "Good news."

He didn't bother to look up as his pencil continued down the list in front of him. "Oh, yeah? What's that?"

"I think I found someone."

"How nice for you." His focus never shifting from his work.

"Not for me, dufus—for you."

He looked up in confusion as his attention skipped from the line of numbers he'd been working to reconcile. "Huh?"

"I found you a roommate," she said before she ducked back out of his cubicle and into her own.

"What?" He jumped up, sending his chair crashing to the floor although he didn't notice. In two seconds he was in her cubicle. He pulled the extra chair over to her desk and sat down expectantly. "Talk to me."

She sorted the papers on her desk for one more second, and then she looked at him as excitement flowed through her eyes. "A friend of mine—Jay Theron—you remember him, he's the guy we met when we were picking out your couch that time. Remember, the ugly yellow thing you said reminded you of your grandmother's..."

"Harmony."

The story stopped, and she looked at him as though they hadn't been sitting in her cubicle the whole time. "Oh, yeah. Well, anyway, Jay's got this cousin. He's from New York or Philadelphia or something. He just moved to town, and he's staying with Jay until he can find a place."

Slowly she tilted her head to one side and looked at him expectantly. He sat, looking at her, waiting for the rest of the story, but she said nothing.

"And?" he finally said, lifting his hand in the air.

"And," she said as annoyance crept into her voice, "he'll be at your apartment tonight at eight—just for a meeting, nothing permanent."

"Oh, my gosh." His eyes closed in relief. "Harmony, you are a lifesaver, you know that?" With no pretense he stood, walked around her desk, and hugged her to him. "You have to be the best friend in the whole entire world."

She smiled into his starched shirt as she closed her eyes and breathed in the scent of him being so close. "Glad I could help."

There wasn't enough stuff in his apartment to clean three times, but Aaron wanted everything to be perfect for this meeting. He arranged the two pillows Harmony had bought for his couch twice before giving up and running the dust cloth over the stereo system. It was silly to be so obsessed with keeping the apartment, but he'd always been the sentimental type.

Losing Mandy was almost more than his over-sensitive side could take—moving would've been the final straw. Carefully he replaced the smooth, ebony marble statue that had mysteriously appeared on his work desk last Christmas. It had stayed on his desk at work until Mandy had come home and announced she was seeing someone else. Then the statue had relocated to this place over his television.

He was sure his receiving it was a mistake, but something about it was so personal, he didn't have the heart to throw it out.

The knock brought him back into the apartment, and he checked the area once more before taking a deep breath and opening the door.

"Hi." A slightly bearded man just younger than Aaron stood there in the hallway. His clothes were less-than fashionable, even a little on the worn side.

"Hi," Aaron said awkwardly, sure this was the guy Harmony had sent but not sure how to ask that of a perfect stranger.

They stood like that for a moment, sizing each other up.

"I'm Drew," the young man finally said, extending his hand. "Drew Easton."

Aaron smiled in relief. "Aaron Foster." They shook hands. "You're Jay's cousin?"

"Yep," Drew said, not moving from the doorway.

"Oh, I'm sorry." Aaron stepped back to let Drew cross the threshold into the apartment.

"Nice place." Drew kept his hands dug securely in his pockets. Weaving his body back and forth, he examined the apartment from each vantage point as his feet carried him across the hardwood floor.

"I just got home," Aaron said, lying only a tiny bit. "I haven't really had time to clean it up much."

"It's nice," Drew said again, stopping to examine the kitchen and the little table.

Aaron fought for something to say. "So, you just moved here?"

"Yeah, from Buffalo."

"Oh? Why'd you move?"

"Too cold," Drew said. "So, the bedrooms are upstairs then?"

"Yeah." Aaron held a hand up in invitation of the stairs. "There's two bedrooms and a bath."

He let Drew go ahead up of him and then followed him, running his hands together with each step. "The rent's not outrageous, but it's a little too much for me to come up with myself."

"What happened to your last roommate?" Drew asked, ducking into the empty bedroom at the top of the stairs.

"I killed her," Aaron said a little too seriously, and Drew turned and arched an eyebrow at him. "No." Aaron laughed, hoping it didn't sound hollow but knowing it did. "She moved out."

"She?" Drew nodded in understanding as he walked down the short hallway to the bathroom. "So, how do you plan on splitting the groceries?"

Aaron shrugged. "We could either buy our own or pool the money. Whichever."

Drew nodded. "And the utilities and stuff?"

"The phone's really the only thing we have to worry about. All the rest is included."

"Wow," Drew said, appraising the situation. "Well, are you... do you have any other prospects?"

"Nope, you're it," Aaron said with a shrug.

"Well, I'll take it then." Drew extended his hand again. "When can I move in?"

"Whenever you're ready," Aaron said, accepting the handshake as gratefulness and relief wrapped across his heart.

"I hear congratulations are in order," Harmony said, leaning on Aaron's doorway with two Dixie cups in-hand the next morning.

He looked up from the computer and leaned back in his chair. "Hey, yeah, I didn't get a chance to thank you this morning."

"Yeah, yeah, but you meant to. I know." She handed him one cup and sat down.

"Champagne on the job?" he asked skeptically. "Harmony, I didn't know."

"Yes, you did," she said as he took a drink. "It's ginger ale."

He nodded knowingly as he pulled the cup down. "Figures."

"Aren't we even going to toast?" she asked, having never so much as lifted her own cup.

"To what?"

She set her elbows on his desk and stared at him thoughtfully. "I don't know. To old friends and new friends."

He raised his cup to hers. "And all those in between."

About the Author

A stay-at-home mom with a husband, three kids and a writing addiction on the side, Staci Stallings has numerous titles for readers to choose from. Not content to stay in one genre and write it to death, Staci's stories run the gamut from young adult to adult, from motivational and inspirational to full-out Christian and back again. Every title is a new adventure! That's what keeps Staci writing and you reading. Although she lives in Amarillo, Texas and her main career is her family, Staci touches the lives of people across the globe with her various Internet endeavors including:

Ebook Romance Novels:
http://ebookromancestories.com

Books in Print, Kindle, & on Spirit Light Works:
http://stacistallings.wordpress.com/

Spirit Light Books Blog
http://spiritlightbooks.wordpress.com/

And…

Staci's website
http://www.stacistallings.com

Come on over for a visit…

You'll feel better for the experience!

Also Available from Staci Stallings

In Print

The Long Way Home

Eternity

Cowboy

Lucky

Deep in the Heart

To Protect & Serve

Dreams by Starlight

Reunion

Reflections on Life I

Reflections on Life II

Ebook Editions

Cowboy

Lucky

Coming Undone

Deep in the Heart

A Work in Progress

A Little Piece of Heaven

A Light in the Darkness

Princess

Dreams by Starlight

Reunion

To Protect & Serve

Made in the USA
Columbia, SC
28 September 2018